ONE BOSSY PROPOSAL

AN ENEMIES TO LOVERS ROMANCE

NICOLE SNOW

ABOUT THE BOOK

Strange men do funny things when you score the last cinnamon roll.

Sometimes he rages about the high crime of jacking *his* precious pastry.

Sometimes he offers you ludicrous bribes to buy it back.

And sometimes—after shattering your faith in humanity—you find out he's your new boss.

I'm not laughing.

My sweet tooth betrayed me and Lincoln Burns is one bad sugar rush.

A coldhearted grump. A mile-wide ego. An eligible bachelor who doesn't "do" dating.

Did I mention Mr. Congeniality runs a fashion empire with weddings in its sights?

Of course he does.

And, of course, weddings make me *gag* after my ex made my heart roadkill.

Every instinct I have screams run.

But money talks, and Lincoln's deep pockets roar.

One big fat bonus proposal lures me into his world.
Somehow, our vicious fights become vivid flirting.
His secrets thrill me in the worst ways.

Then he makes a second proposal.

Pretend we're engaged. Smile for pretty photos like we're soulmates. Dress up like we're actually getting married.

Oh, how I wish cinnamon rolls came with warnings.

It's all sticky sweet heaven until you catch feelings for the bossman from hell...

I: WHILE I PONDERED (DAKOTA)

$\mathcal{T}$he spring sun shines down on Seattle like a sword aimed at my own personal gloom.

I'm sad and hungry—a dangerous combination.

It's been a year to the day since I buried my heart—and the utter scumbag who dragged it through the mud, doused it in kerosene, and burned it to a blackened crisp—and it feels like an eternity.

Some things, you only sort of get over.

Some things, you don't forget.

Hold the pity party, Dakota. You're better off without him. You're a thousand miles from home, smack in the middle of a whole new life, I tell myself.

Eyeballing the gluttonous offerings in the bakery case helps.

It's true. I have rebuilt. Kind of.

I left that small-town dreariness and its regrets behind. I have an interview next week for a job that slaps, and if I don't get it, I'll keep applying until I land something with big-girl pay and a real opportunity to flex my writing muscles.

Without my great escape last summer in a halo of tears, I wouldn't be here in Seattle, practically *drooling* at the sugar-rich delicacies that all seem to have my name on them.

I'd have less time to focus on my writing, too, and I'd still be interning in that one-room closet masquerading as a marketing agency.

Yay, heartbreak.

Yay, Jay Foyt.

His stupidity gave me a whole new life.

"You hungry or did you just come here to admire the goods? Can I get you something?" The barista appears behind the bakery case with a girlish laugh.

"Huh? Oh, sorry—" *Dammit, Dakota, get out of your head.* "Can I get a Regis roll and a small caramel nirvana latte?"

"Coming right up!" She smiles and uses tongs to grab a huge cinnamon roll drizzled in icing. It's so fat I think it crosses time zones. "Lucky lady, you got the last one today! We're a little short. Cinnamon shortage in the morning shipment—go figure."

Lucky me.

If only my luck with pastries would rub off on other things. Like winning lottery tickets or cigar-chomping big shots in publishing ready to snap up my poetry. I'd even settle for a decent Tinder date who doesn't have a fuckboy bone in his body.

Nope. I'm asking for too much.

Today, Lady Luck grants bargain wishes. She delivers the very last mound of sticky cinnamon sweetness in the case and point-three more pounds on my thighs.

I mean, it's a start, right?

I move to the cash register and pay.

"Glad I got mine before you ran out," I say, swiping my card. "I'll be sure to savor the flavor—"

"What do you mean you're out?" a deep voice thunders behind me. "I've been here at exactly this time three times a week since Christmas. You're never *out*."

Holy crap.

And I thought I was having a bad day...

I look back toward the bakery case to see what kind of ogre

2

crawled out of his swamp to rant and rave over a missing cinnamon roll.

"Sorry, sir. The lady in front of you just bought the last roll," the barista says, wearing a placating frown. "There's a bit of a weird cinnamon shortage going around—"

"Are you telling me there isn't another goddamned Regis roll in the entire shop?" The man is tall, built, and entirely pissed off.

"Er, no. Like I said...cinnamon shortage." Barista girl flashes a pained smile. "The early bird got the worm, I'm afraid. If you'd like to try again tomorrow, we'll save one for you."

Barista girl nods at me matter-of-factly.

The ogre turns, whips his head toward me, and glares like his eyes are death rays.

Red alert.

So, he might be just as bad-tempered as the average ogre, but in the looks department, this guy is the anti-Shrek. If the green guy had abs that could punish and tanned skin instead of rocking his Brussels sprout glow, he might catch up to Hot Shrek in front of me.

My breath catches in my chest.

I don't think I've ever seen eyes like amber whiskey, flashing in the morning light.

If he weren't snarling like a rabid wolverine, he *might* be hotter than the toasty warm roll in my hand. The coolness of his eyes contrasts deliciously with dark hair, a furrowed brow, a jaw so chiseled it shames mere mortals.

He might be in his early thirties. His face looks young yet experienced.

The angles of that face match the cut of his body. He's toned like a former quarterback and dressed like he just walked off the set of *Suits.*

He is a Gucci-wrapped cocktail handcrafted for sin.

Every woman's dark vampire fantasy come to life—or maybe just mine.

3

When you're a Poe—distant, *distant* relation to Edgar Allan—it comes with the territory.

I definitely wonder if he woke up with a steaming mug of rudeness this morning to plaster that scowl on his face.

I'm starting to notice a pattern in this city. What is it with Seattle minting grumps who look like sex gods?

Is it something in the rain?

Worse, he towers over me, the picture-perfect strongman with a chip on his shoulder that entitles him to roar at the world when it doesn't fall down at his feet.

Although he's annoyingly gorgeous, and his suit probably costs half my yearly salary, I wonder. What gets a man this fire-breathing pissed over missing his morning sugar high?

Sure, I'll be the first to admit that Regis rolls are almost worth losing your mind over. *Almost.*

While Hades stares, I roll my eyes back at him and follow the curve of the counter to wait for my drink.

Precious distance.

After grumbling for a solid minute, he swipes his card like a dagger at the cash register and follows me around the counter.

Uh-oh.

Surely, he's not going to confront me.

He *wouldn't.*

Oh, but he's right next to me now.

Still glaring like I murdered his firstborn.

He pulls out his wallet, opens it, and plucks out a crisp bill, shoving it at me like it's on fire.

"Fifty dollars," Hot Shrek growls.

"Come again?"

"Fifty bucks. I'll pay you five times its value for the trouble."

"What?" I blink, hearing the words but not comprehending them.

He points to the white paper bag in my hand holding my little slice of heaven. "Your Regis roll, lady. I'll buy it off you."

"Wait, you just...you want to buy my cinnamon roll that bad?"

"Isn't that what I just said? And it's a *Regis roll*," he corrects sharply. "You know, the kind worth dying over? The original recipe cooked up in Heart's Edge, Montana, and approved by a scary burned guy who's been all over the national media and keeps getting cameos in movies?"

I laugh. That's exactly what Sweeter Grind's ads promise about the otherworldly Regis roll, a creation of Clarissa and Leo Regis, two small-town sweet shop owners made famous by some crazy drama a few years back.

"Never mind," he snaps. "You want to make this sale or what?"

"You should do commercials," I tell him with a huff. "Is that what this is? Some strange guerrilla marketing thing?"

I hold my breath. At least that would explain Mr. GQ Model going absolutely ballistic over something so trivial.

Also, it's the one-year anniversary of the most humiliating day of my life.

I need this roll like I still need to believe there's a shred of goodness in this world. What kind of psycho tries to buy someone's cinnamon roll off them for five times the price, anyway?

"Do I look like a comedian?" he snarls, his eyes rolling. "Fifty dollars. Easy money. Trade."

"Dude, you're insane," I whisper back.

"Dudette," he barks back, slightly more frantic. "I assure you, I am not. I need that roll, and I'm willing to pay you generously. I trust you need the money more than I do."

I scoff at him so hard my face hurts.

Rub it in, why don't you? I guess I should up and be amazed you're deigning to talk to us 'little people,' your pastry-obsessed highness.

"It must be nice, oh Lord of the Pastries. What do I get for an apple pie? A laptop?" I shake my head.

His *done-with-your-bullshit* glare intensifies.

"Dakota!" A male barista calls my name and plunks my drink on the counter.

Awesome. There's my cue to exit this asylum and head back

to the springtime sanity outside where birds tweet and flowers bloom and nobody goes to war over cinnamon shortages.

I grab my drink and start for the door.

"Wait!" Hot Shrek calls. "Dakota."

Ughhh.

My name shouldn't sound so deliciously rough on a man's lips. Especially not a man offering exorbitant sums to strangers for their baked goods.

Knowing I'll regret this, I stop and meet his eyes.

"What?" I clip.

"We haven't finished."

"Right. Because there's no deal," I snap, turning again.

Okay. Before, I was just looking forward to stuffing my face with sticky goodness. Now, I *need* this flipping cinnamon roll like oxygen.

If I spite the hottest freak who crawled out of the ogre swamp, I'll have something to laugh about later.

True to the promise I made the barista, I'll savor the flavor while wallowing in a little less of my own misery and reminding myself I'm living a better life now—which apparently includes handsome stalkers begging to throw cash at me.

"Wait. I need it more than you do. I swear," he says harshly, grabbing my shoulder and spinning me around.

I bat his hand away, doubly annoyed and taken aback.

"You're insane. Touch me again and I'll press charges for robbery. It's a cinnamon roll, dude. Calm down and come back tomorrow when they're replenished." I panic chug my latte and walk out the door.

Hot Stalker Shrek is undaunted.

He trails me outside as I stroll into the Seattle sunshine, taking a deep breath.

"Seventy-five!" he calls after me.

"What?"

"Seventy-five dollars."

"Um, no." I speed walk to the bike rack and unlock my

6

wheels with one hand, balancing the Regis roll and the latte in the other.

"One hundred dollars even," he belts after me.

Holy Moses. How high will he go?

"One fifty!" he calls two seconds later.

There goes my jaw, crashing to the pavement.

A chill sweeps through me. I'm worried we're leaving eccentric waters for clinically crazy.

Part of me wants to keep him talking just so he doesn't carry me off to his evil lair. I imagine a storage shed stacked to the ceiling with crumpled cinnamon roll boxes.

"Did you really just offer me a hundred and fifty dollars for a cinnamon roll?" I place the latte in a cup holder on my handlebar and climb on the bike.

He gives me an arctic look, like he knows he's got me now and I've already accepted his bizarro deal.

"You're welcome. You can Uber and still have a nice chunk of change."

I scan him up and down, purposely glancing at his polished leather shoes a second too long. In another time and place, I'd take a nice big sip of my latte and spray it on his shoes but...that's not how I roll.

I have my dignity. I plan to have a little more of it when I'm safely away from here, too.

"This may come as a shock, but not all of us worship money, King Midas," I say.

"What's that supposed to mean?" he says with a snort, squaring his hulking shoulders.

"You're a nutter. Like actually insane." My eyes flick to his wrists for good measure, legit wondering if I'll see a hospital band.

"I am not. Have you ever tasted a Regis roll? Seattle's top food critic described them as—what was it? A category ten mouth-gasm?"

My lips twitch. I try like hell not to burst out into a blushing

7

laugh.

"Man, I am *not* discussing mouth-gasms with you," I say.

"You're missing the point," he says sharply. "Help me and help yourself, Miss Dakota. We never have to see each other again and you'll be three hundred dollars richer."

"Three...hundred?" I say slowly, my mouth falling open.

"You heard me." His eyes flash with hope and triumph, and he starts reaching for his wallet.

Stay strong.

Invisible crucifix.

Latte holy water.

Do not be tempted by Lucifer.

"See, you're not making your case. Just further proving your insanity." I eye him warily. Maybe there's some wild story behind how he stole this suit and he really did just escape some mental institution.

That would be the most believable explanation for what's happening.

Honestly, a lot less scary than thinking guys who look like billionaires want to spend their time reverse robbing strangers for their pastries.

"Five hundred dollars, damn you," he rumbles. "Final offer."

My jaw detaches from my face.

Five hundred flipping smackers?

That's more than my student loan payment this month. Almost half my rent. I'm tempted to sign my soul away, but my fingers clench the bag tighter, demanding me to be brave.

Not today, Coffee Shop Satan.

A smile that's almost comically pleading pulls at his lips.

Damn. Somehow, he's even hotter when he smiles and makes those puppy dog eyes. A face like his should come with a warning.

"I see that got your attention," he whispers.

"Did it?"

"Your mouth dropped," he says, making me keenly aware his gaze is fixed on my lips. I don't even know what to do with that.

He closes the space between us and reaches for my bag, trying to get the drop on me.

"Hey—no! I told you it's not happening, crazypants." I don't like the way he so casually invades my space. I also have a pesky habit of not taking a single speck of crap from anyone. Especially this past year.

But there's also this tiny thought nibbling at the back of my brain that screams this man is no different from Jay.

Just richer, stronger, better-looking, and possibly more arrogant.

Keeping this Regis roll out of his grubby paws is a little win for Dakota Poe against mankind. Against every swinging dick who brandishes his selfish ego like a club.

"I'm perfectly sane. I simply need that roll, and I can't walk away empty-handed," he tells me.

"Y'know, I woke up inspired to write today. But I wasn't planning on getting real-world inspiration shoved in my face from someone so ridiculous."

"I have no idea what the hell that means, but I need the roll and you need money. Do we have a deal?"

"Why am I not surprised you can't follow simple English? Are you one of those guys who paid five hundred dollars for some poor geek to boost your grades too?"

He glares at me like an angry bull.

"Watch your step, Big Mouth. You know nothing about me. Let's make a trade and be on our merry way for the sake of our blood pressure." He gives me a slow, assessing look, his eyes sliding up my body with a weight that makes me shiver. "You're on a bike. Don't tell me you couldn't use a few hundred bucks."

"Orrr I could be so loaded I run a green power company and need to look the part," I throw back. "Plus, biking helps blow off some steam. You should try it sometime."

Scowling, he grabs at my white paper bag again.

I shift away at the last second, slapping his big hand away.

Yeah, I've had it.

Narrowing my eyes, I glare back at him, reach into the bag, and pull out the warm roll. In slow motion, I bite off a massive chunk.

I chew it as loudly as I can, smacking my lips like war drums.

The most mouth-gasmic *"Mmmmm-mmm-mmmm!"* I've ever mustered in my life rips out of me.

Then I drop the bite-marked roll back into the bag, lick my fingers, and wipe my hands unceremoniously on the front of my jeans.

"See? Not everything is for sale. No deal."

God.

I've seen my share of selfish men, but this one takes the cake —or rather, he doesn't take the cinnamon roll I won't let him have. The tantrum brewing in his face when I make it crystal clear he's not getting this roll would scare the best kindergarten teacher pale.

His jaw clenches.

His bearish brown eyes become brighter, hotter, *louder.* I can hear them cursing me seven ways from Sunday.

It's not fair.

When he's majorly pissed off, he's a hundred times hotter than he was at first glance.

His eyes drop to my lips and linger for a breathless second.

His gaze feels so heavy I hug myself, trying to hide from the intensity of his scorned-god look that feels like it could turn me into a salt pillar.

I want to say something, to break the acid silence with a joke, but I'm not sure it's possible.

Should I remind him he's an entitled douchebag?

That he's pretty freaking lucky I didn't spit fifty bucks' worth of roll at his stupid grumpy face?

It doesn't matter, though.

I don't have time to come up with the perfect f-you before

he's turning his massive back to me and stomping off, muttering quietly.

He rounds the corner of the coffee shop and keeps going without a single look back.

Jeez Louise. Shouldn't a guy with that much money and even more ego have a ride?

Whatever.

Not my problem.

I need to get to work.

Rent won't wait for my one-year anniversary personal hell, or encounters with strange men who get in my face about giant pastries.

I take off for the office with three quarters of my Regis roll remaining. I'll enjoy it for its baked perfection, but keeping the precious cargo from Hot Shrek gives me just as many endorphins as the sugar rush.

Captain McGrowly and his mantrum pissed me off so much that I pedal like my life depends on it. I reach the office with time to spare, devouring all the frosted cinnamon goodness before I force myself to deal with the rat race inside.

Just a few more weeks and you'll be out of here. You've got big plans. You can do this.

Later, I repeat the mantra over and over when someone who earns twice my salary makes a mistake that throws the whole project into chaos.

Typical day at my overworked, underpaid copywriting position.

I'm at work past sunset in a desperate bid to fix it.

I wish Cinnamon Roll Luck and the high of my little victory would've lasted longer.

Instead, I'm back in my craptacular reality where the only poetry I write is an ode in sweat to fixing everybody else's problems.

* * *

I'M NOT EVEN UPSET.

I'm not.

It's after nine o'clock and dark when I drag my exhausted butt back to my shoebox apartment. With any luck, I'll be putting in my two weeks' notice soon.

Stay strong, I tell myself.

There's no harm in making a good last impression on my way out the door to greener hills.

I stop to check the mail before heading off to another lonely evening. Courtesy of men who are self-absorbed asshats who make a habit of tripping over their own dicks.

I put my key in the mailbox and turn it.

A pile of junk comes cascading out. I manage to catch most of it before it hits the floor.

Anything that's obviously an ad goes straight into recycling. That leaves five envelopes. A census notice, a flimsy note from a Portland literary journal I can already sense is a rejection, a sympathy card pretending it's just a sweet hello from Grandma, and—

Oh, no.

I stuff the last envelope in my purse and lean against the wall, trying not to scream.

"Hey, Dakota! What's wrong? Tell me you're not just getting home," a bright voice says.

"Oh, hey." I look over my shoulder as Eliza walks over with her usual disarming smile. "Yeah, late night. It's whatever. I just have a few more weeks left."

"Have you had dinner yet?" she asks. Before I can answer, she says, "Let me grab my mail, and then you should come over and try out my new brew."

"It's pushing ten o'clock, Eliza. Pretty late for coffee." My stomach rumbles, though, reminding me I haven't eaten yet and I have another early morning tomorrow.

"Live dangerously."

I laugh as my stomach makes the decision for me. Coffee and

tasty treats sound more appetizing than another lump of frozen franken-fettucine from my freezer. It's also a good way to delay the inevitable.

"Okay, fine," I say.

Eliza pops her mailbox open, retrieves a couple envelopes, and starts pulling me toward her place by the hand. "You have to try the pecan roast. You'll hit the floor."

Strong coffee wafts me in the face before she's even fully opened her door.

But it's not just coffee. Her place is always this potent blend of sweetness and subtle fruity undertones. Everything good in life condensed into mingling foodie perfumes.

"Do I smell vanilla? Delicious."

Eliza grins. "Your favorite. I made a vanilla blend too just for you. Have you eaten yet? You never answered."

No, and I'm about to gnaw my own arm off. I don't want to say that, though.

"What pairs with coffee?" Eliza asks, wagging her brows like it's a pop quiz.

"Uh—bagels?"

She rolls her eyes. "You're a buzzkill, Dakota. Way to ruin my caffeine high."

I laugh. "I'm not part hummingbird like you, living off sugar. Enlighten me."

"Scones! I made a nice fresh batch of huge blueberry ones an hour ago. You'll love them."

She's got me there.

It's impossible not to love living right above a mad coffee scientist who's always after the perfect cup of joe and the best baked bliss to pair it with.

I kick my shoes off and walk through her small apartment, almost as cramped as mine.

There's a daybed and a couple chairs in the main room with a small kitchen off to the side. She goes to the kitchen bar and drops her mail on it.

My studio may be another postage stamp apartment, but her kitchen looks drastically different from mine.

Glass beakers, mason jars, canisters of coffee, a bright light, and tiny potted plants make it look more like a proper lab than a kitchen.

"Are those new plants?" I whisper.

I'm almost afraid to ask.

She smiles. "I'm trying to grow a hybrid bean. So far it hasn't worked out quite right."

"Dang. So you've taken it to the next level? You're growing your own beans in the Seattle gloom to support your habit?"

"Habits are for drunks. Coffee is *life.*" She spreads her arms and waves affectionately at the lab-like kitchen. "You're not looking at a simple hobby. One day, everything I've cooked up here will be the backbone of Liza's Love."

"When you open Liza's Love, I promise I'll read my poetry on open mic night."

"Every night will be open mic night." She wags a finger like it's already written in stone.

"Great. Then I'll be there every night and you'll still be feeding me like a hobo who just lost her last poker game."

Laughing, she heads into the kitchen and pours coffee into three tiny glasses, then piles a plate high with scones. She sets the tiny coffee cups and scones down on the bar separating the kitchen from the living room.

"Tell me your favorite," she demands.

I take a fortifying gulp of the first one and wrinkle my nose. "Oof. That just tastes like...coffee. Needs a little sweetener."

She scowls at me.

I hold up my hands defensively and then sip the second one.

"Oh, my, that's lovely," I mutter, feeling foamy sweetness dancing on my tongue.

"What do you taste?" She watches me excitedly, her hands clasped in front of her.

"Vanilla. Sweet stuff. A little cream. Almost like...a cake flavor?"

Eliza smiles and nods like an approving teacher.

I clear my mouth with water, then take a pull off the third cup, smacking my lips.

"Hmm. Cinnamon?"

"And pecan." She nods.

"Interesting mix," I say, smacking my lips lightly. "The second was my favorite, I think."

"I'll pour you a full mug of birthday cake coffee. Cream and sugar?"

"Just cream."

Eliza opens a cabinet, pulls out a normal-sized mug, and sets to work making my drink to order.

I pick up an oversized blueberry scone from the plate and take a bite.

As always, it's delicious, and I'm starving. I start stuffing my face like a back-alley raccoon before I even notice.

This entire day has been carb-central, and I'm adding to my thighs.

Worth it.

I've also been keeping the mail I brought up with me this whole time. I pull out envelopes and sort through them in more detail, keeping that last one at the end like the poison ivy leaf it is.

The return address is Dickinson, North Dakota.

Too close for comfort. Too close to my hometown of Dallas —a dusty little northern oil town with too many bad memories tainting the good times. It's a place where everyone has a magical love story except me.

"What is it?" Eliza says, noticing the frown on my face.

I shake my head.

"Oh, nothing." I drop the letters in my lap and pick up the steaming mug Eliza set down next to me.

"King Idiot again?"

"...maybe." I pick up the mug and take another sip of Eliza's sublime brew, warming my soul. I slide the letter across the bar. "Toss it for me?"

"Sure thing! You sure you don't want to read it first?"

For a second, I hesitate. But whatever heartless apology or validation seeking thing my ex sent can't be worth the grief. Especially not *today.*

"Nope. Shoot your shot," I tell her, slurping my coffee loudly.

Grinning, she crumples the letter into a messy ball and chucks it into the pink crate with glittery stripes across the room she uses for recycling.

"Score!" She pours herself a celebratory coffee and sits beside me.

"Eliza, I say this gently, but...I don't think you need more coffee." I pat her shoulder.

"And we don't blaspheme in this house."

I laugh. "Will you even sleep tonight?"

She picks up a scone and takes a wolfish bite.

"Eventually. How was your day? Besides the working zombie hours and getting a letter from King Idiot, I mean?"

"Same day, different...asshole." I carefully add that last word, remembering my morning spat at Sweeter Grind. "Actually, that's not exactly true. I ran into a real weirdo at Sweeter Grind this morning—"

"Oh?" Eliza's brows shoot up. "Did he follow you? Did he try to—"

"Yes, he followed. But no. Not the typical harassment like you're thinking. He had a mantrum—a man tantrum—because I was ahead of him in line and snagged the last Regis roll."

"I mean, can you blame him? Regis rolls are *God.*"

For a second, I burst out laughing. If Eliza could build herself an altar of baked offerings like the crazy little coffee Pagan she is, I'm sure there'd be a freaking Regis roll in the center.

"Yeah, but get this," I say. "This dude flips his lid when he finds out the last one just sold out. He yells at the barista and then he tries to buy *my* roll."

"What?" She doubles over laughing, her eyes scrunching up in this funny way that makes me join her.

"Oh, wow. You should've given him some jacked up price just to see if he'd take it. You could have had a nice payday!"

I purse my lips.

"Well...he started bidding. He got up to five hundred dollars without any prompting on my part."

"He—what?" Her mouth falls open. "You're not joking? Let me get this straight. So some rando at Sweeter Grind bids five hundred dollars for a cinnamon roll? Holy crap. You scored the jackpot! I'd be feasting at Le Panier for a week if I had your devil's luck."

"Here's the thing." I take another slow bite of scone and chew, questioning my sanity. "I didn't take it."

Eliza's eyes almost pop out of her head. She slaps her thigh so hard her coffee rattles.

"No way! Why?"

"Because. This guy needed a serving of humble pie. He comes clomping in looking like a model in a three-piece suit and demands the last cinnamon roll in the shop just because he's breathing? Because he's rich? I don't even know, there's just something seriously borked about that. Someone had to teach him a lesson."

"Uh huh. And you, Miss Poe, just happened to notice his suit."

I open my mouth to fire back but the words won't come.

"Dakota. You passed up five Benjamins and the chance to hate-flirt with a hot rich guy, and now you'll never see him again?" Eliza reaches out and gently flicks her fingers against my forehead. "Are you sure you're okay? Like, are you *sure* Edgar Allan's craziness isn't hereditary?"

"Oh, please. We're *super* distantly related." I roll my eyes. "Also, he wasn't flirting. He was pretty horrible. He kept stalking me as he upped his offers, so what else could I do? I took a huge bite of the roll right in front of him just so he'd get it through his Neanderthal skull that he's not, under any circumstances, buying my roll. Being rich doesn't make you God."

She shrugs.

"I mean, I'll give you an A in ethics. No lie, I would've taken the five hundred bucks, though." She flashes an awkward smile.

"It was mighty tempting, but this guy needed a lesson. Trust me."

"Why did you just have to be the one to teach him?"

I shrug.

"Because I could." I sigh. "Okay, because I had fun with it. I needed to brighten up my day."

"Oh, right. I forgot you're coming up on a year since...yeah." Her face softens. "You had a bad day and a pastry-obsessed psycho was an easy target. It doesn't matter, lady. Any idiot who pays that much for a cinnamon roll would regret it. I'm sure you'll never see him again and you saved him five hundred dollars. Tomorrow's a new day. You'll feel better."

"I hope you're right," I say glumly.

"Is there any chance you could wake up more pissed?" She blinks at me.

"Eliza, no," I say, laughing.

"Okay, cool. There you have it, then. Tomorrow has to be better because it can't get worse."

"It's already a lot better with these scones in my belly," I tell her, finishing my last bite.

"How do you think King Idiot found your new address, if you don't mind me asking? Or is your mail still being forwarded?"

"Definitely not forwarded. He probably asked somebody back home. I've told you how gossip flies around Dallas. When the hot guy mechanic got mixed up with a pig and finally got engaged to my friend Shelly last year, nobody would shut up about it for months."

"For sure! So why don't you tell me more about this big interview you have lined up?"

I do exactly that while finishing the coffee and wind up hanging out with Eliza until one in the morning.

Not a terrible way to close out my anti-anniversary.

By the end of the night, I'm grateful that I feel a lot better than I did a year ago.

Eliza works miracles, and not just with her coffee.

I only hope I'll be half as blessed when I finally get a chance to nail the job that will finally set me free.

II: FORGOTTEN LORE (LINCOLN)

I leave work, still preoccupied with the platinum-blond hellcat from Sweeter Grind.

She had an angel's face, an hourglass figure counting down my patience, and the mouth of a demon.

Isn't that how it always is?

Normally, it'd fucking turn me on since I'm sick in the head, but not when it comes to my rolls.

Nobody fucks with Lincoln Burns' Regis rolls.

Yes, I was desperate. Somewhat manic. Unapologetically unhinged.

But *not* crazy.

I wouldn't have offered her five hundred damned dollars for a cinnamon roll if it wasn't life and death.

Right now, those stupid rolls are the only thing keeping Wyatt alive in the grip of his depression. He has just enough strength to fight me off if I try ramming anything healthier down his throat. Not enough strength to run on more than glazed sugar.

When that snapping turtle of a woman couldn't part with her God-given roll, I went back inside a few hours later after putting in some time at the office and bought a bear claw. Long after she was out of my sight.

I said a Hail Mary, hoping my best friend might be in a mood to try his sugar fix in a different composition today.

Then I brought it to Wyatt's tent in the park a few blocks down, marching past rows of human misery in the same situation.

He wouldn't even leave his sleeping bag.

A Regis roll is the only way to get him out of hibernation, and bike chick just had to deny him that to make some pitiful moral point.

When I tried to *pull* him out, he fought me like an ambushed possum. I wound up with a face full of sticky bear claw for my trouble.

I appreciate his opinion, even if it's irrational as hell.

My ma loves the stupid rolls, too. A few times, I've wondered if my sweet, unassuming mother would unalive some poor SOB for the pleasure.

Every time I go by Sweeter Grind to make a sugar drop for Wyatt, I pick up one or two for Mom.

Not today.

All because I was robbed by the one girl in the city who wouldn't have a grown-up conversation about a simple exchange.

Fuck it. Maybe she'll forget about it.

Mother is a little less stubborn than Wyatt when it comes to those rolls, but not by much. I have a while to replay the encounter as I take the ferry over to her place on Bainbridge, standing where the wind can slap me in the face and clear my head like it usually does.

A little while later, Ma meets me at the door with a hug and her usual sunny smile.

"Look who's back! Come on in. Did you bring me one of those heavenly cinnamon rolls today?"

So much for forgetting.

I heave out a sigh.

"I tried. There was some sort of cinnamon shortage—or just the world's worst excuse for incompetence—and then some donkey in front of me bought the last roll in the entire place. She wouldn't let me have it no matter how much money I offered—"

Mom bends over laughing, shaking her curly silvering hair.

"Sweetheart, relax! My doctor would thank you for making me wait for my fix. You don't owe me a cinnamon roll. Your company is plenty."

Right.

She pulls the door open and stands aside for me to enter, then shuts the door once I'm inside.

"I couldn't even get a Regis roll for Wyatt, Ma. I tried feeding him a bear claw and he wouldn't even get out of bed."

She frowns, noticing the slight bruise on my temple.

"Oh, my. Is that—"

"Not his fault. I tried to drag him out of his den when I should know better. He's not well," I remind her.

I always have to when she worries like nobody's business. And she's doing it now, sizing me up, checking me over with the world's sternest mom expression for more battle damage.

"Lincoln...the way you take care of that poor man really is admirable, but he's not your responsibility. He should've seen a professional a long time ago. You deserve more of a life than just working and taking care of that lost soul—"

"That lost soul is the whole reason I'm still alive," I remind her. "I'd be dead without him like I've told you a thousand times. So, yeah, he's my responsibility. He can still find his way back, dammit, and somebody needs to try. Just because we're not blood doesn't mean Wyatt isn't my brother."

She presses her lips together, knowing she'll never convince me otherwise.

"Have you had dinner yet? I made your favorite tonight."

"Ma, I'm a grown man," I say with a frustrated sigh. "I don't need you to feed me."

"My bad for thinking hangry is still your first language." She smiles. "It's pot roast and garlic mash, by the way."

Damn her.

My stomach betrays me, growling like a Bengal tiger.

"...fine."

Whatever. She can still see right through me and must have a psychic read on my blood sugar. Without further protest, I lead the way to the dining room.

She laughs behind me.

"You go ahead and sit, Lincoln. I'll grab everything from the kitchen."

A few minutes later, there's a heaping plate of meat, mashed potatoes, and buttery vegetables in front of me and another plate a third that size across the table in front of my mother.

I barely let her dig in first to save face, listening as she cuts her meat.

"So, besides the stubborn doll who stole your cinnamon roll, have you met anyone lately?" she asks.

Kill me.

The only thing I hate talking about more than Wyatt's latest brush with the abyss is my nonexistent dating life.

"Not doll. Donkey. Big difference," I say, stuffing food into my mouth.

"I could tell she was pretty, though, from the way you said it."

"She looked fine. Just a normal girl," I lie, watching as she waits impatiently for more. "Personality wise, I'd rank her somewhere between roadkill and an ER trip for killer bees."

She laughs so hard she almost spits water. At least someone appreciates my humor.

"You should've asked her out! It would've been interesting, Lincoln. You're not getting any younger."

"Neither are you," I toss back.

"I have a family. You're single."

"You are, too. Technically."

"I'm widowed, son."

"Yeah, sorry. Poor choice of words. That's not the point, though." I scratch the plate as I hastily carve another piece of meat. "You'd still be eating dinner alone tonight if your son hadn't shown up."

She beams at me like the sun.

"Oh, I've already had the love of my life and a smartass son. I just want the same for you, and anytime I don't want to be alone, all I have to do is put a pot roast on."

I take a big bite, enjoying how it practically melts in my mouth.

She may annoy me, but she's not wrong. If she doesn't pack up leftovers on my way out, I'll come back tomorrow.

"All I'm saying is, a little dating never hurt anyone," she tells me. "It's been so long since—"

"Don't. Don't say her name," I snap, pointing my fork like a weapon for emphasis.

The only thing that might ruin this meat is thinking about Regina and her shit.

"But Lincoln, it's—"

"Hardly just that. Ma, you know if I take any girl out, it could easily become a public matter. There are reporters out there who stake their entire careers on capturing a ten-second TikTok clip of anyone like me fraternizing. It would be uncomfortable and messy for us both. No thanks. Running Haughty But Nice is all the trouble I need. It keeps me busy, and that's how I like it."

"I know. I built it, remember?" She hits me with her knowing mom look.

"I know you did. Only, media moved slower in your time and fashion trends could stick around for years."

"Oh, media," she mutters. "You know, there must be a thousand ways to take a girl out without anybody knowing. You're rich enough to have some Hollywood makeup artist fix you up with a disguise!"

I try not to snort mashed potatoes.

"Great idea, Ma. Just what I need, luring some poor girl in so

I can peel my face off in front of her when it's time to kiss like a B-movie monster." I pause. My mother glares, clearly unimpressed with my razor-sharp wit. "You know how the Seattle press stalked me last time I was dumb enough to date. What's the point in making it worse by throwing someone else in the drama? I spend enough time trying to dodge them now. I can't even get a beer without winding up on ten Instagram posts laced with dumbass rumors the next day. Don't people have anything better to do than sling shit at strangers online?"

She covers her mouth, hiding a laugh, even if she pretends to disapprove of rough language.

"Apparently not when it comes to handsome eligible men, or they wouldn't be hounding you, son. Doesn't the new wedding line give you *any* interest in romance? Doesn't it make you want to find a nice girl and settle down?"

I pretend to think about it for five seconds, stroking my chin.

"No," I tell her bluntly, stabbing my fork in another piece of roast.

She stares, frowning, waiting for more when it's a dead subject.

"How about a 'hell no'?" I venture.

She cocks her head. "You know I don't give up that easily, Lincoln Burns. I want grandkids and you're my only child. Don't you think it's about time you deliver for your poor old mom?"

"I *tried* to get your Regis roll, Ma."

"Oh, Lincoln. This is a little more important," she says, so exasperated I almost laugh.

"Is there anything I could ever do to make you happy *besides* grandkids? Something that will make you just as proud? I've added twelve billion dollars to the fashion brand you built, for crying out loud."

Mom's usual easygoing smile fades into a firm arc of her lips.

She shakes her head severely.

"No."

"See? That's exactly why I can't give you a grandkid right

now. You'll just be disappointed for the rest of your life because nothing else will ever measure up. You have to wait for the right moment so you're not disappointed." I fan the slightest breeze on her hopes, hoping to end this as I take another bite of buttery roast. "I can't have my mother disappointed." I grin at her. "Besides, I've gotten far enough to launch such a lucrative line because I keep business and life totally separate."

Technically, that's true. I don't have a personal life.

Not unless you count Regis roll runs for Wyatt and the odd charity event outside work, which is good enough for me.

"They don't mix at all. Period and end of story," I say.

"Lincoln, your story hasn't even started," she says, getting up to put on tea like she always does when she's flustered.

I wish I could say my mother knows best.

I wish I could be the good son and not disappoint her.

I wish I could pry open my heart and give someone a second chance to poison me from the inside out.

But after seeing what a heart-hacking bastard serial killer cupid can be, I'll settle for being the rich and respected *bachelor* son.

* * *

A FEW DAYS LATER, I raid Sweeter Grind for Wyatt's roll.

Bright and early this time.

I can't risk coming too late and finding them sold out again. Wyatt lives on his sugar high and that's how it'll stay until he either snaps the hell out of it or forces my hand into dragging him off to treatment.

The barista makes a drink, hands it to the person in front of me, and rings them up.

"Can I help you?" she asks.

The bell above the entrance dings. I glance over.

A slender blond in a black dress that hugs her body in all the right places walks in. If it weren't for the hair, shimmering like faded spun gold in the morning light, she'd be the portrait of a human raven. There's something about her movements, graceful and birdlike, but with patience and sharp eyes that could be imposing if she settled long enough to stare at you.

Alert. Elegant. An old-world charm in her unfussy dress that licks her skin.

Something innocent and mysterious about her face, her emerald eyes, holds my gaze hostage.

Then she meets my stare, scrunches her nose, and rolls her eyes with all the disdain they can muster.

Bullshit.

It can't be.

With her face twisted into a scowl, I recognize her.

Goddamn if she isn't even more gorgeous scrunched into that dress than she was in jeans.

When she comes closer, I can't help smirking.

"So you've come dressed like a bandit while you're robbing away delicious pastries today? You look like an undertaker," I grind out.

Her mouth drops momentarily, then she tries to shake it off like she's only insulted. The hellcat narrows her eyes at me.

"I have an interview, and no, Captain Dipshit, I wouldn't dirty my hands with you. I'd let someone else scrape you off the ground like roadkill."

Captain Dipshit? Roadkill?

How charming.

That green-eyed little mouth needs someone to bend her over their knee and teach her to talk nicely to strangers.

In another life, maybe that someone would be me, but I'm remembering just how draining an encounter with this woman can be.

"No plans to join any dead raccoons today. Sorry to disappoint you. However, I believe I *will* deprive you of your pre-interview sugar rush. No pastry ever made rivals sweet revenge," I tell her.

27

She gives back this jarring laugh, tossing her bright hair before she looks at me like an angry lioness.

"Revenge for *what?* Because I beat you here last time and bought the last cinnamon roll? How petty are you?"

Excellent question.

She's about to find out.

I flash a vicious smile at the barista. "I'd like every Regis roll you have, please."

"Every—all of them? Every single one?" The poor barista blinks.

"Correct."

"Umm—there are three—almost four dozen today if we're counting what's in the back. Are you sure you—"

"All four dozen, then. A nice easy number."

"Whoa. You and your people must really love them, huh?"

I nod like I have a human soul.

In fact, the damn things are too sweet for me by far. After I drop off a few for Wyatt, I'll put the rest out for my senior staff. They all adore these overhyped cinnamon rolls as much as everyone else in this easily impressed city.

My own satisfaction ends with the roll witch behind me, deprived of her cherished fix today.

I turn slowly, casting a heavy look over my shoulder at her.

"Would you look at that? Some raging asshole just bought the last Regis roll. Maybe he'll share if you offer him an insane amount of money for one—or, better, how about an apology? Or maybe he'll just bite into it and lick his fingers like a cat walking away from a milk truck spill."

She smiles so sweetly, but her eyes are blazing green daggers.

"Nah. I don't hand out exorbitant sums for cinnamon rolls or apologies to jerkwads I never wronged. I make financial decisions with my brain, not my stomach. You should try it sometime," she snarls. "Also, I'm happy for the asshole who got the cinnamon rolls. He clearly must be missing something in his shriveled little ego and needs to overcompensate."

Damn her.

Damn her again for making that little sliver of space between her thumb and forefinger.

Oh, baby girl, if only you knew. No woman ever calls me little.

"I'll have you know, I woke up with a mad craving for a bear claw this morning," she continues, batting her lashes. "I'd hate to think my friends at Sweeter Grind put all that work into Regis rolls that went to waste."

For a second, I want to walk up to her, stare her into the ground, and tell her what's at stake.

How these rolls are the only way to keep a homeless man alive while he's in his funk.

Deprive him, fuck me over for a laugh, and you're single-handedly responsible for starving a veteran. I hope that helps you sleep at night.

Of course, I say none of those things.

This girl may have a taste for tormenting me, and she could be legit crazy. There's no upside to letting her know anything about me or my real need for these rolls.

"Nice cope, lady. You can't prefer a bear claw over a Regis roll. No one does," I growl.

What am I saying? I don't even like these stupid pastries.

I have no earthly idea why everyone hyperventilates over them ever since this little Montana cafe opened in Seattle. I just know that they do.

A voice in the back of my mind whispers, *You know it's not her fault that Wyatt didn't eat. Wyatt had debilitating problems long before you couldn't buy him his daily cinnamon roll.*

"Whatever, entitled douchebag," she huffs out.

For a second, I stop and glare.

"Just what makes you think I'm entitled? Because I offered you a car payment for your cinnamon roll?"

"Nope. You were pissed because I got the last cinnamon roll in spite of my being here *before* you, and then you didn't just offer to buy it. You offered me more than some people make in a week for it. Like I said, I make financial decisions with my brain.

No one who works for their money would have offered five hundred bucks for a freaking roll that would be available again the next day. You need your own hashtag. #BornRich."

What the fuck is she talking about?

"Watch your step. You might have no idea who you're talking to," I warn.

"Oh, I have a pretty good idea. Someone who doesn't get how much money that is."

"You don't think I know it's a lot? Obviously, if someone is willing to pay five hundred dollars for a damn roll, it's important to them. Any sane person would've snapped up the offer."

I hate how good she is at hooking her little claws under my skin.

I can feel my blood boiling.

"Oh, please. Forgive me if I found *my* Regis roll craving just as important as your five-hundred-dollar craving. And who *am* I talking to? Why don't you enlighten me? Are you some European prince? Royalty? Should I curtsy to His Majesty, Grand Duke of Dickheadistan?"

I have to bite my cheek to hold in a laugh. I hope this firecracker moonlights in stand-up comedy.

"You're a riot. And if there is such a country, it sounds like they'd better make you an ambassador. You're fluent in the neighboring asshole dialect."

She shrugs, finally taken aback, glancing away sharply.

"I was being serious. You suck," she says, still avoiding my eyes.

"And you think you're cute," I fire back.

"No, but apparently you do," she says, finally looking at me.

I fold my arms, waiting for whatever bullshit she's about to fling.

She grins. "You wouldn't have said it if you didn't think so."

Fuck.

Cute is an understatement. There's no denying she's gorgeous.

She just happens to be a coldhearted, ruthless, pastry-stealing queen bitch on top of it.

"Sir? I have your cinnamon rolls packed up. Are you ready to check out?" the barista says like a voice cutting in from another world.

"Almost. I need a box of black coffee, too."

The barista nods, moves to the back counter, and preps my coffee.

"I hope all that's for the miserable souls who have to put up with you," the little thief says.

"It's for my staff. I feed my people well so they can keep up with me," I grumble, knowing that's only half true.

"Keep telling yourself that, Big shot." She goes quiet for a minute before clucking her tongue and saying, "You *would* have a staff."

"What's that mean?" I ask slowly.

Why do I even care?

I don't know this chick from Eve and what I know about her, I despise. Who cares what she thinks about me? I don't, and I hope today is enough for her to buzz off.

With any luck, she'll pick a different cafe and I'll never see her again. It's a big city, or at least big enough.

I pay for the coffee and sweets without looking back at that literal green-eyed monster. The barista hands me three neatly packaged boxes of cinnamon rolls and a huge box of hot coffee.

I didn't plan on ordering breakfast for the whole company this morning.

I haven't thought this balancing act through, hoisting the coffee on my shoulders and heading for the door. I try to carry everything, but have to set it all down, reposition things, and try again at the table by the door.

The devil in the black dress lingers there as she waits for her bear claw, watching as I finally manage to get everything stacked in a way so I can trudge out the door.

That's all right, sweetheart. Don't get the door for me. I can manage just fine.

She must read my mind because she smiles at me.

"I'd like to help, but..."

"Offer not accepted. Save your energy for that breakfast you'll pretend to enjoy," I snarl, kicking the corner of the door open and spinning my way out.

Her high-pitched laugh is the last thing I hear.

I roll my eyes, swearing as a broken section of sidewalk catches my shoe. I almost drop hot coffee on my feet three times before I make it back to my car.

* * *

"OH MY GOD. *Oh my Gawd,* this is heaven," Lucy moans as she gnaws at a Regis roll and drops into the seat between Ida and me with a thud.

Apparently, eating for two makes you treat a pastry like it's a wagyu steak.

"Are you okay?" I ask.

She's going to pop any minute, and I'd rather it not happen here. I also wish her the best.

I don't know how this office—especially yours truly—will survive her maternity leave. As my executive assistant, Lucy keeps the place in order so I can focus on what I do best. *Making money.*

"Oh, I'm fine." She takes another bite that makes her eyes bulge. "Say, since when do you sit in on interviews?"

"I told him it wasn't necessary," Ida, my HR director, says with a flourish of her skunk-striped silver and black hair. "It's a senior copywriter position."

"Not *just* any copywriter position," I correct. "This new wedding line stands to make us billions of dollars—if it's marketed properly. I'm personally invested when the talent will make or break us. Besides, anyone we bring on right now has to be fully competent. You're about to go on maternity leave, Lucy, so that means I can't have new hires who need endless coddling. There's no time. Anyone we hire has to hit the ground running."

Lucy laughs. "I love being essential. How will you survive without me around here, boss?"

"We'll manage," I snap, hating that she has to rub her absence in. "Just get back as soon as possible."

"I'll get him a temp," Ida says.

"Ugh, good freaking luck. That never works out. It's usually worse than not having any assistant at all," Lucy says, wincing. "If you really want, I can try to sort your emails and the small stuff from home."

"Like hell. I won't have you working with a newborn. I'm not a complete ogre," I say, raking a hand through my hair.

"Not only that, but it's against the law, boss," Ida remarks. Leave it to an HR director to bring legalese into it and downplay my generosity.

She shrugs. "Hey, as long as I'm getting paid. I'm happy to help however I can when I'm not sneaking in naps."

"Just take care of your kidlet and be ready to put out any fires when you get back. Mark my words. Shit *will* fall apart," I tell them.

"Well, it's nice to be needed." She takes another heaping bite of the roll and lets out a moan of pure bliss.

"Stop that. We're having breakfast before an important interview, not recording adult audiobooks here," I snarl.

Lucy and Ida share a laugh.

"And what would you know about erotic audiobooks, Mr. Burns?" Ida asks.

"Not enough to play into anything that would invite the ire of corporate harassment policies," I say.

"Is that why everyone loves these things so much? They're better than sex?" Lucy twirls the last knob of her roll in her hand, staring at it.

Her words are jumbled because she's still chewing. She swallows loudly.

I don't dignify her musings with a response.

Thankfully, Anna Patel walks in a second later. My marketing head wears her usual bright colors like she just stepped out of a van Gogh painting. Today, it's a vivid yellow dress. Exactly the person I need to whip our focus back on business and not on erotic cinnamon rolls or whatever the fuck.

"Good morning." She hands me and Lucy a copy of the resumé in question before she sits beside Lucy. "I have a good feeling about this candidate, Mr. Burns. She could be the one."

I scan the resumé. The name jumps off the page.

Dakota Poe.

I snort.

"Any relation to Edgar Allan?" I mutter out loud, looking up. I haven't read any of his morbid classics since I was in high school, but you never forget one of the few authors who made sophomore English class interesting. "Did Mr. Poe give up his stint in poetry for a junior level copywriting position?"

Everyone groans.

Apparently, they like my audiobook jokes better.

I'm not nearly as impressed as Anna with the prospect, either. Hell, this is probably one of those social media hotshots who legally changed their name to make themselves look more appealing. I don't need gimmicks. I'll even take solid work over experience at an alphabet company.

"*She* is quite good at copywriting, though it looks like she dabbles in poetry too."

I meet Anna's eyes.

"So, Poe's a woman? How do you know?"

"I checked out her website. She's done rather nice work for smaller companies. I don't think she's worked with an organization this large before, but if she brings the same creativity here that she's shown in her portfolio, she could freshen up the big campaign."

My brows pull down, my skepticism growing by the second.

"How many other candidates are there?"

"Well...I got about a hundred resumés, but only three candidates worth talking to. If the three musketeers don't work out, the only thing I can think of is sending the job requisition back to HR and having it reposted."

"I can repost it if we need to," Ida says.

Lucy sighs. "I hope it doesn't come to that. We need someone now. The clock is ticking to get them trained in."

She points at her bulging belly. The other women laugh.

That's the God's truth and I hate it.

"Good help is damnably hard to find. We'll work with the three you've narrowed down and hope one of them can hack it," I tell them.

"The sooner we get started, the better," Anna says.

"With the earnings potential of this line, I agree, Miss Patel." Maybe I'll catch a lucky break today. I can't afford more delays.

The receptionist peers into the open door. "Your nine o'clock is here."

"Send her in," I say immediately.

She disappears and comes back a second later with a striking green-eyed blond whose black dress fits her like a glove. If this is Miss Poe, she has a ravenesque figure, everything except for the stark white-gold hair that almost reminds me of—

Wait.

Hold the fucking phone.

It's not that she *looks* familiar.

The realization feels like a bullet between the eyes.

What the hell kind of sick, psychotic joke is this?

I whirl around in my chair, glaring at my staff one by one, already trying to suss out the traitor. Only, nobody's hiding a red-faced laugh at my expense behind their hand.

Anna stands, completely normally, and holds out her hand.

"Anna Patel, I'm the marketing director. Nice to meet you."

The green-eyed, pastry-thieving witch flashes a wide smile. "Dakota Poe. It's great to meet you."

Fuck.

Her name was Dakota, wasn't it?

Ida shuffles out of her chair and moves behind me to shake Dakota's hand. "I'm Ida, the HR director."

I can't even bring myself to look at her.

I have no intention of shaking this woman's—*anything.*

This will be a short interview, and the poor girl doesn't realize it. She hasn't made eye contact with me yet.

Lucy grasps the arm of her chair and launches herself—baby belly and all—out of her seat. After the Herculean effort, it would be ridiculous of me not to stand, I suppose.

Biting my tongue, I try not to roll my eyes out of my head as I scramble to my feet woodenly.

Lucy holds her hand out next.

"Lucy Smith, I'm EA to our CEO, Lincoln Burns, but I pretty much run the show around here," she jokes.

"Great to meet you," Dakota says with a friendly smile I've never seen on that face before.

"The pleasure is all mine, but if you don't mind, I'm going to sit back down," Lucy tells her.

"Of course," Dakota says.

My turn.

I suddenly have a horrible need to see how far this punk-ass prank goes.

Slowly, I push past Lucy and extend my hand.

Raven chick looks up with the guarded expression of someone meeting their life's gatekeeper.

Our eyes connect. I wait.

Then comes grim realization.

Her breath hitches, a gasp so tiny I think the women miss it.

She corrects her reaction immediately, but not before I see the way her eyes go wide and round when my face clicks in her memory.

Goddamn, that feels good.

I bet she regrets stealing Wyatt's Regis roll now.

Is she hearing a record scratch? Are the bitter words she said to me this morning playing through her head right now like a cheesy comedy film?

I'd like to help, but...

Because they're damned sure on repeat in mine.

I'm half expecting a laugh track to go off from nowhere and to see *Seinfeld's* Kramer come skidding through the door next.

Poe fidgets with her hands and stands on the other side of the table with her lips trembling. The red, defiant anger I'm used to seeing looks drained from her pale face, her eyes whirling with confusion.

How does it feel to be cornered, Nevermore?

"Have a seat," I bite off, forcing a too-wide smile and gesturing to the table.

Her hands fall to the chair closest to her.

I point to the end of the table.

"We'd like to have you closer. Try over there," I say again, slowly and darkly.

Dakota stares at me in horrible silence, then nods and moves to the end of the table, where she'll be right next to me.

Looks like my sweet revenge could gag an elephant.

Lucy, Anna, and Ida all look at me, tossing curious looks around the room.

"Just sit wherever you're comfortable," Anna says as Miss Poe lingers without quite sitting down.

"She's comfortable there," I say matter-of-factly.

She nods—too briskly—and pulls out the chair at the other end of the table.

I turn my head to Anna again. "Miss Patel, would you kindly bring Miss Poe a cinnamon roll? I believe we have a few left in the box outside and I'm sure she'd enjoy one for visiting us today. Everyone in this city is practically ready to go to war over those rolls."

Anna nods at me and stands.

Dakota throws up her hand, finally showing me a hint of the hellcat I'm used to. "No, Miss Patel. Thank you, but I'm good. The roll looks lovely, but I had a huge *bear claw* on my way in. I really can't eat another bite."

Anna nods again with a polite smile and sits.

"From Sweeter Grind?" I ask.

Dakota looks at me like she's drilling a hole in my head.

"Is there anywhere else in Seattle worth the calories?"

"I believe there are many places in this city where you can get delicious pastries," I tell her. "Of course, the Regis rolls are their signature creation. People will fight over them."

"I suppose that's true," she says awkwardly.

I shrug. "Maybe. Or maybe someone in front of you buys the last pastry in the whole place and refuses to sell it for a stupefying profit. Then you have no choice but to go somewhere else to satisfy your sweet tooth."

She holds my gaze. "Sounds like you value availability over quality, Mister—Mr. Burns, was it?"

"Lincoln Burns," I say harshly, giving a name to the sneer she won't forget for the rest of her natural life.

Such a shame.

She has the right backbone to work long hours on a luxury line. Too bad I have a policy against hiring deranged pastry thieves who put pride over commonsense profit. Even if it's not in the HR handbook, it's my policy, made up right here.

Still, I'm not above making her squirm like a worm on a hook for the next half hour.

Anna and Lucy sit quietly, watching this baffling tennis match of words with muted, wondering looks. Finally, Anna clears her throat.

"So, Miss Poe, I checked out your website," Anna says. "You've done some excellent work. The project I was most interested in was the campaign you did for a local florist last year.

That's exactly the kind of creative edge we're looking for. Can you tell us about it?"

For a second, Poe looks at me. The eyes live up to her namesake, at least. A whole army of ghosts and nineteenth century killers dance in her gaze.

"You heard Miss Patel. Can you?" I whisper slowly when she's quiet for too long. "Expiring minds want to know," I say, deliberately swapping out inquiring for expiring.

I'd love to think I threw her off her game. Knocked her flat with the sheer shock of seeing me here, a hate note from the universe that what goes around comes around in spades.

Only, she smiles, exuding an annoying confidence with teeth that seem too sharp.

"I'd love to," she says, locking those bewitching green eyes on me. "Let's see, where do I begin..."

III: ONLY THIS AND NOTHING MORE
(DAKOTA)

"I'd love to. Let's see, where do I begin..." I say, then everything goes right out the window.

I can't even remember the question.

And it's all thanks to the brute in the suit who's painfully close to me, staring like he's holding my death warrant.

Breathe.

So Hot Shrek—the Grand Duke of Dickheadistan himself—is on the interview panel. So what?

There's basically no chance you're going to get this job, but you can still be the best candidate. You can make everyone else question his decision-making when he hacks up some sorry excuse for shooting you down.

I draw in a deep breath. "I'm sorry. Can you repeat that?"

"I was just asking if you could tell us about the project you did for the florist," Anna says, cocking her head like she's wondering if I'm okay.

Right. It's face-saving time.

The job was for almost no pay and involved thousands of dollars' worth of flowers. I slogged through it the same way I'll strap on my mud boots today, too.

"They were having a hard time competing with the bigger

chain shops. Most of their previous campaigns focused on the flowers themselves. After studying competitors' ads, I realized they focused more on the experience. So I asked the florist, 'Why buy my bouquet from you instead of the place down the street?' She said, 'It will be every bit as beautiful at half the price.' 'Why do I care?' At this point, she looked at me like I was dumb and told me, 'You'll save money. Obviously.' But again, 'Why do I care?' She came back with, 'Duh! You can use that money to fly to Hawaii with your new husband!' And that's what I went with. She gave me the perfect concept, unwittingly. A smiling couple leaving for their honeymoon with the bride still clutching her bouquet. The flowers were almost an afterthought when sentimentality makes brides buy flowers." I pause, stretching my hands on the table. "Copywriting is all about emotion. We all like to think we make decisions based on logic, but really, most people let their hearts do the deciding."

My eyes unintentionally fall on Satan. He's fit for the fallen angel part today with that navy-blue suit stretched over his mile-wide shoulders, a brown tie tucked neatly into his suit that's barely a shade off from his dark, piercing eyes.

What emotional connection does Lucifer have to his cinnamon rolls? I wonder.

I remember how he just offered me one for the ego stroke.

Does he get off on power play involving pastries? Is this how he buys loyalties and seals business deals?

I almost laugh at the absurdity, but it would make a twisted kind of sense.

Careful. You have one chance to pull this out. Act normal, a voice whispers in the back of my head.

"What made you go into copywriting?" Anna asks.

"Copywriting—well, actually writing in general—has been my jam since I was eight years old." I smile. "I started a lemonade stand in my front yard. My first banner was pretty boring and it said something like *Lemonade fifty cents.* The first two hours, people kept walking past. When I went inside for lunch, I made a new banner. *Beat the heat with ice cold lemonade!!!* I remember using three exclamations at the end. I made ten dollars and we ran out of lemonade before sunset. That's when I realized that the words you use matter. Sometimes a whole lot."

"Smart thinking, especially for a kid. What's your biggest achievement?" Lucy asks.

"When I was in high school, I won the Young National Poet's award—"

Lucifer snorts. So loudly I stop mid-sentence, my eyes whipping to him.

"With a name like Poe, it must be in your blood," he growls.

Very funny, prick. You're such a funny man you've made the whole room quiet enough to hear a pin drop.

"You're not a copywriter, are you?" I glare back at him, hoping if I act fearless long enough, then maybe I'll actually feel brave sooner or later.

He glares at me. "I'm the CEO."

Holy yikes.

I almost choke. This maniac runs the entire company?

I had him pegged as some high-level project manager, a midwit with a God complex inflated to Jupiter.

But it looks like he owns his own corporate kingdom to help justify the mania.

Just peachy.

Somehow, this keeps getting better.

"Well, marketing copy has to be original—you can't just swipe it from somebody else," I explain.

Anna snickers.

"Yeah?" Lucifer asks. "I'm not sure what you're implying, Miss Poe."

"Oh, nothing. Just that I'm confident you're better with big decisions than with words. We hope, anyway, am I right?" I shrug, winking at the other women in the room. "You're a little late with the Poe jokes, by the way. The guy who came in second place in that poetry contest swore that it was rigged for me because I'm very, very distantly related to *the* Poe. Nah, dude, sorry. He just lost. I told him to his face to get over it and he didn't like that. Some boys are just sore losers when they don't get their way and never take the hint."

Burns' eyes become brush fires.

Ida notices his death stare and looks back at him, until he notices her and straightens up, leaning back in his seat with a shoulder roll and flex of his arms.

God. It's almost obscene how he moves.

I hate that he's chiseled—one more ridiculous thing that makes him a perfect fit for the royal title I kindly bestowed on him—and he probably uses his good looks to push people around.

"Well, congratulations. That's a real accomplishment for someone so young," Ida says.

I nod. "Thanks. It came with a scholarship in the arts at a public university of my choice. All of my professors agreed I could sling words well enough, and since I started with a lemonade stand, copywriting just made sense."

"You can write copy anywhere," Burns grumbles. "Why here? Why Haughty But Nice out of dozens of other companies in this city that would be thrilled to have you?"

Ugh.

Now that I know *he* runs the place, I'm not sure I want to work here. But I do like holding my own in this interview.

Just suffer through the next hour. Get out of here. Let the chips fall where they may.

"Well, Haughty But Nice sells an upscale product without being over the top. It's the kind of style I appreciate," I say. "I also love that it was started by a busy mom, and the marketing you've been putting out lately has been pretty eye-catching. You produce innovative copy. I'm a creative at heart more than anything else. I'll be an asset here, but I'll learn a lot along the way, I'm sure. A challenge keeps things interesting."

The women smile, impressed with my generous, easygoing answer.

Ogreman frowns, of course.

Obviously because he knows I nailed it.

Nothing I said was kissing up or untrue. It was all genuine—at least, it was when I first walked in here with answers to questions like that drafted in my mind.

"We asked about the florist project because it's the closest to what you'll be doing here," he says coldly. "We're preparing a major launch for a brand-new line of luxury wedding attire, and our current copywriters already have dedicated projects. We need fresh blood. Think you can handle that?"

Weddings?

My whole body stiffens.

I detest them.

They're sentimental fluff designed to keep a sixty-billion-dollar sham industry alive. Plus, there's always a risk your personal investment becomes a catastrophic loss when the groom runs off with his secretary—or you know, a bandmate—leaving you with nothing but your tears.

My face must give me away.

"Miss Poe? Is wedding content going to be a problem?" he asks, snapping his fingers to draw me out of my trance. "Surely, being a Poe doesn't mean you're stuck writing about dreary dungeons and atrocious maniacs, right?"

I keep my face stern and meet his eyes.

"I like writing about the beating hearts of the men I bury under my floorboards only occasionally." I cock my head while the women around us snicker. "It's no problem at all. I can write about anything as the depth of my portfolio shows."

"Very original, Poe," he throws back.

"Not even close. I've been collecting bad Poe jokes for twenty-four years. Unless you've been writing them that long, you don't have one I haven't heard."

"Sorry, but I have to ask... Do you guys know each other?" Anna looks at me.

Oh, crap. Did I come on too strong?

I stop and stare like I'm caught in the headlights.

"We've met," the suit answers for me. "It's becoming a regular occurrence in the morning coffee line. If I'd known it was her, I could have saved us a lot of trouble," he adds under his breath.

"Trouble?" Ida asks.

I smile at her even though I'm breaking inside.

If this is how it's going down, I'd might as well get the last word in.

"He means that this whole interview is just a formality, right? He's already made up his mind," I venture.

"I'm sure he doesn't mean that at all. Do you, Mr. Burns?" Ida asks. When he doesn't answer for a few seconds, she looks at him and bites her lip. "Off-record reminder, it would be highly improper for a publicly traded company to make hiring decisions outside of the structured interview process."

Hot Shrek shakes his head and looks over my resumé.

"No decisions made and no objections lodged. Not *yet.* I'm still eager to find out what Miss Poe can do for us and why she's the best person for this job. Since the next questions are softballs, I won't risk any personal bias clouding the hiring. I'll step out and leave you fine ladies to the assessing," he says, sliding out of his seat.

Without a single look back, he's out the door, moving his hands to his throat like he's adjusting his tie—or making a cross like he's warding off a vampire.

Jesus. What was that?

Lucy rolls her eyes, slurping her coffee. "Nice save, bossman. Now, Miss Poe, can you tell us what you think your greatest strength is?"

I spend the next half hour fielding their questions, talking about my experience, thinking more and more about my potential boss and his rancid attitude. His absence almost makes it worse. I'd rather dance with rabid wolves.

But I survive the final battery of questions, and I'd like to think I impressed them. At the end, they fall silent.

I guess it's over. Time to go home.

As I'm dreaming of tasting the freedom that's outside the door and wondering if any new jobs have been posted online today, a male voice growls over my shoulder.

"The new wedding line is crucial. You'll be reporting directly to me even while you're technically working under Miss Patel. A little spine goes a long way, and yours is made of diamond. Don't make me regret this."

Regret it? Regret what? Did I get the job?

What the actual hell?

The idea of working for this guy feels terrifying.

I'm too stunned to even muster a thanks.

But he stares at me, expectant. Like I'm supposed to fall down and hug his leg. Genuflect. Kiss his ring. Kiss his —whatever.

"I'm hired then?" I ask softly. I need to hear it from the horse's mouth.

Those bottomless honey-brown eyes drop from my face to my lips.

Just like the day he tried to bribe my cinnamon roll away. And just like that first ugly morning, that gaze on my lips makes me tingle.

No, no, no, and no.

He's a professional ass in a tie and apparently my new boss.

He shrugs. "No point in wasting more time pretending it's not a done deal. Are there any last-minute objections?"

He waits while heads shake around the room. I'm glued to my seat in awe at how utterly ballsy and open he is.

"Good. We'll have your background check by the end of the day. Barring any surprises, you can start ASAP. Always remember you can leave just as easily as you came in, so don't get cocky," he says.

"Well, okay. We just need to hammer out the details," Ida says.

"Why don't you get the paperwork? We can take care of it right now," Burns tells her.

"Stop by when you're done and I'll introduce you to the team," Anna says cheerfully.

"That's great. Thank you," I say numbly, my mind whirling with a tornado of thoughts.

Do I really want this? Can I afford to be picky? I know it pays well and the benefits are bomb. Can I afford to flip him off and leave?

The women are nice. Maybe I can just deal.

The ladies leave the conference room one by one, filing out and leaving me alone with Prince Douchenozzle.

"Congratulations," he grinds out reluctantly.

"Thanks...I think?"

The glare he levels could vaporize me several times over.

Yeah. If I want this position, I'm definitely going to have my work cut out for me, and it's got nothing to do with the actual *work*.

Ida comes strolling back in with her laptop a minute later. "We still call it paperwork, but it's mostly digital."

"What do you make at your current job?" she asks.

"Thirty-five thousand a year."

"Wait." Burns throws up a hand, making an exasperated sound. "You make thirty-five thousand dollars a year and you turned down five hundred dollars for a damn roll? And you called me insane?"

Ignore him.

Easier said than done.

Ida scowls at him over her laptop.

"Start her at ninety even with immediate performance incentives, plus the full match in her 401k," he says.

Ninety thousand and then some?

To write?

Is this seriously happening?

"Oh-kay." Ida draws the word out so much it's almost two. "When can you start, Dakota?"

"Soon. I need to give two weeks' notice and tie up any loose ends before I—"

"She'll start Monday," Burns tells her point-blank.

My toes curl up in my shoes.

"But I...I need to give two weeks' notice."

"Why's that, Miss Poe? It's not like they're paying you," he snaps.

Woof. He's so rude.

"Because it's the right thing to do," I say with a sniff.

He waves his hand dismissively.

"So is paying your employees. Your choice, I suppose. You can start Monday with a job that pays more than double your current salary, or you can hang out at your discount agency and keep nibbling at crumbs. I need someone ready to dive in now."

Well, thanks, Mr. Hardass.

He says it in a way that tells me he's not used to having people argue back, much less delay his beck and call.

"Fine. Can I get the offer in writing?" I ask through clenched teeth.

He nods, never taking his eyes off me.

"Have her sign off on it and send it over for my signature." He turns and starts moving across the room, but stops with a hard glance over his shoulder. "Free tip: the next time you're in a job negotiation, don't tell anyone your current salary. It's none of their business. They'll pay what you're worth and nothing else."

Amazing. I never knew it was possible to hate a total stranger this much.

He strides out of the room with the air of a mafia don who's just given his new capo one chance not to wind up dismembered in a dog's dinner bowl.

Ida blinks and laughs awkwardly. "You certainly bring out quite the reaction in our fearless leader."

"So, he's not always like that?"

She twists her lips. "He's a hard worker and doesn't tolerate much foolery, but he's not usually such a jacka—bad guy, I mean. Not usually."

Awesome.

So I get to be the magnet for his lightning storm of assholery.

Why? All because I got to the freaking coffee shop before him and swiped the last cinnamon roll?

What a psycho.

A psycho who's willing to pay me almost six figures to work for him, but still...

Just what will this job cost me if Lincoln Burns stays obsessed with making my life suck?

* * *

"GOOD LORD, I think I'm high on the fumes alone," I say, pushing into Eliza's apartment.

Her laughter echoes off the low ceiling. "Do you want coffee?"

"Do you have more of that sexy vanilla?"

She shakes her head. "I brewed up a hazelnut cinnamon blend, a coconut, and chocolate pecan today. What's your poison?"

"Chocolate pecan."

"Good choice. There's a vanilla scone with your name on it, though."

"When are you opening a cafe?" I demand, giving her a mock-stern look with my hands propped on my hips.

"As soon as I have the money sometime this century. Commercial rent in this city ain't getting any cheaper." Eliza heads for her kitchen coffee lab to start prepping "the caffeinated flight" as she calls it.

49

She's basically my dealer at this point, besides being my bestie and neighbor.

I take a stool in front of the kitchen bar, basking in the heavenly smell of her place.

She returns a minute later with two steaming mugs and scones piled high on a plate.

"How was the big interview?" she asks. "Tell me we have something to celebrate."

"Bonkers, honestly, but—" Big pause. "I got the job."

"Yes!" She puts her mug down to throw both fists in the air and then hugs me. "I knew you'd pull it off. When you said bonkers, you must mean the awesome kind."

"Well..." I clear my throat and take a comically long sip of coffee.

"Uh-oh. Don't tell me it's a traveling job or something. Dakota, if you're leaving me, I'll lose it."

"No, nothing like that," I say with a sigh. I wish it was that simple because at least it'd be a relatable, human problem. Not whatever this thing is with a charging bull who buys cinnamon rolls by the bucketful. "Okay, so you remember the crazy who tried to buy my Regis roll for five hundred smackeroos a few days ago?"

"Yeah?" She blinks at me.

"I saw him at the coffee shop again this morning, and he remembered me. He decided to be an even bigger swinging dick. Before I could even flip him off, he stepped up and bought four dozen Regis rolls to make sure I didn't get a single one."

She stares at me in disbelief.

"Talk about issues! But that means the cray cray happened before the interview then. That's good news, I bet?"

"Um..." I hesitate. "That wasn't the biggest drama."

"Dakota," she presses, setting her cup down and rubbing her weary eyes. "Look at me. I spend at least twelve hours a day every day smelling like a human coffee bean and baking my butt off. My knees haven't taken me on a walk farther than a block for a week. When you have drama and you hold back—no. Girl, you *dish it right now."*

I'm laughing and sympathetic as she takes an annoyed slurp of coffee.

"Fine. He's the frigging CEO, and he was on the interview panel."

I'm hit by a sudden warm mist on my arm. Courtesy of Eliza, laughing so hard she spews coffee everywhere.

"Get out! Sorry." She looks down, grabs a rag, and starts wiping up her mess while she says, "So how did *that* go?"

"About like you'd expect. He kept making unfunny dad jokes about my last name and my interest in joining his lowly copywriter team. He even mocked my poetry scholarship. Sorry, but not all of us were born with a silver spoon in our mouths. Some of us had to work."

"This weirdo owns Haughty But Nice? The whole shebang?" Eliza asks.

I nod.

"Unfortunately."

"They own a lot of lines. Do you know what you'll be writing for?"

I don't want to say it, much less do it. But I kinda have to, so I should just make my peace with it and move on.

"Dakota, hey...you look like you're sucking on a lemon and I know it's not my food. My stuff never sucks." She laughs.

"They want me on their new luxury line. A wedding campaign. Lucky me."

Her face falls. A moment passes in dead silence.

"Oh. Oh, jeez. Can you...can you do that?" Eliza asks softly.

I roll my shoulders in something resembling a shrug.

"I have to if I want that payday. I've written copy for everything under the sun, including a pet cemetery—"

"That gig was so sad. But at least the pets were dead." She shakes her head. "Never a dull moment with you around, is there?"

51

"I can't imagine writing for a wedding being tougher than selling doggy plots," I say miserably.

"Enough! You're freaking morbid, but you really don't like weddings. You have good reason not to, I mean, and—"

"I don't. You're right," I agree with a heavy sigh. I abhor them. "If I'd known they were hiring specifically for a wedding line, I wouldn't have applied. But after I got there and found out the Cinnamon Roll King was interviewing me, I couldn't do anything but beat the odds or blow myself up spectacularly. Now, I kind of want the job just to prove I can handle it. He needs to know I'm not intimidated and he has no control over me."

She grins. "You sure he doesn't? That sounds like a lot of effort for—"

"He *doesn't*. Okay?" I'm surprised at the sternness in my own voice.

"Fair enough. But you're spending a lot of time thinking about this guy," she says gently.

"Not like I want to. He just keeps popping up in the worst places like a bad rash. I've never said anything nice about him."

She shakes her head slowly, her hair swaying loosely.

"No, but after Jay...do you really want another dude in your life who's nothing but bad news? Even if he's not the romantic kind..."

My heart sinks. I ignore her question because we both know the answer.

I grab a vanilla scone and bite it in half.

"It gets worse," I tell her, chewing loudly.

"Um, what? Your coffee shop arch-rival is about to be your new boss, and apparently he's as hot as he is arctic-hearted. How does it get worse?" She takes a long pull off her coffee.

I take a deep breath.

"My new job, of course. I'll be reporting directly to him."

"Oh! Oh, shit. That should be...fun?" She hesitates.

I glare at her.

"Hardly, but it's almost triple my current pay. More than a living wage for once in this city. So, hell yes, I'll do it. I'm signing away my soul on lease if I have to spend the rest of my time there with him riding my ass. I'll put up with a lot for ninety thou."

"Big reward, but I'm being serious now. Are you *sure* you can handle the wedding stuff? Taking the job to make this prick hurt is one thing, but you've done that. Mission accomplished. If it's just going to make you miserable, don't take it. If the asshat will pay you well, someone else will too. You don't have to be desperate."

I smile, genuinely thankful for her insights.

Eliza always has perspective I don't.

I slurp my coffee and set the cup down before I answer.

"Well, it's a little awkward, I guess. But I have to move on at some point, right? It's been over a year. Weddings are a lucrative industry. I can't avoid all things wedding forever if I want to keep my options open—and this one screams 'get in.'"

"Dakota..."

"I know. I'll be fine, I promise. People get jilted all the time. Life doesn't just stop with one awful breakup." I know I'm saying all the right things. I just wish I could internalize them enough to *feel* them.

"True. You're moving on up in the world and you shouldn't let anything hold you back," she says warmly. "You'll get a condo soon and won't even need me feeding you anymore."

"If I get a condo, you'll be my roommate. I can't make scones."

She laughs. "Glad to know you keep me around for a reason. So, you've got a new job title, new pay grade, and soon you'll have a new place. You just have to do a little dance with the devil. Hey, if you play your cards right, maybe you'll come out of this with a new marital status too."

I choke on my scone, shooting her a dirty look when I stop coughing.

"Don't. Don't even joke. There's no way in hell. I don't believe in weddings or marriage or fairy-tale love—not anymore —and this guy will never be anything but my boss. The dickhead is my polar opposite. Oh, plus the internet rumors—"

"Rumors? You Googled him?"

Busted.

"No. Yes. I mean, only *after* he interviewed me and said I'd be reporting directly to him. I just wanted to know who I'm working for..."

Eliza nods, but her smile says she doesn't fully believe me.

"And what do the rumors say?"

"He's loaded. Big surprise. He's also a lot more invisible than most guys with his holdings. The good looks make him a magnet for women who must be sick in the head to overlook his crappy personality—go figure—so he takes a lot of flak for being Mr. Undateable."

Eliza winces.

"That's rough, but who cares, right? You're working for him, not warming his bed. In fact, in HR circles, that's a big no-no."

"Still. It shows you what a fire-breathing jerk he is."

"Are you okay? You're a little red," she tells me, her eyes widening.

"I'm just annoyed." Yeah. More like flustered. Hating that my ticket to financial freedom and a better life involves this bitch-slap to the face. "Even if the rumor mill didn't say he was undateable, his freakout in the coffee shop basically proved it. If I were the sort of girl who believes in cheesy crap like love, I wouldn't date a guy who loses his shit over a cinnamon roll."

"Is that cool, though? Like how will you market weddings? You just said you hate cheese."

"If I ever have a dog die, I'll bury it in my backyard. But that didn't keep me from selling puppy plots."

"You don't have a backyard. Also, *buzzkill.*"

"Good point, but I also don't have a dog." I sigh, sipping my coffee before I continue. "Then there were the lame jokes about my last name."

Eliza sips her coffee. "I don't get what that has to do with anything."

"Nothing, I guess. Just makes him extra undateable. You'd think a man so awful could at least make you laugh... I'm just saying. Why would I ever date a certified bosshole? Why would anyone?"

"He was probably just teasing you, but who are you trying to convince? Me or you, Dakota?" She stares at me, waiting for an answer.

I feel a little dizzy, and I know it's not just the coffee and sweets.

"You, of course. Who else? I won't even joke about dating the d-bag going forward. Since you brought it up, I'm just trying to let you know why it won't happen."

"But I didn't exactly bring it up..."

Didn't she? I replay our conversation in my head.

Wait.

Oh, God.

She's right.

What am I stumbling into? I'm writing for an industry I hate and reporting to a man who might be criminally insane.

Oh, let's count the ways this could go wrong.

It's true that my growing salary means I'll no longer be a disposable intern or busy fixing some creative idiot lead's mistakes. But is there more wrong than right with this job?

It's a decent move up, all right, but at what cost?

Can I actually survive this?

"You got quiet," Eliza urges softly.

"I'm okay." *I hope.*

"Buyer's remorse?"

"Not yet." But I'm terrified once I actually start the job, buyer's remorse might be the least of my concerns.

I finish my coffee and scones while we talk about the latest happenings around the neighborhood.

"I should go. He wants me to start right away, and I have a million things on my mind. The first is how I'm going to tell my current employer I can't give two weeks' notice. Thanks for the coffee and moral support."

"Anytime, Dakota. If you need anything at all, just give me a shout. I've got your back, but I don't think you need it. You look ready."

"Yeah, thanks," I mutter.

I so, so wish that was true.

When I creep back to my own four walls, I wonder how much I'll regret my wishes coming true.

IV: GHOST UPON THE FLOOR
(LINCOLN)

*W*hat a fucking day.

I know I've pissed off the universe when Nevermore, the pastry thief, turns out to be the most qualified candidate we have for the wedding line.

Just my luck.

She might be a black cat disguised as an angel and incredibly naive—why the hell did she spill her salary in the interview?—but at least she has writing chops.

That's what matters.

That's what makes me take a chance on a hire that's one big red flag whipping me in the face.

Her personality might be difficult, but once she's settled into working under me, I'm confident she'll fall in line. If she brings the same spark to her ad copy, she'll also make me money hand over fist, whatever our personality clashes.

When all's said and done, that's the endgame.

I'm ready to get the hell out of here by the time evening rolls around. I grab the cinnamon rolls I bagged up and leave, walking past rows of empty desks. My driver, Louis Hughes, the only employee who's been with the company longer than I have, waits at the curb. I open the door and slide into the back seat.

"Welcome back, Mr. Burns. Home?" he asks.

"Wyatt's first," I say, instantly aware of how he glances back with concern.

"Will do." He pulls onto the street.

By now, he knows the address by heart, even if it isn't on any Google Maps.

I thumb through my email, responding to items Lucy flagged for me. I'm going to be completely boned when she goes on leave. Her organizational prowess makes it infinitely easier to manage this company.

I've made it through five emails when the car stops in front of the familiar, large encampment. There's a typical Seattle spring rain pelting the windows, turning the tents outside into smears of color against the night.

"Here we are. Should I come with you? I'm always perfectly willing," Louis offers.

"I won't drag you out into the rain, Louis. It's just a short walk. Save your fussing for somebody that deserves it. I always come back, don't I?"

His eyes linger on me, dark with worry.

"Are you sure, boss? Forgive me, but this isn't the safest place. The papers said there were four robberies and two armed assaults here last week," he says. "You're a public personality, Mr. Burns. If any bad actors recognized you and took the notion to —well, I might be too late to help if I'm warming my butt in the car."

I chuckle. "Louis, I was a Marine. Plus, far more of those people out there are veterans than you'd think. If trouble goes down, I'm sure I'll have backup."

Frowning, he nods.

"Of course, sir. Sorry to complain. Even after all these years, I sometimes forget you're a little more bold on the streets than Tillie."

"Don't be sorry. Ma needed to feel safe and you always did the job. I appreciate your concern. Give me twenty minutes before you send in the cavalry to find me." I clap him on the shoulder.

Clutching Wyatt's cinnamon rolls, I get out of the car, walking briskly under whatever cover I can find because I didn't bother with an umbrella.

I'm a real Seattleite to the core. Having spent most of my life in this town, the rain feels like my own pulse. Contrary to popular belief, nobody who calls this place home gives a damn about getting wet.

The cool water mists my brows, my hands, the back of my neck like the pure night reaching down inside me, scrubbing away the day's filth—especially my two infuriating brushes with Nevermore.

Out here, it's about what you expect with life on the streets.

Sadly, the Emerald City has a lot of bustling streets and parks and back alleys where this hard life is the only life anyone knows.

I pass a trio of men in worn jeans passing a bottle of cheap whiskey back and forth. Lonely women puffing cigarettes and cigarillos for an extra touch of warmth on a wet night. A once-red tent, now faded pink from the sun, small flower pots strewn around it.

Several tents later, I find him sitting beside a fire in front of his meager home, an old fisherman's cap yanked down over his eyes.

His cheeks are sunken. There are black rings around his eyes.

Goddamn, my best friend looks like shit, and it's got nothing to do with the fact that he's homeless. He's been hollowed out, drained, the kind of tired sleep can't fix.

He's never been this beat down by the treachery that brought him here, and it makes my gut wrench.

I sit down beside him.

"Sorry I couldn't bring you a roll the other day. Like I told you, a greedy crow snatched it out from under me at the last second," I say, pushing the bag toward him.

"It's whatever." He shrugs with his whole body, like it takes that much will just to roll his shoulders. "You bring me one tonight?"

"Half a dozen to make up for the shortage. I hope you're hungry," I say, offering him a thin smile.

Wyatt doesn't smile back. He reaches inside the bag, grabs a roll, and bites it in half the second it's in front of his face.

He's still the most human when he's stuffing his face with sugary carbs, his cheeks ballooning like a cartoonish chipmunk behind his grizzled beard.

He winks at me as he chews, and after a long while, he swallows and says, "Thanks, man."

My stomach drops.

It's amazing how a simple pastry brings him back like watering a wilted plant. Even so, he's getting thinner by the month. Dirtier and more depressed, his once bright pale-blue eyes dimmer as the days wear him down.

I can't fucking leave him like this tonight.

Not without offering comfort I know he'll refuse—but dammit, I always have to *try*.

"When was the last time you ate?" I ask carefully, knowing how much he hates questions.

He slices a dismissive hand through the air.

"Aw, hell. I don't know. A couple days ago?" He stares past me like he's really trying to think.

"Did you eat the bear claw?" I ask, propping one leg on the empty box next to him to stretch.

"Nah." He shoves the rest of the roll in his mouth and shakes his head, taking his sweet time without elaborating. "I traded it to some lady for a couple duck eggs. Scrambled 'em."

I smile, hoping he isn't bullshitting me and actually got some protein into his system.

With Wyatt, unfortunately beggars *can* be choosers.

He's one stubborn SOB. Always has been, and the streets

turned what used to be an asset into a massive liability when the man barely cares about feeding himself these days.

I scan his surroundings, the modest possessions he keeps by the tent. An old canteen, a few empty ceramic pots, a broken bike lock that did nothing to stop some jackass from taking off with a small cart full of his stuff a couple months ago.

Something seems out of sorts—more so than usual.

I can't pinpoint what until my eyes fall on his tattered boot.

A *single* lonely, ripped-up boot.

Fuck.

So that's why he looks worse than usual. He's missing his goddamned leg. I swallow.

"Wyatt, what happened to the—?"

"Asshole with a knife jacked it last week," he says dully. "I clocked him good in the nose, but he shoved me on the ground and...yeah."

I stare at the empty space, anger surging through my veins. "Someone stole your prosthetic? For fuck's sake, why?"

"Why not? I've lost everything else. What the hell's one more fake limb added to the pile?" He laughs bitterly.

It's a ruthless gut punch, and he didn't even mean it to be.

There are a lot of things in his life he didn't mean.

The man just doesn't give two shits anymore—not even about his own life—and that's why that job falls to me now.

My jaw tightens as I look at him, already working on his second roll. If only he wasn't so far up his own ass. I could at least protect him from being preyed on by vultures and punk-ass kids willing to rob homeless vets for drug money.

I've made the same offer a million times. Now that he's one leg short, will he finally be more open? Will he swallow his pride?

"You know I've got an entire heated guesthouse and no company," I say slowly. "If you want to crash, you could—"

"No," he spits back, giving me a scorned look.

There's nothing I will ever hate about this man except for his suicidal ego.

Hell, the rejection was out like a shot, before I even finished. That's faster than usual.

"It's detached. It would be like having your own place," I say, not ready to give up. "It sits there whether anyone uses it or not. Sometimes I wonder why I have the damn thing when nobody visits."

He shakes his head like I'm forcing a ghost pepper up his nose.

"Try your charity on somebody else, Burns. There are folks here with reasons to live who need a good sleep and a hot shower a whole lot more than I do, like Miss Green Thumb a few tents down. You want to help, offer it to her. I'm beyond that shit. Don't need it. I like my tent and washing off at the Y just fine."

I let out a frustrated growl. I can't fucking help it.

I can't help how seeing him give up rips me in two.

Yeah, it's no surprise. I knew he was sailing into rough waters the minute he wound up on the streets. I've also never heard him sound quite so sure about being done until now.

It's not him. He's a fighter by nature.

He *was*, I should say, before that evil bitch destroyed him.

Before he began the slow, agonizing fall into the black pit of misery he's in now.

He'll never get over her, and he can't pull his life back together until he does.

"Look, Wyatt. I'm not here to save you from yourself. We've both been through hell together. All I'm offering is a break from all this for a day, a week...whatever. Take a vacation and come back here recharged. There's no good fucking reason why you can't crash in my vacant guesthouse so we can have drinks together at the end of the day, and you know it."

He snorts dismissively.

"We can do that anyway. You're here now. No point in me

mooching off my best friend or stinking up space someone else could use. Your rich neighbors and maid are gonna think you've lost your mind, moving some random homeless guy in. And fuck, your mom—"

"You're *not* some random homeless guy," I say sharply. "You're my best friend. I wouldn't be here without you." I inhale sharply, feeling ghostly vibrations ripping through solid bone from that day. Even my muscle memory is keenly aware I'd be six feet under without Wyatt Emory. "You saved my life and you can't even crash at my place for a single night?"

He shakes his head like a bull, pulling at his wiry beard.

"It's nothing. If shit went the other way, you would've saved me too. You don't even have to keep up with the cinnamon rolls or my life. Hell, I don't even want to keep up with my life."

That's obvious, and a deep, toxic depression talking. I wish I could somehow reach inside him and rip it out of him like a parasite worm.

I hate that he's his own worst enemy.

Always too proud to accept any help.

Only, now I'm afraid he might be too scarred, too damaged to ever consider it.

Where the hell does that leave me trying to help him?

Do I just throw my hands up and watch a good man die?

Should I bother continuing this conversation?

I hold in a sigh because I'm afraid I'll exhale my soul. Talk is cheap, and tonight, it's damn near worthless.

I doubt it gets us anywhere, except for frustrating Wyatt more, causing him to dig his lonely heel into the ground.

My eyes flick over him, cool and assessing.

Part of me says *make him* get back on his feet. Just haul him off in a headlock and get him help. I'm sure Louis would help me wrestle him into the back seat.

He's on one leg and losing a few more pounds of muscle every month, even if he's still as strong as a pit bull.

It's not like he could run, but the only thing that's kept the poor SOB alive this long is his damn stubborn pride. His agency.

Take that from him—however well intended—and he might break forever.

I reach in my pocket and pull out a phone, holding it out to him.

"If you won't come home with me, at least take this. It's prepaid and has a lot of minutes on it."

He stares at it silently. He doesn't reach for it.

"Damn you, Wyatt. *Take it.* Keep it handy, just in case you need to call me or have an emergency. It's no big deal. I got a deal on it when I upgraded my phone, and yours broke a long time ago."

He stares into the fire for a minute before he reaches out and grabs the phone.

Thank God.

"My number's pre-programmed in the contacts. Number one. Call me anytime," I say.

He doesn't answer.

We sit there in silence for a while together, two old souls set in their ways like concrete.

It's getting late. I should go. But how will he even get back in the tent on one leg without crawling? If I ask, he'll bite my head off.

Maybe if I sit here long enough, he'll ask for help.

He doesn't, though, and eventually I take the hint and leave.

As I'm heading back to my town car on the curve, I wish the rain was colder. It can't dampen the hot fury lashing around inside me.

"I hope you're happy wherever you are, Olivia, you backstabbing fuck." I growl to no one, my fist tightening as I picture Wyatt's ex.

That's another thing we have in common, even if he took more damage from his cheating ex.

As the rain picks up, I mutter a dark prayer to Mother

Karma.

Just this once, I wish that a good man who's suffered so much could find some relief.

I also wish prayers actually came true.

* * *

MONDAY MORNING, I get to the office before eight a.m.

There's already a draft of new ad copy from Miss Poe waiting in my Inbox.

If she thinks a rushed job warrants her salary, she has another thing coming. I'll bring her in and set her straight. I open the document, almost salivating at the opportunity to rip it apart and haul her into my office to chew her out.

Hold the drool.

I blink at the screen, seeing neat lines of ads mocked up with punchy phrases and paired with eye-catching images.

It's damn good. Spotless, in fact.

There isn't anything to sink my teeth into. I can't be disappointed at a job well done.

At least my hiring decisions are spot on, even when they involve a pastry thief in a seductive black dress.

Regardless, I have a meeting scheduled with her today so we can clear the air. I'm not interested in leaving either of us languishing in a hostile work environment—no matter if she's eighty percent responsible for said hostility.

Yeah, I won't admit I'm to blame for how we started out.

This line needs talent, focus, and zero distractions. Something tells me she won't be the one to swallow her pride and make peace.

Time to step up and be the leader everyone respects around here.

If I'm lucky, I'll win her respect, too. She might start looking at me like I'm the boss instead of an inquisitor holding her salary hostage.

Fifteen minutes later, she steps into my office. Her slender legs, curvy hips, and annoyingly luscious ass are outlined in fitted black slacks today.

Her full breasts are hugged by a sparkling silver blouse that yanks my eyes to the tightly formed V on her chest, straight to her cleavage.

Fuck me.

For several heady seconds, I can't yank my eyes off her. My fingers drum against my desk, wondering if I should impose a new dress code, because there's nothing inappropriate about this outfit.

Fuck, Linc. Get it together.

"You summoned me?" She says it too obediently. I half expect her to add *Master* to the end.

Then I catch the cactus-like look in her eye and realize it's all sarcasm.

Damn this insufferable woman.

Damn her lips, too, so full and so sweet it's a crying damn shame they're also full of it.

I never noticed her pout before. Maybe it's just the siren-red lipstick accenting her look today, but hell.

Her eyes, man.

Focus on her eyes. Prove you're a man in control of his faculties and not a gibbering orangutan, I growl inwardly.

"Sit down," I say, motioning to the seat in front of my desk.

She nods, trots in, and sits down before she holds up a notepad and puts a pen to it. "Do you have corrections to go over?"

Good. She's ready to work rather than waste our time trading insults.

I can respect that. Professional, businesslike, blunt.

I never would've guessed she had it in her, but I'm open to seeing another side of her. Too bad we have a very unprofessional subject to bat around.

I shake my head.

"Your copy is clean enough to eat. That's not what I wanted to discuss," I tell her, leaning back in my chair.

She lowers the notepad and pen, her eyes wider and more suspicious.

"Oh?"

"A lot went down between the two of us before your interview." I pause, clearing my throat. "I can certainly appreciate your talent and your backbone, Miss Poe. What I can't appreciate is ignoring the pissed off elephant in the room, that day you decided to make off with my Regis roll—"

"You mean when *you* were harassing me over a flipping cinnamon roll?" she spits, her eyes flashing.

Ah, there's my hellcat, and she's all claws today.

I glare at her like the sucker for punishment I am.

"Actually, I meant you being too selfish to part with your precious cargo even for five hundred dollars." Her mouth opens and I hold up a hand. "Listen, it doesn't matter. I'm not here to re-litigate two regrettable battles at Sweeter Grind. I'm offering you a truce so we can work together like two gears in the well-oiled machine that is this company."

She narrows her eyes, obvious acid on the tip of her tongue.

"Why? If I'm producing clean copy and doing my job, why wouldn't we get along? Professionally, I mean. You can see I do my job, regardless of any past brain-dead debacles."

I pause, shooting her an assessing look.

"Maybe so. However, I still feel we should spell it out so it's an easy working relationship." I hate how she practically glows with the morning light spilling in. "I'll also feel better if you'll accept certain changes to benefit your work here in the interests of minimizing the potential for future conflict."

"Changes?" she echoes, biting her lip. "And what conflict? God, you can't mean pastries again..."

My lips twitch, trying to pull up a smile.

Because the fact that I do probably deepens her portrait of me as textbook psycho.

"For one, you can quit biking to work. We'll share the same ride in my town car and place our coffee order bright and early every morning, well before the cafe has a chance to run out of anything."

She stares at me, incredulous.

"Very funny... You *are* joking, right?"

"I'm doing you a favor. Pastry business aside, I thought you'd appreciate a ride, rather than facing the elements on your—"

"Dude. I happen to like biking to work, thank you very much. And you can't just order me to take a different means of transportation into work. You don't own me when I'm off the clock, Mr. Burns, and just—what *is* your obsession with the freaking cinnamon rolls? Do you have a pathological addiction to cinnamon or something?"

Adorable.

She's strangely alluring when she's red-faced and staring at me in disbelief, her breath coming faster, giving her body this extra pulse that's a delicious hell on my eyes.

Also, it's none of her damn business what I need the cinnamon rolls for. If they were purely for me or the office crew, I'd say so. It's not my place to go around telling Wyatt's tragic life story, though.

So all I can say is, "Sure."

"Huh?" She blinks at me, clearly caught off guard.

"I'm not just an addict, but a pusher," I tell her with a shrug and deadpan delivery. "It's an awful habit I developed in my college days. It happens. Now when I log off as CEO of a multi-billion-dollar company, I spend my nights on the streets, cutting up cinnamon rolls and dealing bagged up bites to anyone who wants a hit."

"Okay. Now you're definitely joking unless you're completely—"

"Insane? Try me, Nevermore. Why the hell else would I offer five hundred bucks for a cinnamon roll?" I fold my arms, glaring until it's almost uncomfortable.

Lame story, but my delivery makes her wonder if it's true for at least a few seconds. More importantly, it diverts her from the real reason.

It's not like I'm trying to keep the man who saved my life alive or anything.

"Your sarcasm sucks," she mutters quietly, heaving out a sigh. "I hope you've got Anna or someone from marketing critiquing my writing. I'm not sure you'd know a good story if it whacked you across the face."

"Ask stupid questions, get stupid answers," I say matter-of-factly.

"It wasn't a stupid question. It was a fair one. You're legit crazy about cinnamon rolls. It's just...weird." Her voice goes up on that last word before she throws out a hand. "You know what? Fine. Keep it a big dark secret. I honestly don't *want* to know."

Miss Poe stares at me like she's trying to decide if I just stepped out of one of her ancestor's short stories.

Say something, idiot. You don't need to scare her.

True enough. She writes clean copy, and I don't want her to walk out of here so rattled she quits on the spot. Especially since Lucy told me this morning that she's starting to have contractions.

"You have to admit, the Regis rolls are worth a princely sum."

"Yeah—they're good. Just not psycho-stalker good." She looks at me, her green eyes glittering and her lips twisting before they purse up in a duck face. "...can I tell you what it looks like to the rest of the world? Assuming you even care, anyway."

"Is there any way I'd stop you?" I throw back.

She ignores that. "I don't think your mantrum—"

"Mantrum?"

"Man tantrum—"

"Hardly, Nevermore. Also, that's a pretty sexist remark and sexism doesn't belong in this workplace. My mother would storm the place like a mad hornet if I let that shit fly," I grumble.

"Nevermore?" For a second, she looks at me, too stunned to speak.

I should apologize. Juvenile nicknames aren't exactly becoming around here either.

I should.

Only, I don't want to, especially when the name suits her.

"Look, Mr. High and Mighty, I didn't want to start my first real morning here debating office power dynamics. I'm pretty sure you'd lose. May I continue?" She ignores the hot glare I level on her and barrels onward without waiting for an answer. "The rest of the world thinks your mantrum over the cinnamon roll happened because you're an entitled prick. You're so used to being handed everything you want that you couldn't handle not being able to get your hands on your morning sugar fix, so you freaked."

I glare at her as she continues.

"Then, when I wouldn't immediately cave and relinquish it for what's probably pocket change to you, it bruised your fragile little ego so much that you just had to clobber me the second time with the only thing that matters to you. The only thing that makes you think you're better. Money."

Fuck, the mouth on this raven.

When she puts it like that, I'll admit, it does sound pretty bad. I want to tell the pastry witch she's wrong, but my brain seizes, tripping over the way she's called me out.

"I called you in here to offer an olive branch, Miss Poe. Not to burn this place down," I warn darkly.

"Oh, okay." She pauses, rolling those eyes like jade marbles. "I have a better idea."

"What?"

"I quit. Effective immediately."

Before I can even breathe, she's out of her seat, heading for the door.

I'm up like lightning, flying past her and blocking the door.

"Quit? You can't just—"

Her look says *try me.* "This just isn't worth it, Burns. I wanted to make this work, but it was wishful thinking, and wishes don't come true."

"Ninety days," I snap off, my mouth moving faster than my brain.

"Huh?"

"Ninety goddamned days," I repeat, pinching the bridge of my nose before I look at her again. "If you make it until then, I'll quadruple your performance bonus. And based on what you turned in this morning, keep that up, and I'm sure you'll make at least an extra hundred thousand. Not from the company coffers, but my own."

There's a long, terrible pause before she huffs out a breath.

"Again, you're trying to buy me. How cute."

I inhale sharply. "Nevermore, I'm trying to make you comfortable the only way I know how. I'm offering you a choice."

She tilts her head with a sarcastic smirk.

"Even *you* can't sneer at six figures for a few months of work. If you're out the door after that, I won't stop you," I say, shaking my head. "I want you here. Working on my wedding line. Not wasting another minute bickering over frigging sweets."

"Ninety days," she repeats to herself, her brows pulling together thoughtfully.

I wait, trying not to make it obvious I'm holding my breath.

I'm not sure when the fuck I started to care this much, or why.

She's a stranger and a royal pain in the ass. Letting her go before she's even started shouldn't feel like losing something critical.

"Well?" I prompt, scuffing my shoe against the floor. "We don't have all day, lady."

"I suppose a quick payoff like that *might* be fair compensation for putting up with your rudeness."

I blink. "My rudeness?"

Does she hear herself? I'm offering to pay her from my own pockets for the privilege of retaining her services—and she's calling me fucking rude?

"That's right. And to help make sure it won't be a problem, *I'll* make the Sweeter Grind run every morning and grab your stupid coffee and your stupid Regis roll. And I'll do it on my bicycle. In the event there's only one Regis roll when I arrive, I'll generously give it up to you."

Not what I expected her to say.

Not at all.

I fucking despise how it's a sane offer—probably a better one than I deserve—and I wonder why.

Is it because she'll give me three months? Even when she clearly hates my guts more than ever?

"Am I such a tyrant you can't stand sharing a car for twenty minutes?" I ask.

She hesitates.

Not good.

"Can I be honest?" she asks softly, looking up with her long lashes fluttering.

What the hell? She's been holding back?

"Are you ever not honest, Miss Poe?"

"When I saw you in the interview, I almost turned around and walked right out. Staying here isn't an easy decision. But I don't want to give you the satisfaction—I *couldn't*."

Her sheer disgust rips through me like an arrow.

"I took the job for the pay—and I'll give it ninety days for the same reason— but that doesn't mean I have any desire to be friends," she says, deepening the wound. "Taking a car together every morning punishes me for something I didn't do. So I'll pick up your coffee, but let's limit our interactions to the office, okay?"

"I'm trying to make amends," I say slowly. "We'll be working very closely together and—"

"Yeah. Right there. It's the 'closely' part that's the problem. We both love our jobs, right? At least, I want to love mine..."

I nod. What's she getting at now?

"Good. Then that should be enough. In fact, that *is* enough."

"What do you mean?" I rake a hand through my hair, fully regretting this stupid peace summit.

"We can coexist as professionals and leave it at that. Frankly, I've never been great friends with anyone I ever worked with anyway and always kept my distance." For a second, she glances away, as if she's revealed too much. Then she continues. "So. How about I write some awesome copy and send it to you for approval or revision? I can check in at team meetings and take notes, or you can mark the document, and I'll correct it. If we just talk business and do our jobs, there's no reason to even worry about being frenemies or whatever..."

"Frenemies?" I echo.

She gives me this fake plastered-on smile I want to yank right off her face.

What the hell would it take to make her smile for real? I must be sick in the head for wondering when I did a pretty damn good job of making sure I'll never see it.

Not that it matters.

"Dakota, this organization is a team. If I can't get along with my own right hand—"

"Um, Lucy's your right hand, isn't she? And you two have a great vibe. I'm just a copywriter."

"You're a highly *specialized* copywriter assigned to a flagship product line who reports directly to me. You are an appendage like my own hand. Care to guess how many other writers fit that criteria?"

"Not really. Since you keep mentioning your right hand, though, I'd see somebody if it's giving you grief. That must be pretty awkward when you use it to—*never mind.*"

"Go to hell, Nevermore," I snarl. "I wanted to set things

straight, not continue sniping at each other like middle schoolers."

She barely holds back a snicker.

"And yet aren't you the one who started the silly nicknames?"

My brow furrows. She makes it painfully hard to ignore her fuckery.

"Miss Poe, you don't understand. If the rest of the team sees us at each other's throats, office morale crashes and—"

"They won't," she clips, slowly walking to the other side of the room. "I promise you my work will get done so efficiently no one will ever question it. I won't even let anyone know about our little agreement, or the fact that I think you're certifiable—"

"Do you always tell your boss who's just given you a huge bonus that he's a nutjob on your first day?" I raise my brows in challenge.

"No. But then again, I've never had a boss who ruined my breakfast before I started working for him, either."

I wish I could just be honest.

If she knew about Wyatt, she'd know I'm not a lunatic chasing his next sugar high and maybe show some remorse for her bullshit.

"We don't know each other very well, but I trust you'll find I never do anything without a damn good reason."

She crosses her arms. "You mean you had a good reason to harass me and buy out every cinnamon roll in the shop the next time you saw me? Were you feeding half the city?"

No. Just the office, plus one brutally obstinate man.

My brain grinds like it's rusted shut. Yeah, buying all the rolls for revenge might have been petty.

I could apologize.

Obviously, I could, but then where would that leave me with this green-eyed pixie who glares up at me like she's smelling blood in the water?

I stare back as something resembling a vacant smile turns up my lips.

"I offered you a roll at the interview, and I had a good reason for needing them that day."

She raises a brow. "Let's hear it."

"At this point, it doesn't matter. I don't answer to you," I snap.

"Right. Because your reason doesn't exist."

"What?" My smile contorts into a frown.

"Clearing the air was your idea, boss. You say you have this wonderful reason for desperately needing four dozen cinnamon rolls, but you can't say what it is. I'd be willing to bet five hundred dollars to a Regis roll the reason doesn't exist—oh, wait! Only one person in this room is rich enough to make a bet as uneven as that, though, and it certainly isn't me."

"It exists," I growl.

"Does it?" I hear her heel tap the floor impatiently.

I glare at her, burning her into the ground.

"It's not your concern, Miss Poe. We should be discussing the vision here and workplace morale in more detail. That will help you understand why I'm bothering with this shit show." I pause as she looks at me, wide-eyed and dripping disdain. "Look. I've worked hard to build an efficient work culture here. I'm not going to watch it get hammered apart purely because we get along like a mongoose in a cobra pit."

"Am I the mongoose or you?" she asks absently.

Inhaling deeply, I don't dignify her question with a response.

"Whatever. I guess I just find it hard to believe a man who's almost criminally obsessed with his breakfast cultivated an atmosphere where people *need* to be friendly with each other. Then again, if friendliness is a job requirement, is it really friendliness or just forced socialization? And do you really think we can just call a truce and forget our run-ins? I don't think so. I've never had so much venom from a total stranger in my life. I've only ever met one man who might be as self-centered as you, and even that might be a stretch."

"Who?" I grind out. I'm a lot of things. Workaholic, yes. Jackass, sometimes. Self-centered, no.

"Huh?" She reaches up, fixing a loose lock of hair, suddenly avoiding my eyes.

"You said you've only met one man as self-centered as me. Who is he?"

She stiffens and goes red, clearly regretting the ammunition she's handed me.

"Oh, so Miss Nevermore has secrets too?"

She's even redder now, and I can't tell if it's shame or anger.

"None of your business," she says quietly.

Too quietly, really.

Why is she so flushed? What happened to her fire?

"See? Sometimes you have the answer, but it's not worth sharing with the world," I say gently.

Her eyes whip to me, hurt and furious.

"I highly doubt it's the same thing."

I shift in my seat, curious who could leave this frosty impression on her.

"Let's make a deal right here. Tell me who beats me in the pompous jackass department, and I'll tell you my reason for trying to jack your Regis roll. We can understand each other, Miss Poe. You go first," I tell her.

Of course, I can't give her the full truth in naked detail. If she answers the question, I'll come up with something.

Predictably, she stares at me in awkward, cold silence.

"Is there a fucking draft in here or is it just me?" I wonder out loud, giving her a stare that could melt the arctic circle.

I already know she won't play ball.

Whatever else this strange blond slip of a woman in black is, she makes a mule look accommodating.

"That's what I thought," I say coldly when she doesn't answer. I've regained control of the conversation, at least. "Now, moving on, I'd like to walk you through my vision."

She glances at her digital watch and then grins at me like I didn't just knock out her soul.

"Sorry. I'd love to stay and chat about your corporate vision, but Anna needs me in a meeting in five minutes and this place is huge. Have a blessed day, Mr. Burns." She turns and strolls to the door, puts her hand on the knob, and looks at me over her shoulder. "Just text me your morning coffee order. I'll be happy to bike it in for you tomorrow. Although, that sounds more like an assistant's duty than a copywriter's. I'm not sure what coffee runs have to do with marketing, but since you *insisted*, I'm a team player."

She throws the door open.

Damn her, I never insisted on anything with the coffee.

"Wait," I call.

She freezes, glancing back in slow motion.

"What?"

"You have a notepad. Just write it down now. Make it a large black coffee with a dab of heavy cream and two Regis rolls." I reach into my wallet and pull out two crisp twenties, which I push across my desk to her. "Since we're not friends, there's no reason for me to have to text you, or for you to pay for my order, and since this is a personal matter, it shouldn't involve a company card. I'll expect my change."

Our eyes clash like two warring cats, all teeth and claws in the silence, snarling for dominance.

"Did you get that or do you need to write it down?"

"Got it. I'm not a moron. I'll remember," she mutters, walking out the door.

Goddammit.

So much for the cease-fire.

I'm starting to think my failure with Wyatt brought her into my life. I'm not a particularly religious man and I don't put much stock in that old saying about God giving his biggest battles to his strongest warriors.

There's something painfully ironic there, though.

Because I couldn't move one mountain of a man, now I've got a stone-cold second peak to deal with. And unlike Wyatt, Miss Poe has the pedigree to make my life a frozen hell.

V: NAMELESS HERE (DAKOTA)

*O*ne week.

I've survived more than one freaking week working for Lincoln effing Burns and I'm ready to live up to my namesake and bury all six-foot something of him under the floorboards.

Except, unlike the crazy in "The Tell-Tale Heart," if I hear his dead heart beating in my head, I just might relish the thought. Because I'll know that I was the one who sent him to hell.

Also, that first 'flawless' bit of copy must've been a fluke.

Ever since our little heart-to-heart in his office, I'm working twelve hours a day and he *still* marks the hell out of every line of copy I submit.

Some of the things he marks are ridiculous, too.

Honest to God, he actually complained about my margins last time.

The worst part is, some of his suggestions are actually good.

It isn't fair. No Neanderthal decked out in Gucci should ever give a fair critique that makes me leave teeth marks in my pen.

The bosshole drives me crazy, but he's improving my writing...which makes it impossible to up and rage-quit this job. I promised myself I'd stick around for ninety days as much as I promised him.

I care too much about raising my game with words in the real world, where it counts.

You can get feedback from any fellow writer on the internet or a well-paid editor, but it doesn't have the same punch as a single line of text that could cause a seven or eight figure difference in sales.

Still. I'd like to settle for punching him if I can't go full Poe on his smug ass.

And since I can't even have that, payback is coming this morning and you'd best believe I'm going to enjoy it.

"What can I get for you?" the barista asks.

"Two Regis rolls, a cinnamon latte, and a large coffee with one cream and six sugars."

"That's...a lot of sugar in the last one," she says, raising a brow.

"I know. Major sweet tooth."

"Gotcha. Can I get a name for your drinks?"

I smile. "Just go with Nevermore."

I pay with the asshat's bills, collect the cinnamon rolls, and move to the counter to wait for the drinks.

A guy sets two hot cups down less than five minutes later.

"Nevermore!" he calls.

"Here. Which one's the latte?"

He points to the cup on the right.

"Awesome." I reach over the counter and grab an empty cup. I pour the coffee with cream and sugar into a clean cup. "Can I borrow a marker?"

The guy reaches into a drawer and hands me a spare. I write *Nevermore* on the cup and draw a raven before I enjoy a nice swift bike ride to the office, delighting in the spring colors and slowly lifting gloom around the city.

He's already in his office when I get to his floor, a workaholic silhouette that looks almost etched into the frosted glass.

Perfect. Maybe he'll take his first sip while I'm still in the room.

I fight back a smile as I enter, and not very well. He notices.

"What's put you in such a sunny mood today?" he asks, wearing his default grumpy frown.

"Am I in a good mood?" I ask like I'm not already dying of laughter inside.

"You are. I don't think I've ever seen you smile unless you were insulting me."

"Sorry. Just hungry. I got your breakfast." I hand him the cup and white paper sack.

He looks at the items I just gave him and back at me slowly.

"Let me guess. You spit in my coffee?"

"No." Only because I didn't think about it. That's not a bad plan for tomorrow.

"Are you sure? Miss Poe, if you've contaminated my coffee in any way, rest assured I will chuck your ass out the door. No matter how talented you are."

He waits like he's expecting me to fall to my knees with some tearful confession.

"It's everything you asked for. Nothing less," I say with a nod.

There isn't much reason I need to be standing here. I should probably leave, but I keep hoping he'll take a drink. Plus, the odds that I could get fired after he practically begged me for three months make things interesting, I guess.

He rips his desk drawer open in a huff and drops the paper sack inside.

Hmm. Saving it for later?

Maybe he really does snort cinnamon icing, and he's waiting to be alone with his precious before he breaks out the credit card.

"Why aren't you eating the Regis roll while it's warm?" I ask.

He stares at me for a minute.

"You spat on my roll?" He sounds even angrier about that than he does the coffee.

"Nope—this office has a one psycho limit, and it's not me. You're just paranoid," I say with an exaggerated yawn.

Good thing, too, because he's hard to look at head-on right now.

There's something about him when he gets mad. He has that scary-hot thing going with the electric honey-brown eyes and granite shoulders and imposing jaw.

I'd bet my next five Regis rolls that eighty percent of the female population would give up their sanity for a ride on him.

I'm just not part of that eighty percent, even if I'll admit he rocks the sleek alpha vibe.

Shame that such good looks are wasted on a selfish ogre.

"Then why do you care when I eat my roll?" he demands.

"Isn't it obvious? You stalked me out of the coffee shop and tried to bribe me over it. The next time you saw me, you bought up every Regis roll in the coffee shop like a middle school punk. But now you finally have a fresh roll and you just...shove it in your desk? What? Come to think of it, I never have seen you eat one."

"I told you, I have my reasons. They may or may not extend to eating."

Huh? That's weird.

For a second, my brain goes horrible places that have nothing to do with my Poe genes. I'm picturing my boss wearing nothing but that tie, the huge roll clenched in his hands, perfectly positioned in front of us—

Dear God. Stop. Surely, he's above a bad reenactment of *American Pie*.

"Miss Poe?" he snaps.

I jump.

"What the hell are you looking at?"

I subtly shake my head in disbelief.

"You. You didn't even want it, I guess. You just had to prove you could get it."

He shakes his head this time. "I had to prove something, all right. There's a little redhead in accounting. She wears low-cut dresses made for sin and she likes cinnamon rolls. I'm dating her."

For a brief moment, I want to slap this redheaded chick, and I don't know why.

Then I remember what the internet says about my boss and it's all I can do not to laugh.

"Nice try, but you can cut the crap. Google says you're undateable."

Oh, what the hell did I just say? Dammit, Dakota, do you really want this discussion?

His grin could swallow me right up.

"Oh, does it?"

"No—I mean, I wasn't looking—"

"Of course you weren't," he says with an amused snort. "And you called me a stalker..."

"Hey! Standard precautions. I was just trying to find out how crazy you actually are before I quit my job for this one."

"How psychotic am I, Nevermore?" His eyes sparkle when he smiles and—damn, they're on my lips again, aren't they?

When he looks at me like that, this cool Seattle office turns into the Sahara.

Shrugging, I continue. "You're a workaholic and extremely undateable, they say. But since that was clear from your mantrum, I don't care. I'm not dating you. And I don't really care if you're a workaholic either as long as you pay me that bonus."

"You're refreshingly honest. I told you what I need the roll for. Now what selfish asshole burned a hole in your heart?"

I freeze, hating that we're back here again.

Hating more that I'm still sensitive to the only man on the planet who's *worse* than Lincoln Burns.

"You didn't tell me crap. There's no chance you're dating a girl in accounting. You're too proud of your 'work culture' to mess it up by pouncing on a redhead with her boobs hanging out. Also, you're Captain Undateable, and even if you weren't...there's no chance in hell she'd have you."

A smile twists his lips that almost scares me.

"Hot damn. Maybe I don't like your honesty as much as I thought," he muses. "For the record, I thought you named me Captain Dipshit. It's hard keeping your insults together, isn't it?"

I'm about to fire back, but the moment of truth arrives.

He picks up the coffee and brings it to his lips.

Oh, yessiree. Here we go.

One second.

One sip.

That's all it takes before his face blanks out like he's just eaten a spoonful of fire ants.

He winces. He sputters. He swallows after the world's longest gurgle, hilariously forced.

Then his eyes flay me open with a slow, sharp look and he says, "Wonderful. I've never had coffee this good, Miss Poe. You're an absolute treasure for correcting my order. I'll be sure to remember it when it's time for bonuses."

Without flinching, I grin.

"Thrilled you enjoyed it. Sometimes you can teach an old hound new tricks. Bye, boss."

"Nevermore?"

I stop, hating that it feels like that stupid name is growing on me like a messed up part of my identity here. A couple of others in marketing have started using it with laughs.

Still, there's a special ragey edge when it's coming from Burns.

"Not my name," I say coldly.

"Poe?"

"Better."

"Why shouldn't I fire you right now for that stunt?" he growls.

"Because HR will tell you coffee isn't in my job description?" I try, hoping like hell he isn't serious.

"You're a workout in patience."

"Crazy coincidence—I could say the same about you." I practically skip out of his office, more exhilarated than I should be.

Yes, I'm being childish, but I'm hardly the only one. I know if I talked to any boss like I talk to him, they should fire me on the spot, regardless of what's in my job description.

But I just can't help it.

He makes it so easy to loathe him with the fullness of my soul.

And he clearly hasn't fired me yet.

What does that mean? Is he a glutton for punishment or am I truly the butt of his bad jokes around here?

As soon as I sit down at my desk, Anna emails a few images for print ads she wants me to align with the copy in today's projects.

The first picture shows a groom running from the altar at full speed. The bride holds her skirts with both hands and chases after him. They're both smiling like they're high on helium.

Bad reminder of what I'm doing here, of what this job really is...

I want to crawl under my desk and die.

I lived this scene.

Trust me, there was nothing cute about it.

Writing wedding copy—even for ridiculously good pay—must be punishment or vicious karma for some cardinal sin from a past life.

Maybe I really do have more in common with Edgar Allan than I realized.

Whatever. I'll support the wedding industry because it's my job, but I'll never buy into it.

I feel sorry for all the poor, blissfully ignorant souls who do.

The worst part is, I'm *blanking*.

I have no clue how to write snappy copy for this image set.

Honestly, I wish I could *forget* images like these. The first thing that comes to mind is: *Run, don't walk, away from the altar. RUN AS FAST AS YOU CAN.*

I scroll to the next image. The same model groom holds his bride against him. Her hands rest on his. Both of their rings are in the shot. A picture I never got to experience.

So lovely. So heartfelt. So vomit-worthy.

Why did I take this job again? Eliza *did* warn me.

I let out a slow, hissing breath.

Sure, I can blame Lincoln Burns for the long hours, late nights, and stupid coffee runs—even if I didn't have to agree to that last one—but he's not to blame for this.

It's not his fault that I have to hide hot, rebellious tears just looking at these stupid photos of an imaginary wedding I never had.

He's also not responsible for my new evening plans to cope with a pound of M&Ms after work.

I'd say Jay is to blame—and he is—but the hard, grisly truth is there's one person responsible for the pain.

Me.

Because once I was naive. Once, I looked at ads like these, bursting with happy couples and happily ever afters, and I bought it hook, line, and sinker.

I swallowed a lie.

Never again.

For once, I have to live up to my new namesake.

Nevermore.

* * *

THE WHOLE TEAM gets an email from Anna, telling us to report to the conference room for an evening meeting.

"Do you know what this meeting is about?" I ask.

Cheryl, a friendly middle-aged woman, picks up her purse and slings it over her shoulder. "No, but we're about to find out."

I grab my notepad and follow her into the meeting room, where Anna and a few other people are already waiting.

"Red alert, people," Anna says, leveling a stare at everyone. The bright crimson blouse she's sporting today adds emphasis to her words. "Our competition just dropped an ad today that's pretty close to what we created last week. We need a fresh concept like now."

"There are only so many ways to promote a wedding. Run it anyway," Cheryl says with an annoyed click of her nails on the table.

"This line is worth a fortune. We're not just phoning the pre-sale in. We need to stand out," Anna says.

"What if we present the anti-bridezilla dress?" I say, tapping my pen.

"Anti-bridezilla?" Anna asks.

"My hometown was known for weddings before it was known for big oil and weird murder mysteries."

Everyone stares at me.

"Sorry. Ignore that last part. My point is, the wedding industry definitely keeps us going. This big movie star, Ridge Barnet, even tied the knot of the century and had it all over the press a few years ago. There are several huge weddings in Dallas, North Dakota, every year. They range from hometown heroes to celebrities jetting in for a destination wedding. They all have one thing in common. The number one thing that makes any normal woman a bridezilla. The alterations aren't right or her form feels off. Something, something, disaster! But whatever the catastrophe, it's always the dress at the heart of it, right?"

Anna rests her hand on her chin, a half smile slowly moving across her face.

"Y'know, that's brilliant. Freaking out over little details never happens with a Haughty But Nice dress. Not when it's crafted by the best designers in the industry using only the finest materials."

I nod.

"Exactly. Use a Haughty But Nice dress to soothe a fire-spitting bridezilla and caption it with something like, 'be a bride, not a dragon.' Or maybe 'Keep calm. Wear Haughty But Nice and carry on.'"

"I love it!" Anna says, scrunching up her nose.

The murmur around the table grows, buzzing with ideas and laughs.

Thank God.

I'd much rather write copy about calming bridezillas than try to come up with a clever way to convince some poor girl she can keep a man around.

After all, the whole bridezilla thing acknowledges the fact that getting married isn't all sunshine and roses. It's one of the most stressful events a person goes through until the big—hopefully happy—day arrives.

"We'll need a fire-breathing groom too," someone says from the back of the room. "Don't forget we sell to brides and grooms alike."

I know that voice.

It annoys me and never has anything pleasant to say.

When did he even come in? And why is he hellbent on making my life harder for the tenth time today?

I turn around and glare. I look right at him, but somehow he manages to see past me with this diplomatic smile for the team. Of course, they look at him like they're in the presence of a freaking rock star.

Asshat.

The royal purple vest under his jacket today draws attention to the broad cut of his chest and the color offsets his eyes.

Illegal. It should be against the law for a man to be this hot and also so heartless.

Also, I'd much rather write bridezilla than some jerkwad who can't figure out he's afraid of commitment until his bride is waiting at the church. There's nothing cute about it.

It's sexist as hell, mean-spirited, and the fact that it's tolerated is ridiculous. I remember the last time I saw a wedding line advertising with a runaway bride...

Actually, I don't.

I try very hard *not* to remember.

But it's Lincoln Burns' company. I'm hardly in the mood to argue with him in front of his staff.

If I do, I'll probably be called into his office for another lecture about work culture and how we need a truce and how I'm being the bad gal for defending myself and blah, blah, blah.

I know.

I know I should just listen and keep my inner bitch in check.

"Uh, I don't know about that, Mr. Burns," a voice says nervously. "The bridezilla concept is cute and all because it takes a known idea to the next level. But groomzilla isn't a thing. It just doesn't work."

"Point taken. If the concept can't sell both lines, it's not a working concept," Burns says, snapping his fingers.

I'm a little surprised he actually took the feedback to heart.

"With all due respect, sir, why?" Cheryl asks. I can tell they're not used to arguing with him, but I'm glad they are. He keeps glancing my way like he's just waiting for me to come charging in.

No, bossman. Not this time.

"It's normal for men's lines and women's to be marketed differently, isn't it?" I say very neutrally.

For a second, his face sinks like he's disappointed.

"I like a cohesive strategy. Something that's fun but immediately lets you know it's us. My mother always looks forward to the Match dot com commercials where the year 2020 and the devil meet up. Our content needs that zing, a relatable story people will look forward to," he says through the laughter in the room.

"Deal! If you pose as groomzilla, I'll write the content," I belt out.

Oh, crap. I didn't mean to say that out loud.

Lincoln's eyes whip to me. I fight the urge to shrink into my chair.

"I'm perfectly willing, Miss Poe, but Shane rightly says groomzillas aren't a thing."

"It's just not in the public mind," I say. "Even if they do exist."

"Then the concept doesn't work." His gaze drops from my eyes to my lips and then travels down.

God, what is he looking at? I hate to imagine he's thinking with his teeth, his tongue.

Heat throbs under my cheeks.

Does anyone else notice him ogling or is it just me?

Well, screw it.

He'll pay for these lingering looks and that damn vest that keeps catching my eye like a kid who's been dared to look at the sun.

I lick my lips.

"I'd love to hear about your idea of a perfect wedding, boss," I say.

"The perfect—" He stops talking as his brow comes down. "What?"

Surprise. He didn't see that coming.

"It might help the team to hear your vision," I say, reminding him of the spiel I walked out on. "Can you describe your idea of the perfect wedding?"

"Why would I do that?" he says, glowering, his body tight like an armed bow.

I give the world's quickest shrug. "If we're going to take a stab at a groomzilla or something else that works, the least he can do is give us something to work with."

His smirk makes me shudder.

"Simple. The perfect big day means a smooth day. Not having to worry about details. That's what people pay a fortune for in this industry, from wedding planners to photo booths to where we come in with fashion. If it were my wedding, all I'd care about is a well-fitted suit and the perfect dress for my bride with every last detail signed, sealed, and delivered. With the logistics solved, we can get lost in each other instead of obsessing over what we're wearing or who's doing what."

Wow.

That's actually sweet.

Not the kind of answer you'd expect from a capital douchebag.

If I'd thought to ask Jay the same question and gotten an answer less spectacular, maybe I wouldn't have been abandoned in a church full of people to announce there'd be no show today. But hey, we might as well not waste the open bar and cake.

My parents already paid for the damn thing anyway.

I wouldn't have wound up in a prepaid honeymoon suite bawling my eyes out while my mother took care of getting everything cleaned up. I wish I could forget that day, and now I've put myself in the one place where forgetting feels impossible.

"Not that the clothes would stay on long anyhow," Burns adds with a wink, not directed at anyone in particular.

Nice save, Captain. That's closer to the answer I expect from a man who's part moose and just as graceful, too.

Why did I have to ask?

I'm positive people are starting to notice the hellfire Burns puts under my cheeks—and yes, I'll own that terrible pun.

The men at the end of the table laugh.

"I think I might faint," Cheryl whispers, prolonging my torture. "Men with a butt like his shouldn't be allowed to say things like that in public."

Oh, lovely. So I'm not the only one who's noticed he's part sculpted steel where it counts. In hindsight, that should be a dead giveaway he isn't living off Regis rolls.

A pang of jealousy shoots through me. Right at the precise second when every woman in the room starts fanning themselves.

I give Burns my best *I'm-about-to-stab-you* look, gathering my words.

"If you need a well-fitted suit and the perfect dress for your bride, you're not exactly oblivious to what you're wearing," I point out.

He starts to roll his eyes but catches himself at the last second. "The average man doesn't care about beading, lace, or ruffles, I'll grant you. Your typical groom rarely thinks beyond a straight tie."

"Women do."

"Some do. Some don't. Our product line spans the spectrum from simple to more extravagant dresses—something for every flavor, but not for every price point. Our upcoming dresses will always be remarkable and bleed high-end confidence."

Oh, I'd enjoy making him bleed, all right, violent little creature that I am.

He cocks his head and continues. "Luxury means status to people who milk their money out of curated social media posts and reality TV. The rest of our luxury buyers put craft and quality first. You can market a luxury wedding line as simple if you focus on the design quality and the clothing itself, made with the finest materials available."

"Craft and quality are features. Not benefits," I say sweetly. "A wedding dress only gets worn once. You don't need it to last forever."

He goes quiet for a moment.

I'm expecting another scowl, a harsh comment, but he actually looks like he's thinking it over.

"The benefit *is* the original design and its unmatched quality, Miss Poe. All our customer needs to do is put it on," he says slowly.

"Not usually true of a wedding dress. You put it on after a corset. It's not a pleasant experience."

"Really?"

"Yeah, unless you're wearing a very simple A-line or a short dress, and even then you might still need a corset holding you together."

"I *know* what a corset involves, even if I've never worn one myself. Obviously," he admits, a slight redness blooming under his trimmed beard.

Holy crap.

He blushes.

I made Lincoln damn Burns blush in a company meeting. That's my kind of payback.

"Wedding dresses need so much structure," Cheryl says with the weariness of a woman who knows from personal experience.

The other ladies in the room nod enthusiastically, including me.

For a second, Lincoln goes stock-still. Then he crosses the room on measured strides, stroking his bearded chin, and sits down beside me.

"You make an interesting point. There's more to this structure aspect than I thought..."

His foot brushes mine under the table, probably from an absentminded sweep of his leg.

My breath catches at the whisper of a touch. I tuck my legs under my chair, pressing my thighs together.

"Sorry, Nevermore," he mutters, though his eyes are anything but apologetic.

His low words and warm breath are only more frustrating.

I ignore him because I can't form words right now, much less a guarded reaction.

"Keep the ideas coming," Anna says, her brown cheeks reddening.

Eyes like dark, worn wood peer into me. "I can't agree more, Miss Patel. No man wants to deal with undoing a corset after his wedding any more than his newly minted wife cares to wear one."

I so wish he'd quit talking about getting naked.

"Join me on the call with Italy this week," he says, looking at me again. "Before we change our marketing, we're going to alter a few designs. I want options that don't require anything more than the dress."

Umm—what? I'm influencing design now? And how am I going to get through this call on something I know jack about?

"I'm not a fashion designer, Mr. Burns. Sorry to disappoint you."

I'm not sorry.

"Doesn't matter," he says. "A more comfortable product falls under marketing research."

Right. But I've been running options through my head—mostly to keep my mind off Lincoln in that vest, talking about removing corsets—and I think I have something now.

A sudden burst of inspiration.

"You know, I think I've got a tagline for the new line. Haughty But Nice: Perfect so you don't have to be."

"Ohhh, I love it!" Anna beams, doing a little dance in her chair.

"So, are we revisiting groomzilla after all?" Burns asks.

"Maybe."

He smiles at me deliciously.

Right. If only he weren't a deranged, cinnamon-roll-obsessed lunatic, and also, you know, my boss.

His gaze falls to my hands. "With no ring on your finger, I have to ask. How do you know so much about the wedding industry?"

There it is.

My biggest shame, tossed into the spotlight for a roomful of people.

Taking a deep breath as the room blurs around me, I glance around, wishing I could disappear. But I manage to swallow the cotton ball in my throat, gather my wits, and glare at him. "The same way you handle this company without direct experience in everything. Google is a miracle worker."

Cheryl's eyes flick from me to the boss and back. She visibly stiffens.

"Are you okay, Dakota?"

I don't answer.

"Excuse me."

I just grab my notepad in a rush and flee the room, but not before I hear Cheryl behind me. "Poor dear. No woman her age likes to be reminded she's still single."

That's not true.

Plenty of women thrive on being unmarried. I'm just not one of them.

Maybe once I was meant to be a wife, but those days ended in a million tears on a small-town day baking under the sun, along with my desiccated heart.

She's trying to stick up for me, I get it, to paper over what a weirdo I am for fleeing, but it just makes this worse.

Oh, and of course I feel the bosshole's searing gaze trailing me as I close the door on my way out.

I need to be alone.

I need to shut myself somewhere dark and lonely and ugly cry. I'd rather not do it in a crowded conference room full of people who'll have a harder time respecting me now even without an open meltdown.

I fling my stuff down on my desk and make a mad dash to the bathroom.

After splashing cold water over my face and fixing my hair, I text Eliza. *Maybe you were right. I'm not sure I can handle this.*

Eliza: What happened?

I'm blotting at my eyes and tapping at my phone with one hand. *The bosshole. He asked me how I know so much about weddings when I don't have a ring.*

Eliza: Oh, God. Ouch. How do you even work for that guy? Did you kick him in the balls yet?

I smile and shake my head at that last part.

He may have it coming, but for once, this isn't totally his fault.

I don't know and no, I send back.

Why not? You're a Poe and last I checked, Poes don't take any crap. They lure people into dingy wine dungeons and brick them up. She adds a devil emoji at the end.

Leave it to Eliza to make me laugh.

A Poe writes about horrible things, but it's fiction, I send. *Also, workplace assault probably won't help me get another job.*

Eliza: True. You can always work with me at the coffee shop.

No, I really can't.

People annoy me like nobody's business.

I think I'd rather paint my place with a toothpick over working retail with customers, with complaints, with an awful need to *smile.*

Ugh.

Sighing, I send her what's really a wish. *Don't worry. If I blow this, I'll figure something out.*

Eliza: When do you get home? I'll brew up a Madagascar vanilla coffee just for you.

Dakota: A steaming hot cup of vanilla bliss sounds perfect right now.

Eliza: Come home early. Don't drag yourself through the rest of the day.

I wince, wishing I could before I add, *I have to power through it, Eliza. I don't have a choice when it's still my job. For now. Catch you later.*

I open the door to the restroom and scan the hall to make sure there's no one around.

The coast looks clear, so I go to the break room and make a quick cup of tea, trying to clear my head.

The pain may be new, but this situation isn't.

Lincoln Burns is a nosy, rude, bad-tempered grumphead. I won't dignify that by adding dangerously handsome.

But I knew that before I took this job, didn't I?

Certainly before I agreed to his ninety-day proposal from hell. And I'm not ready to fly the white flag when I still have over eighty days to go.

I'll get through this.

I have to, if only for my own pride.

If I made it out of a church with a hundred and forty-two people inside before I broke down over the biggest humiliation of my life, I can smile about this, too.

I can put in a few months earning big-girl pay and segue to another position.

Then I can forget all about this cinnamon-snorting psycho and the apocalyptic feelings he's too good at stirring up.

VI: A MIDNIGHT DREARY (LINCOLN)

"*O*kay, I think we're off to a fantabulous start. Class dismissed," Anna says with a wide smile, calling the meeting to an end with a sharp clap of her hands.

I stand, watching my staff file past with the usual mix of wary respect or affable nods. When you're in my position, you appreciate both.

I wait until the last person files past before I start moving.

"Mr. Burns?" Anna calls. "Can you stick around for a minute?"

Shit.

I've been around long enough to know nothing good ever comes from a subordinate asking for my time, even if she's my hardworking and loyal marketing head.

Anna waits a few more seconds until she's sure we're alone.

The look she gives me says *you fucked up* before the words are out of her mouth.

"Something on your mind, Miss Patel?" I urge.

"Well, please don't take this personally but...Dakota Poe is very talented. She hasn't been here long, but I think she has that missing ingredient in creative we've needed for a long time."

I nod slowly.

Get to the point. I never doubted Miss Poe's talents.

"And? You say that like it's a problem," I say, folding my arms.

"I just...well, I hope she doesn't quit," Anna tells me point-blank.

I'm taken aback, even if I don't show it.

"Quit? Why would she? She just got here, and considering her previous position and pay, I'm sure she's happy we've given the stray a new home."

"The pay, sure, but that's not what I'm worried about." Anna hesitates until I clear my throat impatiently, urging her to spit it out. "Boss, I think you upset her. You got sort of personal back there. And if you're going to do it, does it have to be in front of everyone she works with?"

"I said nothing wrong," I snarl back defiantly, looking away and then back at her again. "Did I?"

"Mr. Burns. I mean this as nicely as possible but... Would you be okay if a superior asked how you were fit to oversee a wedding line? Because you're pretty single yourself, last I checked. I mean, you're spearheading the entire line, and in fairness, the same question could be asked of you."

I'm single for good fucking reason, I almost growl back.

"I wouldn't mind answering it," I bite off.

Not true.

I'd very much mind revisiting an engagement that went down in flames.

My heart bristles like it's crawling with hornets, a lying face flashing in my mind I've tried like hell to forget.

Goddamn. Is that what I just did to Miss Poe? Pulled bad memories to the surface?

Perhaps Anna Patel has a point.

"Not everyone has your bluntness. Especially when it comes to marriage," she says softly.

Damn. As much as I want to swipe away her concerns, a small, distant part of me screams she's right.

From the way Nevermore hightailed it out of here, I may have thrown sea salt in an open wound.

"I didn't mean anything by it. I was simply curious," I say.

Anna doesn't say anything, but she holds my gaze with a disapproving glint in her dark eyes.

"Maybe so, but it struck a nerve. And Miss Poe doesn't seem like the sensitive type."

Yeah, she's normally a walking spitfire, but everyone has their breaking point. Their touchy spots. Their defeats in life that they've pushed into a pit and buried.

Maybe more so if your last name is Poe.

And maybe I struck a nerve I shouldn't have like the social porcupine I am.

Dammit, I hate that Anna has to be my conscience. I didn't mean to upset Poe, but I have no idea what I could say to make it better either.

"Relax, Miss Patel. I'll go deal with it."

I've worked with Anna for a few years now. I've never seen the worried hangdog look she's giving me now.

"*Fine.* I'll go apologize if that'll help you nix any plans to pull out your pitchfork and come after me." I straighten my tie like I'm tightening my own noose.

I hope I don't fuck this up more.

Anna brightens and slowly nods. "Good choice. I'm a pretty crummy shot with a pitchfork, but the rest of the mob might aim straight for your balls."

"What a delightful image. Are we done, or do I need to suffer through more of your humor?" I say with an exaggerated yawn.

Smiling to herself and shaking her head, her heels click past me and into the hall.

I trail after her out the door, staying several paces behind her, and decide to take my usual walk through the building.

Downstairs, people are still standing around in busy clusters, holding cupcakes.

Odd. I didn't order cupcakes today.

Through the murmurs, I hear the name Tillie more than once.

Beautiful.

My mother blowing in for a nostalgic hello is the last thing I need right now.

I'd hate it when she "drops by to see old faces" if it didn't make her so damn happy. I have to admit it's an easy morale booster, too, when the entire office knows a visit from Matilda Burns means food and long breaks chitchatting.

Say goodbye to a productive day.

Scowling, I look high and low for raven chick, but don't spot her in any of the people clusters. I move to her desk, only to freeze in my tracks.

Mom is hunched over her in a spare chair, patting her on the back. Poe's face is a crushed red tomato.

Goddamn, this is bad.

Not only do I have to apologize now—and fucking *mean it*—apparently, I have to do it with my mom standing watch like an empathic Doberman.

Before I can back out, their eyes flick to me.

"Mother," I say with a friendly nod before I glance over. "Miss Poe."

Nevermore won't even look at me.

"Oh, Lincoln, you're just in time! I found this precious young thing with a heart sting in the break room. I had to pry it out of her, but she finally told me some thoughtless manager made a nasty comment about her ability to do her job due to her marital status in the middle of the meeting. Can you believe that?" My mother's eyes flash violently like she wants to pull said idiot's throat out with her teeth. "I trust you plan on having a serious discussion with the perp. That's *not* how we do things here, especially to a new hire. When I was in charge, no manager would've dared breathe a single word of that BS."

Fuck.

If only she knew what "manager" went tripping over his own dick.

Of course, Nevermore knows.

Beneath her sad eyes, she smirks at me like the venomous little devil she is behind my mom's bristling shoulder and immediately straightens her face.

Even those puffy eyes don't look quite so devastated anymore.

"I promise I'll look into it," I grind out.

"Tillie knew you would. She told me she's certain you'd never let anyone talk down to your employees like that in your presence," Poe says in an innocent way.

Damn her.

"Absolutely not," I say without hesitation.

Nevermore blinks. Her mouth forms a shocked and appalled "oh," but the shape of her full lips in my mind is far less innocent.

"And yet you were there, sitting beside me the whole time," she whispers.

Mom's eyes lash from me, to her, and back to me again.

"Lincoln Burns. I hope I don't need to be very disappointed in you," Ma warns with a frown that almost rolls off her face.

Fucking hell. Am I sixteen again?

I run this entire company with well over a thousand people's lives in my hands. She can't just come barging in and treat me like a child, undermining my authority.

We have employees who have worked here since I was a kid, and they need to know who's boss. I'll talk about my shortcomings, personal and professional, with my mother later.

For now, I need to deal with the little schemer who can throw me to the lions at a whim.

"We wouldn't want that, would we, Mr. Burns?" she asks too sweetly.

I glare at her.

"And why haven't you introduced me to this precious little

thing before now, Lincoln? You know how much I adore my marketing bees. Without them, we'd never move a dab of honey. Did you know she's a nationally renowned young poet? You should tell me when we get new faces—especially such interesting ones!" Mom says, slapping her thigh.

"Mother, you're retired. Forgive me if I won't drag you out of enjoying retirement for every minor change in the office," I say flatly.

Her face goes blank, her lips form a straight line, and she stares me down.

Here we go. The mom look written large. I haven't seen it this severe since before I left for the Marines.

"I'll make a note to introduce you next time," I promise.

Satisfied, she nods and looks at Dakota. "I hope you can help my son sell wedding wear with a little heart. He doesn't know the first thing about weddings."

"I'm trying my best, but I'm not really an expert, either. After all...there isn't even a ring on my finger, right, Mr. Burns?" She looks up at me with a buttery laugh.

An ugly, strange contrast with the hurt flashing in her eyes.

"Personal experience in weddings hardly matters," I say, leveling my gaze on her. "I'm confident you'll research it the same skillful way you'd research any assignment I give you, Miss Poe."

"True. Your mom told me prom is the last time you really dressed up for a date. That had to be a while ago, huh?"

Did she just call me old?

My stare sharpens, wishing I could melt her like a candle.

"Not quite, I went to the military ball a couple of times."

"His friend's sister wanted to go," Mom says with a muffled whisper.

Dakota laughs.

I've had enough. I push an agitated hand through my hair.

"James and Sally are in the back corner, Mother. They've both been talking about how much they miss the old days when you and Dad were at the helm. Why don't you go share some old stories?" I motion to the older couple from accounting.

"Ah, I'm starting to see why! With the nonsense you're allowing, they might wonder if it's even the same company."

I hold in a sigh.

"Still, you should go say hello."

"I will. Thanks, love." She stands and saunters away with a quick peck on the cheek.

I watch my mom leave with a clenched fist and I take her seat.

"That was evil, Nevermore. Don't think your name gives you a pass to slash up every rule of office politics," I growl.

Dakota shrugs. "Meh, I don't know about that. I kinda thought a strong warning shot was warranted."

"Warning shot? I'll never hear the end of it now." I fold my arms and stare into her soul.

"I'm so sorry." There's nothing sorry in her tone, but fuck if I care.

The little angel Anna Patel put on my shoulder reminds me I deserve it.

"Before you riled up my mother, I came here to apologize," I say.

"Why? You have nothing to apologize for, but I do have a mountain of work. So maybe we can play catch-up and pour out our hearts another time?"

"Dakota—"

She smiles. "Miss Poe."

I bite my tongue, wondering how the hell I could slip.

"Miss Poe—" I correct sharply, but she cuts me off.

"Another time, Mr. Burns. Working."

"Regardless, I'm sorry. Sincerely. I didn't mean to give you an interrogation in front of your colleagues," I say sternly.

She won't even look at me, her fingers clicking on the keyboard.

"'Kay. Look, unless you need to talk about the assignment—"

"I spoke out of turn. I know I made it way too personal, and I'm sorry. It won't happen again. I can be dense with my bedside manner sometimes—"

"Yep, and there wasn't even a cinnamon roll involved today. Imagine that!" she says with a muted glare.

Will she ever let me fucking finish?

"I'm a professional. I'm your boss, and I know you're not here for my personal entertainment."

If you weren't so damn beautiful, maybe my tongue wouldn't get so loose, I think darkly.

This girl obliterates my better senses like no one else.

"To show you I'm sincere, I'll take Sweeter Grind duty next week to make it up to you," I say slowly. "How does that sound?"

"Well, there's nothing to make up for, but whatevs. Knock yourself out, boss."

Her fingers pound the keyboard, drumming this conversation into silence.

Whatever is right.

Even when I try to get along with this moody creature, she freezes me out.

As I turn and stomp away from her desk, I wonder if Ma's concerns aren't valid.

Should I have let this raven into my home?

Is my gamble on her about to win me a hostile work environment?

* * *

AFTER WORK, I sit in my living room, reviewing the latest drafts from the ad team and muttering at everything.

It's bland. Droll. Missing heart.

Everything except the ream of concepts with a name attached that won't stop rapping, rapping at my skull.

Dakota Poe's copy is undeniably on-point. Hell, I can even

tell it's her advising in a few mockups where her name isn't directly attached.

Her concepts are funny, well written, and friendly, if a tad impersonal.

My only suggestion—a real one this time—would be to make the writing more intimate. Still, it's nice working to improve the meat on what's already impeccable bones.

I'm tempted to text her and pay her an honest compliment.

Though after the way she ran out of the meeting today and the showdown after, I'd wager that's inviting trouble.

She's not the sort of girl who gets bent out of shape over an asshole comment or a flippant one-off.

I grit my teeth.

All because I'm realizing, slowly but surely, that I've been a colossal dick to her—and by some freak stroke of black magic, she makes me feel guilty for that.

I pull out the earlier drafts and flip through her previous work. I come across the picture of the runaway groom and frown.

It was a half-baked concept to start with, but Dakota's feedback attached to the image catches my attention.

Yeah, we might want to leave this one somewhere in 1999. Nothing attracts a modern girl to a wedding line like chasing down some loser who doesn't really want to marry her. What if we sell a runaway bride instead? Turn the tables. That's a little more interesting.

Her interview pops into my head. When Anna mentioned she'd be working on the wedding line, she went stiff as a board.

Call me a sucker for punishment.

I pick up my phone and fire off a text. **Not a fan of men who skip out on their own weddings, huh?**

I go back to reading and my phone dings sooner than expected.

We're not friends. It's after work hours. Why are you texting me?

My pulse slows. Another pang of that damnable guilt.

Answer the question, I demand, punching Send. I add, *Please. I'm simply pinpointing where the original concept went wrong.*

It's insane what she does to me, even when she's not in the same room.

I don't think I've ever glared at those three swirling dots on the screen as she types. Her message arrives a few seconds later.

I mean, who *would* be thrilled to have a man leaving the altar? Why even propose to a woman if you're not going to see it through? Better yet, with the time and expense that goes into getting married, how do you make it to the wedding day without knowing you don't want this? Isn't it kinda obvious?

There.

I've pissed her off again.

Texting probably won't solve anything, so I call her instead.

I'm half expecting her to ignore me and let it go to voicemail, but she answers on the first ring.

"Can I help you?"

"Tell me one thing. Am I saying stupid shit again?"

I hear a muffled gasp.

"The only stupid shit is my boss calling me at eleven o'clock on a Friday night. Kind of ridiculous if you ask me, but hey, no one did."

"My bad. I didn't realize it was so late or that you had plans, Miss Poe. I've been going over drafts and lost track of time. Listen, if there's something I need to know about your work on the wedding campaign—"

"Is there a problem with my work?" she asks, venom in her voice.

"Not at all. Your writing is fresh and the concepts are the sort of ass-kicking we've needed for a while. Still, I'm confused by the way you stormed out of the meeting today. I know I was harsh and I apologized for that. It occurred to me the wedding line might be too much if there's some personal reason behind your aversion. Listen, if there's another line you'd rather work on, I can make that happen. I can—"

"I'm sorry," she interjects, soft but firm.

I wasn't expecting that.

"I—I was supposed to be married about a year ago. It didn't end well. End of story. Life goes on. I'll get over it." She pauses, drawing in a long breath before adding, "I'm already *over it.* Seriously. If the ring was worth anything, I would've sold it and taken a writing class."

You're not over a damn thing, I think to myself. The way you fled earlier today and reacted to my dumb ass tells the truth.

Even worse, I *know* that reaction.

It's been years and it still doesn't take much to bring back Regina, and finding her in bed with that pathetic, underhanded little fuck—

"Mr. Burns?" she asks softly.

"I'm still here."

At least now I understand why she was so upset when I pointed out her missing ring like the goddamned lumbering bear I am.

"I appreciate your honesty and the additional context. Again, I regret saying what I did today. Love may be the trickiest business of all," I tell her.

There's a long pause before she says, "Oh, really? Is that why your mom was asking all the old ladies in the office if they had a daughter or niece they could set her up with? She made it loud and clear she wants grandkids and her boy can't seem to get the job done."

I rock back in my chair, gritting my teeth.

What I wouldn't give if I could get Ma to jet off to Maui, the Turks, or the Maldives like an ordinary retired woman in her sixties with all the money in the world to burn.

Anything to keep her and her big matchmaking mouth the fuck out of my office. You'd think that after the hell I went through, she might just accept my permanent bachelorhood.

"Burns? You still there or did Smithers tuck you in for the night?"

I bite back a smile. "For such a sharp writer and someone tired of Poe jokes, I expected better. You're only the ten thousandth person to make a *Simpsons* crack with the name. Congratulations, I suppose."

"If the glove fits..." she shrugs with her voice. "You have to admit, you kinda fit the bill. You're single, loaded, and you like to throw your weight around. You've even got one up over the old cartoon gazillionaire in the looks depar—"

She cuts off abruptly, and damn it, now I *am* smirking so hard it hurts.

"What was that, Miss Poe? Something about my looks?" I wait. Crickets on the other end of the line. "I do put my time in maintaining this body for my health and appearance. It's nice knowing you appreciate it."

"I shouldn't be the one appreciating anything," she whispers. "Your mama has a point."

"She does not. I manage my own dating life very well," I growl, drumming my fingers on my knee.

"Do you?" she snickers.

Why did I call to apologize again?

"What?" I snap.

"They call you Mr. Undateable in the Seattle press," she says. "I'm sure you've seen the Google footprint? Either you don't handle your own dating, or you don't handle it very well. I'm not sure I'd admit the second."

"Stalker," I grind out. "Also, there are things journalists will never know."

"Excuse me?"

"You're Google stalking the boss. Barely a week after you called me psychotic," I remind her. "Does hypocrisy run in the family and precede crazy? Should I worry I'll wake up buried alive next?"

She snorts pure derision. "You think you're so funny, don't you?"

"That makes *one* of us."

"See how antsy you get when someone asks personal questions? And there isn't even a room full of people here." She clucks her tongue like the annoying damned bird she is.

"I apologized and even picked up your coffee duty—you're welcome."

"Which was never in my job description," she throws back.

I'm about to rip out my hair.

"Why did I call you?" I growl slowly.

"If I had to guess, to annoy the hell out of me. Or to soothe your guilty conscience. Guess it isn't working, though."

"You're ridiculous," I spit.

"Off the record, you're a jackass. You're rude, crass, kind of oblivious, and mean," she hisses.

"Tell it to the next person whose cinnamon roll you try to snatch."

"Oh my God. Could you *drop* that already?" She sucks in a harsh breath.

"Why?"

"Because you're just..." She trails off, probably running out of ammo.

"Not a good reason, Miss Poe, and it sounds like your well has run dry. Tell you what, I won't keep you struggling through new ways to insult me. I'll see you Monday to discuss your latest efforts in person."

She doesn't answer.

"Poe?" I move the phone closer so I can check the screen.

She's already hung up.

Glowering, I chuck my phone across the room.

I don't realize I'm hard enough to hit a home run until I stand, my face twisting with disgust.

Why the fuck am I *hard* after that?

Maybe I should see a shrink.

How does this girl get me so worked up like nobody else?

I pace the room like a caged animal, only stopping to stare at the fireplace before I take a few steps the other way.

Enough of this fuckery. Enough of Nevermore, too.

There's a calming predictability in weaving a path across my floor, at least until my eyes catch on the photos.

I get a glimpse of my once happy parents perched above my fireplace. My mother has the biggest, most beautiful smile of her life, and Dad has his arm around her.

She hasn't smiled like that since the day he died.

She may still smile a lot, but I doubt I'll ever see that high-on-life look of hers again.

The next picture houses another ghost from the past, a man I haven't seen for too long.

I'm almost ten years younger, hunkered down with Wyatt in a landscape painted shades of tan.

We're both dusty as hell, two clean-shaven boys sitting around a fire at a base camp about twenty miles outside Mosul.

One more smile that will never be the same again. Wyatt had all of his limbs then and was smitten with his wife.

Less than a year later, he was discharged with a purple heart and no leg from the knee down, abandoned by the woman he trusted most.

Bitterness floods my veins, remembering how quickly the descent came after she left him.

First his addiction to the painkillers—a beast he managed to get a handle on—but only after it cost him everything. He couldn't hold down a job and he'd lost his wife and son.

Now, because he loved, he lives on the street.

Barely alive except for his obsession with fucking pastries.

Love *is* a tricky business, just like I told Dakota Poe.

It's the most hellish, unforgiving, ass-biting business I know with razor-sharp teeth designed to kill.

Some people who get bit wind up torn to pieces, digested, and shat out with all the care of an owl swallowing a mouse.

I can't forget that. No way in hell am I falling into that trap *again.*

I can't end up in a tent like Wyatt or at the receiving end of a knife in my back.

I can't do anything except the only thing I've ever been good at—running this company.

People depend on me.

Mother still receives a pension like countless others who need it even more than she does. My employees depend on their livelihood. It's my job to keep this machine thriving.

Love is a fucking landmine, all too capable of blowing everything to kingdom come.

I've seen what happens when people fall for cupid's schemes, that sneaky little shit.

For every Happily Ever After, there are a dozen hearts fractured and stomped into the ground like shattered ornaments.

I have rules when it comes to women for good reason. Hookups are fine as long as everyone knows it's a hookup, though I haven't even bothered with one-night flings in a long time.

Feelings—relationships—those are for suckers. And if my parents did one thing right, they didn't raise one of those.

I don't date. I damn sure don't have any business being interested in Dakota frigging Poe. Being an employee makes her forbidden fruit of the worst kind, and that's all she can be.

I move to the wet bar and pour a scotch, downing it so fast I almost choke, coughing into my hand.

Yeah, it's that kind of night.

The silvery city lights can't banish the looming blackness that pulls up bad memories like imaginary monsters from my closet.

When you're a boy, it's easy to get through nights like this with a flashlight and a brave face.

When you're a grown man with regrets, obligations, and failures—when you've had your own heart hammered to a pulp and you've seen everyone you care for emotionally mutilated by romance—you need something stronger.

Tilting the glass bottle over the shot glass, I pour two more fingers, down it, and repeat.

I'm on my sixth gut bomb when my phone rings.

Her name flashes across the screen. I almost drop the glass.

What the hell? Does this chick have multiple personalities or something?

"Hello?" I answer.

"I'm sorry I cut you off. It was nice of you to call and apologize. Before you went off with your usual BS, I mean. I shouldn't have egged you on. And shit, I realize it's probably too late to be calling my boss—I'm sorry—fuck, I said shit. Ugh. I'm screwing this up."

"It's fine," I mutter, a crooked smile on my face.

She sighs. "Look, because of the way we met with you going bananas over my cinnamon roll... I sometimes forget I need to be professional around you. I'm working on it. I promise you I am, even if it may not seem like it."

I can't believe what I'm hearing. I didn't think she was built with an apologetic bone in her body.

"It's fine, Miss Poe. My offer stands. I have other lines you can work on if weddings just aren't suitable. You're skilled enough to retain on other projects for the long haul, even if they're assignments I didn't hire you for. We can be flexible."

"No, not necessary. I'm...able to compartmentalize well enough. I'll keep delivering quality copy on the wedding campaign, or wherever else you need me."

"Whatever you want," I say with a nod. "For the record, I'm sorry too for that last conversation. It takes two to tango and I'm a terrible dancer."

She laughs softly before she speaks again, this small, gentle sound hanging in the air.

"So, we're good, Burns?"

"We always were. You're the one who didn't think there was any point in being friendly." Why did I say that? This conversation has been almost civil.

"Right, because you're a psychopath."

"Yes, and the most undateable prick to ever walk the earth, which you know because you spend your free time Googling me." I'm grateful, but mildly surprised I haven't heard her mention Regina, lover boy, or the lawsuit yet.

Apparently, my gag order worked better than I thought.

"Why did I call expecting an adult conversation?" she mutters.

"Easy. You needed to hear the sound of my voice."

Where the hell is my tongue? *Get it together, Burns. Now you're just flirting and she's radioactive. Not to mention she has an attitude the size of Mount Rainier. A girl like Nevermore won't hesitate at all to walk out when things get tough or when something better comes along.*

"Dang, you got me. That's it. I need the majestic sound of grumpy men with tiny fuses to lull me to sleep..."

"Don't call my fuse tiny, lady," I growl jokingly.

She snorts laughter.

"Question," I say, wisely ignoring her crap. "Because you caught me off guard in the meeting today—"

"Oh? That sounds like a first."

"What's *your* idea of the perfect wedding?"

She hesitates. "You're really asking me that, knowing weddings are off-limits?"

"You asked first. Fair is fair, Nevermore. It's just us here. No audience."

"Well, I don't believe in marriage. Not anymore. But on the off chance I'm ever drunk enough to get Vegas hitched or whatever... I think I'd elope," she says.

"Elope? Why?"

"Weddings are all for show. The average groom never does any real work. I'm not willing to go through that for some dude to *maybe* change his mind when we're thousands of dollars deep and on the hook socially. He's either serious enough to get married the minute he proposes, or he can keep his ring."

"You're hardcore," I say without thinking. "I like it."

"No, I'm jaded." She huffs a loud breath. "Like why don't guys spend six months planning what they're going to wear at a wedding or what color the flowers should be? Because someone will do it for them, and then it's 'cute' when ads show her having to chase *him.* I still have no idea how that ever sells a dress. I mean, nothing screams romance from the rafters like the notion that I should *beg* to be good enough for some guy who supposedly wants to be my husband."

She's gone all ranty.

I'm smiling like a dumbstruck fool.

"Damn. That was the wrong question, I see," I tell her, trying to save face.

"Hey, you knew it was a sore spot, bossman."

I chuckle. "It's hard to believe you called me to apologize."

"You're right. But I am sincerely sorry." She pauses. "Technically, you're still a complete freak over breakfast rolls, but we're cool even if we're not exactly friendly. I'll see you next week with less attitude."

"I hope you'll continue being a little psycho, Miss Poe. For the sake of good creative, of course," I say.

"Psycho? Am not!"

"Are," I growl.

"Dude. I'm not the one flipping out over a cinnamon—you know what? No. I'm not getting baited into going around in circles again. I apologized. Good night, Mr. Burns."

She's exasperated and I'm enjoying it far too much.

Shit, maybe I really do have a screw or ten loose.

"You turned down five hundred dollars for a ball of dough for your pride. That's objectively crazier than offering five hundred dollars for said dough." I still maintain if she knew why I needed the cinnamon roll, she'd stop calling me a lunatic.

"I was having a bad day," she says absently.

"Why?" I grip my empty glass, hating that I suddenly care.

"None of your business."

I say nothing, knowing I'm teetering on the edge of another blowout.

"Burns? I just told you—"

"What's the first rule of dealing with clients in copywriting?" I blurt out.

"First rule? I don't know. I was a creative writing major. I only turned to copy and marketing because poetry doesn't pay the rent. I never went to business school."

"How have you made it this far without knowing that?" I scratch my face, far too warm. Blame it on the booze.

"I'm good at writing. I don't do peopling unless I have to."

I pause, thinking over my words, because I mean this and I'm not sure how she'll take it.

"To move up in this industry—to reach your full potential—you may have to get over that," I say carefully.

"I know but...I'm okay with making a steady income and focusing on my poetry. I'm not a ladder climber. I probably shouldn't have bothered telling you that."

"It's fine. I just hope you reconsider somewhere along the way," I say. "You know you're talented, Poe. The first rule of talking to a copy client is this—you have to go three whys deep. Your first reason for refusing to accept five hundred for a lump of flour, sugar, and cinnamon is that you were having a bad day. That could be anything from 'I tripped leaving the house' to 'I just got hit by a truck.' So, if you want to shut me up, give me one more why."

"It should have been—" She pauses. "*Would* have been my wedding anniversary."

"I see."

Dammit, I'm a clod. A total buffalo-brain.

She was left at the fucking altar. I should've known. Also, I have an inexplicable urge to punch the guy who left her stranded and humiliated.

"Mr. Burns?"

"We don't need to go three whys deep," I say sharply. "I get it now."

She's quiet for a heady moment.

"Why did you really want that cinnamon roll so badly?"

Face, meet floor. I made my own bed, didn't I? And I just taught her how to not let up.

"I was starving," I lie.

"Are you on a cinnamon-sugar diet? You had options. There was a case full of bear claws," she reminds me.

I glower at the screen.

"Would you believe I'm allergic to almonds?"

"Not at all."

Didn't think so.

"Fine. You got me. It was for my mother," I say with a twist of my guts. It's not technically a lie. If there were two rolls, I definitely would have saved one for Ma.

I just wouldn't have pitched a fucking fit over it.

"Your mom only eats Sweeter Grind?" she asks incredulously.

She's getting warmer. Closer to the truth.

"She has fond memories of head-sized cinnamon rolls growing up in old Seattle. Sweeter Grind's are the closest, even if they're a newer shop." Again, not a total lie since it's truly why Ma fell in love with them. Still a lie by omission.

"Why?"

Fuck, I have no idea how to spin this further.

"We used to share them when I was a kid," I tell her.

"Oh, and your mom was jonesing for memories to the tune of five hundred bucks?"

"She was having a bad day," I say, amazed I don't trip over my own words.

"Bad day? Really?" Nevermore prompts.

Because it was *her* wedding anniversary. I don't know. Leave me the hell alone.

"She doesn't always enjoy her retirement, I'm afraid," I say. "Especially since my father passed away a few years ago."

There. Hard truth. Now she can buzz off and go torment some other grief-stricken madman on the verge of revealing too much.

"Oh—well, I'm sorry." Her voice is sympathetic and oddly sweet, lacking her usual caustic bite.

"You should get some rest, and I should finish my scotch. We'll talk Monday. Sweet dreams, Nevermore."

Probably not the best goodbye for an employee. Too late.

"You too—sweet dreams."

Bullshit. I don't want her and sweet existing in the same universe.

That's how we got here, sniping at each other, and somehow trading secrets better kept inside the dark chambers of our hearts.

"Good night," I mutter.

When I look down, my screen is blinking.

She's gone like the strange little fever dream she is, fading back into the bottomless night.

VII: UNGAINLY FOWL (DAKOTA)

I wake up in a tangled fit of sheets with a curse on my lips.

All from the kind of insane dream you instantly remember—and regret.

I wore my wedding dress.

Dad walked me down the aisle.

I was walking to meet Jay—what should've happened in real life on that awful day—but when my dad put my hand in the groom's, he wasn't that backstabbing mouse of a man anymore.

The stranger groom wore an impeccably tailored Haughty But Nice tuxedo.

He was taller and broader and more imposing than Jay, and his eyes sparkled like fine polished mahogany. When he smiled at me, *oh God.*

I went from bride to butterflies to butter.

A giddy emotional noodle who couldn't decide if she wanted to break down crying in confusion, or in happy ugly tears for a man who pushes every button.

The second it hit me *who* I was about to marry, I burst into a raven and flew away.

Okay, so dreams are hardly ever realistic, even when they're annoyingly real in other ways.

The raven probably came from my shoulder tattoo. Since I couldn't live down the constant jokes about being an English major named Poe, one day, I decided to just rock it.

I always loved "The Raven," anyway.

The godly tux and Lincoln effing Burns obviously came from the stress I have to deal with at work. Oh, plus the glaring fact that Lincoln was the last person I talked to before I went to bed.

I don't have a crush on my boss.

I don't.

I'm not even stupid enough to think love is real.

Still, it's the kind of dream you have to process.

So, I sit at my tiny table with my notebook, working through the chaos that's my brain the only way I know how. I dive into words, pounding out meter and rhyme and feelings like juggling knives.

When a sharp sound goes off behind me, I almost go tumbling out of my chair.

"You should really start locking your door. Some crazy could walk in." Eliza strolls inside, holding a steaming hot mug with both hands.

My heart leaps at the sound of her voice and I slam my notebook shut.

"Yikes. Thanks for the reminder. Can't believe I forgot to lock up last night."

Was I that distracted from talking to *him?*

I don't want to know. I also don't need anyone else thinking I've fallen so far down the rabbit hole that I'm writing angsty poetry inspired by my cinnamon roll snorting boss.

"You okay? I didn't mean to scare you." She sits down beside me and slides the mug over. "Try it. I'm calling it Raven Blend just for you."

"What? Now you're cracking Poe jokes too?"

"Nope. I named it after your bitchin' tattoo."

I burst out laughing.

God. Eliza's humor reminds me that my encounters with the bosshole have made me overly defensive.

"Sorry. I think I just woke up a little tightly wound today. Probably the new job or something." I pick up the drink and take a long, pleasing sip. "Oooh. Wow, Eliza—*wow.*"

"Perks you up before the caffeine hits, doesn't it? It's two parts cinnamon and one vanilla."

"It's wonderful," I say, praying I'm not developing a cinnamon aversion.

"What's wrong?"

I take another drink. It's good, but not mind-blowing the second time around, and I don't think it's the coffee itself.

"Oh, nothing. Nothing with this drink, that's for sure."

"But you're feeling restless? It's that dillweed you work for again, isn't it?"

I sigh. "No."

"The job? I was afraid writing about holy matrimony all day might be hard. But if anyone can do it, it's you."

"Sorta. Technically, I guess it's psycho-boss. The guy tries *not* to be a twenty-four-seven asshat, and when he tries to be nice...somehow, he's just worse. Or it's just me. After last year, I'm overly sensitive with weddings. I'm also not great at the whole forgiveness thing, especially when it involves dumb remarks from a dangerously handsome, powerful billionaire with my future in his hands. Not forgiving might be safer."

"You knew he was an attractive jerk when you took the job. Too bad you can't get hazard pay for that."

"I know," I say glumly.

"So why did you do it?"

"Huh?" I shake my head. "I guess it just...seemed like the next logical step. I couldn't be a lowly assistant with a sucky salary for the rest of my life."

"I think there's more to it than that. You could've gotten other jobs in this city, Dakota, but you chose to stick it out."

She takes the mug and sips. "Also, it's a nice sunny day and we're not wasting it. How about we talk it out on a bike ride?"

"Really?" I glance up, surprised.

Eliza has always been more of a Pilates or yoga kind of girl. Not to mention somewhat of a homebody on the weekends when she's in full coffee mad scientist mode.

She grins and nods. "Yes! Let's go."

"Let's ride to Sweeter Grind first. My treat."

"I just made you coffee." She gestures frantically at the cup.

"And it's great. But hardly anyone goes to Sweeter Grind for the coffee over other places here. It's all about the baked goods and the atmosphere."

"True. Okay, I'm in."

Ten minutes later, we're bustling downstairs to retrieve our bikes.

"So what did the human dildo do this time?" Eliza asks.

"We were in a meeting full of people, and he asks me how a woman with no ring on her finger knows so much about weddings."

She grimaces.

"God, the nerve. You should have asked him how a man with no game sells so much shit to women."

I laugh hard. She's in fine form today.

"If I had your brain, I would have. He had it coming. Only, he called me up last night trying to apologize..."

"At least, he tried, I guess? You should teach him social skills and charge him out the butt."

He did try.

By the end of our little chat, he actually seemed sincere. That should make me happy.

When we get to the cafe, I go to the counter.

"Two Regis rolls, please."

"I'm sorry," the girl behind the counter says with a wince. "We just ran out."

"Again?" My eyes bug out. "Wait, don't tell me. A tall, growly guy with a black Centurion card?"

She laughs. "How'd you know? We had half a dozen left about ten minutes ago. Same guy bought 'em all up."

The bosshole. I'm a thousand percent sure as soon as she confirms.

"Did he have mocha-brown eyes?"

She giggles. "Yeah. He was pretty built. The guy looked like he could rip you in two, except I've seen him before and he's usually wearing a three-piece suit—not today."

Eliza and I exchange a slow, agonized look.

I hate that I wonder what Lincoln Burns is wearing, too.

"He used to come in and just buy a few rolls at a time, but now he's like...hoarding them? He buys at least half a dozen Regis rolls a few times a week now," the barista says.

Eliza's gaze never leaves me.

"That's Captain McGrowly, all right," I tell her. "And I think we've found the source of his superpower."

What the actual hell, though? Is his mom a cinnamon roll serial killer if she doesn't get her fix?

"I have no idea, but he really likes his Regis rolls," the barista says. "He's been coming around for about a year. Do you want to try something new? The apple turnovers are good."

I nod. "Yeah, we'll take turnovers. Do you have any idea where he goes when he leaves?"

I'm too curious. This is a man who doesn't take sugar in his coffee and stashed the goods in his drawer when I brought them.

The barista shrugs. "I don't know. Sometimes he comes in with a driver, but when it's nice out like this, he takes off on foot. I think he was heading for the park today."

"Is there anything between here and the park?"

"Anything you'd need six cinnamon rolls for? Not likely." She gets into the bakery case and bags up two pastries for us.

I realize how dumb that question sounded.

I just wonder what he's really up to.

Does his mom hang out there? Does he feed the birds cinnamon rolls and think they deserve no less than Sweeter Grind?

Rich people can be nuts, after all.

I pay and grab the paper sack holding our baked goods, then Eliza and I take our pastries outside.

"So what's the plan?" she asks.

"No clue. I say we eat our turnovers and enjoy the spring day."

"Don't you want to find out what he's doing at the park? She said he blew through about ten minutes ago. We could catch him," Eliza suggests.

I pause, rolling it over in my head.

"Sure, but...it doesn't seem like a great idea, stalking my boss at the park on the weekend. Being curious about what he does with a pile of rolls every week isn't the best excuse."

"I vote we live a little, Dakota, and my vote counts more," she says with a grin. "We'll stay back so he can't see us. He has a head start. He may not even be there anymore."

"Maybe..." I hate how good she is at luring me in.

"It's Saturday! And it's not like we have anything else to do besides enjoy the weather," Eliza says.

"Don't make me regret this," I say.

* * *

It's a quick ride to the park.

I've been to the edge of this place a few times before, this open green field with a wooded area at the back. At least what counts for wooded with a few lingering copses of trees in the city.

Once you get past the entrance and a little playing field, the open area is covered in row after row of tents, where the homeless camp out.

We stop and I scan our surroundings. None of the people on

the benches or milling around the edge of the park fit Lucifer's description.

"No sign of him yet. Let's hide the bikes and stay close to the wooded area." I hop off my bike.

Eliza scans the encampment. "Are you sure that's a good idea?"

She has a point. The bikes could be jacked and sold to buy food or supplies by any bad actors in the camp. "We'll stay close enough to see them."

She nods and we move behind the trees, hiding our bikes in some brush.

"This isn't the kind of park I'd expect a dude with a fashion empire to frequent," I say, my brows knitting together.

"What? You mean you're surprised your billionaire boss hangs out in a tent city? I mean, Seattle's no stranger to places like this—it sucks and I feel for the people who live here—but yeah, it's pretty weird for Mr. Moneybags to come strolling through here. I wonder why?"

Your guess is as good as mine.

We trudge on for a few more minutes before Eliza stops, grabbing my arm.

"Hey, wait, I think I see him!" She extends her arm, pointing in front of us and to the left.

"How do you know? You've never seen him." I follow her finger with my eyes and I don't spot him at first.

"I'm guessing he's the only person here who looks like an Instagram thirst trap? That guy fits the description—holy mchottie."

Sure enough.

Lincoln stands in all his sculpted glory, dressed in dark-blue jeans that accent his powerful hips and a button-down shirt with military shoulder traps. There's a Sweeter Grind cup pressed to his mouth.

A few seconds later, he sits on a box next to a man with an overgrown beard and a face smudged with dirt.

Lincoln pulls a cinnamon roll out of the bag and then hands the rest to the bearded guy. They both have coffees from Sweeter Grind.

The entire scene does not compute.

I think my brain crashes and reboots several times before I realize my heart stopped beating seconds ago.

I might be watching the sweetest, most unexpected thing ever.

He's feeding the homeless.

Guilt crashes over me in a tidal wave. Was he planning to feed a homeless guy this entire time with that roll I wouldn't sell him?

"Dakota, is it him?"

"Yep. Good eye," I say, blinking. "You're looking at the dude who throws fits over Regis rolls. I guess he has coffee and pastries with homeless people. I'll *never* figure him out."

"Maybe he isn't as big of a jerkwad as you thought?"

Hmm.

Is it possible?

He did call me up yesterday to apologize. But then again, if he hadn't been such a nosy prick in the first place, he wouldn't have needed any sorries.

"...I don't know," I say, realizing I don't really know anything about him.

"They're talking about a kid," Eliza says.

"You hear them from here?" I look at her.

"My grandma was deaf my whole life. I used to stay with her while my mom was at work. She taught me to read lips. The crazy beard beside him says he'd give up his other leg and both arms to see his son again."

"Other leg? Does that mean he gave up one leg already?"

"I don't know. Can't tell from here, but the best I can follow, it seems like maybe he did," she says.

I don't need her lip reading to process what happens next.

Lincoln drops a hand on the stranger's shoulder. He says

something with a gentle, heartfelt expression. His head is tilted down, and Eliza can't read his lips.

But the other guy smiles for the first time since we've been here, and Lincoln doesn't immediately move his hand. The billionaire jackass certainly doesn't treat the homeless guy like an untouchable.

I'm stunned.

Also, a little humbled.

...hadn't I called him entitled? Repeatedly?

But catching Lincoln Burns in this parallel reality makes it harder to hate him for his rotten behavior.

That's *not* a good thing.

It's like I can feel a big, jagged piece of my defenses falling down and crashing to bits.

They're talking again. I paw at Eliza's arm like a hungry puppy.

"What's he saying now?" I whisper.

"Bossholio's asking—no, more like begging—the homeless guy to...come home with him? What the hell?"

Yeah, I'm lost.

Charity is one thing, but that makes zero sense.

It's hard enough to reconcile this scene with the self-absorbed fiend from the coffeeshop and the prying tyrant at the office. But this is beyond anything I imagined.

Everything I thought I knew about this gorgeous, bad-tempered freak is officially upended.

I don't need Eliza to read lips to know the homeless man isn't impressed by this invitation. He lurches up and shoves Lincoln away with what looks like harsh words. Then he disappears inside the tent behind them and zips it up.

I glance at Eliza. "Ouch. Was he a dick about it when he invited the guy to come stay with him?"

She shakes her head slowly.

"He wasn't. Not at all."

"But—"

Eliza shrugs. "I don't get it either."

With an angry look, Lincoln picks up an old coffee can beside the tent and shoves a wad of bills in it before slamming the lid back on.

"He gives them money, too?"

"Looks like it," Eliza whispers.

He puts his hand in front of his face like he's keeping the sun out of his eyes and surveys the line of trees at the back of the park. When he turns our way, I duck down, even though I think —*I hope*—we're too far away to see.

"Oh, crap. What's he doing?" I whisper.

"Not sure," she says.

But the second he starts toward us, panic.

"Did he see us? Eliza? There's no reason for him to come this way..."

"I don't think so."

"Yeah, well, I've seen enough. Time for that bike ride!" I run back a few paces to grab my bike, hop on, and pedal as fast as I can through the trees to get the hell out of here.

I'm not even sure where I'm going. I just need to stay out of sight, to avoid being caught by Burns after I eavesdropped on such an intimate moment.

I barely remember to look back to see Eliza behind me, straining to catch up.

* * *

MONDAY MORNING, I drag myself out of bed and get dressed.

I'm about to bike to Sweeter Grind when I remember that's not my job this week.

I can go straight to the office today, get to work, and—enjoy a visit to the principal's office, apparently. One look at my phone has me frowning. It's barely the buttcrack of dawn and Lincoln Burns is already in my texts, scolding me.

Come straight to my office when you arrive, he says. *I have your breakfast. We need to talk.*

Awesome.

What now? I send back, my fingers punching the screen.

Lincoln: We'll talk when you get here.

Awesome again, staying mired in suspense.

Twenty minutes later, I get to the office as fast as my body can move those wheels. Anger is a hell of a workout.

Burns leans against his office door, filling the space like an annoyed bear protecting its den.

"Nevermore," he says coldly. "Breakfast inside."

"Thank you." I give him the world's fakest smile.

I walk into his office, brushing his massive chest as I slide past and hold in a sigh.

No bad case of the Mondays ever felt so dire.

He closes the door behind us and moves to his desk with a single word.

"Sit."

"Your wish is my command," I say flippantly, flopping down in the chair across from him. "What's wrong now? You said my work was stellar."

He slides my coffee and cinnamon roll across the table like some grizzled cop in the movies giving the hotshot rookie his badge.

"Your work is unimpeachable. That's not why we're here," he tells me, pushing his massive hands against the desk.

He's good at this whole intimidation act, I'll give him that. Too bad for him that's never really worked on me.

"Why are you so pissed then?" I ask.

"Pissed? Is that what you think?"

"Er—I'm not sure what we're talking about," I throw out, taking a huge bite of cinnamon roll heaven. Mostly so I have a reason to not look at him.

He opens his desk, pulls out a napkin, and slides it over.

"You have frosting on your mouth."

While swallowing, I take the napkin cautiously and wipe my face, trying to decipher that look in his eyes. God, what is his deal today?

Is this about the park?

His nostrils flare as he draws in a deep breath and says, "For someone who doesn't like people rummaging around in her personal life, you have no issue digging in mine. How *interesting.*"

Boom. Hammer, meet head.

The way he calls it *interesting* certainly feels like a cranial blow.

...so he might be a tad better at the whole intimidation schtick than I gave him credit for.

"Umm—you mean because I called you close to midnight on Friday?" I try, praying that's it. "Look, bossman, I'm sorry. I thought it was fine because we just talked."

"Do I hire dumbasses, Nevermore?" he grinds out.

I'm taken aback by the question and sit up straighter, mostly so I don't rock back in my seat.

"Um, no?" I blink. "I'm not sure what you're getting at..."

Is this some weird backhanded insult? Is he calling *me* a dumbass?

"You know what I'm talking about. And because you're not a dumbass, that means you're a terrible liar," he growls.

Holy hell.

I scratch my chin, averting my eyes before I meet the steel trap of his gaze again.

"Mr. Burns, I have no fricking clue what you mean. But let's say I did—which I don't—but *if I did*, we'd be even because you dug first...wouldn't we?"

"No, ma'am. We are so far from even you couldn't get there by jet." He lifts one big hand and places it in the other, loudly cracking his knuckles.

"Can you just tell me what you think I did?" I sputter. "I just...I don't like games. Spit it out."

"Stalking the boss is a serious offense."

My heart skips. I hate how my blush betrays me more than words ever could.

"What? Because of my Google-fu?" An exaggerated laugh falls out of me. "Maybe don't wind up on the internet and I won't read about you?"

I know I'm playing with fire. But I'm going to make him say it.

If he saw me, I want to hear it from his lips.

"How about you and Tweedle Dum following me to the park on your day off? Ring a bell?" His voice is a quiet storm.

Yeah, I'm so *not* ready.

His look cuts me in two, so hot and glaring it's like he's stripping me naked right here in this office.

"The park...what makes you think it was me?"

"You're whispering, for one, and that isn't something you do," he says, stabbing up a finger midair. "Two, you don't think the blond ponytail gave it away? I'd know that hair anywhere, Nevermore. Do not bullshit me."

"Wait, wait, wait," I mutter, waving my hands frantically. "*That's* your evidence? A blond chick in a city of almost a million people happens to be at the park with you, so it must be me? And that must mean I'm stalking you? I'm in awe. I never thought I'd meet Sherlock Holmes."

He isn't impressed.

Neither am I, honestly.

The bosshole leans forward and stares into my eyes.

"Sweetheart, it's not just the hair. Although it's a perfect platinum-gold shade I haven't seen too often—"

"So, you like my hair?" I stare at him.

He rolls his eyes.

"Not the point. You're the only woman who wears a black dress with silver corded straps while biking. Were you going for a joyride or out to a cocktail party?"

"If it were me—and I haven't said it was—but if it *were*, the options are joyride or the library. Keep it straight."

His gaze only deepens until it's bone-deep.

"Nevermore, I'm not a betting man. However, if I were, I'd bet every dollar I own that only you have a raven inked across your shoulder," he says.

Ouch.

Busted.

He knew, and he's toying with me now.

I touch my shoulder, making sure my sleeveless dress is thick enough to cover the tattoo. It is. I've never shown it off at work.

He smiles.

"It's a nice accent on a well-toned body on a sunny day. Between you and me, it was damn hard to look away from," he rumbles, his eyes flipping *drilling* me now.

Heat pumps under my face.

So he's noticed—and likes—my 'well-toned' body.

Eep.

I put a hand on the desk to stop my knees from shaking.

"...so maybe it was me. And what if it was? Am I fired?"

He hesitates for a horrible second.

"Maybe."

What? I bolt up in my seat.

"I thought we agreed to ninety days! And we weren't following you. I swear. That's not fair, Burns."

"Neither is spying on your boss. Unless you're telling me you always hang around homeless sites for fun?"

Prick. I doubt he's serious about the firing threat. He just wants to see me squirm.

"Do you?" I fling back.

"That's my business, and mine alone," he clips, sliding back in his chair.

"Why?"

"Because what I do away from work isn't your concern," he growls, irritation creeping into his tone.

"Why?" I repeat just to screw with him.

"Were you even listening?"

I smile slowly. "A boss once told me I have to go three whys deep."

"I'm not a fucking client," he snaps. "And you should stick to your morgues and haunted houses. You're no comedian, Miss Poe."

"And you're my boss, Mr. Burns," I say sweetly. "You're the ultimate client. But you know how it's none of my business why you were at a tent city inside a public park?"

"Of course I know. That's what I want *you* to figure out."

I try not to laugh. Why does it feel so good getting him worked up?

"It's technically none of your business why I was at the same public park on a gorgeous day, biking with a friend. It's not impossible or even implausible for two people who frequent the same coffee shop a few blocks away to wind up at the same public park, is it?"

Ha. Argue with that.

"Have you been there before? Don't lie to me now. It's very important I can trust the people I work with," he says, towering in his seat as he straightens, his hands clasped in front of him.

I can't help the way my eyes wander to those fingers. For a man who spends so much time in the office, his hands look rough. Worn.

They're the kind of hands that could do appalling things to me in my darkest dreams. The ones I'm totally not having where my boss grabs me, shoves me against the nearest wall, and shoves his hands between my—

"Miss Poe? Are you home or did the ravens make off with your brain today? I asked a simple question," he snarls.

"No. It's not usually a place I go. I'm more the type to head over to Alki Beach or maybe take the ferry over to Bainbridge for the day. But where did you see Eliza and I—"

"That's Tweedle Dum? Eliza?"

I glare at him.

"Where did you see us before we all wound up at the same park?" I ask pointedly.

"Saturday morning? I only saw you at the park," he says.

"Then I couldn't have followed you there. Thanks for proving my point. No stalker, no drama, so maybe let's just get on with our day like grown-ups?"

Like hell, his snapping brown eyes say. *You're not getting off that easy.*

"I must have overlooked you at Sweeter Grind," he says slowly.

"Doubtful. Since we've established I have nice bright hair and a tattoo on a well-toned body you're obsessed with, you wouldn't have missed me."

"Touché." He levels a long look on me.

Why does that make my blood run hot?

"You've seen me go to the park from Sweeter Grind before," he says, his eyes sliding up and down my torso, hot and assessing.

"And I just instinctively knew you'd be there?" I make an exasperated sound. "I don't think so, man. I might like my horror and fantasy but I'm no psychic."

He shrugs. "Maybe you found it on some nosy little rat's social media. You like reading about me."

I snort. "What? Your trips to the tent city are so frequent they're online?"

He's quiet for a moment, deep in thought.

"No. That can't be the case. I've never seen anyone following me or snapping pics, no matter how often I go."

"Then how could I have read it?" I slap my thigh.

I'm so annoyed. And extra annoyed that getting this riled up is a two-way street. It's like we're just feeding off each other's suspicions now.

"How did you find out I was there?" he demands.

I start laughing.

"You took all the Regis rolls again. Duh. We got to the shop after you blew through. I'll admit, I was curious, and Eliza put me up to it. I wanted to know where you went with the rolls and the Sweeter Grind girl said you head for the park sometimes—"

"What is it with you and those damn cinnamon rolls?" he barks.

"You're asking *me*? You're the one who needs at least half a dozen every day..."

"She told you how many I bought? That should be confidential." He sounds mortified.

I laugh helplessly again.

"Nope, everybody knows you're a junkie. Sorry, buddy."

"All joking aside, I don't think you should go back there. Not for work, and not for your personal stomping grounds."

Oh my God.

He's serious, isn't he?

My boss is trying to dictate what parts of the city I'm allowed to visit.

"Yeah, no, that's definitely not your business." I roll my eyes right out of my head.

"Probably not, but this isn't about your juvenile spying. It isn't always the safest place if you're not sure where you're going or who the bad people are there. You and Tweedle Dum—"

"Would you quit calling her that?" I lean forward, flicking a fallen lock of hair over one ear.

"You and your *friend* seem like easy targets," he corrects.

"That's not your problem," I snap.

But I'm actually stunned that he gives two craps about my well-being. Even if he tells me with zero tact.

"Wrong, Nevermore. It's very much my business if I lose my best copywriter and her sidekick to some sneaky fuck looking for an easy payday—or worse."

The way he bites off that last word leaves a yawning silence. Ominous.

"...I doubt I'm your best copywriter, Mr. Burns," I say. "You have people with vastly more experience than me under their belts."

"Your ideas are fresh and funny. That is, when your wit goes in a focused direction with our product and isn't trained on me." He thumps his chest with a hilarious glower, his brow pulled low.

Amazing. He's so far up his own butt that he actually believes his BS.

But he does genuinely care about me getting robbed—or *worse*—and that's unexpectedly sweet.

I take a slow sip of coffee, trying to shake this weird dizzy feeling.

"Are we done here? As much fun as it's been, I have a mountain of work. Can I go?"

His look leaves me anchored in place—and that's when it hits me.

As long as I work here, I'll be answering to a man who can't take a joke or get a clue.

I just wonder what sin I committed in some past dreary life to wind up at the mercy of Lincoln freaking Burns.

VIII: A FLIRT AND FLUTTER
(LINCOLN)

"*A*re we done here, boss? As much fun as it's been, I have a mountain of work. Can I go?" She bats her eyes, utterly oblivious to what it does to me.

"No," I say sternly.

"Why not?"

She has to ask? Like she doesn't know she went peeping through a very dark, private window into my life, and I'm basically letting her off with a slap on the wrist?

"You remember earlier when you said we were even?" I ask.

Nevermore takes a deep breath. Her eyes narrow. Everything is effort with her, the little brat.

"Yes?" she whispers.

"We're not, but we're going to be even very soon."

"Oh, yeah? What does that mean?"

"Did you notice Lucy wasn't here when you came in this morning?" I look down, rubbing at this minor smudge on my desk.

"I didn't have time to notice anything. This impatient nutter pulled me into his office and accused me of stalking and other high crimes."

She gets my eyes.

My very tired eyes, thoroughly exhausted with this sniping back and forth.

"Well, she'll be gone for at least the next eight weeks. Possibly longer," I say.

"She had her baby?" Miss Poe smiles.

"Not yet, but she's in labor from what I understand."

That happy, well-wishing grin on her face fades instantly. Her eyes go wide with grief.

"Wait. Wait, now you want me to play secretary, don't you?"

It's hard to pull back my smile.

She's good at catching on.

"I *do* have some additional work for you in the interim, yes. Don't worry. It comes with additional compensation," I say flatly.

She looks iced over and unamused.

"So I'm going from copywriter to your stand-in assistant?" she asks with a visible cringe.

"No. You're going to be my right hand, and since you're killing it on the wedding line, you'll be doing both jobs. Doesn't that sound like fun? I'll spare you a chance to make more jokes about what my hands get up to when I'm hot and bothered. I've heard them before and they're not goddamned funny."

She glares at me like a desert sun wanting to make me a pile of parched bones.

"It's like a two in one," I continue. "Didn't you tell me coffee duty seemed more like an assistant's role? Maybe now—"

"Don't even try it. You're on coffee duty this week. A deal's a deal!" she throws out with a desperate look.

"Go ahead and move your stuff to Lucy's space. It's a larger desk. You can write from anywhere, and it will be easier if my assistant is nearby," I say matter-of-factly.

"And if I don't agree?"

"Why wouldn't you? I just told you it pays more." Then I remember the day I met Dakota Poe. She turned down five hundred dollars for a cinnamon roll. "Right. I forgot you're not motivated by money like the other ninety-nine percent of the world. You also promised me ninety days. Tell you what, help me out and you don't have to write any runaway grooms. You'll have full creative freedom to flex your muscles and produce whatever you want with my backing."

In half a second, she goes from stiff as a board to a glowing red icon.

"Really? You'd better be serious." She scratches at the corner of her lip, deep in thought. I try like hell not to stare, to acknowledge what her expressions do to me. "But what if Anna gets mad at me because I just came in and can do whatever I want?"

"I'll talk to her. She won't be upset. Anna loves your ideas, and if anything, this just loosens them up."

She puffs out her cheeks and then gives me a satisfied smile.

"Fine. I'll go move my stuff."

Is it wrong that I can think of better things I'd like to move?

Yes, it is.

Still, I'd love to move her against the wall, hold her down, and teach those lips some sorely needed respect.

I watch like the half-mad asshole I am while she stands and walks to the door, her hips pumping, reminding me I'm a slave to thoughts I shouldn't have.

"Miss Poe?"

"Yes?" She looks at me over her shoulder.

"You have me confused. I'm not sure which is nicer—the raven tattoo or the bird who's wearing it," I growl against my better judgment.

She blushes.

"Oh, shut up. That's not even close to appropriate, *Burns.*"

I hold up a hand, hiding my smirk behind it.

"One more thing, Miss Poe."

"What?"

"Since we've already made the mistake of getting personal, we'll be doing a lot more of it over the next few weeks."

"Whatever you think, bro."

"Bro?" My eyebrows fly up and I hold in a laugh. "Did you just call me bro?"

She gives a rolling shrug.

"Yeah, you're a bro. You're acting like a big one today. Ciao."

"Once you get your stuff moved, if I'm not in a meeting or on the phone, stop by my office. I'll show you how to use Lucy's EA Inbox."

She exits without another complaint and a nice view of her plump ass, swaying with every switch of her hips.

Damn.

I don't dare stand before she's gone, or else how much I'm enjoying that view will be on full display. She'll be back soon and I'd rather my right hand not know the full effect she has on me.

Once she's gone, I gently punch myself in the crotch under my desk.

"Ow, fuck," I snarl, ripping my hand up.

Not gently enough.

It hurts like hell, but it solves my problem.

I made a mistake by hiring this nosy, rude, insufferable woman. Every day, I'm digging that hole deeper.

Since I can't fire her, here I am.

Reduced to whacking myself in the balls like a slapstick comedian and praying they're a little less blue by day's end.

It doesn't work for long. I find myself glancing angrily at the clock every few minutes.

I feel like God himself is slamming a door in my face.

You chose this fate, I can hear him saying. *Now suffer the consequences, smurf balls and all.*

* * *

MORE THAN AN HOUR LATER, Poe hasn't come back, but Lucy's emails are being sorted and replied to rather quickly.

I'm equally impressed and relieved.

My EA is damn dedicated, but I can't have her working on maternity leave. It's not right.

I open my office door around noon after reviewing the latest ad mockups sent to me and find Nevermore perched at Lucy's desk with the phone clutched in her hand.

"The image with the logo isn't right. Whatever you choose needs more contrast with the background. This one just fades into it and doesn't pop."

She's quiet for a minute while I eavesdrop.

"Yes, *everything* that appears on the page is part of the ad. If the image and text don't mesh well together, my work doesn't read right. No, that's not acceptable. If you can't find a better pic, try changing the background color. But please send it back to me before you submit it. I'm not convinced this one aligns with our messaging anyway."

I stare at her, wondering how she read my mind. I'm certainly feeling more confident in my staffing decisions—blue balls and all—until her whip of a tongue moves again.

"Well, the bosshole's here and he probably wants something, so why don't you play around while I play secretary to the prince of entitlement?"

My jaw tightens.

How the hell does she even see me? Her back is turned.

And I'm officially a 'bosshole?'

"Can you have it back to me by three? You heard what Burns said. This line is a big deal and the clock's ticking, to put it mildly. If the CEO has inserted himself in the creative process, you can bet it's important. We need these ads in the pipeline and ready to go. The magazines where they'll run have strict deadlines."

She's been here for a few weeks and already talks like a manager? I hide my amusement.

"Okay, four then. Sorry to rush you. I just need to see it before I leave and if it needs a quick tweak, I want to give you feedback before you're out for the day." She's quiet for a minute. "Okay, thanks. Bye."

She drops the phone into its cradle and spins around in her chair to face me.

"You were supposed to come back so I could show you how Lucy's inbox works. You never showed and she's responding to her email."

"No, she's not."

"Yes, she is. I've been CC'd on two already."

"And if I *am* Lucy?" She purses her lips. "Look, the poor girl's busy pushing a bowling ball out of a coin purse. I get that you think you're important, but today, she probably doesn't. The least I can do is fire off responses for her. I assure you she isn't responding to any email on behalf of *the* Lincoln Burns without his input on anything critical."

Fuck, I never thought I'd hear a vagina described like that.

There's the bucket of ice-cold water to the head I need when Dakota Poe is around, I guess.

I clear my throat before I say, "I think you may have just ruined my favorite part of the female anatomy. Also, I had zero intention of letting Lucy work while she's out."

"How? I'm sure you had eighth grade biology once—or were you too busy eating a cinnamon roll to pay attention?"

"Watch where you wag that tongue, Miss Poe." I fold my arms, eyes burning down at her acid little mouth. "You know what I need those damn Regis rolls for and you're *still* going to rag on me?"

A crease forms in her forehead. Her lips form a thin line— almost regretful, but trying so hard not to be.

"What *do* you need them for? I know you bring them to homeless people, which is honestly kind, but I'm still not sure why. You could feed ten more people with a simple loaf of bread instead of those expensive rolls..."

Interesting. Her little spy game still hasn't helped her figure out everything.

"If you're standing in for Lucy, you need to know how," I tell her, ignoring her probing questions.

"Everything has a folder and it's color coded. I'm not a complete moron, Burns," she says sharply, looking up through her lashes.

Goddamn her and that stubborn little pout.

In another universe, I'd grab her by the shoulders, not caring about any bystanders. I'd find a better use for those strawberry lips that doesn't involve endless scorn.

"Did you reschedule the call with our Italian designer?" I ask.

"Her office is slammed. She requested the rescheduling, actually. I found an available time on your calendar and booked it in the system. Pretty intuitive."

"I only take meetings at certain times."

"Did I schedule it when you're free?" she asks.

"Yes. How did you know?"

"She has a recurring space on your calendar for 'no meeting blocks.'"

"What about the invoices? They need to go straight to accounting. Proposals from businesses we've established relationships with get forwarded to me, the proper department, and accounting. Unsolicited proposals can come to me if you think I'd be interested, but only then. Anything else that comes through with an attachment needs to be printed and filed. The filing room is behind Ida's office, and she can show you our simplified system."

She nods briskly, that stark blond hair waving.

"Should I start filing from today? Or do I need to go back and check if Lucy had everything filed through the end of yesterday?"

"Just start with today. If she didn't have it filed through the end of yesterday, she can deal with it when she gets back. If an invoice goes unpaid, accounting will notice and you can print it then."

"Got it."

"Since it's your first day on a new job, let's go for lunch." As soon as the words leave my mouth, I regret them. Private lunches with an employee who gives you a hard-on bigger than a Starship rocket aren't wise.

Too bad she takes her job seriously, though, meaning I have to respect her despite all the hell she gives me.

Even when she gawks at me right now, as frozen as a deer in front of a speeding semi.

"It's tradition," I explain. "Every EA I take on gets fed while they're spending time with me. They should know my thinking, right down to my pastrami on rye. And since you've been sharing my breathing space since I hired you and we never got the chance, we're past due."

"I can't, but thanks anyhow."

I square my shoulders and blink. No one ever turns down a free lunch.

"Why not?" I grind out.

"Lucy's been getting emails since one a.m. I need to go back and work on whatever needs filing, digitally or by hand. Cheryl's sending me a new ad mockup by four and I'm sure it'll need corrections. Plus, I have to write a series of social media posts for Anna, so...double duty, half as much time to chitchat."

Why do I fucking hate that she's armed with good excuses?

My hand balls into a fist.

"Cheryl Helen's been here longer than me. Almost twelve years. Why are you correcting her ads?" I ask.

She gives me a dismissive flick of her hair.

"Yeah, well...I'm not trying to step on any toes, but Anna wasn't thrilled with her last round of concepts. Cheryl is worried about submitting it, and it's got my copy attached. She's just doing the visuals, so I'd like it to look good. The colors are bleeding together, and I'm not sure she sees it. You need an eye for that sort of thing."

"In your professional opinion, is Cheryl's current role a good fit for her?" I ask carefully.

It's not that I'd fire her. If, however, I somehow missed optimizing my human assets, I need to know.

Dakota thinks for a few seconds too long.

"Out with it, Miss Poe. I assure you I'm not looking to reprimand her," I say, leaning in.

"Well...I don't know her super well, but I'm worried she might be going color blind. I've heard her talking about vision issues. Also, she prefers writing copy to graphic work, but Anna said her copy feels sorta dated."

"She's worked here for ages," I say, mulling over what she just said.

"Don't get me wrong. She's very helpful, and she knows a lot. Deep knowledge. I'm glad I'm not management so I don't have to worry about these things..." Poe frowns, a nervousness on her face at affecting any staffing decisions.

"So you're admitting I do hard things?" I say smugly.

Her face jerks up, souring at my mock ego.

There's my little fighter. And if she needs my bad attitude to distract her from fretting over Cheryl for the rest of the day, so be it.

"Someone has to handle staffing, I guess. It's probably easier if he's self-absorbed," she says.

"Again with the selfish asshole remarks? You must rehearse your insults to keep them so fresh," I say with a sarcastic head shake.

She ignores me.

"If you were management, what would you do?" I ask, aiming to pull her out of her own head.

"Well...I guess I'd find some class on copywriting trends and send her to training for a refresh. And I either wouldn't ask her to choose color schemes and images or know that someone needs to check it over. If she's been here for a while, it's not fair to hold her vision against her."

"That's a fair solution, Miss Poe. Find a copywriting course and send it to me, not Anna. Problem solved."

"Is that even a thing? Copywriting classes?"

"How should I know? It's your idea. I just happen to like it, and everyone will benefit from utilizing Cheryl's talents," I say.

With that, I walk past her desk.

"Hey, wait. Where are you going?" she calls after me.

I stop, throwing a cold look over my shoulder.

"Lunch. Are you coming or not?"

Dammit, Burns. Danger, a voice screeches in the back of my head.

I know.

I know I shouldn't when every reckless part of me screams *should.*

"Could you bring me something back?" she asks in a low, awkward whisper.

"Do I look like DoorDash? Join me if you want to eat." This has to be what self-sabotage sounds like.

"Fiiine," she slurs, muttering something less flattering under her breath. I try not to smile. "Where are we going?"

She pushes her chair away from her desk and stands.

"What do you like?"

"Hot Italian beef sandwiches drenched in the salty tears of terrible bosses." Her green eyes flash with wicked delight.

For once, I think she's cracking a joke that isn't meant to flay me open.

"Hot beef sandwiches it is, but there'll be no tears today."

"*Today.*"

"You enjoy watching people cry that much and you think *I'm* the psycho?" I snort, nearly shaking my head off my shoulders.

I don't expect a breakthrough.

Somehow, we get through lunch without wanting to murder each other.

Somehow, we talk like normal human beings about entirely work-related business.

Somehow, we take a step back from holding knives at each other's throats.

A few days later, when I come up for air after dealing with suppliers, partners, and production, we've survived an entire week with Dakota Poe as both executive assistant and copywriter.

Her work remains impeccable.

If she stays on track, she'll single-handedly make this big launch a breeze. That's easily worth more than the private bonus I agreed to pay out at the end of her ninety days.

But tomorrow, I need to check in on Wyatt since I haven't seen him for a few days, so I text Dakota.

When you do tomorrow's coffee run, pick up eight Regis rolls. Make sure you're there early so they don't run out, and don't forget I want you on the call with the designer from Rome tomorrow. Tell her what American women want in a dress.

I hate that I keep a hand over my phone, anticipating her reply. I barely make idle conversation with Louis as he fights our way through late evening traffic.

When my phone buzzes, I bring it to my face so fast I almost drop the damn thing.

Dakota: Psycho hoarder, are you sure I'm the right person to be on this call? I'm not the type of girl who'd pay for a luxury dress. For all I know, luxury dress shoppers might not even care about comfort.

I frown, wondering what kind of dress she picked out once upon a fucked up time. And what kind of shrimp-dicked little coward ruined what would've been the happiest day of her life?

Everyone cares about comfort, and you know the industry. Also, I haven't worn a dress before so my input counts far less than yours, I send back.

Dakota: You're such an asshat.

Lincoln: What did I do now?

Dakota: Don't worry. I'll be there to bail you out.

A smile pulls at my lips, but doesn't fully form.

Are you okay? I start typing. *If this is still bringing back bad memories, I'm more than willing to—*

No.

I erase the text and slap my phone against my thigh.

Nevermore made it perfectly clear she doesn't want special treatment. She wants to fight, even if that means stirring up the phantom pain of a marriage that never was.

I only wish I knew why that scrambles my brain until Louis looks back with obvious concern, and I punch the privacy screen up.

I wish like hell I could stop counting how many times I see her smile around the office. Especially those rare, bright moments when she stops dishing out her hot takes long enough to shut it and listen.

To meet my eyes with her soul.

To grin and laugh before she catches herself and hides her heart away again behind its moat of past hurts and overprotective dragons snorting pure sarcasm.

Dakota Poe's smile is *not* my problem, not my life, and not my concern.

It's just a rotten new addiction I need to stop cold fucking turkey.

* * *

NEVERMORE SAILS into my office in a black-pleated dress the next day.

"Right on time for the call," I tell her. "Pull up a chair and I'll put it on speaker."

She pulls her chair around the desk next to me and sits. Her dress rides up a few inches, exposing a well-toned thigh.

It's like that leg has its own gravity.

My eyes want to jump right out of my head.

Fucking distractions.

A terrible part of me wants that dress up higher, though. A nastier part wants to shear it right off her, all the better to get my hot, tingling hands on her skin.

147

Would she still give me that mouth if these fingers put her in her place?

Would we finally understand each other if we fucked out this suffocating tension at a debased, animal level?

Off-limits, My reason growls. *She's off-limits, you slobbering wolf.*

I shake my head.

"Is something wrong?" she asks, staring at me like I've sprouted a second head—and if I have, it wants to taste her too.

"Not at all," I lie, clearing my throat and shifting my weight.

Like clockwork, the call comes while I'm still trying to quietly kill the hard-on from hell that has me shifting in my seat.

I punch the speaker button.

"Hey, Isabella. This is Lincoln Burns and you're on speaker. My assistant and copywriter, Dakota Poe, is joining us."

"Wonderful. I'm the lead designer on your project," she says in perfect English with a slight Italian accent. "I'll admit I'm slightly confused by this call, sir. I was under the impression our designs were agreed and approved. Now you want changes?"

Next to me, Poe tenses.

"Correct. I'm simply requesting a revision. My marketing team brought to my attention that there isn't much in the way of simple fit comfortable dresses available in our current lines. I'd like to have a couple new choices produced with comfort in mind first and foremost," I say diplomatically.

"What do you mean comfort? These dresses are art, made to your precise specifications," Isabella practically spits through the phone, harsh and offended. "Your bride will be draped in the finest silk that fits like a glove, Mr. Burns. What could possibly be more comfortable than looking like a goddess?"

Nevermore gives me whale eyes, green and unsettled.

"I have a few ideas," I say coldly. "The whole point is trying something new, Isabella. There's certainly no one disparaging your work, past or present."

I hear the woman take a deep breath, and so do I.

Before either of us can fire another barrage, Miss Poe cuts in.

"Hi, this is Dakota. Ideally, we're looking for something that doesn't require a corset bra, full bridal slip, or shapewear," she says. "And you know any full gown requires a full slip or you'll have shadows in the pictures, and no one wants that."

"So you want slip dresses? Three slip dresses? Even then, most women need their shapewear. Very few of us are born perfect," the design lead says with a little less venom.

"That's the point. We want the dress to be perfect so the wearer doesn't have to be," Poe tells her.

"You want me to build the undergarments into the dress? It's unorthodox, but I believe...yes, maybe I can do that."

"Perfect," I say, giving a satisfied nod.

Dakota's eyebrow shoots up and she whispers to me, "How is that better? Being wrapped up like a sausage gets draining no matter where the wrapping comes from."

"You're exaggerating. Why would anyone feel like deli meat if it's tailored?" I grumble.

Her eyes narrow and dagger me.

"You just heard her say very few of us are perfect. Wedding dresses are made with models in mind," she hisses under her breath.

"I have no idea what you want. The only way to do what you're asking for is to go custom, and even then the options are limited," I say.

"If you go custom, what are the options that don't require any puffing or binding?" Dakota asks.

"Maybe a slip dress for a slender woman. A simple A-line with a flowing skirt. I can't really think of anything else you'd wear to a formal wedding," I say, racking my brain.

"Do a long A-line then. If you can make it work, add an option for a train." Dakota looks at me. "How many dresses are in this line, anyway?"

"Five, but—"

"The other two can be anything you want if you add options.

Did you get that, Isabella?"

I shoot her a look from hell. I thought I was the CEO.

"Yes," the designer says, sounding brighter. "It's possible."

Dakota covers the speaker with her hand and flashes an eat-shit smile.

"You have to give the artist some creative room," she explains, moving her hand.

"You have to give them rules as well, Miss Poe. Too much leeway and you'll alienate my customers."

"That's where the customizations come in. Plus, I know Italian silk isn't cheap. I've been doing a lot of reading."

The hell she has.

At least it's a better way to spend her time than reading about *me*.

"Is there anything you don't think of, Mary Sue?" I snap.

I shouldn't be defensive. Her input is solid. She just needs to remember I sign off on any and all decisions around here.

"I've shopped for wedding dresses before," she reminds me with a bitter look. "If you don't want my experience, just say so."

Her statement stirs my insides.

Something ugly and uneven and jagged.

Yeah, I want to punch her asshole ex square in the face even more now. I'm *jealous* that he ever got that close to her, held her heart, and presumably earned the right not to be called Captain Dipshit.

"Your assistant is right. I agree wholeheartedly," Isabella says.

Damn. I half forgot she was still on the line.

Dakota grins at me triumphantly like the spoiled brat she is.

"Fine. Send the amended contracts over, and we'll get them taken care of," I say, hitting the button to disconnect.

With the call finished, Nevermore returns to her desk. Somehow, she still hasn't fixed that extra inch of skin showing on her thigh, and it draws my eyes like a beacon every time I walk by.

"Don't stay too late," I growl as dusk settles in.

She's refused to ride home with me several times. I still

loathe the thought of her biking around in downtown Seattle alone after dark.

Later, I bring Wyatt his Regis rolls and have a coffee with him, but I can't stay long. I have to get back to the office. I have contracts with international turnaround times waiting to be reviewed by tomorrow.

I don't expect to see her lingering, hunched over her laptop when I return.

"Why the hell are you still here?" I say, my shadow falling over her in the office's dimmer night lighting.

She blinks and lifts her head.

"Oh, you're back. Lucy's job is a full-time gig. I'm working on ad copy now. I just wanted to get it right before I take off..."

"You should've just taken it home."

"Maybe so. I lost track of time."

"You're stuck here until I leave now. Luckily, I have a comfortable car and a driver waiting. It's a roomy vehicle, you hardly need to be up in my face for the ten-minute ride home," I tell her.

Her lips twist. She stares at me silently, hopefully mulling it over.

"It's too late for you to bike home. Also, it's raining like hell now," I say, nodding at the steady beads rattling the nearest window.

"Okay, I've tried to explain this before and it isn't getting through. You only *rent* me on salary, bossman. Once I'm done for the day, I don't answer to you."

"Whatever you think," I say, fighting back the needles in my throat.

Must she be so goddamned stubborn?

Is it truly torture sharing a car with me and saving her a wet, dreary, potentially dangerous journey home in the dark?

"What's that supposed to mean?" she asks pointedly.

"If you're so intent on getting mugged and catching cold, it's not on my conscience," I snap.

I need to simmer down.

Tonight, her standoffishness has me more on edge than usual.

She rolls her eyes, but doesn't bite back.

An hour later, I'm surprised when I look up and she comes into my office, holding her shoes in her hands.

"Since I'm not allowed to leave without you, are you ready?" She blinks a few times like she's struggling to keep her eyes open.

What caused her sudden reason?

I flash her a surprised look I quickly wipe off my face.

"Yeah. Let me pack up." I fold up my laptop and drop it in my briefcase. "Let's go."

Downstairs, I send Dakota to the waiting town car. Louis gives me a hand loading her bike into the trunk before I slip in beside her.

In the car, she's an overworked kitten. She closes her eyes and drifts off to sleep barely a minute after she slides in.

Her head bangs the window softly as soon as we pull onto the street.

Damn, looks like the dual jobs I've dropped on her really are taking their toll...

Against my better judgment, I slip an arm between her and the door, gently pulling her toward me.

Her head falls on my chest. I hold her in place with my arm.

There's more traffic tonight than usual. A pothole job takes Louis on a detour that doubles our time to her place.

When we're finally closing in on her street, I'm face-to-face with a new Dakota Poe.

Fragile.

Exhausted.

Vulnerable.

She drools adorably on my sleeve. Holding her like this might be crossing a line I promised I wouldn't, but hell. At least this way she's not banging her head on the cold window.

I don't wake her until we're outside her building.

"Dakota—*Nevermore*—you're home," I say, sharply correcting myself and jostling her gently. "I'll get your bike. Louis, you can stay here," I add, lowering the privacy screen.

"Huh?" She blinks muzzily. I break away a split second before she realizes I'm up in her space. "Oh, thanks. Thank you, Burns."

She climbs out behind me while I walk around to the trunk.

I'm damned glad she accepted the ride now.

A proper late spring rain that smells like the sea pelts my shoulders. It's one of the steadier, long lasting night rains that blankets this city when it can't make up its mind if it wants to be summer just yet.

I watch Miss Poe walk to the entrance of the apartment building before I start moving, rolling the bike behind her.

"Where does this go?"

She points to a bike rack stacked against the old building.

"Do you have a lock?" I ask. *Please tell me you've got a lock.*

She nods, pulling a lock out of her purse.

I secure the bike to the rack and then walk her to the main entrance.

"I can take it from here, bossman. You didn't have to escort me to the door," she says softly.

Rain beads on her brow, spattering around us like a curtain of white noise.

For just a moment, we're in our own silent world of wandering tongues that don't quite work.

"No trouble. You're a heavy napper and I don't want you slipping and falling out here. No judging," I growl, instinctively taking her hand.

You're also cute as hell when you're asleep, I don't add.

Her lips turn up in a smile. Those big green emeralds stare into my eyes, glinting with too many questions.

She tilts her chin up, staring at me like I've turned into someone else.

I don't realize I'm inching closer until my neck is very obviously craned.

Her lush lips are so close to mine I can smell her like never before.

Soft perfume. Fragrant. Cream and honey mingled with something like—mint?

Goddamn.

Dakota Poe *would* smell like peppermint when she's always boldly invaded my world.

I lean in a bit more, smelling her and possibly looking like a freak. I'm past caring.

Only, a harsh warning in the back of my head rears up.

Employee. Off-limits. Idiot.

I snap backward so fast I rock on one foot.

"Whoa, are you okay?" she asks, blinking like she's still coming out of a dream.

"It's slick as hell out here," I lie through my teeth. "Good night, Nevermore. See you around."

Without a glance back, I'm in full retreat like a coyote denied its prey, head down and slipping away empty-handed. Or to keep the coyote analogy, empty *mouthed.*

Fucking hell.

That didn't just happen, did it?

Too close. I came *way* too close to falling on my ass—and I don't mean my sudden pathetic balancing act.

I almost kissed the only woman who's eternally unkissable.

I almost lit a match with my tongue and demolished our lives.

I can't help a quick look back before I climb in the car. I'm not expecting to see her there, perched under the faint orange light and staring after me.

Glaring, actually, before she whips around to face the door, waves a key card, and disappears inside without another glance back.

I just wish I knew why she looked so haunted.

IX: SOME UNHAPPY MASTER
(DAKOTA)

*W*ork is as awkward as you'd expect the next day.

It kind of comes with the territory when Mr. Hyde turns into Dr. Jekyll and almost kisses your face off.

What *was* that?

The soulful eyes, grounding me in the noisy rain around us.

The storm.

The silence as he gazed through me with an unmistakable hunger.

I'd be a filthy liar if I said I didn't feel it too.

Against our better reason, against all sanity, we came one breath away from—

God, who knows? I don't know why I'm surprised. Much less why I'm disappointed.

Isn't this always what men do when they play the game?

Close in, act nice, steal hearts, make promises, and commit.

No, wait.

They actually lead you on and march you through the slow, heartbreaking realization that they don't have the balls to deal with the consequences of their own actions.

I'm dealing with something, alright, hunched over these social media posts and trying to work.

Lincoln comes out of his office around noon and heads for my desk. He's been evasive ever since our brush with human emotions.

"We have a few special projects that need to be done by end of day, Miss Poe. I've already sent you a list," he says neutrally.

I don't look up until he's looming over me.

"I'll look it over as soon as I send this to Anna," I say quickly.

"Be quick about it—and thanks." He turns without a lingering look, marches back to his office, and shuts the door with a deafening click.

Dick.

Also, he's not joking about the extras.

I'm cooped up until almost midnight finishing everything. It's a cool, clear night, and I don't even think about his stupid chivalrous crap while I'm biking home.

The next day goes the same way. Fresh mini projects with whiplash turnaround times.

Sigh.

It's like he's punishing *me* for that almost-kiss.

Does he thrive on this kind of drama?

Does he get some sick enjoyment from everyone whispering about his dating life—or lack thereof?

I wonder.

He's been perfectly frosty ever since it happened. He piles on more work, deeper and higher like he wants to bury me alive.

If he's trying to make me quit before my ninety days—if he's that freaking selfish and petty—screw him. I'm not backing down.

I've maybe slept five hours tops since this started, and I've almost gotten used to it.

I haven't had time to work on my poetry for more than short blocks in weeks.

With Eliza out of town visiting a relative, I haven't even gotten a square meal that isn't reheated in plastic or dripping with frosting and cinnamon.

So, yeah, I'm spiritually committed to surviving this job and the ogre who runs this office.

I won't fall behind, no matter how much I'm juggling.

Lincoln damn Burns won't get the satisfaction.

When Saturday morning finally arrives, work slows down enough so I can peck at my work-in-progress. But Lincoln constantly interrupts me with questions about the wedding line's timeline on my break.

I move between five different documents. When I've had no stupid texts in ten minutes, I pull out my notebook, thinking it's safe to hack at my poem for a minute or two.

I stick the pen into the corner of my mouth and read what I've gotten down so far. Working title, "Ivory Adonis."

She lives between the black of night and shades of grey.
Then comes an ivory Adonis spinning light.
He woke a cold, dead heart.
He woke a heart from a coma marinated in tears.
He was no white knight.
He was soft black stars.
He made a withered heart beat red.
But he was the same.
They're all so lame.
Heartache and shame.
Only, she knows the game.
She lives between the black of night and shades of grey.
But she knows the rules and she can play.
He was no shining knight.
She's not hunting for a wedding night.
Still, he made a withered heart beat red.
Woke from ruined dead.
So they fall down in bed.
With every thrust the darkness falls away.
Bursts of color claim the day.

She owes him her life.
He wants no wife.
She has no shame.
She still knows the game.
A lesson she never learns.
And so she burns.
Burns who? Burns what? Burns me.
But he's her king.
Her fling.
Her boss.
Her loss.

MY PHONE PINGS.

Ugh, not now. I'm on a roll.

He *would* interrupt me while I'm scratching out an angst-ball on paper that's totally not about him.

Okay. Whatever.

I know it's far from perfect. But considering the ivory asshole has me working since nine a.m. on a sunshiny Saturday morning in this godforsaken waterlogged city, I'm just happy to spend a few minutes on something besides a new wedding dress ready to set the world ablaze.

Then again, is it *better* that I'm writing about how Not Lincoln ignites my body?

Holy shit. Why am I writing this?

I take a quick photo of the poem with my phone to save it since I'm old-school and still use paper. Then I pick up my phone with a wince, already wrinkling my nose at whatever dumb demand he's slapping me with.

But it's not his name on the screen—or CAPTAIN, as he is in the contacts.

It's worse.

Jay: Dakota, can we talk? I've been trying to get ahold of you

for over a month. At least give me a chance to apologize in person.

Why? So you can rope me back in and wreck my heart all over again?

Drop dead, Jay, I think bitterly, smashing my phone down screen-first.

But it pings again insistently. Sighing, I turn it over, and hate that my ex isn't done.

Jay: We were together for years. That has to mean something.

I don't want to respond.

I don't want to remember he still exists.

But my fingers move with a mind of their own, and before I know what I'm doing, I've typed out a message.

Dakota: It did once, but you picked music over me. Your truest love. That's what the text you sent said when you left me stranded, anyway. Remember?

I do—it's burned in my brain for life—because I was already at the church.

I'm pinching my teeth together so tightly they could break when my phone buzzes again. I almost fling it across the room. But I do something worse instead.

I read more of his utter bullshit.

Jay: Did you get my cards? The letters?

Yeah. I forwarded them to a local women's prison in your name, I send back with a smile that hurts.

I'm not even joking. I'm just disappointed he hasn't met a nice Lorena Bobbitt yet. He could use a stab-happy bitch to up his game in the bedroom, that's for sure.

Jay: Dakota. Be serious. Why you always gotta be so sarcastic?

Fury churns through my veins, venomous and hot.

When I'm talking to desperate little fuckboys, it happens, I throw back.

I stare at my phone for what feels like five minutes of sweet silence.

Finally.

I think I've shut him up.

Until I set my phone down for exactly two seconds and it buzzes again.

Holy hell. At this rate, I'll scream bloody murder and call the bosshole out of his office, tripping over his polished shoes.

I wish my eyes wouldn't betray me with the urge to read more, but they do.

Jay: See, this is why I freaked. The thought of dealing with a lifetime of that sent me running.

Dakota: Good. Stay gone, little man.

Oh, but that would be too easy.

My phone pings two more times. Great, now he's sending *multiple* whiny texts in a row.

But when I look at the screen with my breath stuck in my lungs, I see CAPTAIN instead.

Hey, can you send me the campaign timeline draft and the latest from Rome? I just left for a meeting in Tacoma, but I have some time and can work from my phone. I just need the file.

Yeah, I send back, relieved it's not more Jay.

I open an email and attach the timeline and the "ivory package." I have no idea why Isabella the designer named it that when most wedding dresses are just plain white. We'll come up with a better name internally...

Try again, Lincoln texts a second later. *Only one attachment came through.*

My eyes do a double roll.

Jeebus. If one went through, they both did. He's probably too dumb to find both.

Whatever. For Mr. High and Mighty, I send the damn email again.

I'm rewarded with another *ping!* that grates on my eardrums.

Jay: Don't you ever think about us, Dakota? About what we could have been? About what we could still be?

Not anymore, I send, gritting my teeth. *And it doesn't matter. You just said my personality sent you running.*

Jay: Really? Even after all the years we spent together you never think where we could be now? I made a mistake. I'm man enough to admit it. You had our whole lives planned out. This doesn't have to be who you are.

Oh my God, *stop.*

But he doesn't. My phone keeps chiming, bringing back the horrible face of a man I don't want to remember.

Jay: You're not some bitchy loner, Dakota. I know you. The caring girl I remember with a mean-ass talent for words has gotta be in there somewhere. I still play the song you wrote sometimes...

I hate having this conversation, but I really *hate* hearing that Jay still carries around any piece of me. Of us.

Assuming he's not just lying through his teeth for sympathy, which is always possible.

But my vision blurs anyway like a heavy, unwelcome rain sweeping in.

Don't. Just leave me alone, I send back with trembling fingers.

Of course, he doesn't listen.

He never did.

Jay: Dakota, please, just one chance. One hour to talk to you, to try. I'm telling you I fucked up. But we don't have to let it end like that.

Yep. I'm fully crying now, ducking down in my chair so nobody else can see the mess rolling down my red cheeks as I bury my face in a tissue.

I could, but I don't want to. It's too late. I'm blocking you, I send a minute later.

Jay: I love you.

Dakota: I fucking loathe you.

Jay: I want you back.

He's...he's drowning me. It hurts to breathe. I muster just enough energy to tap at the screen and send one more frantic F-you.

You don't. You DON'T, Jay, and I'm not interested in trying or being your fucking little pity game. Text me again and die. You're blocked.

* * *

It's a miracle I'm almost alone by the time I log off in a huff, grab my purse, and *run* for the elevator.

I barely manage to scramble on my bike and pedal home, counting every breath and every second until I'm nestled in the sanctuary of my bed.

My ex's comeback attempt by text couldn't be more pathetic.

Except, *I* feel pathetic, wrapped up in the blankets and forced to remember so many times I've spent the last year teaching my brain to delete from my head.

Leave it to this human virus to short-circuit what little memory immunity I had.

Leave it to him to bring me back to the biggest disaster of my life.

* * *

My stomach flutters with a trillion butterflies.

I'm waiting with Dad in the church foyer under a balmy North Dakota sun. Dallas isn't much compared to the big cities, but this small town knows how to make it classy.

There's an antique getaway car waiting for us after the ceremony, on loan from Thelma Simon and the McKnights with their massive car collection.

The decorations are laid out like a dream, all courtesy of Grace Barnet, a local girl who married a literal movie star. She rocks a rustic style to die for and her projects are booked out for months. I think I've been teleported back to my nineteenth century dream along with the church.

The dress I'm wearing is sleeveless and modern and beautiful. I shiver against the breezy air conditioning.

"Let's get out from under this vent before we go blue," Dad says with a chuckle.

I take small steps to the other side of the foyer, heels clicking against the marble floor. The dress is so tight I can barely breathe.

Dad matches my small steps like he's wiping away my jitters just by walking.

Mom comes in wearing a pale-blue dress. She's stunning, but I wonder why her face looks like that.

"Don't freak out," she says with a forced smile. "But the groom and his boys aren't here quite yet, and it's almost time to start. Maybe you should call Jay?"

My stomach sinks and my mind goes off like a rabbit being chased by all the things that could go wrong.

Jay's a big drinker when he parties. His whole band is.

I hope to God they didn't smash it too hard and drive last night. I hope he's okay.

I know—I want to believe—he wouldn't miss the big day for the world.

I pick up my phone to call like Mom suggested, and there it is.

The text from hell.

I'm sorry, Dakota. I have to follow my heart. Music is my life and my truest love. I can't be tied down with a wife. I'm real sorry I didn't realize it sooner, but it's better like this. It's better than if we'd gone through with it and I figured it out too late.

I blink in disbelief.

But the hot tears rolling down my cheeks don't lie.

"Honey, what's wrong?" Mom asks.

I hand her my phone before it falls out of my hand.

"I—I need to go home." The words barely come out in a hoarse whisper. I look at Dad. "My car isn't here."

"I'll walk you to the old Ford. It's yours for the day. Take it wherever you want. Your mom and I will handle everything."

He's fawning all over me with easy words, the kindest he can muster, but it's a day late and ten dollars short.

My stomach shifts from tremors to violent lurching.

I barely disappear behind the truck so I don't have an audience before I squeeze my eyes shut and heave.

When my stomach empties out, I remind myself to take a few deep breaths so I don't choke.

I'm light-headed and probably not the safest driver. Fortunately, it's a small town on a bland day with virtually no traffic.

I get to our not honeymoon suite and slam the door so I can be alone.

The room is paid for in full. Someone might as well use it, I guess, even if it's turned into a fancy-looking torture chamber.

I can't figure out how to get out of the wedding dress by myself, so I —the bride who arrived alone and sick, that has to be rare in this town of ever afters—go to the front desk and ask to borrow scissors.

Back in my room, I cut through the silk and satin like they're prison ties.

I free myself from this damn dress and leave the tattered scraps on the floor.

I'll pick them up tomorrow, or else I'll just leave a really big tip for the cleaners.

Tonight, I live in the hotel bathrobe, collapsing into frantic red dreams.

Dark-grey fog swirls, blowing the wedding away.

I sit on my bed alone, scrolling through my Facebooger feed. A North Dakota wind whips through the fields and howls through narrow alleys, barraging the hotel like my own fist of a heart.

A mutual friend tagged Jay in a post.

A grungy little man who still laughs like he's fifteen and beats the drums, always out of sync except for the rare days when he's sober enough to find rhythm. He congratulates my heartless ex on having the courage to "do the hard thing, but dude, the RIGHT thing. For you and Sam."

Sam?

Aaand that's how I find out Jay has been shacking up with his curvy vocalist since our last winter trip to California. It should've been a huge red flag that he wanted to spend so much time with 'the crew' while he left me exploring Redding alone.

But that grey fog in my head turns literal, swirling through my room.

Everything goes black and bursts into color.

Oh, God. Am I hallucinating from the shock of this day?

Not quite.

I'm on my knees, straddling a warm-blooded Adonis with thighs like carved granite. His mouth moves from mine as he leans over. His grip urges me up, makes me stand, and then his rough lips find the pale pink of my nipple.

He tastes too good as he pulls a fluffy white blanket around me while I'm lost in his kiss.

My legs tighten around him. I gasp.

He moves his head back so I can get a good look at his face, his honey-dark eyes shimmering in the light.

I recognize that face. It's not one I'm supposed to like, much less—

His lips are on mine again, demolishing my thoughts.

His tongue owns my mouth, moving wordlessly and whispering with movement.

"Switch off, Nevermore," I can feel him saying. "Let me help. Let me make you come so hard you never think of his shit again."

I shouldn't.

But that's not what my body wants.

His pure energy, his groan, tastes a million times better than the searing rush of his warm mouth around my breast.

I know what I want.

I just want to be closer to this wild, forbidden man.

Especially as he shoves my legs apart with those workman's fingers that shouldn't belong to a CEO. Especially as he thrusts into me with a hot raspy noise in his throat, his eyes dark with cavernous hunger.

"Go, sweetheart. Ride me to the moon."

"Oh! Oh, Lincoln." I push down, meeting him, pulling him inside me to the hilt.

Burns—no, Lincoln—wraps his mammoth arms around me, holding me in place.

"Goddamn, I love how you feel," he snarls, coiling my hair around his fingers.

He pulls with just the right tension, leaving a delicious burn on my scalp.

Warmth fills me.

A shaky smile is the only answer I can offer.

Then he grips my hips, digs his fingers into my ass, pulls back, and drives into me.

Then he splits me apart into so many spinning fragments I never, ever want to be rebuilt.

* * *

VIOLINS WAIL at me from another world.

My phone, annoying as ever, but at least this time it's not a reckless little boy I'd love to push off the top of the Space Needle.

My body is on fire. I'm so wet I'm in no mood for cinnamon roll duty today. Especially for a man who isn't welcome in my dirty dreams.

I wish he'd get over his addiction already.

Why can't my day start with a nice brisk ride to the office instead of having to make a mad dash for some overprivileged suit's pastries?

Why couldn't I have bought that Bitcoin crap back when I was a pimple-faced part-timer at Amelia's Bed and Breakfast? I could've sold it for a billion dollars by now and had all the time in the world to write poems about good men who don't suck.

I practically crawl through a cold shower and shake off like a dog because...yeah, it's that kind of day.

After blow-drying my hair as fast as I can, I throw on the first dress my hands touch and shove my feet into ballet flats—easier to bike in than heels.

I've just hopped on my bike when my phone pings.

Oh, Lincoln effing Burns, can't you even wait until I get to the office to start harassing me? I pull out my phone. I have two texts.

Lincoln: Extra cinnamon rolls today.

I grit my teeth and don't even cringe at the sensation.

All I can think about is my dream, and him, thrusting like he's staking his claim.

Sad.

Stress does atrocious things to the brain. I shake it off, rolling my shoulders as I type, *Roger. Extra, you sad little addict.*

His reply comes zooming in.

Little? Try again, Nevermore. And is that any way to talk to your boss? I see you woke up in fighting form today. Lose it before you step foot in my office.

I send him a gif of a cartoon cinnamon roll flashing the middle finger—thank God there's a gif for everything—and check the second text.

Please don't be Jay.

Please don't be Jay.

Guess what?

It's Jay.

Dakota. Please just ten minutes of your time? If you let me apologize in person and still find me unforgivable, that's fair. I just can't walk away with silence. Don't you owe me that much?

I owe myself a nice harsh slap to the face for forgetting to follow through on blocking his number.

Seriously. Why would I owe him anything?

He left me at a church full of people on my wedding day.

He was cheating for God only knows how long.

Our time is up. I learned a lot from you, so thanks, I send bitterly.

Like not to trust men—or anyone who isn't named Eliza, for that matter.

How many times did singer girl Sam laugh it up with me oh-so-sweetly? Usually over a bottle of cheap wine at our crappy little rented farmhouse while she was banging my fiancé behind my back.

People. They suck.

So does wasting more neurons on this brutally desperate half-wit.

Jay: Dakota, we can't be perfect. Them mistakes I made bust me the fuck up every day. I can't even sleep. Please. Please give me a shot. Even five minutes.

I gave him the only shot he deserved at a life together.

He flunked it magnificently.

Also, I don't have time to argue, so I shove the phone back into my pocket and pedal like hell. By the time I get to Sweeter Grind, he's texted five more times.

They're all the same trashy woe-is-me messages about how he magically realized he can't live without me and how he was oh-so-wrong.

Gag.

I order the boss' stuff and then move to the counter to wait on the drinks. I don't even know why I replied. Maybe just raw curiosity.

Did Sam break up with you?

Jay: I broke up with her but we weren't even really together. She wasn't you.

I've had it.

With a hurt snicker, I pull up my contacts and block his number.

"Coffee for Nevermore!" A barista sets a large cup down loudly.

I grab the coffee and weighty box of Regis rolls and flounce out the door, but I can't get to my bike.

What now? I think with a huff.

There's some random guy about the same height as Jay with the same mousy-blond hair strumming what sounds like folk music on a six string. He's not the reason I can't get to my bike, though.

A barefoot woman dances around madly a couple feet away, wearing a full-blown semi-formal wedding dress. Loose ringlets cascade down her back with every turn, but she's between me and my bike.

Awesome.

Portland might be the weird capitol of the Pacific Northwest, but Seattle isn't that far behind for the silver medal.

I shouldn't be so pissed. At least they aren't hassling anyone or blocking traffic.

It isn't fair to hate Guitar Man for resembling Jay, either. Betrayal shouldn't course through my blood so deep, but it does.

I try to go around the dancer, but she smacks into me mid-twirl.

The coffee cup crunches between us.

My mouth falls open in slow motion. Then I feel it before I see it.

Scalding liquid runs down my torso, biting my skin through the fabric.

"Ow!" I tumble down on the sidewalk, sandwiched between the pavement and the street dancer, who's somehow landed on top of me.

"My dress—it's ruined!" she shrieks, jumping to her feet like only a bride with a soiled wedding dress can.

I scrape myself off the ground and stumble to my feet, thoroughly annoyed.

"That's probably why most people don't dance around in their wedding dress in front of a busy shop," I bite off.

"But we're getting married!" she says, her lips curled in agony. "And now—*now* I have to do it with a coffee stain."

Perish the thought.

I can't bring myself to apologize. I just glare, my already low empathy tank has no fumes to spare.

"This is where we met," she prattles on, oblivious to my death stare. "Our friend is coming to officiate. You just crashed my wedding..."

Oh, hell. For all that's holy, Jay abandoned me for this kind of utter bullshit. I have exactly zero patience for it.

"Welcome to the club. If it makes you feel better, someone ruined my wedding, too. But if your guy's still here and ready to put a ring on it, I'd hardly call that *ruined*." I'm still holding the crushed cup and I give it another loud crunch in my palm.

Then I move to the trash can in front of Sweeter Grind and toss it.

"You deserved it, bitch! Karma!" she shouts after me.

I don't look back because I have a bigger problem now. I raise the half-attached lid on the box of Regis rolls and groan.

They're spattered in coffee and half their icing was ripped off in the fall. I toss them too and go back into the coffee shop.

There's no chance I'll be on time today. I *dare* Burns to raise hell about it.

"Nevermore?" The guy behind the counter looks up. "You're back and covered in coffee? Tell you what, the new drink is on the house. Nasty spill out there."

I wave my hand. "Don't worry about it. It's a company expense, but I need the same order again..."

"Will do."

This time, when I walk out of Sweeter Grind with my new goods, guitar dude and his panicked lady are standing in front of a guy lecturing them about the evils of 5G wireless signals and trying to sell them what looks like a tinfoil 'shield' stretched over cardboard.

Only in Seattle. I roll my eyes and hop on my bike.

When I get to work, Burns stands outside of his office with his arms crossed like a pissed off teacher waiting for the last straggler from recess to show up.

With a sigh I don't even hide, I walk up to him and shove the loot into his arms.

He snatches the cup out of my hand, sloshing me with a few beads of piping hot coffee for the second time today.

"Sorry about that." Before I can respond, though, he snaps, "Come on in. We need to talk."

What the frick now?

I follow him into his office, glaring at the box of Regis rolls as they land on his desk.

He slams the door behind me and waits for me to sit, silent as the grave.

Cool. What crawled up his butt this time?

My phone goes off.

"Is that important?" He falls into his office chair, pointing.

"I wouldn't think so. You're here." I shrug. "I guess it could be my mom."

Somehow, I don't think I'm that lucky. Jay probably found a dummy number by now to keep blowing up my messages.

He nods.

"Miss Poe, I'll be blunt. You sent me the most unprofessional, inappropriate, frankly crazy fucking email I've ever received in my whole career."

I blink, totally dumbfounded by what he means.

"Don't even try. We both know you're a depressingly bad liar." He crosses his arms again, leans back in his chair, and tilts his head up, spearing me with those stern earthy eyes. "Are you going to pretend you don't know?"

"Don't know *what?*" I'm about to lose my shit. I'm so not in the mood for guessing games today. "I've done *everything* you've ever asked me to, including working two full-time jobs. I get your coffee, your stupid rolls—which I had to buy *twice* today because the first batch spilled—you're welcome. I always reply to your messages promptly even when I'm not on the clock."

I run out of breath, giving him the opening he needs.

"And you think that justifies the bullshit you pulled Saturday?" he growls.

What did I pull on Saturday?

"You'll have to be more specific. With the workload you've

belted me with, I'm running on four hours of sleep most days." And dealing with ridiculous messages from my loser ex. "From what I recall, I spent most of the day writing copy for an ungrateful boss."

"Cute. You expect me to believe that's all you were writing?"

"Huh?"

"You weren't writing copy, were you?"

What the hell? Was he spying on me somehow when I spent five minutes working on poetry?

"We've been through this. You do not own me. What I do away from here or on my breaks is none of your concern."

"It is when it's wildly inappropriate and you send it to me attached to an ordinary work email," he snarls back.

Seriously, *what* is he talking about?

I cock my head, giving him a look that warns I'm a stick of dynamite with a fuse getting dangerously short.

"Mr. Burns—Lincoln—this would be way easier if you'd just tell me what the hell you're talking about. I have no earthly clue. And if you think I'm lying, forget the ninety days. I'll walk right out this door without waiting for a pink slip."

His eyes soften as he uncrosses his arms and wheels his chair closer to his desk. He lays his arms on the sleek wood and leans forward.

"A lesson she never learns. And so she burns," he says darkly.

Wait. What?

I thought he didn't like poetry? Hearing this man quoting anything literary sounds obscene. Certainly NSFW in that angry smolder he calls a voice.

The words coming out of his mouth are filthy, too, making me blush.

They're also—familiar? Startlingly familiar.

But before he even speaks, my heart forgets how to beat.

"Burns who? Burns what? Burns me," he quotes slowly. Lethally. "But he's her king. Her fling. Her boss. Her loss."

Screaming.

Inwardly, I'm flipping screaming my insides out.

My throat closes. I grasp the sides of my chair so I don't fall out of it. The blood rushes away from my head.

For a split second, I think I might pass out. Thank God I'm already sitting.

Deep breath.

I think about the other lines, too shameful to even dwell on.

So they fall down in bed.
With every thrust the darkness falls away.

WITH EVERY THRUST.

Oh, God.

He's read it all and he's disgusted.

And honestly, he should be.

I need to follow through on my threat to quit.

Resign right now.

That's the only way I fix this.

There's no crawling back after this. But first, I've got to stop crying.

I cover my face with my hand. Hot tears won't be held back and they come pouring down my cheeks.

This time, it's not a dream, and I've got no hot imaginary knight to save the day.

My boss knows my deepest, darkest desires.

He knows my pain.

He knows my art, my life, my soul revolves around him.

X: FANCY UNTO FANCY (LINCOLN)

*H*ere we fucking are.

Me, Nevermore, and the height of absurdity.

If she weren't already in tears, I'd laugh.

My temporary assistant-slash-copywriter named Poe sent me angsty poetry about bedding me.

Now that I know she's interested, I'm torn between telling her we should find out just how much color I can burst into her world and apologizing for being the biggest dickhead alive.

I don't even know if sending me that file was an honest mistake.

The lump of pure guilt in my stomach doesn't care.

I have her working two jobs. I'm the man putting her under the gun to market an important new line. Hell, I even have her chasing down my damn rolls for Wyatt.

Mistakes happen. I'm a forgiving man, but we need to talk about this.

Still, there's no denying it would be a far bigger deal if she'd sent that attachment to someone else, though.

Dakota hides her red face in her hands. The neckline of her dress dips into her cleavage as she moves, drawing attention to round globes I hate that I want to maul.

Her rough sniffle keeps my dick in check.

Damn. She's going to pieces and it's my fault.

"Miss Poe, look at me," I say gently.

She doesn't lift her head. She's paralyzed, face buried in her hands and at her wit's end.

"I—I'll just resign. G-go clear my things now." Her broken voice trembles. She hears me shifting, beginning to stand when she says, "I need a minute. Please."

For a few heady seconds, I'm quiet.

"Look at me," I try again.

Fuck. I've slipped into the voice I haven't used since a combat zone, when using it meant saving lives.

She raises her tear-streaked face slowly, meets my eyes, and darts her head down again.

Shit.

I broke her. I made her cry. I left her pride a smoking wreck on the floor.

Lincoln Burns, you absolute jagoff, I think with my lip curling.

"Miss Poe—Dakota—I didn't mean to put you on the spot today. I certainly didn't intend to reduce you to tears," I say, trying like hell to soften my voice.

"I-I'm s-s-sorry."

Wonderful. All my request did was turn her occasional sniffle into a sobbing fit.

"Dakota—"

If she hears me, she doesn't respond.

Do something, you buffalo. Move your ass.

I get up, walk around my desk, and kneel down beside her. I place a hand on her arm and pray she doesn't flinch.

"Listen—I'm not that upset. I'm confident you wouldn't throw around your—your work—maliciously. Assuming this was an honest mistake, you're forgiven," I say, moving my fingers over hers.

Such soft skin, but I can't dwell on that now.

It's almost worse that she's so fragile, so battered, so shredded apart.

Is this really all thanks to my dumbassery? Or was it just the final thread unraveling this smart, gorgeous young woman?

She won't even look at me.

Still, I don't give up. I fucking can't.

I clear my throat and get on with it.

"If you must know, I won't accept your resignation. You still have over sixty days, last I checked. I'm sorry for my fit. You do brilliant work. Hell, most days you work harder, longer, and better than half the senior people here." I pause. "You've become a crucial asset in such a short time. I can't give you up without a fight."

I'm trying. I really am.

Apparently, not well when she sobs harder.

"I can't work here anymore, M-Mr. Burns. You'll think—"

"I don't think anything," I rush out.

"Yes, you do. You think—"

I stop her by rubbing my hand up and down her arm in slow circles.

Goddamn, if we weren't having this melancholy heart-to-heart, my blood would be molten. Even now, I can smell her, and it unscrews my brain in the very worst ways.

"Woman, the *only* thing I think is that you're damned talented. Even that little diddy I lost my shit over—it was creative and well-written. I can see why personal writing gives you rather unique copywriting skills."

"But—" She sobs. "But you were right. It was totally inappropriate. Out of line. And now you just...you *know*. You saw what I wrote about—"

"Miss Poe," I clip, silencing her.

I force back a smile that's beyond inappropriate and immediately regret it when I notice Dakota's whole face is red. She's stiff and sobbing, spiraling into a full-blown panic.

Nothing funny about that.

Not even seeing her go to pieces over me finding out I'm in her most private thoughts in ways I never imagined should make me grin.

"Miss Poe, I know what you wrote. Technically, yes, it is inappropriate since we're both colleagues here. However, I also say it doesn't matter," I growl, pushing my fingers through hers. I don't know if that'll make this worse and I'm past caring. It's what feels right. "Who hasn't stepped in shit from time to time? We spend a lot of time together, and frankly, there's no one else I'd rather argue with."

She looks up at me, moving one hand off her face and wiping her eyes with her other hand.

"Fighting? About cinnamon rolls?"

My lips quirk up into a cautious smile.

"*Especially* about cinnamon rolls. Honestly, your fevered words might be the most interesting thing anyone's ever written about me. Considering the way the press stalks me from time to time, that's saying something." I look at her gently, pausing as she gets her breath back. "I'm well aware I've had you working yourself raw for weeks now. I'm impressed you still manage to squeeze in literary pursuits with the workload I've piled on your shoulders. You're a talented woman, no matter what you're writing. You're a fountain of words—epic and embarrassing words—and the sooner you learn to laugh off this incident, the quicker you can get back out there and make it rain for everyone at Haughty But Nice."

With my free hand, I cross my fingers. I'm hoping like hell the pep talk works.

"Laugh?" she repeats numbly.

I nod.

"I don't get it. If you weren't mad, why did you pull me in here?" She doesn't say anything else, but the accusation is clear. *Rat bastard, you knew this would be mortifying.*

She thinks I toyed with her intentionally.

And it's a fair accusation because I did.

177

"I wanted to shake you up. I just went about it in the worst way possible," I say, looking past her and out the window at an eerily peaceful cityscape outside. "You've heard people say I'm a loose cannon around here. Unpredictable. Demanding. That's how I've kept my crew on its toes—only, sometimes I really am Captain Dipshit as you so eloquently named me a while ago. I can't deny you need to be more careful with the attachments you send out, and I'm sure you'll be the first to agree. I butchered the delivery, though, and I'm sorry."

She looks down, then up again, searching my eyes to decipher whether or not the apology feels genuine.

"Maybe you should use separate devices for work and art," I say. Of course, it dawns on me just then that I could have told her that without letting her know *which* attachment she sent.

I really am a jackass incarnate.

Maybe some warped part of me wanted her to know that *I know* she wants me.

"I'll be more careful. Sorry," she says softly.

"Don't be too sorry. I'm the only one who should be apologizing. I never wanted to upset you. I'm proud of what you've accomplished in the short time you've been here, Dakota Poe."

Her name rolls off my tongue too easily.

And when we lock eyes, I see something new in the unsettled green and gold and ivory of her face. It's the wildness and solitude of her namesake—the roughness and beauty of a girl named Dakota, her soul swept with all the biting winds and harsh sunny days of life.

I hold out an arm. She leans into me over the padded armrest of the chair.

Just like that, I hug her tightly, and I probably linger too long before getting up.

When I'm on my feet again, I grab a tissue and hand it to her.

"You can't go back out there looking like that. The whole company will be after me with pitchforks if they think I made you cry," I say gently.

With a lopsided smile, she takes the tissue and blots her eyes.

"Oh, I doubt that. For some reason, they like you. *Most* people," she adds, leaving me to wonder if she's one of my honest haters.

Not that I can blame her, after today.

"Only because they don't know me," I say, smoothing my tie.

"Right. All of your employees agree you're a total workaholic, but they think you care about them, I guess."

"And what do *you* think, Nevermore?" Another question I shouldn't ask.

Why does it matter too much to avoid?

It matters what she thinks of me, how she sees me.

It matters if she hates my guts like never before.

The slow smile that lights up her face damned near stops my heart.

Yeah. Or maybe it has more to do with the way her neckline plunges down more than anything else, and the terrible knowledge that she's been writing erotic poetry about *me.*

"I think you're a cinnamon-roll-obsessed, mega-entitled freak. Not sorry," she says bluntly.

"A freak who burns you," I whisper.

Bad move. I can't help it. My tongue has a mind of its own.

Her blush deepens and she glares at me, telling me exactly how much I've just fucked up this truce.

"Oh, grow up. We should never mention that again if you really want me to stick around. I won't survive any other way."

Slowly, I nod.

"Consider it forgotten."

"For the record, it's not like it's just me who's noticed you, Burns. Surely, you know the effect you have on single women. But if you ever bring that up again, I'll quit both jobs, agreement be damned. Then you'll have to find a copywriter and an EA who can put up with your crazy ass until Lucy comes back from maternity leave."

"I already agreed to your terms," I say harshly. "And fair

warning—you'll never quit on me, because if you do, I'll publish the poem all over social media."

"You wouldn't!" she gasps.

"Are you sure? I tried to crib a cinnamon roll off you once for five hundred dollars. I think we've established my actions defy conventional logic at times." I wink at her. "Of course, I'm joking."

Her color goes back to normal. She pushes her hands against the arms of the chair and leans forward. "You're despicable."

"Maybe so, but we're back to our usual relations, aren't we?" Are we? I want her to say yes, to razz me like the art brat she is, to show me we're okay.

She stands quickly and starts toward the door.

"Miss Poe? Where are you going?"

"To work. Duh. It's better than being stuck in here with you," she throws back over her shoulder.

She's out the door before I can get up and follow.

Fine.

That's the Nevermore I know. A violent little monster armed with sass and a delectable ass I'm constantly fighting to push out of my head.

Shaking my head, I try to get back to my own work. Not easy.

Soon, I'm throwing open my office door.

She's at Lucy's desk where she belongs, her face buried in some emails.

"Nevermore?" I ask once I'm standing over her.

"Not my name."

"Poe? Dakota?"

"Yes?" She blinks up at me like I should just start using her first name.

It scares me where that could lead.

"I need a new batch of prerelease creative for social media approved by three p.m. Let's change it up this time. Maybe we'll put the happy couple in a bedroom and show the wedding dress on the floor. What do you think?" I ask, never taking my eyes off her. It's a test.

She glares at me. Her eye drops to a fruit basket on Lucy's desk.

Without a single word, the hellcat picks up an apple and hurls it at me.

I'm smiling as I retreat, shutting the door to keep from being pummeled with an orange next. I hear muted laughter around the office as I make it to safety.

Then a resounding *thud!*

Something splats against my door.

Frowning, I open the door and find a stream of sticky plum juice running down my door to a couple destroyed fruit corpses on the floor.

"You're keeping the janitorial staff extra busy," I say, shaking my head. "Was that necessary?"

"Yes, and legal," she grinds out. "Last I checked, there's no HR policy against food fights."

She picks up her desk phone, still daggering me with green-eyed mischief.

"Now what are you doing?"

"Calling for cleanup like you asked."

"But was it *necessary?*"

She narrows her eyes. "Very. Also, I'm not out of fruit."

Little damned minx.

Damn if I'm not thrilled to see her back in fighting shape, though.

With an exaggerated sigh, I shut my door and head for my desk. She's fast with good aim and I'm not risking a banana barrage to the head.

Honestly, I don't care how childish it looks to anyone else.

The way I touched her hand lingers in my mind.

If only I'd walked my fingers higher.

If only I'd caressed her face, traced my thumb over her lips.

My cock throbs as I lean back in my seat, caught in a vision of those pert, strawberry lips sucking my thumb.

Even now, after the crap that went down, I'd still like to stroke that delicate skin where her neckline keeps falling.

I'd like to satisfy this weird fuck-fantasy we both share and run my hands over her tits, up her dress.

Fuck, what I wouldn't give to grab her panties—black lace or dotted with ravens, no doubt—and tear them off her so I can *feel* what she really thinks of me.

Shit.

How the hell am I supposed to keep my head on straight now that I know she wants me?

It has to be the first poem anyone's ever written about me, and that wasn't some soapy love and loss piece.

That was an 'I want to fuck you because you excite me' cry from the heart.

Or maybe that's my own projection talking.

Still, there's no denying one thing.

Miss Poe excites me in a way no one else has in ages, even if I'm interchangeable to her like she said in the poem.

They're all the same.

Either way, it's going to be damnably hard not to try stealing her away, alone, now that I know she wants me to feel her teeth in a different way than I ever imagined.

And isn't that the problem?

Even if I didn't have an unbearably large, complicated machine to manage, I know too well that messing with romance only fucks with your head.

Wyatt will never be the same man after the way his ex-wife abandoned him.

I'm sure Dakota isn't a similar self-centered witch, but my parents were married for over thirty years. They adored each other. Their love for me sprang from their own.

When they weren't working, everything they did was for our

family, and it was beautiful and perfect until the day my father died.

He left a bottomless abyss—complete with pendulum since I can't get Miss Poe off my mind—in my mother's soul.

Then there was *her.*

Regina Swann.

Once as graceful and bright and kind as her name might suggest. I was in over my fucking head.

I believed in an us that never existed, totally unable to imagine she'd kiss me in the sweetest way when I came home. Right after having another man's cock in her mouth two hours earlier.

She was a walking demolition.

The woman, the siren, the nightmare who taught me beyond any doubt that I'm not cut out for love. The murderer of hearts who made me a rabid monster.

I'm a razor-sharp businessman above all else. Besides assessing marketing that plays on the right emotions, I'm not in the business of love.

My one true mistress is sweat. Equity. Work.

I don't dream of anything besides chiseling my mark on this world in everlasting stone.

I don't get mixed up in relationships anymore. Why bother when they're glaringly predictable?

Sooner or later, they all end the same way.

Heartbreak.

Bruises.

Devastation.

As I break out a mineral water and stare out at the city, I realize there's another reason why I call her Nevermore, Poe fluff aside.

She might invade my fantasies, but she won't invade my life.

For my sake and hers, Nevermore is all Dakota Poe can ever be.

* * *

I KNEW it wouldn't be easy.

For the most part, Dakota avoids me after our conversation about the poem. When she does talk, it's like her tongue is glazed over. So fucking icy I want to shiver.

I'm back to wondering if she spits in my morning coffee.

Weirdly, being ignored makes me crazier than anything she's ever said to me.

Ironic.

Anna Patel calls a marketing meeting on Thursday and asks me to sit in. Of course, there's a vacant chair beside Nevermore.

I hesitate a second too long, leaving an opening for this junior copywriter to step past me toward the seat. I can't even remember his name.

Jake? Jeremy? James?

He's a newer kid, and he's damn near undressing her with his eyes so obviously that if she ever looks up from her laptop, she'll feel buck naked.

The punk thinks he's sitting beside her.

Like hell.

I speed up, stepping behind him and grabbing his shoulder.

"Why don't you take the seat beside Miss Patel? I may need to talk to my assistant." It's not a question. My words are professional, but my tone is barbaric.

I've never felt so uncivilized in the office, and fuck, it has *everything* to do with the hot prick of jealousy coursing in my veins.

"Oh, sure thing, Mr. Burns!" he says, fear flashing in his eyes before he scurries off without looking back at me.

That's what I thought.

I sit down beside Dakota, grateful she's oblivious to my territory marking.

Until she laughs, leans over, and whispers, *"Behave."*

"Why?" I ask, flashing her a clueless look.

"You practically gave the poor guy shell shock."

I'm not sorry.

He *should* be scared when he tries to usurp the boss' seat—or his woman. Let him drool over a hundred thousand other beautiful women in this city.

"You're welcome, Nevermore. From the looks he gave you, I think he writes angsty poetry about *you*. If he's able to write at all. Is he any good?"

I've never noticed his work when he's assigned to a less pressing line under Anna. Hell, like most new hires, I half forgot he even worked here until now.

"He's where he should be, I think. We don't collaborate a ton," she says diplomatically, hiding a rosy blush on her cheeks.

"He should do more writing and less eye-fucking," I growl in her ear, leaning close.

What the hell is wrong with me?

My nostrils flare at her scent. It's bad enough that I practically tossed the boy on the floor, and now I'm low-key smelling her like a Neanderthal with a rose.

"Mr. Burns, shut up!" she hisses.

I can't help smirking as her green eyes roll with shock.

"Did you see how he looked at you?" I whisper, undaunted. "If he was looking for his muse, it damn sure wasn't interested in PG-13 poetry."

She's bright red but she grins.

"You're such an idiot. Jim does *not* write poems about me. I doubt he even *reads* anything that isn't a bargain thriller. I mean, that's usually what he's got his nose stuffed in during lunch."

Her quip shouldn't make me happy. At least Nevermore isn't impressed with his reading habits.

"Takes one to know one with writers, I guess. You are a Poe and a literary princess," I tease.

Her eyes lock onto mine harshly.

"Boss, I will stab you with my pen," she whispers.

"Doubtful."

"Want to bet?"

"I do. I'm the guy who's signing your checks and your first performance bonus is coming up fast. Wounding me now would be monumentally suicidal."

"You sure? It didn't stop me from nearly hitting you with an apple," she says. "I'm still sorry I missed."

I snort, shaking my head. "Thanks for reminding me I should put you on an improvement plan."

Dakota picks up the pen beside her laptop and jabs me in the center of my hand with the butt end.

Fuck.

I blink away the sudden sharp sensation.

"Damn you, are you out of your mind?" I snarl, shaking out my hand under the table.

"Seems to be the theme around here, Lincoln."

Damn her again.

My urge to flip her over my knee and slap some respect into her plump ass eases ever so slightly when I hear my name on her lips.

At least she's back in fighting form. I'm about to demand a meeting in my office after this one when I look up at the room, now full with several late stragglers slouching against the walls.

All eyes are on us, and I realize we're no longer whispering.

"Are you two, um, ready? We should get started," Anna says awkwardly.

"Of course." I nod. "Sorry. Take us away, Miss Patel."

"He started it," Dakota mutters under her breath.

The few people in earshot burst out laughing.

Wonderful. This insufferable woman twists my balls so tight I'm accidentally giving the entire office gossip machine plenty of grease for the next year.

"Okay, everyone, let's hear some updates on the wedding line. Let's start with you, Martha," Anna says, pointing her pen at the easygoing brunette in the corner.

I try not to glare at the slender blond next to me. I should be avoiding Nevermore, not sparring with her out in the open.

One by one, the team checks in, and they're all making progress. Several people have completed new ad sequences with samples for us to review on the screen.

The designs are mostly promising.

Jimbo's comes up somewhere in the middle. It's a passable image, but the man can't write his way out of a paper bag. I haven't seen sales copy so bland since I bothered to read Chicago Transit billboards at the airport.

Dakota even corrects his grammar twice.

When it's my turn, I offer the best feedback—the blunt kind.

Fifteen minutes later, I'm far from done, but I wait while a couple others pass around my comments. I'm not expecting two tiny fingers pinching my arm. My head whips toward Dakota.

"Will you stop?" she whispers.

"What? He's my employee. He has to produce content I'm happy with. This is shit."

"You only gave one or two bits of advice to everyone else. You're singling him out," she whispers.

"Hardly. If he wants to write, he needs to learn."

"And you need to learn a little patience with the people you hire, Burns," she says harshly.

I kick back in the seat, rolling over her words in my head.

"Come to think of it, he came in here on an internship. You're offered a job by default at the end if you don't fuck up. I don't even remember interviewing this guy," I say.

Fine.

Maybe I *am* being overly critical because I didn't like the way he undressed my woman—my assistant and best copywriter—with his beady little eyes. Or maybe he just feels like a waste of resources.

"When I'm done playing EA, I'll review his writing and work on coaching him up to snuff," she says politely.

I shake my head like I've just been kneed in the stomach.

"That's Anna's job. I'll mention it to her after the meeting," I bite off, staring her down.

When I look at the front again, there's someone else's work on the projector now.

The image shows a glowing bride with her well-dressed groom holding her hand. They're besotted with each other. Everything about the shot bleeds luxury through rosy filters and fine-tuned colors.

"...here, I think you'll agree this is a lovely mockup. Perhaps we should outline the words in a brighter hue so your copy shows up clearly, Dakota," Anna says.

That's what I catch, anyway. I'm sure the rest of whatever she said went right out the window, blurred into a Charlie Brown grown-up monologue of toots and whistles.

Fuck me. Where is my mind?

I'm afraid to answer that when one glance at Nevermore tells me.

When Anna stops speaking, everyone looks at me.

Shit.

"I agree wholeheartedly, Miss Patel," I say, like my brain isn't grounded on Nevermore and the way her dress is riding up every time my eyes flick to my side.

Her muffled laugh pulls my eyes right back to her as Anna plows on.

"You weren't listening, were you?" she asks.

"I didn't care to elaborate. Key difference," I whisper back.

"Is that everything?" Anna clears her throat loudly as she watches us across the long table. "Does anyone else have any parting questions or concerns?"

There's a low chorus of 'noes' and 'what's for lunch?' comments flying around.

Anna's face pulls tight, her lips flattened in a straight line.

I've worked with her long enough to know she's not happy, and I hate to think I'm halfway responsible. She seemed content with everyone's progress this week.

No sense in bottling it up.

"Something wrong, Miss Patel?" I call loudly.

She hesitates, glances down, and then back at me with worried eyes.

"No," she mouths, and it's not the people beginning to stir and file out with their own conversations that's drowning her out.

It's quiet and not convincing.

"Are you sure?" I press.

She taps her pen off the conference table. "I know everyone is working hard. The ads are coming together nicely, but there's a segment of the market I still think we're missing. I just want a little more oomph behind the ads for A/B testing—"

"How about a personal endorsement from our fearless leader? That's enough *oomph* to be *oof*," Dakota suggests with a laugh.

I lash her with a cutting look.

"What?" I'm never involved in the ad campaigns. I certainly don't put myself in front of cameras willingly. Not even cameras I control.

She shrugs like she's serious.

"C'mon, boss. You have the looks. I bet you'd sell this new line to women who are already married if you just asked nicely enough. You have the whole lady-killer vibe," she says matter-of-factly.

I rake my eyes over her, unsure if this is a real suggestion or more of her unfunny bullshit.

"There's exactly *one* lady I'm aware of killing," I whisper harshly.

She glares at me.

"Dude. Why do you think the press and people after easy views on Insta follow you around? Attraction is a marketing superpower—"

"I'm no model," I grind out. "If you're serious, Miss Poe, we can always explore hiring talent."

"We could. But if you *really* cared about the wedding line, you'd model the men's line yourself," she says with a flick of her hand, wearing a grin I want to bite off her face.

"Slam dunk, Poe! Way to throw down the gauntlet," our college intern says, flashing some ridiculous hand sign.

"That kid annoys me," I whisper to Dakota.

"Good. You annoy most of us, but we just bite our tongues because you're the boss. And he's hardly a kid. He's almost as old as me," she says.

I don't like being reminded how young she is, even if my cock strongly disagrees.

"You're far less annoying," I say.

She beams, stifling another laugh.

"Wow. I think that might be the nicest thing you've ever said to me."

"Not true. I've told you plenty of times you're as talented as you are beauti—" I choke off mid-word and slam my yap shut.

Too much.

Too late.

She stiffens slightly, biting her bottom lip, and then she edges over, making more space between us.

I want to laugh at the effect I have on her that's impossible to deny. A twisted part of me enjoys it, but I hold in my amusement.

We're still in a meeting with several stragglers around, and I need to be professional.

"Well then, Miss Patel, what are your thoughts? Since Miss Poe says I'm such an irresistible ladies' magnet, should I consider modeling the groom's wear?" I'm joking, of course.

When Anna nods with a wide smile that shows her teeth, I almost fall out of my chair.

"Not a bad idea. It's very original. Possibly the next best thing to suiting up in Haughty But Nice attire for your own wedding—"

The room goes silent. Everyone who's still here has their eyes glued to us.

Anna's gaze becomes laser-focused on—I'm not sure what. Her mouth forms all kinds of shapes, but nothing comes out.

"Miss Patel? Anna?" I prompt.

She holds up a finger and remembers how her mouth works.

"Holy crap. That's it!"

"What's it?"

"Your wedding."

"What damn wedding? I'm not getting married," I say with a snort. "Has my mother been here again? Is this some high-pressure prank to make me settle down?"

A couple of the older employees laugh knowingly.

They get it. My sweet-as-pie mother becomes an unpredictable assassin when it comes to my love life—or lack thereof by choice.

"No, but you and Dakota hit it off pretty well, right?" Anna says, her dark-brown eyes glowing with something I dread when she speaks again. "So, call me crazy, but what if you two staged a wedding? What if you got all dolled up in a photo shoot in Haughty But Nice wardrobes? It's a unique, interesting angle that could send our sales through the roof."

Goddamn. It's worse than I thought.

"You're crazy!" I snap.

Dakota jerks up in her seat. I almost think she's more horrified than me.

"Anna, that's, um—a big yikes," she spits. "That's just...a bridge too far."

That's putting it mildly.

I can't believe we're even having this conversation.

I'd slam my dick in the door ten times before I'd ever get married—even *fake married*—purely to move my products. And if I *were* getting married to sell clothes, it certainly wouldn't be with a frigging employee who already lives in my head.

"Not happening, Miss Patel. You know I welcome exotic ideas within limits, but this breaches them all," I say.

Dakota leans in closer. "Aside from the you and I part...it's not half bad. What if I did a few shoots with the intern kid?"

My eyes pivot to the side of the room where the scrawny kid sits with a smug smile.

Dakota and him? That's even worse than copywriter Jimbo.

Fuck that.

"You need a man who looks the part if you want to sell, Nevermore. Not Peter fucking Pan," I growl.

"Me and my big mouth," she groans with a delirious eye roll.

"Guys, calm down, it's just a thought!" Anna says in my ear. I hadn't noticed her getting up and moving next to us, taking the vacant seat. "No one expects you to get, like, married-married. Just *fake* married. And not even married but fake engaged."

"Do we make Hallmark movies now?" Dakota asks with a laugh. "Fake Married for Fashion. Sounds like pure cheese..."

"I agree, it isn't dark enough by half for you," I quip.

With a loud huff, she picks up the pen again and leans over. I can feel her breath as she whispers, "You want to see dark?"

You have no earthly clue, you little firecracker.

I slide my hands under the table, shifting my pants so my unruly dick isn't pitching a tent.

"I'm joking, of course. This whole idea is laughable," I tell her.

Dakota lifts a brow and nods.

"Guys, just give it some thought," Anna pleads. "A fake wedding announcement for the marketing campaign with you both doing photo shoots would be a sensational endorsement. It's a unique spin, considering your social media clout, Mr. Burns. We could even work up some wild story about how the whole line was inspired by your love. Can you imagine the sales?" Her eyes are huge, gleaming with excitement.

For once, I regret how Anna can be a human Rottweiler when it comes to ideas.

I wish like hell she'd drop this one.

"Personal endorsements have worked out insanely well for other brands," Cheryl says from the corner, looking up from her phone. "I bought three years' worth of perfume last Christmas because the owner wouldn't stop talking about how awesome her life is on TikTok ever since she started wearing her own stuff."

"That's cool and all, but marrying my bossasaurus—*fake marrying*—was never in the job description. That's just too much," Dakota says.

"Bossasaurus, huh? I like it," Anna says with a grin. "See? You two already bicker like a real couple all the time. Are you *sure* you don't want to give it the teensiest little try?"

The room bursts into laughter and frantic whispers. Even a few of the people who'd stepped away before are back in here.

Goddamn, do I hate how fast word travels in this office.

Dakota's face is painted crimson when I look back at her.

My chest clenches like there's a caged animal trying to get out.

This must be killing her.

Sure, it's not like the heartbreak in my office when we had that little chat about her poetry. I could bring the color back to her face by letting her know how talented she is and then infuriating her with a few thoughtless remarks.

But we're in a crowded room today.

She's justifiably mortified at this, the dumbest shit ever, and anything I say will just make it worse.

Anna shrugs and her eyes meet mine. "I know it's not your style, boss. I respect your concerns. I just hope you might mull it over. This could be the difference between this line doing well and a Vera Wang breakout success."

Dakota bites her lip. "Nothing will ever tie Vera. We're not even in the same category."

My jealousy bone twitches.

"Why's that, Miss Poe? We're a luxury line with a damn fine

product, even if we don't have their international presence and we're a bit more localized," I say.

"When I say Hershey, you think chocolate. When I say Vera, you think bridal," Dakota explains slowly. "And when I say Haughty But Nice...you think high school mean girl or real housewife of King County. Your other lines are pretty well known in the regional market, but if I mentioned this brand back home in North Dakota? Bridal wouldn't be the first word that comes to mind. Until it is, Vera isn't your direct competitor."

Damn her, she's right.

Marketing this line could be harder than I realized in a crowded space—especially when we're a mostly local entity native to the West Coast.

I also hate considering that Anna could be right.

We'll have to flex our creative muscles like never before, but I'm still not fake marrying an employee.

With Dakota being Dakota, me being me, and our entire working relationship resembling a fucking dumpster fire, that spells one word, and one word only.

Disaster, written out in blood-red.

XI: MY BOSOM'S CORE (DAKOTA)

"**S**o, you'll do it?" Anna asks. "Because we're not a breakout success until we're butting heads with the big boys and girls. Right now, we're the dusty back of the rack at an Alfred Angelo bridal store."

"Nope. Not even if he were the last man alive and this was the last job on earth," I say, drumming my fingers on the table.

"Oh, please. If the rest of the world was in ruins, there'd be no more of those damn rolls to fight over," Captain Snarlypants says. "I hate it just as much as you, but it would be very *colorful* marketing, wouldn't it?"

"Would you shut up?"

"I could, but I'm enjoying you flustered too much, Nevermore."

Ugh. He would.

"Miss Poe can stop panicking, and Miss Patel can quit badgering us," he continues. "Obviously, it would be grossly inappropriate for me to marry an employee—fake or otherwise —and Miss Poe has already said she's not interested. Keep bringing it up, Miss Patel, and I'm afraid *you'll* be my decoy bride."

She gives him a horrified look.

I meet his eyes suspiciously. Is he *defending* me? Really?

Anna folds her arms in front of her chest with an annoyed *humph!*

"I'm willing to take one for the team, but I'm not sure I have Dakota's special chemistry with you, bossman," she says with a knowing smile.

Yikes. Isn't that the truth and the entire problem?

"I'm not sure what chemistry you're referring to," Lincoln lies. "However, this engagement ruse was your idea. Since Miss Poe isn't interested, if I'm crazy enough to let you do this, you'll have to step up and play ball."

How is it that something so outlandish makes me feel so jealous?

I stand up, glancing around at the growing audience we've collected with worry. I hate being the center of attention almost as much as I like being smiled at by a pack of coworkers who feel like wild coyotes right now.

"Meeting dismissed. This time for real. You can all go eat and stop gawking," he grumbles.

Thank God.

My cheeks haven't felt this hot since he read my poetry about bedding his grumpy face. And he's referred to the thing that should never be mentioned like the top-notch asshat he is several times during this joke of a meeting.

Why is this my life?

But I'm painfully aware I brought some of it on myself. I should've kept my mouth shut about Lincoln modeling the groom's line.

People walk out of the room around us. Anna starts to leave, but Lincoln says, "Not you, Miss Patel. Stay."

I study his face.

He's all simmering emotion, this strange frustration and amusement etched in the shadows of his face.

Naturally, it only makes him hotter, which is the last thing I need.

196

I hope he isn't too harsh with her. It was a fascinating idea, even if it is a little out there. I just didn't want to be involved with it beyond stringing words together.

"Thanks again, Anna. It's a cool idea, but Mr. Burns is right. Using actors or models would probably make more sense if you guys move forward to avoid any drama." I head for the door, eager to get the hell out of here before I'm roped into whatever's coming next.

"It was a whole year before Mr. Burns would even crack a joke with me," she tells me quietly. "Nothing like the way he does with you. I don't think he'd open up enough with an actress for the sham to be believable. I know you're just coworkers, but you two look like a couple. Seriously. You play well off of each other."

I nod like I'm swallowing a frog and double my pace out the door.

It's a huge relief when I reach my desk—for all of four seconds.

My phone vibrates before I lay it down. A new message from an unknown number. Frowning, I tap the screen.

Dakota, can we talk?

I'm going to be sick.

Who is this? I send back, though I'm sure I have a good guess.

Who do you think? the stranger replies.

I'm so not in the mood for this. That's probably the only reason I respond.

Didn't I block your number, dickhead? What, are you on burner phone level stalking now?

I frown so hard it hurts, waiting for his pitiful reply, which needles my hand when it buzzes a few seconds later.

Jay: I hardly think you can call me a stalker. I didn't talk to you for months.

See? Pitiful.

Pinching my jaw tight, I reply and hit Send so hard I have to shake my hand out.

LOL. Right. And then you pop up like I owe you something. Bye, Jay. Don't waste our time trying this BS again.

New number, blocked.

My phone makes it clear it isn't done tormenting me for the day when it vibrates again. *Damn how many numbers can one guy have?*

But this time, I'm in luck. It's a slightly less annoying, fairly less cruel man.

Lincoln: Dakota, you can take off early today? I'm not a big enough tyrant to make you hang out for our four o'clock after the way that meeting went. Also, I need you to pick up a package for me while I have a late call. Take the company car. I'll send you an address where I'll need you to drop it to this evening.

Beautiful.

How gracious of you to give me the evening off.

But since I'm working two full-time jobs, his permission really doesn't matter unless someone else wants to manage Lucy's inbox, follow up on the contracts, do the filing, or approve a new round of Facebooger ad copy for a wedding line that's only going to be moderately successful because we don't embark on marketing techniques from the asylum like sham engagements.

Argh.

Stop me from screaming.

He's right about one thing, though. That meeting was beyond mortifying when weddings mesh with my life like an acid bath.

...so, filing it is. Then I'll follow up on the contracts and hope the copy is passable enough to give it a quick thumbs-up.

Actually, since I have the CEO's permission, copy can wait until tomorrow. I may need to hunt down Eliza, if she's back from her trip to make me a stiff espresso shot or five before I can dredge up the nerve to deal with tomorrow.

I spend an hour rifling around in the files, and when I come back, I start following up on contracts I haven't received signed copies of and forwarding Lincoln proposals to review.

He passes my desk on the way to his office and pauses. "You're still here?"

"Umm—as kind as it was for you to offer me the afternoon off, I can't keep up with both Lucy's job and my own and take time off to play post lady."

"After that meeting, I'm surprised you care." His eyes narrow in the usual scary-hot way.

"What can I say? Your money's good. It keeps me from exploring the dark corners of my mind in lyrical form and accidentally dropping it in your inbox so you can keep laughing at me after you said you wouldn't."

The harshness in his expression fades.

"Point taken, Miss Poe. I'll do better."

I glare at him.

"I really do need that package picked up," he says, his voice weirdly gentler. "Leave whenever you want, but make sure you can grab it and meet me at the address by six thirty."

"Does Lucy always pick up your personal packages?"

"No, but she has been known to do me small favors like this when needed. Believe me, I don't make this sort of thing a habit. Since you already intruded on this part of my life, you'd might as well be included."

Is he talking about—oh, right. The park. The homeless stuff.

I'm annoyed that my curiosity rises.

"Careful, Burns. You're starting to rhyme. Next thing I know, *you'll* be the one sending me poetry," I say.

"Careful what you wish for, Nevermore," he grumbles, trying oh-so-hard not to break into a smile before he turns his back.

"Hey, wait. What did I intrude on? Can you at least tell me?" I ask.

He barely pauses to throw a dark look over his shoulder.

"You'll know when you get there."

Jeez. Who can turn down that sort of mystery?

I fly through the contracts as fast as I can because now I want to find out what this package is. I forward the last proposal to Lincoln and knock on his door.

"I'm ready, but I'd rather not take the company car. My bike is here. How big is this package, though?"

"Take the company car," he insists. "I'll drop you back here when we're done tonight."

"We? So you're going to be there, too? Where are we going?"

"You have the address."

"What are we doing?"

I watch his face tighten, his eyes hardening at me for pestering him.

"You'll find out when you get there, Dakota, like I've told you repeatedly."

Dakota.

I don't want to acknowledge what hearing my name from that mouth does to me. I'm tingling.

"You're not going to tell me anything? Not even a hint?" I venture.

"I've told you everything you need to know, now scram," he growls, swiping a hand at me.

I don't say anything, but my face must speak for me.

Just when I'm expecting him to slam the door in my face, he stops and smiles. His eyes soften.

"What the hell is it now, Nevermore?"

"Has anyone ever told you that you're a horse's dick?"

"You, on the day I met you. And I'll take that as a compliment considering their size. We have a lot in common."

Oh my God.

No.

Just.

It takes *effort* to make my tongue work. It feels frozen by all the awful thoughts conjured up by my boss' hint that he's packing below the belt.

"Okay, just...making sure you know," I say quietly.

How lame.

"I knew there was a reason I keep you around, so I can stay well-informed about my endowment," he says.

"Happy to be of service. Okay, it's package time then." I start moving with a blush, hoping he won't latch on to that last word.

"Stop at Sweeter Grind and get at least three Regis rolls," he calls after me. "Hell, get six if they have them."

I stop moving just long enough to shake my head and look back at him. "You need rehab. There must be a cinnamon addiction program somewhere. I'm worried it's a bona fide health crisis at this point."

"Just bring me the damn rolls," he barks.

I put two fingers to my forehead and salute him.

"Will do, Captain." Then I spin around on my heel, ready to leave.

"Dakota?" Oh. He isn't done.

I look back over my shoulder, waiting as he stares at me strangely. Longingly?

"Yes?" I've stopped breathing, counting the seconds.

"I like your dress today," he says sincerely.

Holy crap.

I smile before I can help it.

"Oh. Well. Thank you."

I'm not even sure what to make of that and I don't have time to wonder.

Before I drop dead, I race downstairs to the smiling driver who's already waiting to open the door for me. I climb inside the jet-black town car without a fuss.

I'm glad I do, even if it brings me back to that rainy night he took me home. On the inside, it's luxe leather, almost limo-like.

"Hi," I say.

The driver turns and nods at me over his spectacles before we're moving, looking vaguely surprised. "Hello. You must be the lovely Miss Poe. Mr. Burns told me I'd be chauffeuring this afternoon. It's a pleasure."

It's not the first time. He's an older man, the same driver who took me home that night, though I didn't introduce myself then.

"We've met, haven't we?" I ask.

"Certainly," he says with a low laugh. "Technically, I'm supposed to be invisible. Mr. Burns is a busy man with a big company to manage. He doesn't make a lot of small talk."

"That's sad," I whisper too loudly.

"Eh—it isn't half bad. He pays me better than any other place would in this town. Special delivery, I hear?"

"Right. Do you need the address?" I settle into the cushy seat, wondering why I feel so jittery.

"He sent it to me earlier. No worries, I'll get you there. I'm Louis Hughes, by the way. I've been with Mr. Burns for a long time."

That gets my attention.

I offer a muted "Thanks," but that's not what's on my mind.

Does Louis know Lincoln's origin story?

Does he have insights into what makes the man tick that most people don't?

I wonder.

And I wonder a lot of things as the car slices through the cool, dark night.

Like what the hell happened to make Lincoln Burns such a rude enigma wrapped in the grumpy mask he wields like a shield against the entire flipping world.

* * *

"ARE you sure this is the right place?" I ask roughly twenty minutes later.

"Yes, ma'am. This is the address," Louis says.

"But it's...a medical supply store?"

"Yes, ma'am, I do believe you're right." If Louis is as surprised as I am, he doesn't show it.

I'm so confused.

"What does Lincoln need here? He's like the poster boy of

good health." *Or a genuine underwear model.*

"I believe he's been here before, so it isn't the first time," Louis says cryptically.

I wait, but the man never elaborates.

My brows knit together.

"Okay, well—maybe it's something for his mom." That's the only rational guess I have.

"Could be. I'm not sure. Mr. Burns is an exceptionally private man when it comes to his personal affairs," Louis tells me.

More like a walking vault. But since there's only one way to find out...

I tell Louis I'll be back soon, climb out, and head inside the store.

There's an older lady in a wheelchair being pushed by a woman wearing pink scrubs. A large, older man with silvering hair behind the counter hands them a bag and they're on their way.

"Can I help you?" he asks.

"Yes. I'm here to pick up an order for Lincoln Burns."

"Ah, Mr. Burns, sure. I'll go grab it. One minute." He disappears behind a door marked Employees Only and comes back holding a long box. "Usually, it takes a little while longer to be properly fitted, but since we had the measurements on file and verified, I used those per Mr. Burns' instructions. However, if this is uncomfortable or he has any trouble walking, just let us know so we can adjust it ASAP."

He? Fitted for what? What are we talking about?

"Umm, okay—what is it?" I ask.

The guy stiffens and scratches his chin. "You don't know? You'll have to ask Mr. Emory or Mr. Burns about that, I suppose. Privacy regulations are awfully strict."

"Emory?"

He looks at me reluctantly and shrugs.

My gaze drops to the box. A sticker with a barcode stares up at me.

Emory, Wyatt, pros. is typed above the bar code. *In care of Lincoln Burns* is handwritten under it.

What the actual hell is going on?

So maybe Burns only pretends to be a workaholic and he's actually part of some bizarre art cult. I shake my head, knowing better than to get caught up in a writer brain story.

But if the box says Wyatt Emory, whatever I picked up isn't for Mrs. Burns, and it's not for Lincoln either. What's he doing and who's Wyatt?

I try to remember if I've ever heard that name before, if Lincoln ever slipped, but I'm totally blanking.

I know one thing.

Burns has a cinnamon roll obsession like no other, and he needs another batch. Are the two pickups tonight related in some weird way?

I've got a sixth sense twitching that almost knocks me flat.

Lincoln's obsession with Regis rolls and the homeless must be tied to whatever's in this box I'm holding. Although what a cinnamon roll has to do with a medical supply device, I can't even fathom.

"Where to?" Louis asks once I'm back in the car.

"Sweeter Grind, please."

My phone buzzes.

Dakota, this can't go on forever. You gotta talk to me at some point. We grew up in the same fucking town. Our parents are still friends. Have a heart!

Oh, no, he didn't.

But he did.

Jesus. He's never going to give up and leave me alone until he runs out of dummy numbers, is he?

Were. They were friends, I send back bitterly.

Jay: Is that really how you want it?

I purse my lips. I know the worst thing I can do is keep giving him attention.

The second worst is letting his comments infiltrate my head, and I'll be damned if I'm letting my crappy, cheating ex have that kind of control.

My fingers fly across the screen. *No—but you made your choice. You made it like this in front of the entire town. Don't put it on me, asshole.*

My phone buzzes again before I've had time to shove it back in my purse. I don't even look at the message. I just roll my eyes and type a response.

Are you done? If I block your number again, are you just going to harass me from another phone? You left me high and dry. Plus you had your sidepiece the entire time. Just stop.

I flip the screen down and don't look at it again until it vibrates. I'm relieved when I see Lincoln's name until I read the text.

Lincoln: That was a loaded message, Nevermore. Don't block my number and make sure you get the cinnamon rolls. I'm on my way now.

I blink and look at the message again.

Oh, crap. Can this get more embarrassing?

The only safe thing to do is brush it off, so that's what I do when I send, *Sorry, bossman. My bad, that wasn't for you. I have to ask, what's in this long slender box? The guy at the supply store wouldn't tell me. I'll get your stupid rolls.*

Lincoln: You'll see. And make sure you do get the Regis roll even if you have to buy them off some crazy biker chick.

I snort, thankful he doesn't dig at me over the hate-text meant for my ex.

Dakota: Whatever. You're the psycho.

Lincoln: Dakota, are you okay?

I frown, wondering what he's getting at. The message meant for Jay?

Dakota: I'm fine. Why?

Lincoln: You're slipping. First the wrong attachment, now you're texting the wrong person. What will you do when it's a client instead of me?

Ah, there it is. Any illusion that he cares about my well-being vanishes when I realize he's just sending me his usual BS.

Oh, please, I punch in. *The only people who text me besides Eliza are my boss and moron ex-fiancè.*

Another minute of silence.

Another reply that leaves me floored when it finally comes, rattling my hand like a mini earthquake.

Lincoln: You're better off without the little shit. You can do a million times better. I'm sorry he cheated, Dakota.

Holy hell. My throat goes tight.

Thanks, I send back. *I just wish he'd f-off and leave me alone.*

When my phone pings again, I can't help but smile as I read.

Lincoln: Say the word and I'll shut his yap for you. No dismemberment involved, unfortunately, but fully legal, of course.

I actually laugh. When I look up, the car slows as we pull into a familiar, cramped side street lot parallel to Sweeter Grind.

It's evening, not long before close, so the place isn't as packed as it is in the mornings. I go straight to the counter.

"Can I get half a dozen Regis rolls, please?"

My phone buzzes again.

Lincoln, chill. I'll text you as soon as I'm back in the car.

But the vibrating barely stops.

"Regis rolls. Got it." The barista boy behind the counter kneels down in front of the bakery case and pops back up with a tense look. "Uh...looks like we're out."

Oh, God. Not *this* mess again.

"Let me guess...cinnamon shortage?" I ask, pained.

"Nope, we just cleared out the last rolls we had about an hour ago. We could make more, but it's an hour until close."

"Do it. I've been instructed not to leave without Regis rolls even if I acquire them at insane prices from a biker gang. How long will it take to make more?"

"Maybe thirty minutes? Only thing is, you'll have to buy them by the dozen. New rule for orders like this after two o'clock," he tells me.

"Fine. Hang on." I pull my phone—*now buzzing again, argh*—out of my purse. "You're sure it'll just be half an hour?"

"For sure. Made fresh. They just have to defrost for ten minutes before I can pop them in the oven," he says with a grin.

I have four new messages I don't have time to read just now.

Lincoln damn Burns, get a life. Ideally, one that doesn't revolve around pastries.

I'll catch up on whatever's so important in a minute.

Right now, I need to know if he's willing to buy twice the cinnamon rolls and wait half an hour, so I text, *I can only get the rolls by the dozen. It'll be half an hour before they're ready. Are we good?*

Sure, if you are, he replies a minute later. *What's a Regis roll? Are you ever going to give me another chance?*

Wait.

That's *not* Lincoln.

Frick.

I did it again, scrolling up as bile rises in my throat. Sure enough, Jay sent three more messages I missed while ordering.

Dakota, it was a year ago. Talk to me. We can work this out.

Yeah, no. Opinions and bad behaviors can be worked out. Leaving a woman virtually at the altar is pretty much final.

You owe it to me...to us...to all the time we spent together.

Right. If only he'd thought about what he owed me before blowing our wedding off to chase his dumb music and his dumber bandmate's ass.

I never asked him to give up his band. Not in a million years.

Old me would've even followed him to California in a heartbeat if he'd asked me to stay like the lonely, loyal puppy I was. He didn't.

Just give me a chance to explain. If you still hate me after that, fine.

Oh, jackass. I don't need anyone's permission to hate you.

I block his number. Again.

Ugh. I might have to take Lincoln up on that offer to shut him up, whatever it involves.

Then I move to the next message in my box.

Lincoln: Is he still harassing you? Don't try to convince him you're better off without him. He'll try to prove you wrong. Just block his number. Life is too short.

Cute. Now I'm getting advice about handling rotten exes from the bosshole.

Dakota: Thanks, but I've been blocking him. He just keeps finding new numbers. You have to buy twelve Regis rolls tonight and they won't be ready for half an hour. Is that okay?

Lincoln: Yes. Do whatever it takes for the rolls. If he keeps finding new numbers, let's put an app on your phone to send unknowns straight to archive. The security is pretty good at deleting anything made with Google or other quickie tools as spam.

Is that a thing? I didn't even know.

Also, what is happening? Lincoln Burns is really helping me? Not just scolding me or having a laugh at my expense with some foot-in-mouth swipe.

Thank you. We'll try it, I text.

I drop the phone back in my purse.

"Yeah, I'll take the dozen. Can I get a latte for the wait?" I finally confirm for Barista Boy.

"Of course, no problem."

I pay for the order and move to the counter where my drink slides across momentarily before I sit down at a table and wait for the rolls.

My phone goes off again. I doubt it's Jay this time. He may be ridiculously fast, but I'm sure he hasn't had time to spoof a new number yet.

Lincoln: I think you'll understand why I need the cinnamon rolls tonight.

Dakota: The same reason you need the mystery package? You're so weird.

Lincoln: I don't want to risk you freaking out when you arrive, so I'll tell you now. The mystery package contains a prosthetic leg.

I stop cold. *What?*

Dakota: Why, pray tell, am I traveling around with an artificial leg?

Lincoln: Just don't mention the damned leg. He hates that.

Again, the mystery deepens. I realize this must all tie back to his weird charity pastry runs, but a single prosthetic? Apparently for someone very specific?

He? I send back.

Lincoln: You'll see.

Dakota: You'd better not have an imaginary friend, or I swear I will go full Poe on your butt.

There's a pause before his next message sails in.

Lincoln: I have something worse—a very mouthy assistant.

Damn him. But maybe, for once, I deserved that.

Dakota: Meh. You knew that when you hired me, and I was just supposed to write copy, remember? If I'd known I'd get stuck babysitting you all day, I never would've taken this job. No matter how well it pays.

God help me, I'm smiling. I'm also hyperconscious of the few people milling around Sweeter Grind watching me and wondering what's gotten in my head, so I hide my smile behind my hand, nibbling at my knuckles.

Lincoln: Liar. You belong to me, Miss Poe.

Oof. I wonder if that was a slip or intentional. A normal boss would say *you belong here,* but this is Lincoln Burns and he's—

Yeah. He's not making this suffocating tension any better.

I don't respond this time, although arguing with Lincoln does make the evening go faster. It's a warm, clear night. My favorite kind of moon rises high out the window, slowly, casting a pale-yellow sheen over everything that feeds my Gothic fantasies in this city.

Well, Gothic-ish.

I try not to think about the fact that I'm meeting up with my boss under the moonlight to deliver a freaking leg.

He might be an irredeemable vampire of a man, but if it's meant to be moody and romantic, the weirdness outshines everything.

My phone hums again.

Lincoln: Anna isn't giving up on her fake marriage idea, you know. Word gets around. Other people think it's a good idea too, even if they won't come out and say it.

Dakota: Other people like...?

Lincoln: Half the marketing team. Plus design.

My heart sinks. I wonder how many of my coworkers are whispering behind my back, hoping I'll take the bait and fake it with Lincoln for their amusement.

With a sigh, I text back, *Do you want me to call a talent company and set something up?*

Lincoln: Fuck no. The last thing I need is a high maintenance model hanging around and trying to seduce me. Wouldn't be the first time.

I roll my eyes. He can't go ten minutes without brandishing his ego, and the worst part is, I know it's probably true.

I just wonder why his dating life seems so hollow if he has a harem of supposed supermodels lined up. Most men with his looks and his money would barely poke their noses in the office. They'd be too busy banging and breaking hearts in one bad fling after the next.

Dakota: Well, best not to keep the people waiting. Congratulations on your fake wedding, boss.

I'm not game. That's for sure.

Lincoln: It's not my fake wedding. It's Anna's and it's still not happening. Even if I'll admit I can't stop thinking about the interesting opportunities it might bring...

Dakota: So why are you texting me about it? Does Anna scare you that much?

Lincoln: No. He sends a red-faced emoji with smoke coming out of its ears.

I laugh.

Ten minutes later, Barista Boy calls my name and gently places a box on the counter. I grab it and head back to the car.

"Are we going to the park now?" Louis asks once I'm back in my seat.

"Are we?" Would I really be taking a leg and cinnamon rolls to the park? "Lincoln texted me the address. Hang on, I'll get it for you."

I pull out my phone, find the address, and read it off to him.

He pulls back on the road, goes up a couple of blocks, and takes a left turn. Sure enough, before I can blink, we're back at the encampment in the park, not far from Sweeter Grind.

Nothing about this makes sense.

"Are you sure we're at the right place?" I ask again, uncertain.

"Once again, this is the address, Miss Poe," he says.

"Maybe I got it wrong?" I pick up my phone to call Lincoln so I can confirm the address.

But before I do, I see Louis' dark eyes in the rearview mirror looking back at me.

"I doubt it. He comes here a lot after picking up his rolls. There he is now!" He gestures at the passenger window.

My eyes follow in the direction he's pointing.

You can't miss him.

Like a gleaming diamond in the velvet night, the ivory Adonis stands in front of a ragged tent, crisp and cool in a three-piece suit. There's my modern Gothic.

It's oddly beautiful, even if it's also just *weird*.

But not that weird, is it? I think back to the time I saw him when I was in the park with Eliza weeks ago. This was definitely the spot where I saw him talking to that homeless dude and hinting at a million secrets.

What will Lincoln Burns show me tonight?

I wonder.

With excitement burning through me, I grab the cargo and climb out of the car, stepping into the moonlight that rolls out like a bone-white carpet, leading to the answers I crave.

XII: ENGAGED IN GUESSING
(LINCOLN)

I can't believe I let her in on this.

Hopefully, Wyatt doesn't rip my head off in the process.

The town car pulls up as I walk toward her, an added quickness in my step.

I don't want her alone in the dark here, even with Louis looking after her.

Most of the people aren't dangerous. They've been dealt a shit hand by life, but chaos always draws bad actors. Drugs and alcohol also run rampant here, creating a volatile environment where anything can happen in the blink of an eye.

As soon as the car stops, she steps out, balancing the medical supply box and the Sweeter Grind rolls. I move in, holding my arms out as I catch up.

"Give me the heavier box," I say.

"You'll have to get it. If I try to toss it over, I'm going to drop everything."

Placing my hand under the large box on the bottom of her stack, I slide it out.

"Stay close," I warn her, casting a wary glance through the dimly lit tents and squaring my shoulders.

"What if I don't want to?" she whispers.

"Do it anyway. This isn't always the safest place."

From the corner of my eye, she grins like the wicked little angel she is.

"Mr. Burns, are you *worried* about me?"

Damn her, I am.

I also hate to admit I'm having second thoughts. I shouldn't have brought her. Part of me wants to stuff her back in the car with Louis and tell him to take her straight home.

What was I thinking? If it wasn't for that meeting across town—but even I need a little honest help sometimes.

"I'm worried about getting smacked in the face with a lawsuit," I lie, glowering at her.

She laughs like the spoiled brat she is.

"Okay. Whatever you say, bossman. I'll try not to make you five million bucks poorer if I get stabbed."

No fucking comment.

I lead her to Wyatt's tent. It's only a short distance, thankfully, and I move with her like I'm back in the service. I only escorted VIPs a few times at an airfield, but I know enough to make an effective bodyguard.

Even when I'm the dolt who put her in a place where she *needs* protecting.

I hear Wyatt before I'm even at the mouth of his tent. A deep wheezing comes from inside, followed by a deep, rattling cough that almost sways the tattered canvas, and a gurgling sound that scares me.

Dakota stops when she hears it and meets my gaze, her eyes wide.

"Umm—is he okay?"

Fuck, I hope so.

I tap on the tent with my fingers, "knocking" the best I can.

"Wyatt? You good in there?" I call, pushing the front of the flap aside.

He doesn't even leave it zipped, assuming the zipper itself isn't broken.

A pale, rough face pops out before I get a good look inside. I jump back as Wyatt sticks his head out and spits.

Christ.

I hook my arm around Dakota's waist, tugging her back just in time to miss a thick loogie that lands near her feet. I hope being a Poe means she isn't grossed out easily.

My attention flicks back to my friend as he stumbles out of the tent a second later, trying to clear what sounds like wet cement in his chest.

"I'm fine, Burns. Who you got here?" His eyes peer through the darkness, trying to focus.

"A friend," I say generously. "Her name's Dakota. She's a copywriter at the office and she's also filling in for my assistant while she's out on maternity leave." I look at Dakota and motion to Wyatt. "This is Wyatt Emory. We served together years ago. We're war buddies, you might say."

"Hell of a place to make friends," Wyatt says, shaking his head with a lopsided smile. "I came out looking better than this guy, didn't I?"

I'm expecting pure awkwardness. All tension, unease, and subtle revulsion showing even if she's too nice to insult him.

Instead, Dakota laughs.

The same easy laugh I always hear when she's dealing with my shit—at least the kind that doesn't leave her wanting to wrap her hands around my neck.

"You sure did! Bet you're a better runner, too. I can't imagine Lincoln jogging," she says.

I fold my arms, hiding a smile.

Her words are so sincere I don't know whether to be touched at how empathetic she is or pissed that she implies I'm in worse shape than Wyatt. I take off my jacket and drop to the ground beside him, spreading the jacket out for cover before I motion.

"Do you want to sit?" I glance up at her.

Her puckered face says not really, but she wordlessly smooths out her dress and sits on my jacket, sweeping her long legs to the side.

As usual, they're a delicious torture for my eyes. Too bad I didn't come here to ogle this raven-stamped girl who drives me to the edge of madness.

"I brought you something," I tell Wyatt once she's settled.

"Aw, fuck. Not necessary. I can feed myself," Wyatt says with a coughing fit I hate at the end.

"Not just the rolls. You'll be happy when you see it, trust me." I open the prosthetic box and pull out the contents.

For a second, he's speechless. Frozen. His eyes bulge like marbles, glinting in the faint light.

"You're shitting me, right? That's too damn expensive even for you, Lincoln. I could've got one from the VA anytime and waited," he says coldly.

Easier said than done without a mailing address, I think bitterly.

This is what drives me up the fucking wall with Wyatt, his uncompromising pride. It's the best part of who he is and it also makes him his own worst enemy.

"The VA can take up to a year. It's nothing," I say sharply.

"Bull. I would've waited."

"A year is a long-ass time to wait for a leg, Wyatt," I remind him. Especially when he'd still have his real leg instead of this engineered metal if he hadn't gone and saved my sorry ass.

"He makes like a gazillion bucks a day. He can afford an arm and a leg here and there," Dakota says lightly, trying to be funny.

I give her a wry smile.

She's trying to help, dammit, but I wish she wouldn't. Wyatt's moods can be unpredictable, and if he gets pissed or unruly, he could chuck the prosthetic into Elliot Bay for all I know.

My worries are unfounded, though.

Because Wyatt chuckles loudly until he runs into another hacking fit that has him doubled over, choking up phlegm.

I suddenly regret bringing him the new leg because it doesn't go nearly far enough. He needs treatment, professional help beyond anything I can offer. At least a bottle of medicine and a chest X-ray for that nasty infection.

I'm about to grab him when he straightens up, holding out a hand.

"Sorry, ma'am," he tells Dakota before meeting my eyes. "She gives you hell. I like her already."

"How do you know she gives me hell? You've barely met," I say with a snort.

"I can tell. Good pick, Burns. You need a chick who keeps you honest."

"Don't go getting too attached," I mutter under my breath, hoping she can't hear. "She just works for me. That's it."

Wyatt gives me a knowing smile under his bushy beard.

"Whatever, my dude. I always had girls who just worked with me meet up at homeless parks after sunset, too."

I shake my head fiercely, trying to form a response.

At least he's not truly on death's doorstep yet, however ugly that cough is. If the assholery in his sense of humor ever goes, then I'll really worry.

"He's not lying," Dakota says. I almost wince knowing she heard us. "No good looks or bags of money could make up for his sterling personality, right? I'm here because I was mandated...and because I want to be."

"In that case, you should let her go home. You can't hold her hostage, Burns," he growls.

I gaze at Dakota.

She bites her lip, her green eyes sparkling like gemstones in the moonlight. She's a portrait of dark beauty that fits my melancholy spirit too well tonight.

"She'll survive—won't you, Nevermore?"

"Nevermore? You've even got a nickname? Shit." Wyatt squints at me, calling me a *dumbass* without saying it.

"It's cool. And I don't really have a choice because I need a ride back to my bike," Dakota cuts in, offering her support.

"Well, hell. I'm glad you finally found yourself a hot one you'll appreciate whenever you pull your head out of your ass," Wyatt says. "Better than wasting your life away at the office and chasing after me."

I smile painfully, shaking my head.

"Man, it's not like that. I told you. She's an employee. Nothing more."

"Yeah, and I'm Paul Bunyan." He stands up straight and turns to Nevermore. "Hey, Dakota, since this guy insists you're his model employee, you wanna date me instead?"

What the fuck? I could club him with that fake leg.

Now, I feel worse. I didn't bring her here to take ridiculous advances from what's supposed to be my best friend.

By some miracle, Dakota laughs it off with high, sunny humor I'll admit I'm becoming addicted to.

"Sure," she says.

What the double fuck?

"Dakota?" My head snaps to her.

"Yes, bossman? You look troubled."

Damnation.

Maybe I should be feeling sorry for myself, instead of these two boneheads double-teaming me tonight.

"Don't call me bossman," I snap off.

"Why? Everyone else does."

"You're not—" I catch myself before I finish that sentence, ignoring Wyatt grinning like a wolf.

But she's not like everyone else, is she?

I never once asked Lucy to get involved with Wyatt and his troubles. Not once in the two years he's really spiraled down.

Dakota Poe is *just* an employee who has unprecedented access to the darkest chasms of my life.

Why?

"What's got your tongue, Burns? We've got a few strays roaming around here," Wyatt says, ribbing me in the side with surprising force.

I whack him back playfully as Dakota laughs louder, clenching her sides.

"Are you two done having fun?" My eyes flick to my tormentors, one at a time.

"Hmm, I dunno. Fun is pretty hard to come by," she whispers with that spear of a tongue before calling, "How about you, Wyatt?"

"Nah. This is more fun than I've had in a while. We've got him riled up. He always has a tell," Wyatt says with a smile I haven't seen in months.

Oh, shit. Here we go.

"Wyatt, *do not*," I bite off. "Don't go there, or I swear I'll find a better use for this leg that involves your head—"

"Look at his ears," Wyatt says, fearless and pointing. "They're redder than a cranberry."

Smiling, Dakota leans closer, inspecting my mutinous fucking ears.

I'm torn.

Torn between reaching out to touch her and swatting her away, or making good on my threat to slug Wyatt with his own prosthetic. In the end, I do nothing but glower.

"You're right! Holy moly. Those things could shame a fire truck," she says with a messy giggle.

"Now you know. His ears always light up like Christmas when he's embarrassed. Or lying," Wyatt adds with a *fuck you* wink.

I so regret coming here tonight. Almost as much as I regret bringing Nevermore along for the ride.

"Dakota has something for you," I say.

"Way to change the subject," Wyatt points out, scratching his beard. "Don't think we're done with you yet."

Dakota stands and steps up to my side, holding out the box of Regis rolls for me to take.

"Have you had dinner yet?"

She shakes her head.

"Take one," I tell her. "You might get hungry before we're back and we've got plenty to go around."

She opens the box, grabs a cinnamon roll, and passes it to me.

I also take a roll before passing it to Wyatt. "Rest are yours. Just leave one for my mom."

Without hesitation, Wyatt hoists a big roll from the box, bites a gaping piece off, and swallows. His table manners may suck, but there's no table here and I'm just glad he's eating like he always does.

"How's your ma doing, anyway?" he asks, chewing loudly.

"She stays busy with her day trips and angel investing. Basically okay, but, you know..." I don't elaborate, taking a big bite of my own roll.

"Sorry. I know it's been hard for her," Wyatt says, smacking his lips.

"She's a nice lady. What's the problem?" Dakota asks carefully.

"Nothing," I snap, hoping she'll take the hint as I stuff more pastry into my mouth.

"His ma was the happiest lady anybody ever met before his old man passed," Wyatt says, eyeing me. He knows to leave it at that.

"She seemed very bright passing out cupcakes at the office," Dakota says.

Wyatt chuckles. "So, Nevermore met your ma?"

"Not like that," I rush out. "Mother still drops into the office from time to time. She's never taken to retirement well. Dakota works there, so—"

"Lookie there. His ears are all red again." She points at my face, the little scoundrel.

I glare at her, swallowing a lump of pastry.

"I should fire you on the spot."

Compared to us, she nibbles at her Regis roll, pulling off a small piece at a time and stuffing it in her mouth. "But you won't. Because no one else is going to wait half an hour for Sweeter Grind after work to fetch your precious grub."

"Burns, you *idiot*," Wyatt mutters. "You've got the poor girl doing your dirty work now?"

"Dirty work?" Dakota asks.

"He knows I can't resist a good cinnamon roll from that place, so when he wants me to talk, he brings a box."

"Oh," she says softly.

Yeah. Now you know, and you can leave me the hell alone about the damn cinnamon roll mystery, I think miserably.

Wyatt leans closer to me and whispers, "Don't be like me, man. Wisen up before it's too late. She's a good one. Can't let the wrong bitch trash your life."

"She's just an employee," I flare, hating that his brain flips back to his own bitter past.

His situation was more complicated than that, of course, even if Olivia was a self-absorbed banshee.

"Just don't fuck it up," he tells me.

I'm annoyed that he won't believe she's just an assistant and that he's comparing Dakota to his ex, even if he means well. She's a firecracker, yeah, but she's not underhanded.

"She's not Olivia," I whisper harshly, looking up to make sure Nevermore stays glued to her phone.

Wyatt nods firmly, already chomping on another cinnamon roll. He bites off another big piece and coughs. I regret not bringing him some water.

"Wyatt, are you taking anything to help with your cough?" Dakota asks, her eyes brimming with concern.

"No. I'm fine. It's just a cold."

"Are you sure? It sounds a little rough," she tells him gently.

"It's a shitty chest cold, but I'll survive. I've had worse than this, right, Burns?"

His eyes flicker in the moonlight. They feel like magnets drawing out my soul.

"He has." I don't say more.

He certainly isn't wrong.

How could I ever forget? Reaching for his hand, groaning as he pulled me from the debris.

That deafening explosion.

That panic as I threw myself on top of him, shaking him, blood fucking everywhere.

That improvised tourniquet I struggled to tie around his flesh, sure that he was about to bleed out, cursing God and the universe and everything in existence because I was sure he'd just given his life for mine.

Fuck.

Wyatt, stay. Stay with me, goddammit. You don't leave like this.

I bite down on what's left of my roll so hard it hurts my teeth, snapping me from those thoughts. I don't care to relive that day, and Wyatt sure as hell doesn't need to, either.

Stay with me.

Isn't that all I've been asking him to do for years?

Still trying to save him when I thought that was long over while I waited to find out if he lived under an unforgiving sun, smoking a cigarette a few paces from a field hospital.

Dakota pulls a handful of peppermints from her purse, stands, and brings them to Wyatt.

"Here. My gift. If it ever gets too bad, try these," she says, handing them over.

"Thanks. I will," he says, clearing his throat loudly.

She returns to her seat beside me. I'm still bewildered he actually took the mints without fussing.

"Do you always travel around with mints?" I ask.

"Only since I started working for you."

I snort.

"What? Why does working for me require mints?"

"Because when I miss lunch, I can always suck on a mint and tide myself over," she tells me.

Wyatt lets out a bark of harsh laughter. "Damn, dude. Let the girl eat. No wonder she's so skinny."

"I've never told her to skip lunch once. She does that on her own," I insist, leveling a look at her like I'm suddenly on trial.

"But you *do* give me impossible deadlines most weeks. Especially since I started juggling two different roles."

"Like hell," I growl, angry that it might be true.

"You do," she says, wearing a teasing smile.

"Then they can't be impossible by definition, Nevermore. I don't need to be a writer to know that. If they were, you wouldn't keep meeting them."

"Yeah, because I skip meals and get six hours of sleep on a good night," she mutters.

I stop and stare. Am I that awful?

Is that why she's mixing up texts with me and apparently her fuckwit ex?

Guilt roils my guts, and I hate it.

"You're depriving her of sleep too?" Wyatt gives me a sterner look this time. "Goddamn. Nevermore is gonna drop you like an old shoe."

"Old shoes are easier to drop than bad habits." I look at Dakota. "If the timelines are unrealistic and you're truly that frayed, why haven't you said anything? I'm not a monster. I can make accommodations."

She shrugs slowly, squaring her shoulders before she looks at me again.

"Like you said. They're not technically unrealistic. As long as I find the time..."

Damn her.

I glance up at the moon, high over the bay now, and back at her with a roughness in my throat.

"You never mind jumping down my throat about anything else. Why haven't you just told me you're not a drone and you'll get it done when you can? I care about your lifestyle habits."

"Because I like getting paid. Besides, it's not all bad. A nice pile of work keeps me from having time for poetry, and you *know* how that goes, so—"

That wins her a smile.

"Liar. I'm willing to bet you still find time for that. Why can't you find the time to eat and sleep in when you're not worshipping your ivory Adonis?" I tell her.

She doesn't answer.

Wyatt gives us a lost look.

When we both notice, we burst into laughter.

* * *

LATER, back in the town car, Dakota looks at me with a question hanging on her lips.

"So, Wyatt's the reason behind your pathological cinnamon roll needs," she says.

"He'll stay in his tent for days without eating. He won't come out for anything else. Regis rolls are too sweet for me, but he loves them."

She gives me a wary look. I can't tell if she thinks I'm being sweet or stupid.

"It isn't healthy, I know. He's not well with his diet. First it was his Banh Mi obsession, the same sandwich from the same particular Vietnamese shop every day. He spiraled down from there. I'm hoping we'll progress back to protein and vegetables at some point, but for now, I can't let him starve."

I'm aware of how pathetic that sounds.

Every week, I question whether or not I shouldn't just knock him out and *drag* him into treatment. But if I take that last tiny ounce of freedom, of will, of pride he still has...what the hell will he have left?

"Are you guys really just war buddies?" she asks.

Where do I even begin? We are, but we're not *just* war buddies like your average comrades in arms who serve together, make it home without a scratch, and laugh about it years later.

Without him, I never would've come home in one piece.

"Are you in a hurry to get home, Nevermore?" I ask, steepling my fingers.

She looks at me for a long second and shakes her head.

It's terrible how I love watching her hair cascade down her shoulders when she lets it hang loose, how much I wonder what it would feel like tangled in my fist.

My eyes flick to her mouth, heart-shaped and mellow pink in the shadows.

Goddamn, do I really want her alone?

It's late. The night yawns with danger. I may feel like I owe her an explanation, but is it worth the risk of what could happen if she's with me—too close—without another soul around?

I don't answer that. Instead, I lower the privacy screen.

"Louis, take us to my spot," I say, knowing he'll understand exactly what I mean.

"You got it, Mr. Burns."

I raise the screen again and meet her wondering eyes.

"Patience. I'll tell you everything soon," I promise.

She nods, but she's also—laughing?

"What's so damn funny?"

"Why are you so freaking secretive? You're like a Bond villain or something. Was introducing me to Wyatt so terrible?"

It wasn't, even if it wasn't my brightest idea.

I rake her with a cautious look.

"It's not a big secret. Not really. We're just diving into a lot of sensitive subjects tonight," I say, hoping like hell that'll satisfy her.

Dakota nods emphatically.

"I get it. Telling you about Jay wasn't easy, either," she whispers.

"Jay? Oh—the shitbag." Knowing the prick's name somehow makes him more real. More loathsome. I don't want a jackass who left her at the altar having a name, a human face.

It's too fucking horrible.

Knowing he *exists* and how much he hurt her makes me feel

like I owe him a complimentary facelift, courtesy of my knuckles.

"Yeah," she confirms.

"If he calls you again, tell him I'll slap him with a harassment suit," I snarl. "If that doesn't work, I'll fly to your oil town and tie him to a goddamned rig."

She smiles, her eyes glowing with gratitude for a crime I haven't even committed. Yet.

"I think I can handle him without my boss fighting my battles. But thanks, Lincoln."

"Tell me one thing—how the hell do you leave a girl stranded on her wedding day and then start texting her like it's no big deal?" My fingers curl into a fist I bring to my jaw, scratching my face with my knuckles. "I can't wrap my head around that."

"I shouldn't have said anything." Dakota sighs and looks away from me. "It isn't important..."

Nevermore, you're wrong. What he did to you was pure bullshit.

She's right, though. I don't need to rub it in.

I don't need to welcome hurt memories to dance on her heart.

Damn.

"My apologies. I regret if I've said something stupid again. I do respect your privacy, even if I don't always show it," I say, leaning forward in my seat.

She's quiet for a minute before she finally meets my eyes again.

"I appreciate it. It's okay."

The car jolts to a stop at the base of the scenic lookout when she stops speaking. Dakota falls forward next to me. I throw an arm out to catch her.

Somehow, I stop her from falling, but her breasts press snugly against my hand.

"Umm—" She blushes, but makes no effort to move more than gravity pushing her back.

Not what I need.

Not at fucking all.

She's so cute, so delectable, I could kiss her.

And the way she looks at me, flushed red with full lips, her perfectly palm-sized breasts teasing my hand...

No, sir.

She's just my employee. How many times did I say that to Wyatt?

Yeah, I don't believe it either, but I still need to pull my head out of my ass right now.

"This is our stop. Stay there," I tell her, getting out and rounding her side to open the door for her.

"Have you been here before?" I ask as she follows me up a winding, hilly sidewalk to a platform.

"Yeah. Maybe once after I first moved to town."

"The stars aren't as impressive as the North Dakota flats, I'm sure," I say. "Still, when you see that view of the city and the ships at night, you can't help falling in love."

"That's kinda beautiful. I'm a small-town girl at heart, but I always love a pretty scene."

"How do you like Seattle?"

"I love it, honestly. The arts are alive here in a way that's totally different from Dallas. We have a lot of creative, crafty people there, but it's pretty rustic. Out here, you get all the flavors. Modern, historic, experimental, international..."

She's speaking to my soul. I'm not quite sure how to handle that.

Damn if I can't resist the urge to slide an arm around her waist and pull her closer when we've reached the top of the overlook and its platform.

"It's a narrow path up here. Watch your step and stay to the side," I say, pretending that's the only reason I've put my hands on her.

She smiles.

"You're worried about me again? Or are you still freaking out about me lawyering up to leave you penniless?"

"This is America, Nevermore. We all live in fear of frivolous suits, but I'd rather you not fall, all legal wrangling aside."

"You're such a charmer," she says, dripping sarcasm. "But honestly, you're not the ginormous jackass I thought you were."

"Thank you. I think," I say with a smile.

"When you tried to attack me—"

"Attack you?"

She rolls her eyes. "Well, when you *accosted* me for my cinnamon roll, I thought you were just some entitled rich prick."

"And what do you think now?" *More importantly, why do I care?*

"You're a grump. You're demanding, focused, and sometimes just rude. But deep down? After what I saw tonight with your friend, I'd call you a sweetheart." She looks at me. "Don't let it go to your head," she adds quickly.

"Bah, I liked the first part. You're giving me more credit than I deserve."

She laughs as I sit down on the bench with a breathtaking view of the night. It's a small seat, almost a ledge if not for the safety railing, and she stumbles.

I swear, I'm not *trying* to pull her into my lap and lock my arms around her.

"This isn't inappropriate. Obviously, I'd like to stop you from going over the edge."

She curls against my chest and smiles up at me, a pretty splash of moonlight in her eyes.

"Of course."

Then it happens. Something that can't be trumped up to accidents, however unlikely.

She lays her small hand over mine, nervously at first.

I bristle.

"Let me guess. You're wondering who Wyatt is and why he's so important?" I say, desperate to keep talking so I don't let my mouth get other ideas.

"Yeah." She nods firmly. "You said 'war buddy,' but it's more than that, isn't it?"

"He saved my life in Iraq." I close my eyes and I'm back there again.

Hot flashes of death light up a sky reeking with black smoke.

My skull feels dislodged from the deafening improvised blast.

I breathe in Dakota's flowery, faintly minty scent to blot out the stink, holding her tighter, anchoring myself to the present.

"Wyatt should've been okay. Our unit ran into a trap, a buried bomb," I tell her slowly. "The armored carrier was ripped open like a tin can. I was pinned under something—" I shake my head. "A huge piece of steel, I think. I don't know how it never crushed me, but there was an opening, and he still had his wits. Wyatt dragged it off me and carried me out. We were almost to safety when the second explosion went off. Another fucking bomb, hidden just a few paces away like a landmine. He lost his leg because he was ahead of me. A few bruises and a concussion aside, I walked away fine. The leg wasn't the worst part, though. For saving my life, he lost his own..."

"I'm sorry," she whispers, folding into me like melted butter.

"The rest, it's a long story," I whisper.

"It's okay. I get it now. He saved you, so you keep him in cinnamon rolls and prosthetics..."

"I'm trying to keep him *alive*. Everyone else gave up on him a long time ago. The leg was just the trigger for what Wyatt lost later." I pause, inhaling slowly. "Some of it was his fault. A lot of it wasn't. Regardless, he loved his wife so much. He...he almost bled the fuck out that day. I kept telling him to stay, to pull through for Olivia and their boy. I've never seen anybody fight so hard in physical therapy, but he came through it."

I lose my train of thought. Or maybe just my words.

Nevermore watches me softly, her green eyes twinkling in the night, all moon and stars and roaming questions.

"Olivia left him broken. She blamed his addictions, but she

was cheating long before that. Before the accident," I tell her slowly. "She filed for divorce and won custody of the kid easily. She said he had PTSD, and technically, she wasn't wrong, even though he was getting treatment. She said he couldn't be around their son unsupervised."

"That's brutal," Dakota whispers, bowing her head.

"Yeah, well, the judge went by the book and threw out any context, so that was that." I have to stop because it still puts me in a blinding rage. "Right? Wrong? Who the fuck knows. I'm not here to play social worker or argue morals. I just know Olivia Emory kept the kid, the house, and a lot of their shit. Wyatt was cleaned out, left homeless with no job and no people. It's a damn miracle he got off the opiates when he hit the streets. I helped him with that, before he left my place after crashing a few weeks. Even now, I have plenty of room, but he's a hard-nosed fuck. I can't make him stay with me."

"It's sweet of you to try. It's really kind how you care for him." Her fingers find my brow.

She's stroking me.

Touching me like a big, angry animal needing to be soothed.

For fuck's sake, she's not wrong.

Maybe I am tonight, as hard as that is to admit.

"It's not sweet. It's responsible, and I owe him my life. Bringing him his daily sugar rush and making sure he can walk is the least I can do. That divorce annihilated him. It drove him to drinking, bad habits, and took what little hope he ever had. He's basically an alcoholic wreck, and I can only do so much."

I glance away sharply. It's not her problem, but putting this shit into words makes it feel like she should share it.

I don't want that.

I don't want her to shoulder this boulder I've been heaving back and forth for years, a task that feels like it'll only end when the very thing I'm trying so hard to stop finally happens. When I walk into the camp one day and find Wyatt's cold, stiff body.

"I understand. I...I wanted to die after my wedding. I didn't get out of bed for days," Dakota admits with a sad sigh. "My mom finally threatened to send me to the Larkin's farm to clean stables if I didn't start moving and doing normal things." She pauses and smiles. "I wouldn't have minded cleaning horse poop so much. My town is kinda famous for animals, and there was this old horse named Edison. He'd always escape and drive his owners crazy, but it was always entertaining for everybody else. One time this tiger got loose, and Edison even helped track it down—"

"Tiger? What the fuck?" I wonder if I heard her right.

She just smiles sheepishly.

"Nevermore, you come from a weird place," I grind out. "Is it a coming-of-age rite for every Poe to grow up in *The Twilight Zone?* I'm surprised you didn't stay."

"It wasn't an easy choice, but...if I had to rejoin the living, I decided it couldn't be in that little town. It couldn't be Dallas anymore no matter how lovely the people were to me," she tells me, her eyes misted with memories. "They saw my worst humiliation. Plus, cool animals aside, I never totally meshed with small-town life. I started applying for jobs everywhere after that mess, and a shipping company in Seattle was the first place that called me back for a marketing gig."

I don't know what to say to that, so I opt for nothing, running my thumb over her hand instead. Sometimes, silence can be more eloquent than any words.

"Love can be cruel," I whisper after a while.

I hold her tighter.

Her blond hair shimmers under the night lights, somehow brighter when it's laced with shadows. Her eyes dance when she looks at me and says, "It can. But it doesn't always have to be so painful."

I snort loudly, spoiling the moment.

"You really believe that?" I don't mean to tell her she's naive, but that's probably how it sounds.

Regina's face flashes in my mind, her eyes wide with horror

and still trying to lie. Even when I caught her butt-ass naked, draped over another man's dick.

I'll never believe love is anything magical.

It's an invisible fucking serial killer of hearts and dreams, but I hold my comments because I can't crush this girl. If she's still clinging to a shred of something better—holding out for her prince—I can't be the asshole to cut the last thread.

She bites her full bottom lip. For a moment, all I want to do is the same.

My eyes linger on her lips and I think she notices.

Because she tilts her chin back, angles her head, and leans in closer.

Oh, fuck.

Is she asking for—

Yeah. She is.

And I hear a voice grabbing my brain like a tennis ball, squeezing, and growling, *Burns, you better fucking not. Run.*

My body doesn't want to listen, straining against my thoughts like a wild horse.

I move closer, cradling her in my arms, peering down like she's breakfast, lunch, and dinner.

Her scent isn't doing me any favors. Cinnamon and peppermint waft up my nose, mingled with something uniquely Dakota.

Delicious.

Dangerously fucking delicious.

Her eyes flutter shut with a soft rasp of her chest. She's tense and still so soft, her breasts heaving—yes, heaving, and I always thought that sounded ridiculous before.

Not now.

Dakota Poe is asking for my lips, my tongue, my teeth and she's utterly serious.

We're almost touching already, barely inches apart.

All I have to do is shut that second mouth in my brain, the voice of sanity, and seal the deal.

All I need to make that happen is to kiss with a passion I've never had.

I close my eyes, still fighting internally, and move my mouth to hers.

Our lips barely brush before I jerk back.

She's fucking electric, like a static spark in my soul.

Have you ever kissed anyone who's too fucking good to be kissed? You come in hot, expecting perfect poise and control and a tongue primed for its best moves, only to get one second in.

One measly second before you're frozen in disbelief, thrown back like you've been hit by the very best kind of lightning.

I know she feels it too, her eyes open now, big and green and glistening. Her mouth is parted with awe, her cheeks flushed, red as apples and begging me to take another taste.

Deeper. Longer. Sweeter.

I'm about to do that, ignoring the hard-on aching to bust out of my pants, when a noise like the world ending stops me.

Some fucking donkey who needs a muffler whips into the tiny parking lot, blasting noise, and then peels out again with a grating screech.

Dakota jumps back, blinking.

Just like that, the moment is gone.

Probably for the best, though I don't fucking believe it.

I can't get mixed up with a woman who works for me. Even a beautiful one who tells me off when it's warranted and can handle anything I throw at her.

"Sorry. Umm—I should—I should get—" Her mouth won't work, still hanging off her face and looking so delectable.

"It's late. We should go," I finish for her.

"Right."

"We'll go to the office and pick up your bike, then I'll have Louis drop you off."

"Why? I always take my bike."

"It's way too late for you to be biking home, and you know I won't have it," I say with a shit-eating grin.

I know there's something different in her when she doesn't fight back.

I help her back to the car and do exactly what I said.

I should be happy for the interruption caused by the clunker with Satan at the wheel.

We only half kissed.

Nothing fucking happened.

I let her go quietly, watching as she locks up her bike and disappears inside her place, with my life no more complicated than when we arrived.

Only, I'm not relieved at all.

The entire ride home has me clasping my knee, staring anxiously into the night. I need a stiff drink to take this tremor out of my hand, but I know that won't cut it.

I needed her full taste, dammit. Not the hurried sample still lodged in my core, her lips glued to my brain with the same ruthless question.

Why didn't I kiss Nevermore like a man when I had the chance?

XIII: IF BIRD OR DEVIL (DAKOTA)

"Can you look at these before I have to show them to Anna?" Cheryl asks, handing me a bulging folder.

"Sure." I open it and thumb through the old-school printouts. Even from a few slides, her copy reads much sharper than before. I smile up at her. "Nice job. You're getting better."

"Oh, thanks! I started stalking Twitter trends just like you showed me."

I nod. "See? All you needed was a little inspiration. You always had the writing chops."

"Oh my God, I'm so glad you came to work with us, doll." She leans in with a beaming smile. "I thought I'd been at this too long to learn any new tricks."

"I'm happy I could help, Cheryl." My heart flutters.

It's nice to feel like I've actually helped someone.

Cheryl's eyes trail behind me to Lincoln's office.

"Hey, I can't help asking... Have you given any thought to the fake marriage thing?" She suppresses a laugh. "It's the talk of the whole office. Everyone's waiting on tenterhooks to see if you and Burns tie the pretend knot."

Yikes.

"Tell them not to wait up forever. It's not happening. I wish

Anna would just drop it," I say, unable to keep the irritation out of my voice. Mostly because I'm pissed. I don't *need* to be reminded how hilariously interesting it would be to get engaged to my hot cactus of a boss. Or how badly I wanted him to kiss me again that night, how my body ached to the bone when he did, and how he's not actually a total Saguaro cactus at all.

Ugh. He's a man who secretly helps his homeless best friend.

He's a man who makes me brittle with his smolder and he takes me apart with a single muted kiss.

I hate that I wonder why he stopped, regardless of the idiot with the bad muffler.

Did kissing me disappoint him? Did it scare him? Was it just too flipping much?

"Sorry if I struck a nerve," Cheryl says sheepishly. "Anna told me she's just using it to tease Burns since he hates it so much. Or maybe she hopes you'll both just do it to shut her up."

I roll my eyes. I like Anna well enough, but what the hell? Is this multibillion-dollar company junior high school again?

"Ask Anna how much she likes being teased," I hiss.

"Oh, I think the boss already did that, doll. He tore into her a couple days after that meeting. I don't think she meant anything nefarious by it, though. She just thought we'd gain tons of traction, and isn't that the goal these days?"

She isn't wrong.

Still. Some lines can't be crossed just for internet clout.

"Mr. Burns is rather strict about not fraternizing with the staff. He was probably upset by the suggestion," I say, grateful that my boss is a decent guy in the office when he's not hellbent on pissing me off.

"No, he was pretty adamant that Anna should apologize for embarrassing you and also make sure you didn't feel like she was told to apologize," Cheryl tells me with a frown.

"What? Why would he do that?" My eyebrows shoot up.

Cheryl shrugs. "I don't know, but he went in pretty hot."

Interesting. I honestly don't know whether I feel protected or annoyed.

Then, as if saying her name calls her, I hear the click of high heels and a voice that's definitely running on a double shot of espresso.

"Party at Dakota's desk!" Anna runs up and rests her hands on the walls of my cubicle. "Is Mr. Burns in?"

"Yeah, but he's still on a call, I think."

Cheryl picks up the manila folder from my desk and hands it to Anna. "I have some new social media copy."

"Great!" Anna opens the folder and starts flicking through it, laughing intermittently. "These are cute. Way to step up the game, Cheryl. The wedding campaign's on track—well, aside from one thing." She lifts her head and looks at me pointedly. "I just wish we had a *unique* hook. A personal touch. Something Vera and the other big brands couldn't top to save their lives."

I try not to glare at her. It's painfully obvious what she means.

"Careful. I told her the boss demanded an apology," Cheryl says with mock humor like she's trying to diffuse the whole thing.

It's not working.

Anna smiles down at me.

"Sorry. It's a nonstarter," I say, hating that I always feel compelled to apologize.

"Dakota, everyone notices how you two play off of each other," Cheryl says.

"He's ripped and loaded. Just bat your eyes and go along with it. Hell, maybe push for an extra performance bonus. Do you have any clue how many ladies in this office would love to be in your position for free?" Anna says sweetly.

Heat throbs under my face. I bury my head in my hands, willing myself to disappear before I open my eyes again.

Didn't work.

I'm still here, being tormented by people who are supposed to be on my side.

"That's enough, you two," I say, trying to lay down the law. "I have my reasons for not wanting to be a stand-in bride. We're just not interested and I—"

My desk phone rings, grabbing my attention.

I pick it up with a heavy sigh.

"Lincoln Burns, CEO, this is Miss Poe speaking. How can I help you?" I say with rehearsed politeness.

"Miss Poe, this is security. I've got a delivery with your name on it. Should I send it up?"

"What is it?" I freeze in my seat, grateful Anna and Cheryl have at least gone back to chattering among themselves.

"Can't tell, but it's pretty long. Light weight. Came in a box. You want me to open it?"

Oof, yeah, as long as it's not a bomb.

"Sure, open it and then send it up," I say.

A few minutes later when the elevator opens, a guy wearing a building security uniform steps out with a bulging bouquet of puffy purple hydrangeas. "Dakota Poe?"

Oh, no.

He stops and glances around. A few heavy seconds pass while I'm frozen in my seat before I finally clear my throat enough to say, "Right here. That's me."

Unfortunately.

He storms over and shoves the flowers in my face. "Can I put these down?"

"Um, sure." I start rearranging stuff on my desk to make space like I'm trying to bury my own shame.

I gesture and he sets the flowers down in the empty space I cleared. I have one good guess who they're from and it's already making my stomach heave.

"Ohhh, gorgeous! Just the splash of color you need, Dakota. Who are they from?" Cheryl asks, her eyes wide with excitement.

I try not to cringe. I should've known it was hopeless, hiding my anti-gift from one of the office big mouths.

"I haven't read the card yet," I lie. I find it buried between the flowers and pluck it out, unsure if the lead weight in my belly is mostly anger or dread.

Anna giggles obnoxiously. "We know who they're from! I think that's his way of saying he's game for a little marketing magic."

Desperation, thy name is Anna Patel.

"You do, huh?" I flip the card open only because I want to prove her wrong.

"Bossman has an eye for lavish gifts," Cheryl says.

"I wish," I mutter.

And I actually do wish Lincoln was my secret admirer when I read the blocky words scrawled inside the card.

Can we talk? stares up at me, along with a new number.

Anna can't see the name. I'm starting to believe she really thinks it's from Lincoln with the way she giggles. It's just incredible how the boss might be the least annoying person here today.

"What's going on out here?" Speak of the devil. His voice drops low as he comes around my desk. "Flowers? Who are they from?"

"Like you don't know," Anna says, giving him an exaggerated eye roll. "I knew you'd come around. That email you sent the other day about scouting talent with the model agency was a dead giveaway."

He glares at her.

I think a full thirty seconds passes where Lincoln's dark eyes flick back and forth. It's like I can see him contemplating her termination.

"Oh, well...maybe he doesn't know. Sorry for assuming," Anna squeaks, then grabs Cheryl's arm. "We'll get out of your hair, Mr. Burns. Lots of campaigns to polish up. Later!"

They both scurry to the elevator like fleeing rats.

It's so ridiculous it takes the edge off, and I almost laugh.

Then Lincoln's intense gaze lands on me and lingers until the elevator dings shut.

"Who are they from?" he asks, his voice low thunder.

I hold my hands up, trying to find the words.

"Dakota? You have a hot new date or what?"

Holy hell. The look on his face is one long silent scream of jealousy that makes me shudder.

"Why do you care?" I say with a shrug. "They came from somebody back home."

A little white lie painted purple. That's all I've got.

Even if we've been on better terms lately, I'm not about to explain that my stalker ex keeps sending me unwanted flowers. For all I know, Lincoln might be ludicrous enough to follow through on his threats—though having Jay wrecked right now is very, very tempting.

"I don't care, Nevermore. Just curious." He rolls his big shoulders, a tension pulling through him like a cord.

"Don't waste the mental energy. They're for charity," I say, refusing to meet his eyes.

"For such a bad liar, you're bold," he rumbles, leaning over me.

My heart skips a beat as I look up, defiantly meeting his swirling brown eyes.

"What? Why would I lie about this? It would be cooler if they *were* for me." I know I'm playing with fire, strumming his jealousy strings.

"Cool. Right. Whoever they're from has trash taste. Hydrangeas are overplayed and barely remarkable. They shout friend zone, not romance," he says, and I'm surprised he talks like he knows his flowers.

I bite my tongue so I don't laugh. Also, he isn't wrong.

"I told you. They're just for charity. Down, boy," I say playfully.

"Charity? Only because you don't like them, and you know

I'm right. Whoever sends this shit to a girl wants to make her drier than the Sonoran desert."

The anger in his voice, his stance, has me feeling something and it's far from dry.

I swallow thickly before I say, "Yeah, well, why are you hating on my flowers so much? What's not to like?"

He glares at me and then looks away as if I've touched some nerve.

Weird.

"They don't strike me as Poe flowers," he says.

"Poe flowers? Do I even want to know what that means?" I squint at him.

"Not bold. Not *you.* I'd have picked a dozen red roses with their thorns still on the stems," he growls confidently.

I push back into my chair.

Whoa. Am I that obvious? I hate that he has me pegged, but not as much as I hate wanting flowers from a man like Lincoln Burns.

"Because roses aren't overdone or anything," I bite off, trying to save face.

"You prefer something more exotic? Fine. Maybe something dark blue and fragrant from a rainforest in Bolivia. Regardless, I don't see light purple being your thing."

I look at him, my brow pushing down.

"It's not intense enough," he explains, his jaw tightening with a hot look that cuts right through me. "You're all bold color, Nevermore. Not washed-out pastels."

My heart stops like a stuck clock. I'm horrified because that might be the nicest compliment any man has ever given me.

"They're just flowers, dude," I whisper. I can't even fake being angry. "Who wants to go blind looking at a little splash of color?"

Again, a lump lodges in my throat as he gives me the heaviest look ever.

"You," he says. No hesitation.

Oh my God.

"What-ever, Dishonest Abe," I say, snapping my face to the side and rubbing my cheek, wishing I could wipe away blushes.

He chuckles. "Very on point today with the banter, sweetheart."

I look back at him with an annoyed blink.

"Did you just call me sweetheart?"

He shrugs both shoulders, a brash portrait of a man with no regrets.

"Why shouldn't I? I know you better than the little gnat who sent those," he tells me.

Crap. If only he were *wrong.*

How did I almost marry that loser, anyway? Jay never said anything half as sweet as Lincoln.

Granted, I was young and stupid and stuck in a pretty narrow dating pool. Too young for the big moody hero-men in town, who always had their sights set on some other lucky girl.

Maybe I dodged a legit bullet when the asshat didn't show up at the church.

I'm still up in my head and slow to react when Lincoln grabs the bouquet off my desk.

"Hey! What do you think you're doing?" I snap.

"Since they're for charity, I'll handle these for you. Unless you had a specific charity in mind to give them a new home?" His eyes drill into me, knowing damned well I don't.

Even so, my mouth drops as I stare back at him.

"As a matter of fact, I know someone who could use them," I say. He doesn't make any move to give them back and I fold my arms. "Lincoln Burns, if you give my flowers to another woman, I'll cut your balls off and bury them under Eliza's floor."

He throws back his head and lets out a barking laugh.

"Hell of a way to treat your friends, much less your boss. Why not *your* floorboards, Nevermore? Or is having my balls up in your business too much for you?" The way he smirks almost skins me alive.

Holy shit. This man. *This conversation.*

All things that *should not* be happening.

"It's logistics, you freak. Eliza's also my neighbor. I don't live on the first floor, so burying it under my floor wouldn't quite work—"

"So you'd rather have your bestie driven nuts by my balls haunting her? Didn't the man in Poe's story start hearing the dead guy's heart? I wonder what sound my jewels would make if you followed through on your little threat." He looks at me grimly and steps forward, fully invading my space. "I think they'd be shouting *Nevermore* all the damn time."

I try to give my best dead-eyed nod, but I can't help laughing.

This is so dumb. Though I'm impressed he paid attention to something besides making money and growling at people long enough to remember "The Tell-Tale Heart."

"That's...creepily well thought out. And also incredibly stupid. Have you ever chopped people up before, Lincoln?" I wonder out loud.

"Nope. Never had to think like a lunatic until your crazy ass showed up. Must be rubbing off." His lip curls slightly as he looks at me, unmistakable desire heating his eyes.

"Meh. I've never had a boss steal my personal property before either, but here we are."

"Not stealing, Dakota. I'm delivering it to the homeless. There, I found you a good cause and saved you some work."

I'm about to scream.

How can anyone be such an insufferable dill weed and also Mr. Generosity all at once?

"You sure? I doubt Wyatt eats hydrangeas," I tease.

His brows furrow and his eyes go incandescent.

Sweet Jesus.

Before Burns, I never knew a man could send you to heaven or hell with a single look.

"I know I'm right," he says roughly. "Some loser bought you flowers you don't like. Also, it's not Wyatt I have in mind."

"Oh? So now you're trying to seduce some poor homeless lady with flowers? Dude. Why don't you start with a hot cup of tea? I'm sure that'd get you laid a lot faster."

He smiles darkly.

"Some women are old-fashioned. They don't date before a man's given them a real gesture. And for the record, you're the one who brought up getting laid. Fuck, you make me sound like some comic book villain."

"Well, when you look the part—"

"Poe, if I didn't know better, I might think you're just jealous. You've got the most eligible man in Seattle running after you all damn day right now. Why ruin a good thing, right?"

Does he hear himself? I could punch him. Seriously.

"Oh, please. I could care less if you're sending flowers to Vladimir Putin. Just as long as they're not mine anymore. Have at them, I guess."

It comes out pretty harsh. He gives me a hangdog look that melts me right down.

"You said they were for charity, Nevermore. I'm being charitable."

"They were for *me* to donate. Not have my boss steal the show," I say sharply.

"Are Anna and Cheryl still giving you a hard time?" he says, giving the flowers a small shake. "I told her multiple times to back off. If she isn't listening—"

"It's okay," I say quickly, not wanting to cause any real trouble for Anna. "Nice way to change the subject when you don't have a comeback, though. You did that with Wyatt too."

"You didn't answer my question." He glowers. "Are they pushing? I'm serious when I say nobody here has a right to keep clawing at you when I've already vetoed the idea."

"No," I huff out. "But I'm sure you need people here with a little backbone. I mean, you put up with plenty from me, so why not Anna?"

I try to smile sweetly to distract him and fail.

"You're such a shit liar," he grumbles, shaking his head.

"Funny, because I haven't lied to you. Anna hit me up again, yeah, but I can hold my own. I don't need teacher to step in," I say, my tongue flicking between my lips.

It's kinda involuntary. I don't mean to razz him. But I guess it does something because he turns abruptly, clutching the flowers to his chest.

"Lincoln? Wait up, I didn't mean to—"

"I heard the whole thing," he says, glancing over his shoulder. "I saw Anna and Cheryl in front of your desk before I came over here, both of them giggling like eighth-grade girls. They even gave you crap about the flowers. With some attitudes around here, I *do* need to play teacher."

Eep. We're back to scary-hot Lincoln. The Viking Lord in a suit look that turns my tongue to stone.

"It's honestly no big deal," I whisper, pleading with my eyes. "Please let it go. Don't say anything to Anna and Cheryl. They're good people, even if they're a little extra sometimes..."

He stares back at me for a long, heady moment.

"Does that mean you like working here then?" he asks gently.

After a long second, I nod. Sincerely.

"We're the island of misfit toys, right? I belong here. I hope so, anyway."

I wonder how he'll take that, but he smiles.

He gives me an honest freaking smile that's about as rare and gorgeous on him as a sunny day in a Seattle November. God.

"Me too, Nevermore. Thanks for the reminder. This place feels like home for good reason." With that cryptic comment, he stomps off to his office with my bouquet swinging from his hand.

Overgrown bear. I still never know if I'm getting the short-fused grizzly or the oversized teddy.

But with the flowers out of sight and out of mind, I realize sometime later that I must feel better.

I go back to sorting contracts and printouts, trying not to

dwell on how much raw power Lincoln Burns has over my emotions.

* * *

AFTER SIX O'CLOCK, Lincoln comes out of his office with my bouquet in one hand and his laptop bag in the other. He glances over at me.

"Good night, Nevermore."

I look up, shooting him a look.

"Seriously? You really won't tell me who you're giving my flowers to?"

"They're donations, aren't they? I told you, they have a home. Unless, of course, they aren't really for charity and you want to tell me who sent them." His gaze hardens.

I glare back with arctic defiance.

"They're for charity. The rest is none of your business."

If he's fazed by my challenge, he doesn't show it. He just turns his back and starts walking.

Ugh.

For some unholy reason, curiosity eats at me like a dog with a bone.

I want to know who he's giving my flowers to. So as soon as he gets in the elevator, I decide to do something stupid.

I get up and run for the elevator, squeezing into a corner before I mash the button just in case he's still lingering in the lobby.

Nope. I get to the first floor just in time to see him outside, climbing into the company car as he says a few words to Louis.

I'm too late.

There's no way I'll catch up with him on two wheels.

But when I see a flash of yellow driving by, I just can't help myself. I throw myself outside and gesture for the cab.

Water splashes my shins as the taxi swerves to the curb, spraying the afternoon rain puddles before stopping.

Awesome. Now that I'm drenched, I guess I'm committed.

I climb into the back seat and look around.

Lincoln is two cars ahead of us now, wedged between a sleek sports car and a service van for a cable company.

I point in front of us. "Follow that town car, please."

The guy in the front seat laughs and looks back at me in the mirror. "Just like the movies, huh? As long as you're not expecting me to break any traffic laws..."

"Whatever. No. Just follow them!"

I sit back, remembering to breathe. The driver's reaction reminds me how crazy this is.

Here I am, openly stalking my lunk of a boss who gets in my face about mystery flowers and then seemingly has the perfect place for them. Not something that would rustle anybody normal.

But a normal person would *run*.

Far, far away from this stupid crush after the half kiss that night overlooking the city that almost detonated our entire lives.

I'm not normal, though.

I'm a freaking Poe.

So I let my brain feast on all the crazy possibilities involving Lincoln Burns and that bouquet as we drive for about fifteen minutes in slow traffic.

We pass Sweeter Grind without the town car stopping, and then wind around the city for a few more blocks.

The other end of the park, I realize.

Oof.

Was he serious about giving my flowers to the homeless? But why would Wyatt want hydrangeas?

I'm totally baffled.

"You want me to make the block before I pull in, so they don't know you're stalking them?" taxi driver asks, looking back at me with a nosy grin.

"I'm not *stalking*," I lie. "I just need to know where he's going. Important business."

The guy throws back a big belly laugh. Yeah, I don't believe me either.

"Ma'am, that's textbook stalking, but don't worry. I won't tattle. You sure you don't want to make the block?"

I shake my head fiercely.

"No. Just pull in and keep your distance from the other car..."

I hear driver boy snicker loudly to himself again. One more reminder I'm being ridiculous, but when you're in this deep...

I watch breathlessly as Lincoln slides out of the town car, nodding at Louis before he starts walking toward the row of tents.

Huh. Maybe Wyatt likes hydrangeas after all? I suppose it could brighten up his space or something.

I wait at least another minute. Once Lincoln seems far enough away to avoid seeing me, I pay the driver and slip out the back.

I think I get five strides down the sidewalk before the cab engine roars behind me—he'd better get that checked out—and Lincoln spins around to face the deafening noise.

There's only a small group of people walking and riding bikes between us. His eyes find me easily through the crowd.

Oh, crap.

There isn't even time to get away before he's coming toward me with a frown. His body is as straight as an arrow, jaw set and shoulders squared.

Here it comes. The cost of this dumb decision. I should've just logged out and went home and let some mysteries remain unsolved.

"How did you even hear that car?" I ask as he closes in, deciding to try brushing this off as nothing.

He doesn't stop until he's right in front of me, barely a few inches apart, looking down. "You shouldn't keep following me here, Nevermore. It isn't always safe."

Ah, it's lecture time. Awesome.

"Chill. I just wanted to see what you were doing with my flowers, and since you wouldn't spill the big secret..."

"I told you," he growls, his eyes dark with distrust.

"And I didn't believe your non-explanation, bossman. You didn't exactly elaborate," I mutter.

That wins me a smirk, even as he folds his arms.

"I told you enough. Are you calling me a liar, Dakota Poe?"

"Depends. Why does Wyatt want my flowers?" I say, flicking back a loose strand of hair.

But Lincoln stops me. He reaches out, swats my hand away, and tucks the hair behind my ear with slow, measured practice.

My toes scrunch up in my shoes.

It's insane how even the simplest touch makes me a flaming mess.

"He doesn't want flowers, and neither do you," he says, his eyes reaching into me.

Oh, God.

Stay strong.

"So, you *do* have a homeless girlfriend?" I ask, hating that I feel a flick of jealousy. I don't even know her and she probably isn't real, but I already want to claw her eyes out with my nails. I'm just annoyed she might exist. But part of me also wants to slap him for allowing his made-up girlfriend to remain homeless.

"Poe, you're a rotten sleuth. Of course not. You think I have time to date after you went snooping through my bullshit on social media?"

I cock my head, staring up at him, hating how good he is at putting on the mystery man air.

"Then why are we here? Do you just like driving me bonkers?" I huff out a loud breath.

That twinkle in his eyes—the way the evening lights catch and shine—says he just might.

"I'm here to see Wyatt. You're here because you're a freaky

little stalker." He sighs, suppressing a laugh. "Can I be straight with you?"

I glare.

"Sure. I'm trying to think of a time where you've been anything less than blunt..." A breeze blows around us, fluttering more of my hair loose for him to fix.

"I don't care that you followed me. I care about your safety. You came here once when I knew you'd have somebody around and I was expecting you. I wouldn't have let anything happen. But if I don't know you're here and you come snooping around—"

My laugh cuts him off. "C'mon. I'm not some damsel in distress who needs Burns-man to the rescue."

Again, his mahogany eyes darken with an overprotective look that makes me shudder.

"It's not funny. You can take care of yourself, but you're from a small town and you don't spend much time in places like this. There are lot of good people here and a few fucking rats." I should be touched at how uptight he gets about my well-being, I guess.

"But you just said it. I *can* take care of myself. You're also my boss—not my freaking bodyguard—so what does it matter if I decide to take my chances?" I smile up at him sweetly.

He doesn't roll his eyes, even if I can feel his frustration curdling the air around us.

"Dakota, coming here alone after dark to spy on me isn't a choice. It's dumb as hell," he says bluntly.

Harsh. But I can't say he's wrong.

I knew this was a bad move the minute I rushed down the elevator.

"Would you walk in front of a charging bull for kicks too?" he asks. "You're too smart for that shit. Too intelligent to get hurt, all because you have something to prove. That isn't the woman I know—the one I hired who thinks before she trips over her own feet."

He's scowling, practically grinding his words, and it's so hilariously intense I feel weirdly touched. Dallas was mostly a sleepy town growing up, and nobody ever got growly about my decisions or my safety. Not even Jay.

"Are you listening?" he bites off, his eyes still drilling through me.

"Yeah, daddy dearest. I heard you loud and clear through all that grumping." I'm blushing the second it's out, realizing how I've butchered my choice of words.

If there's one man on the planet I should *not* be calling daddy, it's the beast in front of me who has my entire future in his hands.

"I'll show you real grumping, if I need to," he says, scratching his face to hide a slight, adorable redness under his scruff. "If my right hand needs a lesson on common sense, so be it."

"*Temporary* right hand. And I'm thinking the one that's attached to you is just fine unless you're like, into a sock or a fleshlight or something."

He snorts and his lips *almost* turn up in a smile.

"Dammit, Nevermore. Are sex and murders all you think about?" He snorts again, shaking his head sharply. "And for your information, I only need to worry about one right hand. The other works just fine and it doesn't fly solo. I put it to work on whoever's getting me off."

Gah.

My face is on fire. My next breath shakes me to my core.

How did we wind up talking about Lincoln's sex life again?

I'm just grateful he doesn't extend the torture when he glances around the park, looks at me again, and says, "Since you're already here, come on."

"Where are we going?" I ask, trying to catch up since he's already moving.

"You'll see."

I follow Lincoln to the familiar row of tents spaced apart, but this time we stop before we get to Wyatt's. We're in front of a faded pink tent instead.

He bends down and places the flowers in an empty coffee can in front of it. As they're settling, I notice there's a tiny note attached to the wrapping paper.

"What are you doing?" I whisper, my brows pulling together.

In the distance, a grinning Wyatt waves to us.

"Burns? It really is you. Come on over. I brewed up something good," he says.

I give Lincoln a puzzled look.

"Don't say anything. They're for Meadow, the only person besides me who bothers to check in on Wyatt. She's young and kind of cute. I know he likes her, so what's the harm in dropping a few flowers on his behalf?" He shrugs. "She likes plants. He calls her Miss Green Thumb."

My lips turn up in a smile and I almost fall over.

"You...you big idiot. You're playing matchmaker?" My lips quiver because I still can't believe it.

Every time I think I have this man figured out, he bowls me right over again.

"Quiet. Don't let Wyatt hear," he grumbles.

I nod and don't mention it again as we walk, still trying to bite back a smile.

"Come on already. Damn, you guys are slower than snails and that's coming from the guy on one leg." Wyatt sits on a few stacked wooden beams in front of his makeshift campfire.

"He's impatient today," I say.

"He's in a good mood if he's brewing coffee. I haven't seen that in months. We're going to have to pick up the pace." Lincoln's steps grow into a jog.

I struggle to keep pace.

He reaches the campfire before me and drops down on a box. I slow down and catch my breath as I approach them. Smoothing my skirt, I'm about to take a seat on the big crate beside Lincoln when Wyatt looks up with narrowed eyes.

"What the hell, man? Are you gonna let her ruin that pretty dress?"

But before he even finishes, Lincoln shrugs out of his blazer and lays it over the space next to him. *Smooth.*

"Lincoln, that's okay, you don't have to—I'm fine."

I am so not fine. Seeing my grumphole in a suit acting chivalrous makes me feel things I should *not* be feeling in any universe that still makes sense.

"Wyatt's right. Sit down, Nevermore."

I can't even say no. I just drop down beside him, leaving a sliver of space between us.

"Here. You have to try this." Wyatt ladles out a dark liquid in a disposable cup he takes from a sack beside him. He passes it to Lincoln first.

My nostrils flare as I catch the scent. Fragrant coffee, and it smells like it's strong enough to peel wallpaper.

Lincoln sniffs the cup and smiles.

"Smells mighty good." He takes a small sip. "Damn, I like it. Tastes smoky."

I swear I see Wyatt standing a little taller, less hunched over. He's proud of his brew and it's just...nice. Insanely nice to see this broken man care about something besides pastries and basic street survival.

"You want some, Dakota? I don't have cream and fancy stuff to go with it," he warns with a shine in his eyes.

Honestly, black coffee and I don't get along, but I can't stand being rude.

"Yes, please. I'll give it a shot. Just pour me a little," I tell him.

With a friendly nod, he ladles that jet-black rocket fuel into a second cup and passes it over. I'm a little afraid it'll melt my throat. It smells like Eliza's whole apartment after an entire day of cooking up batch after batch of rich espresso and pourover concentrate.

"What trouble are you two in tonight?" Wyatt asks.

Linc takes another hearty pull off his cup, totally unruffled by the potent drink.

"What else? I came to see you. Dakota's just stalking me."

"I am *not*, Wyatt. I...I came to see you too." I stumble over my words, realizing how weird that sounds. "I was hoping you might have a story or two. I'm a fiction writer—a poet, really—when I'm off the clock. I'm always looking for inspiration. How could I know we'd both show up at the same time?"

Lincoln doesn't even look at me but lets out a sigh that says, *Nevermore, you suck.*

"Pure coincidence. Always the best kind." Wyatt ladles himself a drink and glugs down half the contents in one gulp.

"Exactly," I say matter-of-factly.

Wyatt's eyes trail from Lincoln to me. "By the way, if you are stalking him, I don't think he minds. He likes it."

"*Pffft*," I hiss. "He wishes I cared enough to stalk him."

Wyatt chuckles.

"I'm right here, you know?" Lincoln stiffens and takes another swig of coffee. He glances at me sharply. "Can you check my office email while you're here? I'm expecting a proposal."

"Sure." I pull out my phone and open the EA inbox.

I'm pretending to focus on the screen, but I notice he leans closer to Wyatt. "What the hell are you doing? I'm her boss. Are you crazy?"

I couldn't say what Wyatt is, but Lincoln is definitely off his rocker if he thinks I can't hear. If I suck at lying, he's a terrible whisperer. His voice has that deep, resonating boom that could carry through a thunderstorm—or even the Fourth of July.

"I'm trying to help you, man. Lighten the fuck up," Wyatt growls back.

"Oh, yeah? And how would you feel if I hinted to Miss Green Thumb that you've got a beating heart?" Lincoln says, flashing me a conspiratorial look.

"Burns, you leave her alone. I swear to fuck..." Wyatt finishes that thought with a vicious glare.

I try not to giggle.

It's like watching two standoffish bears in a library trying to keep it down and failing comically.

Will they notice if I slide to the edge of the crate? This conversation isn't for me, as funny as it is, and I don't want to eavesdrop when I shouldn't. I'm also well aware of how important it is to Lincoln when his friend has a good day.

It takes me all of one minute to see Lincoln doesn't have any new important emails.

I slide the phone back into my purse, taking tiny sips of the coffee. It's definitely too much for my taste. I try not to gag.

It's bitter without cream, but the smoky undertone is interesting. I'll have to tell Eliza.

I drink half of it one baby sip at a time and feel like that's an accomplishment, considering it's black and strong enough to wake up an elephant.

"...you're just too chickenshit to admit the obvious. Ask her on a real date and stop worrying about your little rules and that great big redwood jammed up your ass," Wyatt says as I look up.

I bite my bottom lip to keep from laughing at that one.

Yeah, right.

Lincoln Burns might grind every gear I have, but he's one of the richest, hottest, and most eligible men in the entire city. Heck, probably the whole country when you consider the billionaire dating pool.

He's not going to date a girl like me who fights him at every turn and hails from flyover country. He's also not the dating type, even if that's something I seem to attract in men.

Even Jay Foyt needed a year to figure out he wanted me enough to ask me out. There's no way I'm the kind of girl Burns dates. Never mind the whole he's-my-flipping-boss factor and therefore off-limits.

"I'm her boss," he snarls at Wyatt like he's just read my mind. "Besides the ethics breach, there's a thick fucking HR policy put in place by my mother, no less, against—"

"Dude, whatever," Wyatt says slowly, flipping him the finger.

Yikes. That's one way to put it.

He'd probably do a better job getting Wyatt off his back if he just admitted I'm so far out of his league I couldn't buy tickets.

Wyatt looks at him again, an expression of brotherly annoyance on his weathered face.

"Man, an alligator-filled moat wrapped in barbed wire and guarded by pissed off HR hawks couldn't keep me from a chance at the good life. This is a golden opportunity—a chance, at least —to have a life outside the office with a beautiful woman. I don't get you, Linc."

My pulse quickens as I wait for a response, but Lincoln just shrugs.

Torture.

Maybe if I remind them I'm here, I can shut down the awkwardness and avoid a brawl over my non-dating life with my boss.

"This is interesting coffee, Wyatt. My friend Eliza could learn from you."

Lincoln looks up quickly and jerks away from Wyatt like they weren't just discussing me. He won't meet my eyes for a long second, but when he finally does, my heart stops.

Lincoln's eyes are as pitch-black as the smoked coffee swirling in my cup and infinitely stronger.

His look is fraught. Questioning. Conflicted.

A stare that splits me in two and strips me naked.

I may bury myself in words until I'm crushed, but after Jay —*because* of Jay—I never believed in hot-eyed looks that could stop time.

Now, I wonder.

I wonder about a lot of things I should be chasing out of my head.

Ideally, before Lincoln damn Burns pulverizes what's left of my heart.

XIV: EACH SEPARATE DYING EMBER
(LINCOLN)

"*E*liza, huh?" Wyatt asks, pulling Nevermore from what looks like a trance.

Not just her.

It's the kick in the ass I need to rip my eyes off the mellow, curious thing next to me. I've been staring, and not politely. The only thing hungrier than my eyes tonight is my blood, which seethes like it has an active current every time I stare at Dakota Poe too long.

Even at night, she's like the goddamned sun.

This indecipherable, overwhelming sight that burns so small yet still has this undeniable power over my entire world.

When the fuck did that happen?

When did I start gnashing my teeth with denial? If I'd never date her—if I *can't* damn well date her—I shouldn't be growling it like a man holding in secrets while he's being waterboarded.

Wyatt's practically a brother and always will be. Though after the shit he's been suggesting tonight, I'm sorry I didn't write out a full-blown love declaration for Meadow to find with his signature forged at the bottom.

"Eliza is my friend," Dakota says vacantly, turning the coffee cup in her hands and staring into it. "My downstairs neighbor, really, but we get along great. She's obsessed with inventing new coffee flavors, and she's always experimenting."

"They any good? The coffee itself, I mean," Wyatt says, wagging a finger. "Here's my rule: if it's no good black, then it's no damn good at all. Don't think you can cover up a shitty weak brew with an assful of sugar and half a teat of cream."

Dakota blinks at him and then bursts out laughing.

I shake my head like it weighs a hundred pounds.

He's always had a way with words.

"Dakota wouldn't know good coffee. She likes her lattes sweet enough to kill and loaded with cinnamon or salted caramel," I grind out.

Predictably, Nevermore glares, but ignores my crap.

"Eliza hits the jackpot sometimes with her stuff. The rest could use some work, but I mean, that's part of the process. Darker roasts aren't her strong suit. I think she's been working on that, though." Dakota fingers the corner of her lip, deep in thought.

I hate how adorable she is.

But not nearly as much as I fucking *loathe* the angry ache she puts in my balls. Why did she have to crack a joke about beating off with my right hand again?

I haven't jacked off in ages, but tonight, it might be the only way I'll ever get to sleep with her up in my head.

"How would you know anything about dark roasts? I've gotten your coffee order before. It's milk and sugar with a splash of coffee thrown in."

"Shut up," she says, rolling her eyes to the moon.

"Creative. Remind me why I hired you to write copy again?" I know I'm being an asshole.

I'm taking out everything Wyatt stirred up on her, and if I have any sense, I should sew my yap shut.

"Um, apparently so you could make me pull double duty as your assistant while your real one went on maternity leave?" she throws back with the usual venom.

That shouldn't make me smile. I hide it behind my coffee cup as I take another long pull off the drink.

"You got a boyfriend?" Wyatt asks, reloading his cup with more coffee.

Dakota looks at me just as I swallow.

She doesn't say anything, but her eyes are bright. Nervous.

They make me wonder why.

"Wyatt, she's out of your league," I say numbly. "Stick to girls who like to garden and can put up with your shit."

Wyatt chuckles and gulps his coffee. "Relax. I wasn't asking for *myself*."

"Wyatt." The look I throw his way could flay him open.

He holds a hand up.

"Hey, no harm, no foul. Just askin'." He looks at Dakota. "You want a story before I hit the hay? Oh five hundred will be here soon enough."

"When was the last time you were up at oh five hundred?" I ask.

"Tomorrow. Busy day."

I stare at him, glowering, wondering what sort of story he's about to tell.

"Hell if I know, Burns. But your girl doesn't want to hang out all night in front of my tent, so take her home after this." He stops and takes a deep breath, holding his hands in front of the fire like the drama queen he is. "Okay. So, I moved around a lot as a kid, and I lived a year or two in this little mountain town called Heart's Edge. They had this spooky old mine everybody always said was haunted, so one time me and my friends went exploring, not knowing these weird military contractor guys were setting up shop—"

"She's not my girl—keep your facts straight," I interject. "That goes for your damn ghost story, too."

"I'm really not," Dakota adds with a glassy look. "I just work for him."

She rips her eyes away from me.

Damn. Why does she look hurt?

"But you aren't working now and you're having a good time. You laugh a lot and you smile real pretty," Wyatt tells her, always the charmer.

She doesn't deny it, just gives back a friendly smile.

"Where are your friends, anyway? If you're not his girl, you must have more fun with them than your worn-out old boss who can't handle his tail being pulled." Wyatt gives me a shameless grin.

I'm so close to decking him square in the face tonight.

So close.

Dakota shrugs. "Eh, I haven't been here that long. I've kept my head down, mostly. Eliza's really the only new friend I've made."

"Where you from?" Wyatt asks.

"Dallas, North Dakota," I answer for her. "Odd little place that's barely on the map like your mountain town. They've got a lot of oil, movie stars settling down, and even the occasional tiger."

"So you were listening when I told you about it." Dakota looks at me and smiles, raising her brow.

I snort, but wonder if I'm digging my hole deeper. She shouldn't look so impressed that I listen to her.

"How long have you been here?" Wyatt asks, a question I don't know the answer to.

"About eight months come June," she answers.

"You should have made more than one friend by now," I say, sipping my coffee. "What, no poet groups worth their salt around here?"

"I'm a working writer. You'd be surprised how hard it is to relate to the self-appointed starving artists who relish their part-time jobs and rolling out of bed at noon every day to hack at a few words. Also, I really like the girls I work with, but I haven't been at Haughty But Nice long enough to socialize a ton. At my old job, no one really talked to anyone. And if they did, it was because they were trying to cut you down. A real crab-in-bucket place. I like Anna and Cheryl but we work a lot. There isn't much time to hang out."

I nod at her, feeling a twist of guilt because *I'm* the reason she doesn't have the free time to socialize.

"Yet you have time to stalk the boss," I say, trying to brush it off.

"Someone has to keep you in line and Wyatt's a busy guy," she says with a nod at my friend.

Damn her, I laugh.

"Yeah, speaking of busy, I was just getting to the good part so pipe down and listen," Wyatt says, shifting back into full bard-mode. With his wide eyes and grizzled beard, he certainly fits the part. "So everybody had stories about the mine, especially this cool old lady who owned the inn, Miss Wilma..."

We listen as Wyatt drones on about getting pumped up on local legends and pushed into mischief by his friends. It won him a close encounter with a mountain lion who decided to settle into that old mine and came flying out after him when one of those late-night contractors started running a jackhammer somewhere deep in the old mine.

All this time on the street may have made him more dramatic, but I've got to admit, it's hard not to wrap a protective arm around Dakota by the time he's wrapping up.

I also know there's a darker edge to his story.

That Sweeter Grind place was founded by a couple sisters from Heart's Edge, and their locations have partly taken off thanks to the notoriety of that little town's craziness in the national press.

"Linc, you disappoint me," Wyatt says. "With Dakota being new and all, why don't you take her for a ride in that fancy car and show her around? Like I said, I've gotta hit the hay. Oh five hundred and all." He stands and lumbers back to his tent.

I watch him unzip the flap, crawl inside, and zip it back up, blotting out the world.

Don't get me wrong.

I wouldn't ever wish for Wyatt's anguish, but there are times when I envy him for being able to disappear at the flick of a zipper.

Also, I make a mental note to kick his ass for egging on Dakota the next time I visit.

"Now that you've had your ghost story, guess that's our cue to go," I say.

"Your friend has a knack for storytelling. He sucked me right in. Umm—what should we do with the cups?"

"You have any coffee left?"

She nods and hands me a lukewarm cup that's still half full.

I gulp it down—one more caffeine hit for the road never hurt —and stack her cup inside mine.

"It's dark, so stay close," I say, reaching for her hand.

It's raw instinct. I'm not sure how she'll respond.

She laces her fingers through mine, twining our hands together with a tightness that surprises me.

"You know what I hate about you stalking me?" I ask as we walk through the cool, oddly quiet night.

"What?" she clips, already over my crap.

"You had fun so you'll keep doing it," I say with deadpan delivery.

"Oh my God! Stop. I am not stalking you. I don't stalk anyone, especially not you. I wouldn't even stalk you if we had a zombie apocalypse and you were the only person left alive who I could trust not to eat my face." She makes a frustrated sound. "Get over yourself. I just wanted to see what you were doing with the flowers..."

"I gave them to a homeless person just like I said, didn't I? And I still haven't acquired a taste for human faces. Sorry, that's a deal breaker," I tell her, fighting back a smirk.

"You're so dumb sometimes."

I lash her with a look. "And you could learn to take a joke,

Miss Tight-ass. I'm in charge of a forty-year-old fashion power-house and I still ham it up."

"Oh, what-the-hell-ever," she whispers. "You did surprise me playing matchmaker. Who knew?"

She's right. It is out of character, but I couldn't resist.

Besides, Wyatt got even without knowing what I did, so I'd say winning him a little attention from something that isn't a cinnamon roll is fair game.

"Did you have fun, Nevermore?" I ask her more seriously.

"Yes! Thanks for letting me hang out. You could've just run me off."

"Purely for Wyatt's sake. The company is good for him," I tell her, frowning because I'm barely a better liar than she is. "It's still early. Should I show you around Seattle or have you seen most of it already?"

For a moment, she hesitates, looking at me like she wonders if I'm setting her up for another kiss neither of us can bear mentioning.

"Fine. What can it hurt? Let's cruise."

Her smile hooks my gaze as we walk. I quicken our pace, leading her closer to Louis and the waiting car.

"Damn you! I told you for the last shitting time—" A huge guy in a stained wife beater shirt comes barreling out of the last tent before the sidewalk, swinging a bottle of whiskey and waving his arms at someone else still inside. "I'm tired of this shit, you bitch. Try me again and I will *burn* this whole fuckin' place down."

Dakota gasps and leans into me, damned near jumping into my arms.

I lock a protective arm around her.

"It's okay. He's just drunk and angry. I've got you," I whisper, picking up the pace as I shepherd her out of here.

I don't blame her for being scared, even if there's no direct threat.

It's nothing I haven't heard here before.

Life in the camp is hard. It's an explosive stew of hurt people, and a few of those people are one bad argument and too much booze away from violence.

I'm almost dragging Dakota along with me. Three paces later, we've passed the guy, and I look back to make sure he isn't moving on whoever's inside that tent.

Sure, I mind my own business. Though if I thought he was putting anyone in danger, I'd step in to stop it after a quick call to the police.

Dakota doesn't move away until we've reached the car, and I make no effort to let her go. Wyatt's words from earlier echo in my ears.

In an alternate universe where tonight was a date, this could be a chance for a life beyond work with a beautiful woman. Wyatt doesn't know she's also brilliant.

There's some truth to it, dammit.

Trouble is, it's the most *dangerous* truth. There are days when I wish I'd lost my leg in Iraq instead of him.

Then I wouldn't have seen the ravages of love with Wyatt, with my mother, with Regina.

I wouldn't have taken a dagger in the back from someone who fed me poison from her lips wrapped in promises.

I love you, Lincoln. Now and forever.

My brain throbs, remembering the most toxic phrase of my fucking life.

I should just bring Dakota home. Call it a night and not indulge fantasies that can only grind what's left of me to a nub. But a promise is a promise, and I've always kept mine.

When we reach the car, I throw open the door for her.

"Do you see why you shouldn't follow me here alone now?" I whisper gently once I'm in the seat next to her.

"Y-yeah. I'm sorry," she says glumly.

"That's not an I-told-you-so, Nevermore." I'm actually *glad* she followed me today. "Just a nasty reminder that this place can ambush you."

She nods slowly. The soft city lamps catch her hair and light it like rose gold.

"I get it. I'll stop stalking you now."

I give her a serious look.

"No need to do anything so extreme."

She smiles. "If I'm not supposed to follow you here because it's unsafe...what's the alternative?"

"Next time, before you turn into the park, call me first. Tell me you're behind me," I say.

"And you'll do what? Give me a raise for eavesdropping?" she jokes hopefully, raising her eyebrows.

"Nah. I'll tell you to get lost or escort you in."

"Oh, Linc, you're hilarious tonight," she says with a small snort.

"Only Wyatt calls me that," I growl.

"And me," she says insistently.

Brave girl.

I pause to mull it over before I give her a firm look and say, "Okay, Nevermore. And you. I suppose it's fair considering what I call you—and Linc is a big improvement on Captain Dipshit."

Damn if we don't both laugh at that.

Damn if I don't fall deeper into her while her face screws up, her cheeks glow, and her green eyes catch this honest, happy fire that traps me in the sweetness that is Dakota Poe.

We drive around Seattle for over an hour—probably to Louis' delight and fat overtime pay—and when I'm out of places to show her, I take a chance and throw my cards on the table.

"Do you want to come back to my place for a glass of wine?"

She gives me a worried look. I'm about to tell her I misspoke when her lips turn up.

"I dunno. Can you cook? I'm about to gnaw my own arm off."

"I can order the finest takeout this city offers. Pizza or Thai?"

"I can do DoorDash on my own and you didn't answer my question," she says with a smile. "Do you cook?"

I shift in my seat before I glare at her.

"For you, Nevermore, I'll surprise you." That's putting it mildly. I haven't done a simple spaghetti aglio e olio in ages and hope I remember how.

Her laughter echoes through the back of the car.

"So, that's a yes then? Linc, you'd better wow me."

Goddamn, do I want to.

And you'd best believe I don't mean with food.

* * *

DAKOTA STANDS against my balcony railing, peering out at the night sky after dinner.

She sips from her wineglass when she's not wearing a permanent smile.

I'm feeling mighty proud I put it there. Thank God I remembered how to make that stupid pasta without burning the garlic into a rancid mess.

Deciding to try my luck, I step up behind her, closing the space between us.

"Fair is fair, Nevermore," I say, feeling my blood heat when her eyes catch the city lights.

"What, you're asking me to cook for you now? I suppose it's a fair trade," she says.

"Might take you up on that someday, but that's not what I'm getting at," I tell her. "You know who I gave the flowers to and why. When will you tell me who sent them?"

She goes quiet, staring out over Puget Sound and the few pinprick lights from passing ships.

Fuck.

I don't want to ruin this, but I have to know.

"They're from *my* stalker," she says finally, her eyes meeting mine. "And not the fun kind who puts up with all of my crap and always breathes cinnamon rolls."

"Someone's stalking you for real?" Everything inside me

turns to steel as she nods. "Dakota, talk to me. I'll get you a protection order ASAP."

Hell, I'd love to do more than that.

Like use every resource I have to hunt down whatever worthless ratfuck would do that to her, and have a nice, long talk with my fists.

I'm not a violent man.

I've only lost control *once*.

It should say a lot that she brings out baser impulses I've tried to bury, searing my vision red every time I imagine her in danger. It should run me off.

But when she turns to face me fully, running is the last thing on my mind.

"Lincoln, I don't think he's truly dangerous. Just really, really annoying. He won't give up. And I think he found some website to buy phone numbers by the boatload because every time I block one, he finds a new way to come at me," she says glumly.

My jaw tightens.

Dangerous or not, that's not something any stable man would do.

I don't like the sound of this one fucking bit. Silencing a growl, I pull her into my arms.

"Who are we talking about? A bad date? Some asshole ex-boyfriend?"

She clutches her glass so hard I see her fingers go white.

"The idiot who chickened out of marrying me." She trembles slightly when she says it.

That only pisses me off more, turning the red I'm already seeing into ruddy murder-darkness.

"We'll get a restraining order. They can cover digital harassment like the sort this little pissant is engaging in. Plus, if he's calling you from random numbers and sending shit to the office, it's a corporate security issue, too. I won't stand for having my people threatened and attacked at my workplace. It's a safe space. We can't let this go on."

She shakes her head, her soft hair spilling down her shoulders against my hand.

"I—Lincoln, please don't take this the wrong way, but... I don't want your help with this. I can handle it." She swallows. "If I have to keep blocking him, so be it. Maybe if it escalates, then—"

"If it escalates, I'll break his face," I snarl. She looks up at me, her green eyes wide and glistening. I clear my throat. "Sorry. Not really. Not unless he was about to hurt you, I mean."

Truly, I meant what I said the first time, and the fact that I'm willing to go that far almost scares me.

"Linc..."

"If you change your mind, I'm here for you. That's what I'm trying to tell you. I've got your back as a boss and..." I pause, unsure what to even call this ball of tension and banter and gentleness between us. "As a friend."

She looks up at me, but not before swiping her cheek, catching a tear.

"Thank you. I appreciate that, even if you're being a little harsh."

"What's wrong?" I urge, pressing my finger to her face, wiping away the wet grief she doesn't need to hide.

"W-what do you think?" she stammers.

"I'm not a mind reader. Talk to me."

I shake my head.

She bites her bottom lip. Another tear falls, bigger and angrier.

"It's just... I mean—okay—s-so I know I dodged a bullet not marrying the asshole. But why do you think it took him a whole year after the wedding to think he made the wrong choice? Like what made him *leave* in the first place?"

It's like I can feel the stone pelting her heart, the way this boy shattered her.

Even if he was her age, he's a fucking *boy*.

267

No man would ever abandon a beautiful, smart woman after promising forever.

No man would come crawling back like a snake a year later, angling for a shot at killing what's left of her heart.

I wipe her face with my hand again.

If I ever see this guy, I'm going to kill him. Straight up annihilate him and expedite him to hell.

Who waits until their wedding day to leave a woman? And *this* woman? He'll never find anyone else like her, and he doesn't deserve her.

But right now, she's crying in my arms over *his* damage. I wish I could erase him from her memory, her whole life.

"I-I'm sorry. This is so embarrassing. God, what's wrong with me?" She presses her face into my chest while my hand runs through her hair.

"Nothing's wrong, Nevermore," I whisper.

I mean it.

There's something completely fucked in his head.

She needs to know she's wanted, that she's not crazy for hurting or confiding in me. She's damn sure not crazy for aching to feel desired.

I've never wanted anything so badly in my life.

She wants it too. I know because she said it in verse when she slipped.

It's not like the night I missed my chance thanks to a dumbass driver without a muffler. When I wait for her to look up with my eyes burning, she doesn't lean in or tilt her head.

She doesn't know it's coming.

There's a halting second where I just hold her. Her surprise grows when my arms drop from her shoulders to her waist, pull her in, cradle her tighter, and I can't hold back.

I press my lips to hers like a man who's starved, even knowing full well she's just as ravenous.

In a split second, she opens her mouth and whimpers against my lips.

All soft, pleading sweetness.

She's fucking shaking.

I'm not sure if my heart is still beating, but I won't miss my chance.

I'm not missing another opportunity with this woman. Not tonight or ever.

With a hot rumble in my throat, I push my tongue in her mouth, slowly and fiercely.

I'll show her she's not some pitiful conquest. Not a mistake born from emotion and all the weird turmoil around us tonight.

I need her to see she's *cherished.*

Her teeth graze against my tongue. I groan now, dipping in, tasting her fully and loving and hating it because I know I'm already addicted.

Goddammit, Dakota.

Her arms tighten around my shoulders.

I feel her nails pressing against my shirt, scratching, begging.

With a rough sound, I move in, pushing her against the wall, taking what's mine and exiling every doubt from my brain. We're way past reasonable thoughts.

We're two mouths, two bodies, two souls drawn together by a thread of pure lust. When she gives me those soft green eyes, I break, driving my tongue against hers as it flutters softly against mine.

This is it.

All I have to do is grab her, toss her over my shoulder, and—

Clank!

There's a sharp, fragmented noise that startles us both.

Something cold and wet runs down my back.

Dakota jumps back, breaking our kiss, blinking in confusion.

"Nevermore?" My voice is ragged, far more desperate than I want it to be.

"Sorry. Oh, the wine," She bends, trying to collect the remnants of her wineglass.

"Leave it. You could cut your hands."

"Leave it?" she echoes.

I nod, and this time when I pull her closer, I'm far more demanding. I'm not losing her over a broken damn glass I'll sweep up later.

She doesn't hesitate, at least, folding her arms around my neck.

Her lips find mine automatically.

Our tongues meet again, twined and hungry.

It's getting hard to breathe. Even the air itself with this woman—that Dakota hint of mint and sweetness—makes me feel more intoxicated than the two glasses of Cabernet I tossed back earlier.

"Oh, God," she moans, leaning into me, her knees going weak as I kiss her off her feet.

My grip on her tightens, shoring her up, my fingers tingling with pins and needles. I need to feel her, roam her bare skin, squeeze her nipples, plunge into her drenched depths.

These hands need to take her apart and claim every piece.

I swallow something hard in my throat, moving away from her mouth to kiss her jaw, then igniting a neat line of fire down her neck.

"Linc, what are you doing?" she whispers with an innocence that makes my cock seethe.

"The fuck does it look like?" I snarl, nipping at the space under her ear with my teeth.

She shudders so intensely she almost falls over.

"Do—" I stop to run my tongue along her jawbone.

"Oh."

"You want—" My lips swipe across the top of her neck.

Her arms tighten around my neck. She's trembling.

"Me to—" I trace my tongue down her skin before I breathe out, "Stop?"

"O-only if you want to." She draws in a deep breath, staring with wide, needy eyes.

Is that an easy out for me, or does she think I'm not enjoying this?

"I'm asking what you want, woman," I rasp. "Tell me now. Sixty more seconds of this and I can't hold back."

"I-I wish this could last forever," she whispers, her lips pursed in a biteable pout.

I chuckle. "You being poetic or trying to tease me into the ground?"

Our eyes lock.

"You choose."

Enough.

My choice is fucking sealed, written in the lust churning through my veins.

I lower my head, pressing my forehead against hers like I'm marking her skin. "I can't make this night last forever, but I'll make it memorable."

Again, she shudders, tempting my hands to start tearing off clothes. I don't care if they're a shredded heap on the floor soon, I'll replace them all.

"Do you say that to all the girls?" she whispers.

I move one hand to her hair, running my fingers through light-blond silk. I shove my lips to hers again, taking her mouth good and deep before I answer.

"Not until now. I've never said that shit to another living soul."

It's all she needs to hear.

Her hand comes to my face, covering my bottom lip, her finger lingering. Stroking. Teasing. Caressing me to sin.

She leans in, her tongue tracing the inside of my lip before I feel the harsh tip of her teeth.

I'm out.

I'm no longer in my own fucking body in this state.

With a rough snarl, I scoop her up in my arms, toss her over my shoulder, and start moving with my hand grabbing her ass.

Dakota lets out a messy squeal.

"Lincoln! What are you doing?"

I don't answer. Not with words.

I just carry her to the outdoor sofa behind us and fling her down under me. I need to cool off in the night before I self-combust. I pull her on my lap, already addicted to the soft contrast of her hair in my hand and all the ways I want to take her apart.

"Look at me," I whisper hoarsely.

"What?" Her eyes are glowing.

"You heard me."

The moment she does, I twine her hair around my fingers. I clasp it and pull, firmly but gently, worshipping the way her head falls back. Her eyelids flutter shut and a gasp slips out of her.

I almost come in my pants.

"Goddamn, Nevermore," I whisper. "*God fucking damn.*"

The side of her face moves against my chest and she wraps her arms around me. We stay like that for a fraught minute, both of us trying to breathe, obsession running like a current in my blood.

"It's a beautiful night," she whispers.

"You have no idea," I growl back, making sure she knows I mean what's laid out in front of me.

I've been on fire since our lips met, and the way she's pressed so snug against me isn't helping one bit. But the smile she gives me a second later makes my desire go nuclear.

"Now who's teasing?" Her eyelashes sweep low and her face glows red.

I have to devour her. *Have to.*

Have to do it right now in the quiet hole of night while I'm a flaming wreck, leaving any grim consequences for morning.

"You drive me insane," I tell her.

"Oh, please. You have no idea what it's like to be at arm's length—always a kiss away from disaster every day."

Away from you, she means.

Her confession makes my entire being throb.

"No, but I do know what it's like fighting tooth and claw to keep an enticing woman away even after you know she's thought about fucking you. Hell, after knowing she's *written* about it."

She blushes and bites her lip and I am so completely gone.

I grab Dakota's waist, my fingers digging into her skin, raw hunger strumming every nerve I have like a heavy metal ballad.

"It was totally inappropriate," she whispers.

"That's a funny way of saying it was hot as hell," I growl back. "I only gave you shit about it because of the effect it had—"

"Effect?"

"You don't know? You don't know how many times I've jacked off to being your Ivory Adonis, Nevermore? And I'm not a man who makes a habit of using my hand." My voice is rough gravel being tossed around. "Even before you butt-emailed me that poem, the times I thought about it—"

"No way!" she hisses, shaking her head in disbelief.

"What?" I narrow my eyes.

"You're just playing it up now. I can't believe you thought about *that* with me. I'm just average and you're..." She swallows thickly without finishing that thought.

I smile like the devil.

"Average isn't a word I'd ever use to describe you. I only wish you knew your own worth, Dakota Poe," I whisper, moving in.

"What worth?" she whispers faintly.

My nostrils flare as I inhale her, my soul bristling at how close, how aroused she is.

Her stubborn disbelief makes me want to show her how wrong she is. A lesson in red madness that'll take all night and leave us both spent.

"Now, you're just pissing me off," I whisper. "You refused to sell me a cinnamon roll for five hundred dollars. You're not intimidated by me, and you're so beautiful it almost knocks me on my back. When I tell you how special you are and you don't believe it...you don't even know, Nevermore. You cannot comprehend the shit I want to do to you to prove it."

I feel her shudder.

"God, you're shameless, Mr. Burns," she whispers.

"Don't call me that."

She blinks at me.

"Mr. Burns. We're past that. I'm Lincoln when we're alone like this, and nothing else," I breathe against her lips, my cock throbbing every time I remember how much I love hearing my name on her tongue.

"...do you think we'll be alone like this more than once?" she asks eagerly.

"You think we won't? You're the one who wants this to last forever. I'm no poet, but forever usually means more than one night."

"Fair point, Romeo." She picks up my hand and kisses my fingertips, slowly and softly and one at a time, turning me inside out.

I close my eyes and sigh.

It's all I can do to delay shredding her clothes, throwing her under me and spreading her legs.

"Enough talk. We have a lot of night left and very little patience." I kiss her forehead.

"Promise you're okay with this?" she whispers.

I reposition her in my lap so I can seal that promise on her lips, pushing my tongue deep into her mouth.

I write my vow on her person and steal it with a stolen whimper pulled from her lungs.

I sign the fucking thing with my hand on her tit, finding her nipple, and pinching it like it's already mine because —*goddammit, yes*—it is.

I promise by devouring Dakota Poe until she's a quivering, red-faced, hot little mess.

I'm almost blue from the frustration in my balls spreading by the time I rip myself away from her for a few ragged breaths.

"There. I promise, Nevermore," I say sternly.

She looks at me and smiles before her mouth joins mine again in sticky sweet bliss.

I hold her as close and as tight and as jealously as I can.

I wish I could keep this moment pure, innocent, special. But with my body starved for hers, I don't have a prayer of being a choir boy tonight.

My hips rear down against her, pressing into her like an animal in a mating dance, my cock growing harder by the second. We're both in a fever, rolling on the sofa, taking our turns on top and bottom with a storm of biting kisses.

"You even fight me for kisses," I muse, pressing my hands against her back when she's on top of me, staring into her eyes.

When I start to shift her over so I can push my hand between my hard-on and her leg, she moves first, swings a leg over mine, and straddles me.

Fuck.

A hoarse sound grinds out of me as I move my hands to her hips, dragging her against me greedily.

"You'll slaughter me," I tell her, deadly aware this can't end anywhere else but my bed.

"Slaughter? Did I do something wrong?" Her emerald eyes go round with mischief. "Should we—I mean, I—we—umm—should I stop?"

Does she hear herself?

Should the sun not rise tomorrow?

My teeth are bared as I take her lips again, moving my tongue in and out, languidly but fiercely, leaving no doubt what I want from her.

"...but you said I'm driving you crazy," she whispers when I break away.

"Only in the best way, Nevermore. Have me committed, just as long as I get you naked." I can't believe she's still giving me nervous eyes. That little screwball did a real number on her.

I've got to convince this woman she can trust herself, trust her own emotions, trust the fact that she's hot perfection any man would feel eternally grateful for.

"Sorry. Lincoln, I just—"

"No more excuses. Shut up and kiss me again," I growl, fisting her hair and helping guide her mouth to mine.

My lips find hers again. I relish in the sweet, unsure way her tongue traces mine.

Every movement.

Every sigh.

Every heartbeat.

Every nip.

Her teeth catch my bottom lip as she has a burst of confidence and then falls away trembling.

I'm about to complain, but her mouth moves to my neck. She kisses and explores me with a frenzied interest that tells me she's wanted to for a long damn time.

"Oh, God," she moans, clutching my shoulders for support.

She has no clue.

How badly I want to be buried inside her with her body thrown around mine. Her kisses are a flash flood in the desert.

Sweet as heaven, but they won't come close to quenching the thirst, the animal need driving every inch of me.

Her small fingers brush the skin under my shirt collar. She pulls it down.

Cool night air tickles my skin and then the warm caress of her tongue.

Mania, your name is Lincoln Burns.

Inhaling sharply, I cup my hands under her ass and stand, keeping her in the same position as I urge us upright.

"Where are we going?" she asks in a tiny voice that says she already knows.

"Inside," I answer.

I'm not fucking waiting for her legs to work. I lift her again, pull her into my arms.

She starts at the base of my neck with the sweetness of her

tongue, her teeth, and the full glory of her tease. She's made it up to where my neck meets my jaw by the time we're moving through my place.

With a lot of deep breaths and miraculous focus, we make it upstairs to the hall outside my room.

Her fingers come to the top of my shirt. She runs one over the bare skin of my throat and then places her other hand on the top button.

"If I were to push this out of the hole—"

"I'd be offended if you didn't," I say.

That's all the encouragement she needs.

She's smiling like I've never seen as the button pops free.

I open the door to my bedroom and lead her to my four-poster bed, dropping Dakota in the middle of it.

"Straight to the point, huh?" She blinks up at me, always using that damned mouth to tease even when it's not on me.

"I plan to make you squirm," I promise.

"Um, I think you've already done that..."

I try like hell not to grin because she hasn't seen anything yet.

I take my shirt off slowly, my dick pulsing, fully intent on teasing her back.

She stares at me longingly, her mouth slightly parted in raw curiosity.

As I slide the shirt off, she crawls to the edge of the bed, sits up on her knees, and runs her hand down my chest.

I close my eyes and sigh.

"So gorgeous," she whispers.

"Not half as great as yours, and it'd be a shame if it was."

She laughs. "But you haven't seen mine yet!"

Yeah, that's a problem I plan to rectify soon.

"We can fix that. Come the hell here," I order, tugging her up and reaching behind her. I unzip her sundress halfway and work the straps down her arms.

My eyes are glued to hers until the dress slips down. It falls under her chest, revealing a lacy peach bra that looks like it was custom designed for sin.

That's saying a lot from a man who's been more involved in women's fashion than ninety-nine percent of the male population will ever be.

She crosses her arms in front of her chest like she wants to hide, fresh uncertainty on her face.

"I always thought you'd wear black. Interesting choice," I tell her.

"Yeah, I...I don't have a body like yours. Or the models you've probably dated."

"Fuck models and fuck *that*. I wouldn't dare have you ruined. You're perfect the way you are," I say, sincerity vibrating my voice.

"Umm—I just mean I don't think I have a body like the kind of woman you're usually with." She looks down like she's searching her own imperfections.

"And yet I've never wanted another woman like I want you." The wild truth of that burns my throat.

She casts a slow glance at me like she's trying to figure out if I'm being honest or just putting her on.

Enough talk.

Enough games with words.

I just smile, take her hand, and hold it to my mouth, kissing her palm slowly, furiously, madly.

By the end of this night, I swear to everything holy that Dakota Poe will know what she does to me.

She'll finally understand just how deliciously remarkable she is.

XV: UNCERTAIN RUSTLING
(DAKOTA)

I think I'm on fire.

Lincoln takes my hands in his, peels them away from my sides, and drops to his knees beside the bed, kissing the edge of my lace bra.

He traces down the curve, brushing his tongue against the hard peak of my nipple.

I'm flipping electric.

Falling back, I wrap one arm around his neck, pulling him closer.

His hands join his mouth on my breast, sucking and teasing, detonating me in slow motion. The only thing between us is the peach lingerie now.

My eyes close and my head drops low.

No man should ever make me feel this good.

"Oh. Oh, Lincoln," I whine, mouthing those words more than speaking them.

My legs are already jelly.

I'm not sure how much longer I'll even keep my balance, but I just know I need more. I'm drenched in pleasure, edging on breathless, and he's barely begun.

It feels divine but it's still not enough.

Reaching behind my back, I grab my bra clasp, helping free my offering for this devil's tongue.

His hands move to my arms, grabbing my wrists. He stills them before moving them aside, pulling his face off my breast.

"I promised to make tonight last, sweetheart," he rumbles, his eyes restless with dark-brown desire.

"But I kinda need this now," I whisper, brushing my breasts against him.

"Not yet," he clips. And then I understand—his tongue goes to work against my other breast, sucking and rubbing and lashing me to bliss.

God!

I'm clenching his head, my nails digging at his scalp, needing to hold on before Lincoln freaking Burns sweeps me away with a fever. He finally reaches behind me and hurls my bra away. It hits the wall somewhere on the other side of the room.

I'm down on the bed again, falling under him, and he's still tasting me. Still licking. Still scorching nerve endings I never knew I had.

It was never like this before.

Never, ever this intense when I've barely gotten started.

I'm so in the zone, soaked and buzzing.

It's heaven on Earth. It's also like being yanked out of a perfectly warm bath when he suddenly lifts away.

I glare up at him.

You weren't supposed to stop.

But he returns with a feral smile, kissing down my belly and only stopping when he comes to the waistband of my panties.

"P-p-please. Take them off," I sputter.

"Not yet," he warns again with a slow laugh.

I want to punch him.

But I also want him to take his sweet time, to rend me in two, to make me *remember* what he's doing long after I'm just another memory.

I know this won't last, but I've made my peace with it.

One smoldering night with Lincoln Burns is worth a thousand nights with forgettable men.

In a single slow breath, I feel strong hands clutching my thighs. He parts them with ease and I fall flat on the bed. I'm on my back with my legs in the air.

Lincoln stands still, clasping one ankle in each hand as he rises. He presses his lips to the arch of my foot.

The sensation makes me giggle.

Soon, he's winding up again, kissing my ankle and moving up the inside of my leg one soft kiss at a time. By the time he reaches my thigh, I'm clawing at the sheets.

Keep going.

Oh, God.

Please.

I swear he can read my mind.

Because Lincoln moves to my other leg, pushing his mouth against my inner thigh. He kisses down the too sensitive inside of my leg, adding an unexpected nip of teeth.

I'm shaking.

Desire courses through me like a relentless wave, too strong and too serious to even let me laugh this time.

Lincoln turns me gently, slowly, so I'm now vertical on the bed.

His massive, shirtless bulk climbs over me, making me feel a hint of his weight, his power.

He brings his mouth to mine with a claiming stroke of tongue.

Hotter than ever.

He kisses me with depth and meaning and a message I can't ignore.

Tonight, I own you, he says with every kiss. *Tonight, Nevermore, you're due to be fucked in ways you never knew were possible.*

My nails dig at his shoulders. I trace his lips with my tongue.

His mouth opens, and I glide in, chasing after his demanding tongue.

My hands go to the button of his pants. He puts a hand over them and breaks our kiss.

"How many times do I need to tell you? *Not yet.*"

His eyes are glinting so hot it *hurts.*

"You'll give me a heart attack," I whisper.

"I'll resuscitate you then. I think you see I know a thing or two about CPR." He gives me an evil wink right before his mouth crushes mine again.

This man.

This absolutely cocky, brash, chiseled man.

I try to match his passion as his tongue caresses mine, as his teeth graze my bottom lip. I'm rewarded with a guttural "fuck" thrown from his mouth.

Yes. Please. I so want you to.

But he means what he says about taking me apart on his terms. When he moves away from my mouth, it's to kiss a neat, burning line from my cheek to my ear. His hands find my wrists and shove me down, pinning me to the bed while I push back against him.

"See? Told you I'd make you squirm," he growls.

I'm about to protest, but his tongue traces my earlobe and shoots down, attacking my throat.

I whimper.

"You're so goddamned gorgeous when you light up," he mutters, and then his mouth is back on mine. His arms slide under my back and he pulls me closer, a glimmer in his eye that says he wants to make every last bit of me shine like the sun.

And he's closer than he thinks.

I'm utterly soaked. Trembling and aching. Too close to an explosive end without even having him inside me.

That's never happened before with a man.

Not even close.

With a throaty sigh, I wrap my legs around his waist, arching into him.

Thunder boils up his throat and his face screws up.

It's almost that scary-hot look I see around the office—except ten times more intense—and I nearly come on the spot.

Somehow, I buck against him again, pushing my legs around his.

With a snarl, he pushes me down and flips me around. His thick hands find my zipper and he rips it fully down. I help shimmy the dress away as he slides it out from under me.

My turn now.

When my hands move to his pants, Lincoln doesn't stop me. I unbutton his slacks and push them down.

I gasp at the bulge outlined in his boxers.

Considering he's Big Dick energy incarnate, I should've expected as much.

But seeing it in the flesh is—*holy hell.*

"Are you just going to stare, Nevermore, when you like what you see?" he whispers darkly.

Oof. I think I need a paper bag to breathe into.

Especially when he pushes me back and takes my nipple in his mouth again.

With almost nothing left between us, the flick of his tongue feels a million times better than before. My head rolls back as I moan loudly.

It's hard to touch him, even though I want to, like I'm laying hands on some rare, exotic beast.

I stroke his back with my hands.

Down, down, down...until I hit the elastic waistband.

I tug at his boxers and he lets me—thank God—pushing them down. Then my hand circles around, brushing against his hard length.

Eep. He really is huge, angry, and pulsing so hot against my fingers.

He goes stock-still.

I'm not breathing as I clasp his girth, marveling again at his size, and start ever-so-slowly sliding my hand up and down his length in steady pumps.

"Dakota."

Hearing my name on his lips releases my breath.

It's the *way* he whispers my name, equal parts harsh and awestruck, that sends goosebumps racing across my skin.

For a second, he lets me stroke him quietly.

His eyes never leave mine, two earth-toned storm clouds crackling with lightning.

The sex in the air is so thick it's stifling.

But he finally moves, placing his hand over my arm and moving it gently away from him. He threads our fingers together, kissing my knuckles, and shifts his weight as he pushes me back into the bed.

He's on me like a wolf, his hungry erection rubbing against my opening.

I take a deep, ragged breath so I can force out the words, "Wait. *Not yet.* I have to make you squirm..."

His eyes smile down at me, even as his face remains a stone mask.

"You think I'm not wrecked on the inside, woman?" he whispers. He laughs once. "Nevermore, you always surprise me. I like it."

He's not lying. I can see how honest he is as our eyes lock in a fraught stare, both of us asking for the one thing with the same silent demand.

"Lift your cute ass," he orders.

I do, pushing up on my feet.

Again, his rough hand comes between my thighs, grasping my panties in the middle.

In one swift flick of his arm, they're gone, flying over his shoulder in a ball.

Our eyes fuse as his lips come home to mine. I watch him tear open a condom with his teeth—he must've pulled it out of his pants' pocket when I was distracted—and then he's *there.*

All swollen, angry head at my entrance.

A guarantee of Lincoln Burns' darkest intentions.

My fingers flatten against his torso, feeling his body drawn like an arrow. My legs wind around his waist, pushing against him, begging him to do it.

For a breathless minute, we're frozen just like that, until his powerful hips roll forward.

Oh, shit. Here it comes.

He slides into me with a single slow, punishing thrust.

I bite down, clenching my teeth, because it's almost like losing my V-card again as I stretch to take him. We become a whole new feeling made flesh.

I couldn't put it into words to save my life.

We're coiled tongues and stalled breath and insatiable silence.

We're flesh and steam and mingling smells, his masculine citrus and pine against the flower and mint that always shadows me.

We're two battered hearts, our souls beating out of us, desperate to join.

I bare my teeth, panting, scratching his chest *hard* as I ask him to do his best, his worst, his everything.

"Damn you, Lincoln Burns. If you don't—"

One harsh movement of his hips shuts me up fast.

He grinds into me, slowly at first and then faster, *faster*, finding a rhythm that was always meant to reduce me to ash.

"Oh!" I'm gone. Too infinitely lost for words.

He kisses me roughly, shoving his tongue against mine as his cock glides in to the hilt.

"Goddammit, Dakota," he growls as his mouth breaks away with another powerful thrust.

Is it wrong that this sex feels a little scary and that excites me?

The man is a human battering ram working in slow motion to take me over.

A human wall of muscle and the sweetest cruelty.

Yeah, I won't last long at all, and I'm already too out of sorts to even be embarrassed.

My face screws up as I arch to meet him, throwing myself against him, my O coming like a racing wildfire.

Then it happens—he pulls away at the very last second.

I open my eyes, a question hanging on my lips.

"Not yet," he whispers. "I told you, Nevermore, you're going down on my terms."

He smiles, moving to the edge of the bed. After a weightless second, I follow.

That's where he guides me into his lap, pushing my legs apart. I slide over him with defiance in my eyes as his gaze locks.

If he thinks he's in full control...think again.

When I wind around him, I'm smiling like a madwoman.

"Careful what you wish for," I tell him.

"Like what? Watching every sexy bit of you shake while you come on my cock?"

Speechless.

Yeah, if I've learned anything by now, it's how ridiculously good he is throwing me off-kilter.

And he leaves me dizzy as his hips lurch up, slamming into me, raking this divine friction over my clit.

I clasp his shoulders, holding on, pleasure tearing me in two like a flimsy sheet of paper.

Again, he thrusts, his rough fingers coming to my jaw, tilting my face up just as he rocks into me again.

"Look at me. Give me every bit of those green eyes when you go off," he growls, his stare beaming pure dominance into my brain.

His hands move back to my hips and stay there, guiding my movements so I match his.

Soon, our pace quickens, and I don't have a single solitary prayer of holding on.

"Oh! Lincoln. I'm going to—"

He looks right through me, fingers digging into my ass, his thrusts coming faster and harder and deeper.

"Tongue," he commands.

I give back a whine. My eyes roll up in my head and I'm going, going—

Gone.

The second he leans forward and takes my mouth, swiping his tongue against mine, I'm vapor.

He swallows every breathless moan I give, every whimper, every fractured part of me going to pieces on his hardness.

My hands move up and down his back frantically to the back of his head, scratching him, joining us closer, deepening the kiss that destroys me as he sends me to nirvana.

My body clenches around him.

The room goes bright with white-hot fireworks.

I'm coming so hard I forget my own name.

Holy shit!

I'm an awestruck mess.

Time condenses.

My pussy experiences miracles I never fathomed until I was struck down by Lincoln "Zeus" Burns, sex god.

The craziest part is, he's not even finished.

I'm barely coming off my high for air when I see him staring, waiting patiently, letting me breathe.

Or maybe *not so* patiently.

His breathing is different now, his massive chest rising and falling, his face screwed up and his mouth pulled slightly open.

"Lincoln?" I venture. "I-is something wrong?"

"Yeah. I'm enjoying this ride so goddamned much I never want it to end," he rumbles, twining my hair around his fist.

Then it's on.

Another hard round where he crashes into me, making me ask a thousand times how I could ever hate this man.

Kiss by kiss, he's wearing me down, making me worry I won't ever be able to hate him again.

What then?

What the hell happens when we're back in the office, trying to pretend this never happened, and—

"Dakota!" He bellows my name, a smolder in his eyes, the unmistakable look of a man—a wild animal—who's losing control.

Oh, God.

My heart races.

I don't even try to hold back as he wraps his arms around me and flattens me against the mattress.

As he thrusts back inside me with claiming teeth at my throat.

As he reaches down, finds my clit, and rubs with maddening intent.

As he swells, as he whips me around like a doll, as he breaks me down for any lesser man, past and future.

With one last cry of "Nevermore!" he fills me to the hilt.

He releases so hard I swear *I feel it* through the latex.

But a second later, I can't feel anything else as my body ignites a second time.

Sweet, searing chaos swallows me up and doesn't spit me out until I'm nearly blacking out.

"Damn, Dakota. Dakota, fuck," he mutters a few minutes later, alternating my name with curses.

We're both flopped down on the mattress and he's holding me. He runs his fingers through my hair, slow and still so sensual, his eyes calm mocha seas that could go unruly again at a second's notice.

"Did you enjoy that?" he whispers.

"Do you have to ask? Um, yes. God, yes." Heat pumps under my face, but I don't have to worry. It's just the two of us and a long, dark night ahead where I'm sure he'll deliver a lot more to enjoy. "Honestly that was... Gah. I can't even compare it to anything else."

"You're beautiful when you look like a cherry, Nevermore," he says with a torn laugh.

He caresses me a few more times, pulling softly at my hair— that seems to be his new favorite thing.

Then he stands, and the moonlight spilling in splashes his naked body.

He's really, truly, undeniably glorious.

But I bite my lip, suddenly nervous.

Is that it? Am I wrong about tonight? We had sex and now he's going to get dressed and go about his evening?

And isn't that what Jay did, always going back to his dumb video games, where he'd spend half the night yelling at strangers when he could've been holding me?

My heart slams my ribs. I wonder if I'll *ever* trust a man again.

Lincoln looks back, his face that broody mask again. I still wonder what secrets, what doubts, are stewing inside of him.

"Are you leaving?" I venture anxiously.

"I need a shower to recharge. You want to come with?"

My heart flutters back into place.

"Umm, I would, but...I'm not sure I can stand." Embarrassing, but true.

Laughing, he rejoins me on the bed, tucking me neatly into the huge, protective arch of his body. "How about we just lie here until your legs work? Then we'll clean up dirty."

I'm smiling so hard I want to cry.

Thankfully, I don't. I just kiss his cheek instead.

"Oh, I like that. I like that a lot." I'm quiet for a heady minute. "That was the best I've ever had," I finally say, working up the confidence.

"Same," he throws back.

I do a double take.

"Okay, now I *know* you're lying."

"You think I ever lie about anything besides Regis rolls?" he asks with a grin.

Laughing, I roll my eyes.

"I find it pretty hard to believe a man like you hasn't had more—uh—attractive partners."

Why, yes, that is my own terror speaking.

"Believe what you want," he says casually, right before he melts me with another kiss that only Lincoln Burns could ever give. "Now, I have to ask, did your muse get any fresh inspiration?"

I stare at him for a hot second.

Then I snap my head down and sink my teeth into his arm.

"Hey!" He pushes me off him, laughing. "Did you just bite me?"

"Yep. Because I warned you to quit talking about that stupid poem."

"It wasn't stupid," he says firmly.

"It was."

"I liked it. Best words anybody ever said about me." He thumps his chest once for emphasis.

"Oh, God. You had to say that, didn't you? I was crying, Linc."

"And you're not crying now. I still love that I have my very own blond stalker writing poetry about me—and she's a freak in the sheets, too."

I elbow him playfully in the side.

"I'm *not* your stalker."

"Shame. I adore your type of stalking, Nevermore," he says, kissing me deeply before I can even blush.

Slowly, but surely, those kisses lead us to our feet and then to a master bathroom that could fit three of my freaking apartments. It's a sleek, modern design with sparkling glass, a sauna room attached, and spotless white tile gleaming next to midnight-blue-and-gold cabinets.

He takes my hand and leads me underneath a stream of water that pours from *two* waterfall showerheads. I think I've gone to another world while Linc gently washes my back.

When we get out of the shower after so much more kissing,

he dries me off with an oversized towel. He wraps me up in it neatly before lifting me off my feet again.

"What are you doing?" I ask.

"Nothing you won't like. Trust me."

Smiling, I bat my eyes.

"Why does that make me so nervous?"

"Don't know. You worry too much, Nevermore."

We sail back into the bedroom, where he sets me on the edge of the bed and unwraps the towel slowly, one side at a time.

Then he's kissing me again, only stopping to drop to his knees. His mouth moves to my belly button and slips down.

"What are you doing now?" I ask breathlessly.

He answers, but not with words.

When his tongue finds my clit, I understand.

God, do I *understand.*

His tongue flicks back and forth, sweeps inside me, moves like he's writing his name inside me.

Lincoln grabs my thighs and holds them apart, pushing me against his face, bringing me *home.*

"Oh. My. Whoa," I mouth slowly.

"I'm coming for your muse, sweetheart," he whispers, stopping just long enough to look up at me with fire in his eyes. "Hold the fuck on. Lie back. Let me give you colors worth the words."

He grabs my legs the same way he did earlier and resumes his position after I'm flat on my back.

Then it's just his mouth, my pearl, and a scream lodged in my throat.

His tongue is relentless, gliding down my seam, taming my pussy with wild abandon.

With trembling legs pressed to his face, his beard and his heat and his unforgiving mouth throw me into the hottest climax of my life.

* * *

I BLINK my eyes open and wonder why I'm sleeping on a cloud.

This bed is a sort of soft I didn't know money could buy. I'm nestled under a fluffy white blanket that might as well be a marshmallow. The furniture around us is marble-topped.

Why am I not in my apartment again?

Oh, right.

The best hours rush back to me. My mouth drops open.

Oh, shit. I'm *that* girl.

The girl who sleeps with her boss—and relishes it.

I'll face the fallout later, but right now, I wouldn't trade last night for anything.

I need to get dressed and make excuses so I can get home and freak out about how much I've blown up my life.

Rolling to the side of the bed, I start groping around on the floor for my clothes. Nothing touches my hand. I pull the comforter across me and sit up to look. The floor is clean.

Huh?

I scoot to the other side of the bed and try again. I find nada.

What the hell? Where are my clothes?

I jump out of bed and quickly search around the entire bed. Everything is just gone.

I spot a plush white bathrobe lying near the foot of the bed, though.

It's ginormous, but I tie it around me anyway, unlock the door, and start searching for Lincoln. I'm going to have to swallow my pride and ask if he's seen my clothes, I guess.

As I move downstairs, I think I hear—whistling?

Yep. Definitely whistling.

I follow the sound and find him in the kitchen, which could rival Eliza's place with heavenly cinnamon and vanilla perfuming the air.

"Morning, Nevermore." He holds his arms out.

Umm—what? I blink.

Am I still asleep and dreaming? Either way, I walk into his embrace.

He hugs me tightly and kisses my forehead.

"Did you sleep well?"

"I did. But, uh, have you seen my clothes?"

"They're in the dryer. By the time we eat, they should be ready," he says, his eyes shining happily.

Sweet Jesus. What universe did I wake up in?

"You...you washed my clothes?" I say slowly.

"Yeah. Thought I'd do you a favor." He shrugs like it's nothing.

My jaw scrapes the ground. But before I can say anything, there's a loud *ding!*

The oven timer.

Lincoln strides over and pulls out a tray of huge, piping hot cinnamon rolls. "Give them about five minutes and I'll get the frosting on."

He cooks?

Well, I knew that since last night, but...he bakes? He makes me freaking cinnamon rolls?

"You made us rolls?" I ask, disbelief ringing in my voice.

"I wasn't sure what else you usually ate for breakfast." Again, he shrugs like he isn't demolishing what's left of the stuck-up suit I used to think he was.

"Who are you and what have you done with Lincoln Burns?" I shake my head, my hair lashing my shoulders.

"I'm a thoroughly satisfied man this morning," he growls, swatting my butt.

I jump. Heat burns my face and I double over laughing before I look up. "Jeez. If I'd known you just needed to get laid to act like a human being, we could've adjusted your attitude a long time ago."

He stiffens.

"That's not why—"

I smile. "No. Of course not. Sorry. Bad joke."

"You cleared my head, Nevermore." He nods. "I woke up thinking maybe we should reconsider Anna's idea."

"Anna's idea?" Oh, what? The idea hits me like a Mack truck. "You can't mean—the fake engagement thing?"

"Yeah. That 'thing,' as you so eloquently put it," he says with a snort.

I'm not sure how I'm still standing.

"Are you crazy?" I toss at him.

"Dakota, if you're interested, I could use a lot more of last night in my life—"

"Sex?" I interrupt.

"*You*, but sure, the gravity defying sex is great, too."

My heart rivets. My face is on fire. My everything short-circuits.

"I mean, I guess I *would* like that. I'd love spending more time together, if only that charade wouldn't create a million other problems."

"Worrywart," he whispers, stroking my hair. "Where's my spitfire who tells me to go to hell on a daily basis? She disappeared when I kissed her, and I don't want that. I like her."

I wonder if he's right.

"Sorry. I haven't been in this situation too many times—"

"Situation?" His eyes search mine.

"With a man—like that, I mean. And the last time I was, it didn't end well. I'm just afraid if you're serious and things get out of hand with this goofy engagement trick..." I trail off, my brain spinning too far to finish.

"You still think you're unlovable? Listen to me," he whispers, tracing my cheek with his finger. "There's nothing fucking wrong with you, Dakota. That little ant who ran out on you just had his head up his ass so far he could spit into his own throat."

I laugh at the crude statement.

"But what does spending more time together have to do with Anna's scheme?" I ask.

"It's too soon to talk to HR about this since we don't know how serious it is—"

"Oh. Right!" I say too eagerly.

He's right. We don't.

I'm still convinced this is just a crazy hookup and my rabbit brain is making a mountain out of it.

"We'll need excuses if anyone notices a change in our demeanor. Need to explain why we're spending so much time together. Anna's fake wedding shit gives us the perfect cover. Plus, I think you agree it's a crazy-like-a-fox marketing plan. It could give the wedding line unprecedented reach."

"This is really fast," I whisper.

Not to mention *intense*.

Me, men, and engagements—fake or otherwise—don't normally get along.

Don't get me wrong.

I'm as much fun on a date as the next gothy poet chick. I look okay in a wedding dress—as good as any short, slightly awkward girl with white-blond hair is, anyway.

But it's the combination.

The skyrocketing stakes.

The alien feeling of *caring* again and bracing for disaster. I know how it ends and the potential final chapter of this situation *scares me.*

My brain says *run, Dakota.*

Run fast. Run far. Run to safety.

"Dakota?" he urges.

"Can I think about it?" I whisper.

"Can you think while wearing pretty dresses and taking pictures with me?" His eyes scan me up and down. He's as relentless as ever. "I think I'm going to request another dress design."

Why did his eyes roam my body as he said that? He doesn't think I'll do justice to the current designs?

"Why's that?" I wonder, searching his eyes.

"Because I know exactly what I want to see you wearing," he says without a shred of doubt.

The way he says it reminds me of last night. Memories of

being held as he pummeled me into the mattress invades my mind.

"Yeah? What *do* you want to see me in?"

"Something that hugs your curves and shows some skin. Without showing too much skin that's for my eyes only," he adds with his brows pulling down.

I smile. "You like leaving something to the imagination, huh?"

"Yeah, makes me want to tear it off you like a candy wrapper. But I like that everyone else has to keep guessing, too, and only *I* know."

The jealous look he gives daggers me. Three cheers for scary-hot men.

"Possessive much?" I joke.

"Not usually."

He doesn't elaborate until I urge, "Why now?"

"Got cursed by a girl with a raven tattoo," he says with a comical shrug.

God help me, I step closer and kiss him again.

When I try to pull away, he places his hands behind my head and keeps me there.

"See? This is why we should try. If we're faking an engagement, we can do this to our heart's content and no one will think twice."

I hate that his madness has a certain logic that *may* make it worth a shot.

"But Lincoln, if I have to be in it before I can decide, then I can't really think about it, can I?"

"Not if you plan on talking yourself out of it," he throws back.

"What if I don't want to fake an engagement with my boss who doesn't know how serious we are?"

"Do you know how serious we are?" His stare hardens.

For a second, I hesitate.

"Um, how can I? I never thought this was even possible. Aside from not being anywhere near your league—"

"That's bullshit and you know it," he cuts in.

"You know what I meant. The only man who ever showed any interest in me before is a loser starving musician who won't stop hounding me. It's safe to say I'm out of the league of someone who's worth—whatever Scrooge McDuck numbers are in your portfolio. Not to mention a guy who's the talk of the Seattle paparazzi."

"That boy was a worm, and if men don't approach you, it's because you're intimidating." He thumps his chest lightly. "What if you've met the man who isn't afraid?"

It's freaky how well he has me pinned down.

"How intimidating can I be?"

"You're beautiful and feisty and hurt. That's a lethal combination. Nobody wants to be shot on sight trying to pick you up. Men—no, little boys—are scared to approach you."

Somehow, that makes me smile.

"You're scared right now. Don't be," he whispers gently, sweeping me into his arms.

But I step back, stunned at how well he reads me now. "You know my history. I don't know, a fake engagement, even one where the people closest to us know it's just a ruse...it's a lot."

"It's a lot for me, too," he says with a heavy look. "You're not alone in the broken hearts club. I was engaged once."

I do a double take as his eyes focus on me.

"Her name was Regina. She danced ballet, everybody loved her, and I put a ring on her under the radar so we could avoid the press. She was also a pathological liar."

My heartbeat quickens. I hate this Regina already.

Especially when I see subtle lines deepening across his face, hinting at just how much damage she did.

"I came home early to surprise her with tickets to Broadway and an evening flight to New York one day," he says, anger curdling his voice. "I found them together. In our bed. She was draped over him like a fucking sheet, naked as the day she was born."

I gasp, a quivering hand coming to my mouth.

He must realize I'm about to fall over because he grabs me, holds me so gently, and touches his forehead to mine.

"That's awful, Linc. My God. It's almost worse than what happened when Jay left me," I whimper, my heart aching for him even if deep down, a selfish part of me is glad it didn't work out with this cheating bitch.

"Don't, Dakota. There's no need to compare," he says gently, his eyes glowing in the morning light as he peels back to look at me. "Hurt isn't a contest, sweetheart. It's not about better or worse. We all walk away with battle scars and bad memories. It only matters whether or not we let that shit rule us. It only matters if we let yesterday ruin tomorrow."

I'm almost crying now.

I never imagined he had it in him to be so deep, to peel back my layers, to find my core, my soul, my truest heart. But that's where he is now.

That's where he's always been destined to wind up, now that I know Lincoln Burns shared my uniquely rotten agony the *whole freaking time.*

"Can...can I ask you something?" I whisper.

"Hell yes." He strokes my hair.

"Why weren't you afraid of me, Lincoln?"

He chuckles. "Like you don't know?"

"That stupid poem?" I'm blushing.

"No. That stupid cinnamon roll. The first day we met," he growls. "Dakota, I wouldn't have been able to stay away from you forever if we kept butting heads. This would've happened faster if I wasn't your boss, believe me."

"Oh. I always thought you saw me as an annoying nerd then."

"You are," he says fearlessly. "But you're a beautiful, feisty, and talented little nerd. You're the whole damn package. So if I send Anna an email letting her know that her idea is brilliant and the extra push we need to compete, will you be pissed?"

I think for a long second before I slowly, but firmly shake my head and whisper.

"No."

"Good." He kisses my forehead. "Now, are you going to help me frost the cinnamon rolls?"

"Sure."

We finish the rolls together and sit down at the table.

I haven't noticed until now, but right in the middle of the table there's a bouquet of bright-blue flowers with violet centers. Instead of the normal baby's breath mixed in with a bouquet, I see midnight-black and smoky grey feathers. The ribbon is tied up with a crystal raven.

I smile before I force my face straight.

Yesterday wasn't planned. He couldn't have had time to order flowers...

I'm baffled.

Lincoln picks up a roll. "Are you going to keep pretending there is nothing on the table?"

He takes a manly bite and looks up from his pastry.

"For me?" I ask cautiously.

"Do you see anyone else here?"

I reach out and slide them over, loving their scent. "They're beautiful. Seriously."

"I thought it was high time somebody gave you flowers you'd like after I jacked the ones you hated," he explains.

Mentally, I'm speechless, but I manage to say, "Oh. Oh, wow. I love them."

"Look at the card." He gestures.

I don't see a card. There's a flat piece of cardboard with three small plastic objects glued to it. One silver, one blue, and one black.

It takes me a second before I ask, "So, the feathers are—"

"Pens, Nevermore." He grins and nods.

Oh, crap.

My heart bursts into a million pieces. Even my parents never gave a gift that's so me.

"Lincoln. This is amazing. But how did you get flowers here?"

"Favor."

"What favor?" I ask, laughing.

"I gave the word and my driver put it together this morning. I tipped Louis extremely well."

"That man might be a miracle worker. Almost as much as you," I add, turning away because if I meet his eyes, I *will* be in pieces.

I only wonder one thing.

How messed up is it that my fake engagement is already turning out better than my real one?

XVI: THRILLED ME (LINCOLN)

I stare down at my phone, wondering if I've reverted back to age fifteen.

Mom: Lincoln Burns, you tell me how you let this happen. How is it I find out from Cheryl that my only son is getting married to the beautiful new copywriter? Come home for lunch!

I snort, shaking my head as I type back, **Cheryl was also supposed to tell you it's a ruse, Ma. It's marketing. Not matrimony.**

Her reply flies back like a bullet.

Mom: Regardless, this is the closest I've ever seen you to love since that wretched woman. Come home, Lincoln. We need to talk.

I mutter about ten curses, swiping a hand over my face before I hit her contact and call.

Let's get this over with. Because if we keep texting, this shit will go back and forth all day.

Word travels too fast in this office. I just sent the email to Anna last night letting her know that Dakota and I decided to go along with this madness.

How the hell did Cheryl even find out? And why did she have to tell Mother the instant she heard the news?

"Are you on your way?" Mom says breathlessly, picking up on the first ring.

"No, Ma. I'm working. It's the middle of the damn day."

"I guess your lovely assistant didn't forward your change of plans. You're visiting your elderly mother, so hop on the first ferry over to Bainbridge."

My brows pull down. "For the record, you would've slapped me if I'd called you my elderly—"

"I'm glad you know your boundaries. I taught you well. Now, prove it by having lunch."

"There isn't much to talk about. It's a harebrained idea marketing drummed up to sell the new line. Anna pitched it as a weird sort of personal endorsement that will catch eyes, and she's right. We're new to the wedding scene. We don't have a chance in hell of competing with the big players unless we're bold and a little unorthodox."

"Mm-hmmm. Sure. Do you ever watch the Hallmark channel, Lincoln?"

I actually laugh. Do I look like I have time to binge-watch love stories?

"You know I don't, Ma. Why even ask?"

"Because. Half of their movies start out with a fake relationship and end with a baby," she says defiantly. "Now, since you agreed to this and that lovely young lady did too—I'm holding out hope. Unless you paid her to do this? Oh, Lincoln. Please tell me she's not just in it for the money. Although plenty of great love stories start off that way, too!"

"Ma!" I'm so annoyed I could spit.

She laughs. "You're just offended that I asked. I'll see you in an hour, son."

"I'll *think* about it. You can't just tell me what to do," I mutter halfheartedly.

"Do not disappoint me. And fake arrangement or not, I should have Miss Poe over for dinner soon. We have a spectacular wedding to plan." She sighs. "I just wish your father was here to see it."

"There's nothing to see. It's a fake engagement and there'll be wedding photos with no wedding."

"No wedding?" She sounds aghast. "Well, we'll just see about that. Are you on your way or what?"

Damn her, she's insufferable.

"Fine," I grind out, ending the call as I stalk to the elevator.

* * *

ROUGHLY AN HOUR later after a ride through traffic and a ferry hop with the cool breeze hitting me square in the face, I open Mother's front door.

She rushes over to hug me like she hasn't seen me for ten years.

"You're finally engaged. I don't have to live forever."

"Fake engaged, Ma. And you won't die on us since Dad checked out early."

She squeezes me tight before her embrace softens and releases me.

"No one lives forever, and your father didn't go willingly, of course. He'd never do that. It was just his time."

Yeah. The last thing I want is to relive Dad's untimely demise.

"Why am I here again?" I ask.

"Because I'm excited for you, Lincoln." She claps her hands in front of her chest and then pinches my cheek. "Fake or not, you're finally moving on."

Fuck.

A terrible part of me wonders if she might be right, and if I am...what then?

"I've said it a dozen times and you're still not listening. I'm not getting married. I'm not even engaged. The crap is a marketing ploy, and nothing else. I don't plan on getting married for a few more lifetimes."

A little pitchfork digs at my brain as my words turn over.

If that's true, why did I tell Dakota we'd spend time together without any bystanders sniffing around until we find out how serious we can be?

Seriousness has its limits when I've sworn off marriage to the grave, right?

"Come here, dear. I need to show you something." She takes my hand and leads me to my father's study. The same room has served as the family library for years. It's barely changed since the day Dad died like a weird sort of memorial to him frozen in time.

Shelves line the soaring walls, overflowing with books.

The entire space breathes with a literary soul, whispering in ink and old pages, dreams and ideas and bygone wisdom. I'd spend whole afternoons here growing up, my nose stuffed in a volume bigger than my head, teleported to Narnia, Neverland, and Middle Earth.

I wish like hell I was in a fairy tale now.

Then I wouldn't be standing here, watching as Ma moves to one well-organized shelf and starts pulling out books for some big lecture. Looks like she's milling around in fiction.

Sometimes she pulls a book out, scans the front cover, and replaces it quickly. When she's done rifling through them, she has a stack of paperbacks in vibrant red and white and pastel colors that she needs both hands to hold.

"Here. Read at least three of them," she says with a severe librarian look.

I look down. The first book on the stack has a man so airbrushed he can't be real with a woman in his arms and a grinning pig behind them.

Hog Fights Under City Lights: A Second Chance Romance by Emily Bristol.

"Aw, Ma, you're kidding, right? I don't have time to read romance novels. Can't you skip to the point?" Yeah, I already regret coming here.

"These are all fake relationships that turned into happily ever afters. I met Dakota at the office the day I brought cupcakes. You could do worse, you know. Oh, and I hope you found whoever was so rude to her and taught them some manners." Her left eye twitches with this funny little tic she has when she's mad.

Considering the rude asshole was me, I'd say the lesson was received.

Also, Nevermore's new name should be Snitch.

She holds the stack of books out for me insistently.

I make no effort to take them.

"At least choose one!"

"Ma, this is insane. Sure, life imitates art sometimes, but real relationships aren't based on lies and..." I pause, my eyes flicking to the top cover again. "Pigs who *smile*, apparently."

"Boy, where is your imagination?" she mutters under her breath before dropping the books on a table. "Fine. Be that way. But if your 'marketing stunt' opens the door for you even a little bit, I'll pray you don't mess this up."

"There will be no messing anything up. It's not real," I tell her. "I want you to acknowledge that, Ma. Prove to me you're not losing it."

She folds her arms and glares.

Okay, fine. Maybe I took it too far.

"And I'm waiting for you to acknowledge I want grandbabies, Lincoln Burns. You let a few more years slip by and you won't be a spring rooster anymore."

"It's spring chicken, Ma," I correct. "And maybe you should adopt."

"That would make them babies. I said *grandbabies*," she tells me with all the seriousness of a judge reading out a life sentence. "That means you need to adopt or get laid."

I jolt back. Did she really say that?

"Ma, my sex life is none of your business," I snap.

She laughs. "You're turning red."

"What? Like hell." My hands move to my ears where I feel that telltale heat from two little traitors attached to my head.

"See? You're thirty-two years old and you still can't lie to me." She laughs like she's possessed and then stops suddenly, leveling me with a wide-eyed look. "Waitaminute. I *know* that look, Lincoln. You *did* get laid. Was it Dakota?"

She claps her hands together.

Yeah, fuck this. I'm out of here.

Turning my back, I stare at Seattle's distant outline across the water, wishing I could teleport back there. I'm not even pretending to answer her question.

The whole point of agreeing to Anna's insanity was also to protect Dakota's reputation if anyone ever found out about us. She may be a firecracker, but she's as fragile as blown glass. I won't have anyone breaking her when she's already cracked from that assclown who hurt her.

"It was her, wasn't it?" Mother asks quietly.

"Why would you say that?" I turn slightly, looking over my shoulder.

"Because. If it wasn't, you would have just denied it until you were blue in your face. You're miffed but you're not even putting up a fight—"

"Ma. You're being ridiculous."

If there was ever an evil smile, she's wearing it now. I try not to wince.

"Well, now. This might just be easier than I thought!" Her unfriendly smile blossoms into a grin like she's already visualizing Dakota with a basketball-sized stomach.

Please. Someone put me out of my misery.

"I could've lived my whole life without hearing that, you know. Save the fireworks, Ma. You're not getting grandkids next year. It's just not in the cards," I tell her firmly, scratching the back of my neck.

I feel like there's a spider trying to burrow under my skin.

"Whatever you say, dear. Brunch?"

"I already ate this morning."

She frowns. "We'll call it tea if that makes you feel better. But come sit and talk to me."

"We've been talking, Ma. Hasn't been helpful."

The stare she hits me with says I don't get a choice.

"Look, what you're overlooking is the fact that these cutesy books and movies about fake relationships blossoming into something real are just stories. This is real life. We're both professionals and while I can't speak for Dakota, dating isn't on the agenda. She's been burned before and I... You already know."

Mom stops midstep with a sad look. "*Who* hurt that poor girl, Lincoln? And yes, we know who hurt you."

"Can we not go there again? We've only been through it a thousand times." I shake my head bitterly. "My point is, don't get too attached and overprotective with Nevermore—Dakota, I mean. It's all a farce."

"I'm not. I'm just curious." She picks up her pace, scuttling around the kitchen while I linger at the breakfast bar.

"It's not my story to tell, Ma. You know I won't violate an employee's privacy like that and I'm damned sure not dating her." I ball my fists on the counter and stretch my arms. "You should be happy your rules are still ironclad."

"Oh, rules, fools." Again, she hits me with those puppy dog eyes. "You're a good man, Lincoln. Sometimes too good for your own well-being and mine."

A few minutes later, we gather at the table. I help carry a snack tray into the dining room while Mom pours piping hot tea.

We're dancing around the greatest betrayal of my life—my clusterfuck of an engagement—and I hate that even years after the carnage, it still has the power to suffocate this room like a goddamned mammoth.

For years, the same song and dance.

Mom pleading for me to let it go while I insist I already have. Then I go right back to my safe life with zero room for love, for sex, for anything.

That begs the question. If we're both damaged goods afraid of anything serious and I've admitted this isn't a romance story, what am I doing with Dakota Poe?

I just know I'm craving more of last night.

With her, I need it a million times over.

"You're doing a fine job with the company. I'm proud of you," Ma says, setting down half a sandwich. "But I don't know where you got the idea that work is everything. We raised you to know better—"

"And I'm here right now with you, in the middle of the workday."

My eyes fall on the picture hanging behind her. It was their fortieth wedding anniversary. Ma wears a blue sequin dress dancing with a light in her eyes as she stares at my father adoringly. Dad wears a perfectly fitted tux and a smile too big for life on his weathered face.

His arm is snug around her waist. Her head is pressed against his chest.

A dagger goes through my chest.

Growing up, people always talked about how vibrant Mother's smile was even as she aged. A few weeks after that picture was taken, I lost my father to a brutal heart attack.

It took about a month to realize Mother's gorgeous smile died with him. Her old pure love cast in bright-white teeth was eventually replaced with a new smile, a quieter one where her mouth always stays closed.

It's never been the same since.

My mother has a lot of smiles: the kind ones, the wicked kind, the frustrated kind, and the slow, nostalgic kind she wears when she thinks nobody's looking.

She just doesn't have *that* smile anymore.

Watching Dad's unexpected departure take a piece of her soul was almost as bad as losing him.

She still refers to their fortieth anniversary as her farewell party. Dad died on a charter flight coming back from a business conference. He was gone before the plane even landed for help.

To her, their last anniversary was the closest thing to goodbye.

Even now, I peer at the tired eyes and subtle smile across the table from me.

One more good fucking reason why I'll never get married.

I don't care what they say; it's not 'better to have loved and lost.'

Better to be safe from that pain, that agony, that destruction.

Better to spend your life making money and bringing order for thousands of people, with a dab of debauchery thrown in when it all gets dull.

Mom is living proof.

Ditto for Wyatt.

I'm damn sure not making the same mistakes.

Mom sips loudly from her teacup and sets it down with a heavy look. "Lincoln, dear, I don't mean to be morbid, but what happens when I'm gone someday? Who's your family then? You have cousins out east, of course, but they have their own lives."

"There's Wyatt—" I stop myself, hating that I have to wonder if he'll even be around.

"Ah, yes. That heartbroken, troubled man who—"

"Saved my life," I cut her off before she reminds me what a lost cause he is. "I owe him my all, Ma. You know that."

"...son, you know how much I love that you care but...just how long will he be around? If he chooses not to help himself, I mean. He lives rough and doesn't take care of himself. Who will you have left if I'm gone and you just can't turn Mr. Emory around?"

"My company. My team," I grind out, hating that her question darkens my whole head.

"Haughty But Nice?"

Christ, isn't that enough?

I nod and slurp my tea.

309

"Well, as your mother, I'm holding out hope that she-who-won't-be-named didn't ruin you forever. And I choose to believe this little game with you and Dakota might just be the fire under the butt you need."

"You watch too many movies. There's no such thing as true love—"

"Yes, there is," she says fiercely, drawing up in her chair. "I know. I had it once."

"You did." My voice softens with this gentle grief I haven't acknowledged in ages pushing up. "And you haven't been the same since—"

She sets her cup down with a loud *clink!*

"So? Lincoln, that doesn't make our love any less real. It was so real and beautiful that I still have a punk in a fancy suit across from me talking like a smartass." She sniffs loudly.

"Sorry." I hold my hand up defensively.

Her face falls before she looks at me again.

"It's okay," she whispers.

"Ma, look, I'm trying to let you down easy before you get any ideas. If you keep believing this is going to magically morph into a real relationship...you'll wind up pretty disappointed."

"I've been around the block, Lincoln Burns. I'll manage." She pauses, staring into her cup before she says, "My only question is, can you handle a teensy bit of surprise in your life?"

Can I?

Her question haunts me as I finish my tea, wondering why I feel so goddamned annoyed that I can't answer it.

* * *

SATURDAY MORNING, I find Dakota perched at her desk, diligently working.

There's something wrong with my brain.

Even the way her little fingers move nimbly over the keyboard does terrible things to my cock.

I know how those hands feel. This woman could be gargling mouthwash with two-day-old bedhead and I'd still want her under me.

"I hope you're not planning on giving me more work," she says as soon as she looks up.

"What the hell? I don't even get a hello?"

"Only if you promise you aren't task dumping. It's the weekend." Her little pout makes my teeth ache, stricken with the urge to bite her.

"Scout's honor," I say.

"Somehow, you don't strike me as a Boy Scout."

"I was a Marine," I mutter. "Does that count for anything?"

She hesitates.

"Hmm, well, I suppose."

"Listen, I got an email from Anna. The photographer wants to do our first shoot next week. I know you hate weddings, so I thought we could take my boat out today and try out the setting alone as a trial run. The clothes are already aboard. You can choose a dress you like before the shoot and you'll have a chance to get used to everything without the pressure."

She casts a longing look and sighs.

"Linc, I know what you're trying to do and I appreciate it, but it's not necessary. I know what I agreed to. I won't mess up the shoot."

She smiles up so bravely, my bright girl with the sun in her hair and determination set in her face.

"What if I just want to see you again on my boat?" My body tenses.

"At least you're honest. Usually when a man 'just' wants to see you again, there's some flimsy excuse."

I narrow my eyes.

"You criticizing my game, Nevermore?"

"More like calling it out."

Brat. I see the smile she's trying to hold back.

"Well, fuck, I want to see you again regardless. It's a nice day on the water, but I do think it's a good idea to prep for the photo shoot. I'll pick you up in a few?"

"Sure," she finally says, glancing around.

It's always a skeleton crew in the office on the weekends and everyone on the floor already went home. Even if they haven't, my mind says fuck it.

I lean down, cradle her face, and pull her lips to mine.

She moans real sweet for me as I drink her deep, my tongue hinting at exactly what I intend to do.

* * *

LATER, we're on the open water, cruising the Puget Sound while Seattle's evening lights are just beginning to twinkle in the distance.

"Jesus. When you said boat, I thought it'd be some James Bond speedboat. Not a hotel with a hull," she says, whistling quietly into the wind as we stand on the top deck.

"Got it. I knew you were obsessed with size, Nevermore. Ever heard the phrase that it's not the size of the boat but the motion of the ocean? Thankfully, I'm blessed with both."

"Idiot!" She whacks me playfully in the arm, laughing.

"Has work been awkward since we committed to the wedding hoax?" I ask, shifting to a serious tone.

She shakes her head, her hair whipping around delightfully. "The only people making dumb jokes about it are Cheryl and Anna, and I'm pretty used to that."

"Why are they giving you shit?"

"Well, Anna's convinced we have chemistry—the real kind—and Cheryl agrees. She's a huge sucker for romance movies."

"No wonder she's best friends with my mother," I groan, raking back my hair.

Dakota's green eyes catch mine a second later.

"And what do you think, Nevermore? Does their teasing ruffle your feathers?"

She blushes, but her face is tense. "Chemistry is a loaded word. I think I'd call it energy potential."

"Energy potential?" I snort. "You sound like a physics teacher."

She bites her bottom lip, oblivious to how it makes my dick lurch in my pants.

"Well, we definitely have potential for—umm, *inspiration,* as you put it before—but I kinda thought it was a one-off. You said you didn't want it to be, and that's why we agreed to this whole wedding farce, besides the marketing benefit. But this is the first time we've really talked outside work since it happened..."

"Yeah. I'll admit I can be an idiot sometimes," I say slowly.

Laughter sputters out of her. "No argument there!"

"Careful, hellion. Are we cool, though?" I stare at her, needing her to say yes.

"...I don't know, Lincoln. You tell me."

"I hope so. If I've upset you, let's lay it out, here and now."

"No. We're good," she says softly, her eyes searching mine.

"I want to believe you, but you are a Poe. I can't dismiss the possibility that you're planning to murder me in my sleep and bury my heart under the neighbor girl's floorboards. You're just waiting for one more round of the best dick of your life," I say with a slow smile.

Her grin stretches from one red ear to the next.

"I won't murder you—even if your attitude might deserve the death penalty. I still need you to sign my paycheck."

I laugh. "Glad you have one good reason to keep me around."

The distance between us closes and we're standing toe to toe. She props her hand on her hip.

"Thanks for reminding me I've been signing stuff for you a lot lately. I could probably forge your signature."

"All this fluff and you still won't mention the real reason you like having me around, huh?" I lean closer, audibly inhaling her scent.

I feel her weight shift. She leans up on her toes, flushed scarlet as she gives in, brushing her lips to mine.

Here we go.

Growling, I pull her in, mashing her perfect tits to my chest. One hand skims down the small of her back, stopping to toy with the upper curve of her ass.

"Do you want to see the wedding line or do you just want to fuck? They sent several dresses in your size," I rasp against her ear, adding a nip of my teeth. "I'd love to see you in them before they're on the floor. But if you'd rather skip to the best part, I'll hardly complain."

"God, you're just..." She trails off, trembling in my arms, overcome with the same desire coursing through my veins. "...I don't particularly like white. Fair warning."

"You're beautiful in any color. And you never finished that thought about me, Dakota Poe. What do you think I am?"

"Bossy. Way too flipping bossy for your own good. One day it'll give you a bruising," she whispers.

"As long as it's you leaving marks," I say with a shrug.

Then I take her hand and lead her to the upper cabin near my suite, where the two largest cabinets with the clothes are set up.

"Oh, no. Are we doing that thing where you tell me what to wear and I have to do it because girls and weddings and you're my boss and blah, blah, blah?" She makes a funny face.

"We are. I want a private show with you modeling everything for me. Don't bother going anywhere between dresses, I want to see you changing." My tongue flicks across my lips like the fucking serpent I am.

She hesitates, and I smack her delectable ass lightly.

"Everything's in there. My tuxes, too." I point to one door and use my thumb to gesture behind me. "Let's change separately for this first round and I'll meet you in the room in fifteen minutes?"

"Sounds good." Her shoulders are high and her spine straight as she marches into the cabin where I had the gowns laid out for her.

I'll hold off on round one before I see her naked. If it happens too soon, there's no way we're getting through this little trial run.

Fuck.

I still hope this isn't too much for her, like a buried mine detonating and heaving up bad memories.

I put on a black tux and barely manage to tuck my raging cock into my charcoal pants during the impatient fifteen-minute wait before crossing to the main suite.

When I do, I stalk across the corridor like a tiger and knock.

She answers the door immediately. My eyebrows dart up when I notice she's still in her black sundress.

"Don't tell me. You're backing out?"

She scans up and down my body with her mouth slightly open.

"Classic look. I like it a lot! But what else do they have over there?"

"Navy blue and seersucker, I think, but first I want to know why my bride isn't dressed?" I glare at her.

"Your decoy bride, you mean?" She smiles. "Honestly, I spent all fifteen minutes trying to pick a dress..."

I smile and shake my head.

"You're not Cinderella getting dolled up for the ball. Try them all. That's the whole point," I tell her.

She gives a rigid shrug.

I wonder if it's so simple. Her reluctance to choose a dress might be connected to her hatred for all things wedding related.

"You're okay with this, right?" I grab her hand, pushing her thin fingers through mine. "You don't have to do anything you don't want to. No money ever minted is worth your tears, Dakota."

She gives me a slow look, something dark and melancholy spinning in her eyes.

"That's really sweet but...you don't need to treat me like a victim. I'm fine, Linc. Everyone has crap to deal with. Go try another tux on and I'll be dressed in fifteen minutes."

She gives me a firm look, a promise set on her face.

"All right, I'll hold you to it." I lean over and kiss her before I exit.

This time, I choose a cream tux I didn't notice before.

Fifteen minutes later on the dot, I knock on the door again.

When she doesn't answer, I nudge it open since it's unlocked.

My jaw instantly hits the fucking floor.

Dakota stands in front of a full-length mirror in a long white dress. Pale silk flows around her like a foaming waterfall. She'd be beauty incarnate, Aphrodite come down to smack every man ever born with her glory—especially *this* damn man—except for the fact that her jaw is clenched so tight her temples bulge.

Her reflection in the tall mirror beams back glossy eyes.

My heart crash lands in my gut. I have to do something.

"I thought you hated white? You look like you could be the swan in some Russian ballet. Nice change from the raven schtick, Poe," I say, playing up the sarcasm.

She whips around at the sound of my voice, turns to face me, and smiles. It doesn't touch her eyes.

Damn.

"That's a really nice color for you," she says softly, her eyes trailing down my body. "Your chest is accented." She scans further. "Oh, and your legs. They look powerful in those slacks." She meets my eyes. "That's the one for sure. Anything less would do the photos a disservice."

"Glad we settled that." I brush my hands together like our work is done and close the space between us, wrap my arms around her, and twirl her to face the mirror again. "Do you know how fucking hot you look right now?"

She doesn't answer, just glances away quickly.

"Sweetheart, why do your eyes look so sad?" I whisper, grabbing her and pulling her into my embrace.

"I just—*I don't know, okay?* I'm probably overreacting..."

I thought she might get upset no matter how much she prepared. Seeing herself decked out in a dress when the first time was so traumatic can't be easy or controllable.

That's why I arranged this—to help her and help me—but still. I can't handle seeing Nevermore in tears, and her eyes are only becoming glossier.

"I want you to look at me and listen." I wait for her eyes, gently urging them to meet mine with two fingers under her chin. "You're beautiful, Dakota Poe. God himself wouldn't change a single solitary thing about you."

Her face screws up. A muffled sob falls out of her.

"I-I'm not sure. But thanks." She sniffs again, staring up like she's seeing me for the very first time. "Thank you, Lincoln. That might be the nicest thing anyone's ever said."

I smile.

"I'm only stating the obvious, woman. I know you can see the effect you have on me," I growl, pushing into her belly, making her feel my hard-on.

Red excitement fills her face.

"You weren't thinking about the dress, were you?" she asks.

"Technically, yes, if thinking about ripping the damn dress off counts."

"That's my point."

"Nevermore, that's what every man thinks when he sees a wedding dress worth anything. That's half the reason we agree to get dressed up and march down the aisle." I search her eyes. "Now you know."

She laughs, wiping her cheek.

"There must be *some* good men out there still."

"Yeah, and they're all boring as hell." I lean in and kiss her neck. "Wanting to make love to his wife doesn't make a man bad."

I leave a string of kisses down the side of her neck until I've reached her clavicle.

"Mmm. Fine. I guess you can be pretty convincing." She sighs.

She has no goddamned clue, but I aim to enlighten her.

I gently spin her around in my arms, pulling her tighter so her silk-clad bottom rests against the seething bulge she felt a few minutes ago. I kiss the spaghetti strap of the wedding dress.

"A wedding and a marriage aren't the same thing. Not wanting to stand through a long ceremony on full display doesn't mean you don't value the marriage." I push the strap over with my hand so I can kiss the bare skin under it. "Girls are so weird. If my bride wanted a sixty-second ceremony so she could get me alone, I'd think it was the hottest shit ever."

Nevermore giggles and her eyes come alive again in green witchfire.

Finally.

I kiss her from her shoulder to the back of her neck, trailing my mouth down her back until I meet the section of dress where the pearl clasps begin.

She wiggles her ass against me, freeing her baser instincts.

I'm so damn ready, bringing my hands over her breasts.

She whimpers.

I smile, knowing that sigh would be a lot louder without this dress in the way.

I'm about to ask if I'm a bad person if I need to destroy it right now, but before I can she turns to face me, closes her arms around my neck, and brings her face to mine.

Her tongue meets mine with a hunger and an urgency and a mad glint in her eye.

I take her then, matching her passion with my own pressure.

She moans against my mouth, pouring sticky heat against my tongue.

I can't unclasp the pearls fast enough.

Her hands go to my waist. She undoes my pants and they fall down around my ankles.

A second later, her back is free, open for my hands. I shove the dress off her, freeing her in all her snow-white glory tipped with pink.

The way she shivers as the dress falls is so sexy and enticing I almost come in my pants.

Enough.

I'm done wasting time doing anything but making her sweet ass entirely mine.

Placing my hands under her rear, I lift her to me, aligning our bodies perfectly. Warm, molten heat between her legs glides against my skin.

"You're so fucking wet for me. You make me obsessed, Nevermore," I whisper.

My body pulses like an armed grenade.

I take a few clumsy steps to the wall with Dakota in my arms and push her against it.

"Dakota, can I—"

"Please?"

It's all she has to say.

My hand moves down and I grab her panties, shredding them off in one swipe. The noise is loud, feral, a voice for the unhinged desire splitting me in two.

"Spread your legs," I tell her, already grabbing my cock, shocked at how hot it feels in my hand.

I don't wait.

Not the fuck today.

A single, powerful thrust pins her to the wall and I groan, only holding my eyes open to watch hers roll.

"Lincoln!" My name comes from deep in her throat, all husky fire.

Her grip around my neck tightens as she gives me those nails like the fuck bunny she is and leans forward to kiss my lips with total greed in her eyes.

Yeah, sweetheart.

Give it up.

I'll shake you right down.

But she lets go of my neck as the kisses slow, even as I pull at her bottom lip with my teeth, sucking it into my mouth, holding her hostage.

My forehead rests on hers.

Our eyes meet, molten pools drawn together like magnets.

I rear back and thrust into her again, claiming her sweet little cunt.

It's on.

Each stroke comes faster, harder than the last. I stir her from within, reflecting the storm that's ripping me apart from the inside out.

"Oh. Oh! Oh, shit," she whispers, her breathing ragged.

"Dakota," I whisper, forcing my eyes open as I dive into her again to the hilt.

I have to *make* myself hold still.

Goddamn, it's really not like it was with anyone else.

Sex with Dakota Poe is a meditation in lust. It takes more control to hold myself together than it does to send her crashing over the edge.

She holds her hands above her head, pinned against the wall with mine, her whole being vibrating. She's about to come and I know it, her green eyes huge and gleaming.

"Let go."

"W-what?" she whispers.

"Let it fucking go. I want to feel your pussy twitch when you blow. Suck me off without using your mouth," I growl, pushing my head to hers, thrusting again for good measure.

A frustrated whine spills out of her and I know she won't last long.

"Don't stop!" she gasps through worn breaths.

Woman, like that's even an option. You will dismember me if I stop now.

I reposition my arms so they're between the wall and her head for extra leverage. Then it's just a frenzied collision of hips, of sweat, of muffled breaths and muted curses and two desperate bodies melting into one.

I mean to fuck her straight through her first O when it hits, to make this last, but she tightens around me. It's like pure silk squeezing the angry tip of my cock, urging me deeper, faster, harder.

"Dakota—fuck!" I'm roaring for her.

"Don't stop, please!" she whines again.

I won't deny her.

Her arms are fused around my neck, bolting me to her flesh. I lunge forward, letting her engulf me, filling her to the brim with a sound that's less than human tearing from my throat.

There's barely a second to brace for the fire fountaining up the base of my spine, lashing my brain like a whip.

Her orgasm, her heat, her everything quickens.

Her beautiful body clenches around me, and she lets out all the breath in her lungs with a light squeal.

The silence after is glorious and so intense I'm sure it shames the creation of the universe.

"*Never-more.*" I push it out of my mouth like two separate words.

Then I release so hard and fast I'm blinded.

XVII: FANTASTIC TERRORS NEVER FELT BEFORE (DAKOTA)

"*L*inc! You left the door unlocked," I whisper.

His fingers don't care.

We're in his office at eleven o'clock in the morning; he's behind me, and his thumb is on my clit.

The minute I walked in, he summoned me to his desk without a word and pulled me onto his lap. What started off as slow-burn kisses became my dress strap pulled down and Lincoln's tongue tracing my raven tattoo.

"A broken heart. I don't like it, even if I love how you taste," he growls, gingerly circling my ink with his finger.

"Maybe it's a work in progress," I tease back honestly. I'm trying like hell not to reveal any wild hopes that he could give me a reason to alter this tattoo someday.

Five minutes later, he has me bent over his desk against my better judgment, my panties flicked aside before I can even protest.

"Is the door your only complaint, sweetheart?" His breath is heavy and so, so enticing against my neck.

Then his thumb moves again, tracing agonizing circles.

I grit my teeth.

"God. You're just—you make this so hard."

"If you wanted hard, all you had to do was ask." He pauses. I sense him shifting behind me before I hear a zipper opening. "Guess you'd better get me the fuck off real fast."

Bye, brain.

This is demented.

Anyone could walk in while we're—*ahem*—and land us both in a world of hurt.

"Lincoln, we shouldn't."

"Does your little pussy agree?" He inhales sharply and there's the crinkle of foil tearing.

I shudder as I imagine him sliding the condom onto his cock, no doubt seething in his hand.

"That's what I thought, Nevermore," he mutters.

He thumbs my clit, bringing his free hand to my mouth, positioning his wrist against my lips.

"Bite down if you're worried about the noise. Look at the city out the window. It's a beautiful morning. Far too pretty to waste being nice when you looked like a pinup the second you stepped through my door."

Oh, God.

He pushes into me with a guttural sound.

I whimper.

I've never done anything like this. Sex was never risky before Lincoln Burns, and I'm worried I'm already addicted.

I bump his desk gently as he drives into me—and then not gently at all.

His hips slap mine, each stroke coming harder than the last, hellbent on dragging my pleasure out of me, kicking and screaming.

It doesn't take long.

I see pink and red and so much white. His fingers are still on my clit, rubbing me mad, pushing me to the edge so fast it's almost blinding.

"Shit!" he whispers. "Listen to your pussy, sweetness. Listen to my thrusts. *Let. Go.*"

My mouth pops open. My core tightens like a coil made of fire.

I sink my teeth into his wrist, too awestruck to care about leaving teeth marks, the pleasure ripping me out of my body and—

Knock. Knock.

Oh, no.

There's someone at the door and I'm coming uncontrollably, biting him, trapped in a red, red ecstasy that won't let go.

"Yeah?" he calls behind me, his voice ragged.

I know he's close. I'm clenching him so tight he doesn't stop thrusting.

He can't.

"New shipments are in from Europe, Mr. Burns," a man's voice says. "You said you wanted to know immediately. I tried calling but everything's going to voicemail."

Yikes.

If I wasn't stuck in an orgasm that turns me inside out, I'd be horrified.

"Five minutes," he growls back. "I'll be right with you."

"Great." The doorknob clicks. "If you just want me to leave the spec sheets, I'll—"

"No!" He roars, grabbing my hips, slamming in so deep my whole body thumps the desk. "Just. Fucking. Go."

Fitting words because Lincoln is already gone.

For a hot second, his cock swells. I hear a frantic sound like he's covering his own mouth as he grinds against my hips and releases.

Holy fuckamole.

Edgar Allan Poe could rise from the grave and walk in right now and neither of us could make ourselves care.

He's groaning against his hand.

I'm leaving a full imprint on his wrist.

We've forgotten how to breathe.

And this fireball detonates through us for minutes that feel like years, storming our bodies with unrelenting bliss, making me *feel* him coming as much as I know he feels me.

When he finally pulls out, I think I need to be scraped off his desk.

"Linc. That was—God." I have no words.

Honestly, he does a better job of summarizing it than me. I watch as he tosses the condom in the trash, tucks himself back in his pants, and hovers over me, brushing his lips so gently against mine.

"That was what you get when you trust me, Nevermore," he whispers with a kiss. "If you're a good girl, there's a whole hell of a lot more to come."

* * *

THE NEXT DAY, I knock on Eliza's door with my elbow.

My hands are full, clutching my laptop and holding a small disposable cup of campfire coffee.

She opens the door with her eyes narrowed. "I *knew* I was being haunted. What brings you back to the land of the living, ghost girl?"

"I brought you a present to make up for being so busy."

With a silly smile, she throws the door open.

"Come in! Why are you never home anymore? I almost thought you skipped out on me and moved."

"I'm Lincoln Burns' full-time fake bride. That means lots of time with my faux fiancé, taking pretty pictures."

Ugh, I can't hide anything. A rosy red blush betrays me and my mind instantly goes to the photo shoot a few days after the yacht cruise.

How sweetly Lincoln cradled me against his mile-wide chest.

How good he smelled, cologne and man distilled into the best scent.

How fast we raced back to his place, tearing at each other's clothes before we even stepped off the elevator to his penthouse floor.

"Holy crap, lady. You and the bosshole?" Eliza looks dumbstruck.

I just hold out the small cup of coffee I brought along, courtesy of Wyatt after our latest cinnamon roll visit with him this morning.

Eliza takes it and turns it around slowly. She sniffs and jerks back.

"Wow, that's strong! What is this stuff?"

"Lincoln's friend, Wyatt, he makes this brew. I thought you might find it interesting—"

"Wait, Lincoln? You're on a first-name basis now? Wow. You *are* spending quality time with the boss. Are you sure it's just fake?"

"...I'm not sure what it is," I answer honestly. The sex is truly the most intense experience of my life. My face goes hot at the thought. "That's not my point, though. Wyatt brews this coffee over a campfire, and whatever he does, it always comes out with this smoky flavor. It's pretty good when you add a little creamer to take the edge off. I started bringing my own after it choked me the first time. Try it!"

She sniffs the cup again and smiles.

"Maybe I will. But first, why are you blushing?"

"Blushing?"

I'm not sure why I bother playing dumb. She sees my scarlet face.

Eliza laughs and levels a look that's determined to make me fess up.

I shrug. "Oh, I don't know. It's a warm day. Just try the coffee. Then I have some pictures to show you."

With a frown, she finally drinks from the paper cup. Her eyes widen comically.

"Whoa—I—*oh, mama*. This *is* good. I don't know why I never thought of a fire roast before, but it does give the bean a nice smoky undertone." She stares at the cup, transfixed. I almost think she's forgotten about my Not Relationship with Lincoln. Until she looks at me again. "So, do you think your fake fling with the boss is leading you anywhere besides cool experimental coffee?"

I sit down on her small love seat.

"Not a clue, Eliza."

"How'd it happen, anyway?"

I fill her in on everything, deciding there's no sense in hiding the truth. The flowers from Jay, the ridiculous proposal, the nights in Seattle, the moment one blinding kiss turned the whole world into a waking dream when I opened my eyes.

"Amazing," Eliza whispers when I'm finished, shaking her head in awe. "You guys are a thing."

"I guess we are..." I nod slowly. "And I love it."

She smiles. "Would you love it more if you could put a label on it?"

Would I?

"I don't know. I'm not even sure if it should be anything besides what it already is," I say carefully. "He's still my boss, Eliza. This is pretty taboo as it is, and it's also the kind of thing that follows you if it goes sour..."

"Aw, I don't think he'll come after you if it isn't meant to be. *He* agreed to this fake engagement so no one would question it, didn't he?"

"Still, what if HR finds out it's not all fake when we're off the clock?" I swallow, worry balling up in my throat.

"Cross that bridge when you get there," she says simply.

"It's not like I can stay away from him, so...maybe you're right."

"If you can't stay away, trust the chemistry."

I stare at her. "Do you have some catchphrase for everything?"

"Yep. It's what I do. You have a lot of time to think while you're waiting for the bloom on the perfect pour over or steeping cold brew." She grins smugly, her eyes flashing.

"Eliza, life isn't as easy as coffee. I've just stacked all my chips in one place and obliterated boundaries. If this doesn't work out, it could get ugly."

"But what if it does? What if penny boy decides he's game to take you on a real date the whole world knows about?"

Oh, God.

The minute she says it, I tense. Hope and nervous horror knife through me. *What if Lincoln did do that?*

"Penny boy?" I whisper.

"You know, Lincoln? Abe? Penny? Never mind!" She throws up her hands, laughing.

"You come up with the goofiest names," I say, cracking a smile that takes the edge off.

"Yeah, my other talent. Now you said you had some pictures?"

Right. I turn on my laptop. The company images aren't synced up to my phone so we'll do this the old-school way.

"You have to promise not to scream first," I warn her, wagging a finger.

She crosses her heart with her tongue stuck out the side of her mouth.

Oh, Eliza. With friends like you, who needs trouble?

I press forward anyway.

An image comes up on the screen with Lincoln in a cream-white tux, holding me like I'm an absolute treasure. I'm wearing a simple white dress, resting my head under his chin, a bouquet of bright cornflower clenched between us.

Even though I've seen it ten times, my breath still stalls.

Is that really what we look like together?

Do cameras ever lie?

God. We could be shooting for a *Pride and Prejudice* reboot. And why not? Darcy was the original billionaire bad boy.

Eliza lets out a scream that would be earsplitting if it wasn't for her palms pressed to her mouth.

"Hey, you promised not to scream! Covering it still counts." I elbow her in the belly playfully.

She skids back, a messy laugh falling out of her.

"Dakota, that's...a big deal. You're wearing a wedding dress. The suit has you cradled against him. You both look like you just found your stars. Like, I'm over the freaking moon for you. You wouldn't have allowed this in a million years if you didn't feel something. Not after that annoying little blue jay..."

I shake my head, even as my heart flips.

"Let's not get carried away, okay? I'm a copywriter for an apparel company. This is a marketing gig and it's over in a few more shoots. When it's done, I think I just want to lay low and let fate do its thing. I don't want to get my hopes up."

"No, but—look at him! He's *eating* you with his eyes. I don't buy him thinking this is just a dumb marketing ploy. Not in a million years."

I wish I shared her confidence.

I manage a tense smile.

"He told me his mother got after him. Apparently, she's pulling for us and told him it's like a romance movie that needs to end with grandkids for her." I smile with my cheeks heating again.

Eliza blinks at me.

"He told you that?"

I nod. "We laughed about it later."

"Dakota! You shouldn't wonder anything."

"Come again?" I look at her, not following.

"You've got a dude telling you about his cute little fights with mama. A dude who also looks at you like you're his hottest fantasy come to life." She leans forward and flicks me softly between the eyes. "Dakota, you don't *fake* that stuff. Lincoln

Burns is basically your boyfriend and I hope to God you're ready."

I barely remember to rub the bridge of my nose, too stunned by the insane possibility she might be right.

And if she is?

Oh, crap.

* * *

It's eight p.m. sharp when Lincoln emerges from his office. I came in late to catch up on some work after that heart-pulverizing morning talk with Eliza.

"Why are you still here?" He stops at my desk.

"Lucy's emails took the whole day. I didn't start ad work until after four."

He leans against my desk, a tower of a man who still looks hot even when he's at his most mundane.

"I appreciate the commitment. Are you coming home with me tonight?"

I do fairly often these days. It's practically habit now.

"Is that an invitation?" I look at him slowly, trying to play it cool but failing.

"Always," he growls.

I giggle. "Well, okay."

"I'll be ready in an hour or so. If you get to a good stopping place anytime soon, could you order us some dinner?"

"Will do."

He moves closer to me, bends down, and kisses me. "I told myself after I dealt with that last proposal I'd get a reward."

"Let me guess—I'm your reward?"

"Since you're the hottest thing in my life? *Yes.*" He kisses me again, showing just what sort of reward he has in mind.

And I'm happy to oblige, savoring his tongue against mine, the brash way he moves inside my mouth. I can't peel my eyes off him until his back is turned and he's heading for his office, shooting one last longing, heated look over his shoulder.

God.

This man.

He's a human chess piece and it's scary how easily he's put my whole heart into checkmate.

An hour later, after work is done and we're in the town car on the way home, I say, "I shouldn't work so late. But my hardass boss has me doing double duty..."

"He pays you well for both jobs. Plus, certain duties that come with one hell of a bonus." The way his eyes rake me up and down promises perks infinitely better than money.

"Maybe, but why do *you* work so late all the time?"

"Contracts tonight. They keep the money rolling in so I can pay my employees—particularly beautiful ones who are mighty serious about salaried hours."

His words make me smile.

"Thanks, but I don't just mean tonight. Word is you've been all work and no play for a long time." Yes, I'm pushing now. A little more determined to figure Lincoln out.

He gives me a long look before he speaks.

"Blame it on the Corps, I guess. The military made me crave hard work and the devil's hours. Also, my mother retired not long after my father died. There was plenty to do at the office and long hours were necessary in the transition. Working like hell helped me," he says, an odd hardness in his voice.

"Helped how?"

He sighs. "It was easier to deal with my old man's death if I could keep my parents' legacy alive. If I didn't have spare time on my hands to dwell on the grief, it didn't need to hurt so much."

His eyes darken, russet-brown dimming to walnut.

"I'm sorry, Lincoln. I can't even imagine..." I reach across the seat for his hand.

He takes my fingers and squeezes hard.

"It's whatever. The business does better every year, and Ma's good work lives on. I'm damn proud of that," he says.

"You should be."

He reaches for the door and pushes the button to roll up the privacy screen. "Working around the clock also kept me from getting into other trouble—"

"Other trouble?"

"You know what happened with my engagement falling through, but it's not just that. If I've learned anything from my parents and Wyatt, it's that relationships are fucking hard, and losing them is death. I decided I didn't have the time or will. Not until a chick with a raven tattoo invaded my life and started sending me erotic poetry."

I grin. "Are you saying you could give up the workaholic loner life?"

"I'm telling you I'm bewitched, Nevermore."

He runs his fingers through my hair, a subtle tension in his face that makes me burn.

Poor Louis barely has time to stop in front of the building before Lincoln pulls me out, ferrying me up to his place.

* * *

HOURS LATER, after we've shared another magical night, Lincoln's tongue traces the inside of my mouth. He pulls away, brushing his lips against mine.

My arms are still clasped around his massive back, slowly guiding my hands to his butt.

"You still taste like wine," I whisper.

He kisses me again.

"Is that good or bad?"

"I don't care what you taste like when you kiss me, just as long as you do."

He rolls off me and pulls me beside him. "Nevermore, you wore me out."

I touch his face, running my hand through his thick hair, fully aware my heart is rabbiting in my chest.

I'm so close to saying something I can't take back, but I want him to say it first. I'm not brave enough to go it alone and it frustrates me.

"I could stay here in bed with you forever, you know," I tell him, picking weaker words.

He presses me closer and holds me tight, a possessive glint in his eye.

"Me too, sweetheart. With you, the world stops. I just wish it stayed paused longer," he says with a heavy sigh.

He drifts off to sleep, and I'm left floating in this perfect haze of nerves and questions and what-ifs.

Sweet baby Jesus.

I never knew I could feel as happy as I am when I'm in his arms. He adores me, showers me with wine-flavored kisses, and the sex—*the sex!*

It never fails to leave me the best kind of sore, like Lincoln still wants me to feel him with every step I take.

But a voice in the back of my head whispers like rustling leaves, *You're letting your guard down. Nothing this great ever lasts.*

I tell it to shut up.

It's my natural pessimism speaking, old wounds wanting to talk crap.

It has nothing to do with me—with us.

Six feet something of chiseled muscle sleeps peacefully beside me like a lion, graceful and honest.

A man this powerful couldn't lie if he tried.

Nothing could break him.

He's strong, brave, intense, and for now, so loyal.

And as long as I'm with him, nothing will hurt me. I mean, he goes to a tent city multiple times a week to check on his friend and drops everything when his mother calls.

There's a reason for his madness. It's why he fights so hard to protect the people in his life.

"This isn't like before," I mouth to that annoying little chicken inside me.

Lincoln Burns isn't Jay.

It isn't fair to let past fears poison our present. Especially when there's a chance Eliza's little celebration for me isn't premature.

I kiss his shoulder, letting my lips linger on his skin.

"I love you," I whisper, confident he can't hear me when he's out cold.

I only wish I'd said it to his face.

Maybe tomorrow.

Bravery takes time—and so does love—but I'm making progress, right?

I just have to believe there's no ugly 'other shoe' about to drop.

* * *

"Aaand that's a wrap! Great job, you guys," the photographer says.

He's a tall, lanky man who almost looks like a scarecrow when he smiles and holds up his long thumb.

"Oh, thank God. My feet are about to fall off." I hold up one leg, bending my knee to show off the six-inch white heel paired with the dress today.

Lincoln draws me closer and whispers, "I'll make the effort worth it later, sweetheart."

"Promise?" I lean back against him.

"Cross my heart and hope to fucking die," he rumbles in my ear, brushing his stubble against my neck.

His heat only adds to the warmth falling down on me in lovely splashes of sunlight. It's a breathtaking day in the park. We've gathered half the marketing team for this shoot, early summer in Seattle in all its sky-blue, gold, and green glories.

A bright light flashes in my eyes as I melt into him.

Ugh, it's like I'm destined for a migraine today.

"Hey, I thought we were done?" I ask, scowling at the photographer man.

"Sorry. That was way too authentic not to capture!" He smiles sheepishly.

"Are we finished?" I look up at Lincoln, imploring him to call it good.

"Yeah, we'll have material for months. Let's pack it in." He snaps his fingers at the photographer. "Come on, let's take a walk."

He moves to my side and takes my hand. We start for the sidewalk.

It's honestly sweet how this is a normal park and sectioned off for us, but he still escorts me like a bodyguard in Wyatt's neighborhood.

Ch-ch-click!

My ears throb at the noise that follows us.

"Jeez. He's still taking pictures, isn't he?"

Lincoln smiles. "Can you blame him? Might be his only shoot for weeks with a beautiful woman." He lowers his voice. "If he wants to rip that dress off, he's not the only one. Of course, he'll hurt for his trouble."

Lincoln's fist swings up, joking but not joking.

"You're so bad." I laugh before I can cover my mouth.

He stops moving and leans forward, staring at my lips. "I'm not bad. I've just been cursed by a little soul stealer," he growls.

I think that goes both ways when I tilt my chin up.

His cool mahogany eyes sparkle with sun glitter as he comes closer.

"Are you sure you want to do this here? We're not that far away. The team could see us, you know, and—"

"Their problem," he bites off. "Not ours."

And just like that, he ignites my whole mouth. It's a sunny sweet kiss that reaches down inside me and strums *all the feels.*

Butterflies. Weak knees. A fluttery moan.

Wherever Lincoln Burns just brought me, it's a place where I'm not thinking about work or anything else. Not until a voice interrupts from behind us.

"Dakota! Holy shit, Dakota, I found you. Finally."

You know that moment in bad horror movies where everything seems fine, and then the lead turns around to find a monster with a mouthful of hellish teeth drooling on their shoulder?

If I had a choice, I'd take ten of those monsters.

Because when I whirl around in what feels like slow motion, I'm praying I'm hearing things. I'm *begging* all the gods of coincidence that I'm not about to see the owner of a voice I never wanted to hear again.

"What's wrong?" Lincoln growls, his arms drawing tight around me as he senses my panic.

"Dakota," the voice calls again, this time closer.

My gaze focuses and—there.

There he is.

His shaggy blond hair hasn't changed a bit since I last laid eyes on him. It flops up and down in front of his face as he runs toward us, wearing flip-flops that *splat* on the sidewalk with every step.

"I...I don't know what to do!" I whisper, clenching my teeth.

Lincoln drops my hand, hooks his arm around my waist, and pulls me closer. "Whatever you want, Dakota. I've got you."

It's like he already knows how bad this could be.

But it's worse when Jay finally stops, standing right in front of me in a red t-shirt and khaki cargo shorts.

"Damn. I thought I'd lost you." He hits me with this awful, too-wide smile before his eyes flick to Lincoln. His brows dart down in confusion like he didn't notice the man holding me until now. "Oh. Shit. So this is why you've been ignoring me? To shack up with your fucking boss?"

His sneer cuts me in two.

Instant rage.

I'm about to ask what business it is of his—why he's even here scolding me as if he wasn't screwing his bandmate—but something else knocks at my brain.

"Wait. How do you know who my boss is?"

His lip curls and he rolls his eyes.

"You kidding? Your mama told the whole town of Dallas you've been crushing on the guy you work for. Dakota, c'mon, you're not this kind of girl."

I hear Lincoln's teeth grind.

Oof.

I'm highly annoyed at Mom for blowing what little I've said about Lincoln way out of proportion.

Also, he's here, in Seattle, after harassing me for weeks.

Did he come halfway across the country just for this pathetic in-person shot at changing my mind?

"Jay, we broke up a year ago. You left me. You can stay gone."

I'm awestruck that I'm not shaking. I think the two protective arms wrapped around me have a lot to do with that.

"My band has a six month gig in Seattle," he explains like I should care, pushing his hair out of his eyes.

"Nice. It's a big enough city for both of us."

"Dakota, you don't mean that. You can't keep hooking up with your boss. You'll regret it." His face drops like he's genuinely hurt. For the first time, his words sound more desperate, more sad. "I'll turn down the gig for you. We'll move home and get a place just like we planned. I'll teach music. You can write for the oil company. We can still fix our mistakes."

For a second, there's an ice-cold silence.

Then I've absolutely had it.

"Our mistakes? *Our?*" I scowl at him. "Are you fucking kidding me, man? Also, FYI, I am *not* hooking up with my boss! I'm in love with him."

Oops.

Too many things happen at once.

Jay stumbles back like he's just been shot in the chest.

My heart flies into my throat like a drunken hummingbird.

Lincoln turns to stone and draws a rough breath.

Oh, God. Me and my big fat mouth.

Jay straightens and hurls an angry look at me.

"Bullshit. You're still hurt, I get it," he says like he's trying to make himself believe his own delusions over my words. "Some people back home thought you'd been sleeping around—only way you could've gotten such a cushy promotion so soon. But shit." He holds out a hand. "You know what? It doesn't matter. We'll get through this. We can—"

I'm shaking.

Hot tears of fury sting my eyes.

"Holy shit, Jay. Do you *ever* shut up? Do you even hear the crap coming out of your mouth right freaking—" I stop mid-sentence as everything blurs.

In one movement, Lincoln swings forward, shifting me behind him, standing toe-to-toe with Jay and towering over him at least a good foot and a half.

"She's had enough, you fucking maggot, and so have I." His voice is all war, so intense it scares me. "Listen. You may have gotten away with disrespecting her when she was yours. That's over now because she's mine. So I'm going to give you one chance—and only one—to walk the fuck out of this park politely. Exit her life with your face intact. Comprehend?"

I'm not sure who goes more pale—Jay or me.

It's devilishly satisfying to see him stunned speechless for once in his life. He's the kind of man who always talked too much.

"Are...are you threatening me, man? Dude, you don't own her!" Jay spits, drawing up, his face a hurt, frightened sneer. Even though he's shorter, and probably sixty pounds lighter, he holds his ground.

"I never claimed to, asshole. You weren't listening. However, I do know you're a selfish, brain-dead prick who threw her away like she was fucking trash, and you couldn't even spare her a second glance until you came crawling like the worm you are. You shouldn't have shown up here. I may not own her, but she's mine as long as she'll have me. She's appreciated. She's *cherished*. What's very not appreciated is some little college shit—"

"I graduated two years ago!" Jay squeaks miserably.

Lincoln snorts, baring his teeth.

"Oh, my bad. Post-college shit, I mean, poking around our business. Dakota needs a man in her life. Not a chickenshit little boy who already ran out on her once. And if you thought you'd come here just to rip her heart out all over again, I will fracture your shoulder."

Jay gasps, trembling with ugly, impotent rage.

"Y-you can't say that shit! Who the hell do you think you are? She's supposed to be my *wife!*" His voice cracks horribly on that last note.

My stomach heaves. I feel sick.

Lincoln lets out a vicious chuckle.

"Is that what you think? You really are delusional. You left her, *dude*." He snarls that last word.

"Nah, I just...I needed to get my head together. I had to figure things out."

"That's something men do *before* they propose, Einstein." Lincoln's hands ball into fists at his sides, more like rocks than human appendages anymore.

"You should talk! You're taking fucking advantage of her. She's screwed up in the head and she's just sleeping with you because you're the boss. That's the only reason. She still loves me. She always will. So if you have any sense you'll—"

I'm too paralyzed to even scream as Jay cuts off.

Lincoln flies forward, plowing into his chest with one massive hand outstretched. Jay falls back and hits the ground, fumbling around in his pocket as he slowly pulls himself up.

"I told you, watch your fucking step around my girl. Last warning." Lincoln is fearless, his eyes pinning him down. "Here's your chance. Show me you're not totally stupid. I'll kill you before I let you trash her in public again."

Jay stares like an angry dog.

I open my mouth to yell a warning just as he springs up, something metallic glinting in his hand. The two men collide in chaos.

A few bystanders scream.

"Don't hurt him, you lunatic!" I scream at Jay. "For the love of God, don't—"

I throw myself between them just in time, just as Lincoln plants his fist into Jay's nose. There's a sickening *crunch* and he goes down with a howl, the knife he was holding clattering into the grass next to him.

I'm panting with my heart lodged in my throat, clutching Lincoln's arm.

Holy shit.

Holy shit!

"Fuck," Lincoln mutters, staring down at the broken mess on the ground before he looks at me. "Are you okay, Dakota?"

I bury my face in his chest, the sobs coming harsh and broken and free.

One big arm closes around me. His other hand strokes my hair.

"I'm...I'm...I'm fine!" I manage on the third try.

He holds me tighter, his eyes shifting back to Jay like judgment incarnate.

"You're lucky as hell I didn't do worse. Stay the fuck down until the cops arrive," he orders, taking a stride forward to plant his foot on Jay's chest.

His jaw is clenched like an angry god, chewing on the urge to slaughter my ex like it's bubblegum.

I take half a step back. Just enough to see what's going on around us.

Anna, Cheryl, and the rest of the crew are either rushing in or already surrounding us, staring at the scene with their mouths open.

Jay coughs and moans miserably under Lincoln's foot.

I can't even stand to look at him.

Something tells me whether he pulled a knife or not, Lincoln would've busted his nose anyway, and...I don't even know what to think about this.

Another nightmare begins when I notice all the horrified faces around us.

So much for faking anything.

The awkward HR conversations Lincoln wasn't ready to have are coming, fast and furious. And I know this is so not the way he wanted it to happen.

Save me.

Anna, dressed in bright pink today, stares for another awkward moment before she looks up and says, "Oh. I didn't realize there was actually something between you two..."

"There's nothing, Miss Patel. Just call the damn police," a steel voice booms, furious and conflicted.

My heart stops.

I drop my hand that's still touching his waist. He won't even look at me, this silhouette of rage.

Nothing? *Nothing?* And in front of the whole team?

I wish there was a sniper in a nearby tree to put me out of my misery.

It feels like last summer at the church all over again.

Except somehow, this is *worse.*

He just told me he cared about me and changed his mind in less than a second. Or else he's just lying to cover our asses in the most hurtful way possible.

I fucking hate men.

I get three steps away, struggling to walk in these stupid heels, before I burst into tears.

Great.

Now I hate myself too.

A pair of arms find me a few seconds later. Cheryl, determined to keep me from falling, whispering soft words.

"It's okay, Dakota. Deep breaths." She gives Anna a desperate look, who's also at my side.

"Why don't you guys go for a ride in the company car?" Anna asks. "I'll sort this out. Everything."

Oh, how I wish that was possible.

XVIII: LENORE? (LINCOLN)

I could cut out my own goddamned tongue.

As soon as the words left my mouth, Dakota shirked away from me, sobbing into Cheryl's arms.

I am a supreme dumbass. A miserable, unthinking fuck.

That's what happens when you run your mouth without thinking first.

Worm boy pissed me off, yeah, but he triggered something deeper.

Another time. Another place. Another heart broken and another clown begging for pain.

Only, that time I lashed out like a gorilla. I did serious damage to that cheating asshole, and if it wasn't for that last-minute settlement, he might've ended my career.

Is that what I'm doing again?

Throwing hands at a man because I'm too afraid of being hurt again? And no, I don't mean the knife the little prick pulled. At least this time, I'll be covered legally since he tried to come at me with a weapon.

I wish it was just him.

Hearing Nevermore say the l-word detonated ten tons of raw, emotional violence in my gut.

It came down on my head like an avalanche in red.

I'm in a relationship with my employee.

Well, fuck, *was* in a relationship. I'm sure she'll have every reason to hate me now after this ironic malfunction.

I stood up for her, and then I turned around and did the same shit he did.

I'm not even sure I deserve her any more than the gibbering heap they just dragged off in handcuffs.

I've officially lost control over a woman.

Something I swore would never happen a second time.

Clearly, I couldn't stand to watch him hurt her. But it turned me into that violent, bristling ball of pure rage I swore I wouldn't become after a woman betrayed me once. After I watched everyone I love have their hearts shredded by tragedy.

I vowed to live like a calm, focused shell of a human being, and now I'm out like a hermit crab, snapping at everyone.

Worst of all, hurting the woman who drew me out in the first place.

"Okay, guys—show's over. Nothing else to see here. So let's grab some rides back to the office," Anna says with a nervous look at me.

She's a good team leader. The folks clustered around us listen and start moving.

Her eyes stay on me though, waiting for an explanation I don't have.

"What are you looking at, Miss Patel?" I snap. "Your concern is noted. However, I would have done the same thing for you if some maniac accosted you with a knife. It was nothing."

Nothing.

Right.

I've got to sort this out, but first I need to stop lying.

Anna purses her lips. "Bossman, I appreciate you'd try to stand up for me, but honestly? If you did it by telling someone I was *yours* and then that there's no relationship, I'd resign ASAP. I wouldn't even know how to handle coming in the next day."

I get the sense that she isn't done.

"But?" I urge after a silence.

"Well..." She looks at the ground. "I saw what you were like before he came charging in."

I glance away from her, hating what's coming next.

"...maybe you didn't want everyone to find out this way, but I'd man up and apologize," she says.

"Apologize for what?" I bite off.

She smiles nervously, glowing in the sun.

"There was nothing fake about how you two were acting during the shoot, and especially not after it. I'd bet every dollar I own she'd still be here crying if Cheryl hadn't left with her..."

Fuck, that guts me.

The coolest girl I know couldn't play it cool after my words machine gunned her heart.

This is why people shouldn't mess with relationships.

They crawl up in your head and go ballistic, leaving nothing but smoking debris behind.

I also know damn well Anna's right. I have to apologize to Dakota and soon. I'm just not sure if it'll matter.

If Dakota told everyone I didn't matter to her when I needed her, I might not forgive and forget either.

"Hey, um, Mr. Burns?" Anna meets my eyes.

"Yes?"

"I know you're my boss. I'm sorry if I'm speaking out of turn, but I really hope you—umm—fix whatever it is you've done. She's very talented. The wedding launch won't be easy without her around, and then there's the whole engagement interview we promised a couple publications. If people find out it's all a sham now—"

The entire company loses credibility and it damages the line.

Goddamn, how deep did I dig my grave?

I put my foot in my mouth one time and risk losing Dakota and an entire product line.

My phone vibrates in my pocket. I reach for it with a frustrated scowl.

Please be Nevermore.

Then again, I haven't pulled the words together for a proper groveling yet. I have no idea what to say. There's no easy way to make this better.

Please don't be Nevermore.

I glance at the screen.

WYATT flashes up at me.

Oh, shit. It's the burner phone I bought him that he's never used, and probably never would unless he's in real trouble.

I flick the green icon.

"Wyatt? What's happening?" I lash out, my heart having a fit in my chest.

"Is this Lincoln Burns?" a woman asks.

Oh, boy. Wyatt, what the hell do you have going on?

"Yes, speaking," I say.

"My name is Jennifer Green. I'm a nurse with Seattle Memorial—"

"Nurse? Is Wyatt okay?"

"Your number is the only contact we found in his phone. He had no ID. The girl who made the nine-one-one call—"

"Nine-one-one? What the hell happened?" Sweat rolls down the back of my neck.

"I think you should come here immediately," she says carefully.

"Okay, on my way. Where?"

"Intensive care."

Shit. That poor dumbass has finally done himself in.

Dark scenarios flash through my brain, each more terrible than the last. Some screwball at knife point trying to jack his prosthetic again. A robbery over his coffee can cash. What if he went foraging and fell, or—

"Fuck!" I'm growling, running across the park, pulling up an Uber on the way.

Wyatt, how could you? How many times did I tell you to just crash in my guesthouse? Hell, you could have stayed in the main house. Why end up in ICU for your pride?

"Wait, sir, before you hang up, could you tell me his last name?" The nurse is still on the line. "I don't have a way to trace his family without it."

"His name is Wyatt Emory." I rattle off his date of birth and hang up, dragging a hand over my face.

What else can fuck me over today?

* * *

I STEP in the elevator and punch the button for the ninth floor.

My stomach lurches, ready to barf up lunch.

I have no idea what to expect or how bad he is. I always *knew* this might happen, but it doesn't soften the reality one bit.

Please be alive.

Please be mendable.

You can't fucking die on me now.

The elevator opens and I head to the nurses' station. "I'm here to talk to Jennifer Green about Wyatt Emory," I tell the man behind the computer.

He swivels around in his chair. "Jennifer, you've finally got someone here who might know something about your new intake."

"Are you Mr. Burns?" A slender brunette comes to the counter.

"Yes, how is he?"

Her mouth forms a tight line. "Are you family?"

"Brothers." It's not a lie.

Once a Marine, always a Marine, and for us, it's a brotherhood bound in blood.

She nods. "He's not in good shape, I'm afraid. He hasn't been conscious since he was brought in for the infection."

"What infection?" I ask.

"He has severe pneumonia. Looks like the type that creeps along for weeks and takes a sudden turn for the worse if it goes untreated," she says.

"Who called him in?"

"You can talk to her. She's still hanging around outside his room."

"Can he not have visitors?"

"It's ICU. Only family goes in. Since she was the only person here, I offered to give her a few minutes, pretending not to notice if she went into his room. But she doesn't want to see him. It's a little odd. She rode here in the ambulance with him."

"Have you called his ex-wife? His son should know."

She shakes her head.

"No. We only pulled up his information before you got here. A former wife came up but I couldn't find a contact."

"I'll find her. What room is he in?"

"Nine twenty-two, the very last door at the end of the hall. You're welcome to visit, but he's not conscious. I just want you to know." She points to her right.

I nod. "Thank you."

When I reach his door, I find a familiar face in worn flannel and scuffed jeans, one cheek smudged with dirt. Probably from her nonstop gardening.

"Meadow? I'm glad you came," I say, shaking her hand. "Thanks for calling nine-one-one. You did the right thing."

She nods. "I was so scared. When I couldn't wake him up this morning...I thought he was gone. He was barely breathing. They told me on the phone how to check his vitals. I felt a pulse, but not much." She shakes her head. "He even gave me flowers a little while ago..."

"I heard," I mutter softly.

"He's had that terrible cough forever, and it rained hard the other night. His tent sprang a leak and he insisted he was going to fix it, but the last time I saw him awake, he was white as a sheet." She sighs.

Dammit, I know that frustration.

Why the hell didn't I just drag his ass home with me a long time ago?

Because I was busy with Nevermore, of course, one more epic catastrophe hanging over me.

"He's such a nice man. I hope he makes it through this," Meadow says, looking at me sadly.

"He's strong as a bull. He'll pull through, I think. I've seen him survive far worse than pneumonia." I'm putting on a brave face.

Deep down, I'm scared shitless that Wyatt's extra lives are up.

"In the war, you mean?" she asks.

I nod firmly.

"He tells me stories sometimes..."

"Yeah? He doesn't usually talk about it."

She shrugs. "Sometimes he needs to, and my daddy was a soldier."

I cock my head. She gives me the far-off look I've seen a hundred times. It says her father probably never made it home.

"I'm sorry. Did he die in action?"

There's pain in her expression, despite her shy smile.

"He killed himself. The insurance doesn't pay that way, so we lost everything. Mom couldn't handle the streets well, so...she's gone too."

Wow, fuck.

This girl just summed up a tragic life in two sentences, and somehow she's still smiling.

"I'm sorry, Meadow."

"It's okay. We all just put one foot in front of the other and keep on moving, right?"

I nod. Wiser words today.

"I'm going to go check on Wyatt. When I leave tonight, I can give you a ride back if you need it?"

"The nurse said I can sleep in the waiting room." She rubs at her weary eyes. "I think I'll take the offer. It's more comfortable."

I nod and push open the door to Wyatt's room.

He's not bleeding, but he looks as bad as he did that day in Iraq. The ventilator and tubes are plugged into him like a human battery, the color drained from his face.

The nurse said he looked rough, but now her words have emphasis.

I move to the bed, clasping his arm with one hand.

"Hey, it's Burns. Wake up soon. You're missing out on your next cinnamon roll," I joke with a boulder building in my throat. It's the only thing I can stand to say.

I'm only in the room for five or ten minutes. He's virtually comatose. What he needs right now isn't my company, dammit.

I go back to the nurses' station after stopping to give Meadow a few encouraging words I wish I believed.

"Where's Jennifer?" I ask the guy at the desk.

"She's making her rounds right now. It could be a minute before she's back. Is there something I can help you with?"

"I just want to know if there's anything that can be done for Wyatt that hasn't already been tried?"

"You're next of kin, right?"

"His brother," I half lie.

He nods. "Let me pull up his chart for the doctor's notes..."

"He's got IVs, and he's on a ventilator. There are some other things we could try, but Medicaid won't pay for it, and I don't even know if he's got that."

"He has VA insurance, but—fuck, I'll pay for anything it doesn't cover. Spare no expense."

"Okay. I'll talk to his doctor and find out more for you. Do you have an ID?"

I'm so goddamned done with this.

My friend is dying, and I'm caught in this red tape. But I've already taken out enough rage today for one lifetime, so I'm not going to hound this guy who's just doing his job.

"I own Haughty But Nice. I'll pay cash for whatever he needs. Send me the paperwork for a payment method, take my card, whatever you need. Just make sure he has the best care. I have to track down his son, but I'll leave you my number. Call me for anything financial."

He opens a drawer, pulls out a form, and hands it to me. "This is a guarantor's form. Just get it back to us soon."

I promise I will.

By the time I'm stumbling outside, drawing thick breaths, I'm wrecked with a hundred regrets about not doing more for Wyatt Emory when it mattered, even if I had to twist his arm.

All the regrets in my life are catching up, threatening to crush me under their weight.

Dakota Poe feels just as lost as Wyatt, and after this fucked up day, I wonder if I'll ever find my way home.

* * *

THE NEXT DAY, I'm on my way back to the hospital with red eyes after a sleepless night, but I've finally found Olivia's number.

I need Micha at the hospital. Money aside, it's all I can do for him.

Maybe Wyatt will fight for his son, because he's sure as hell not fighting for me.

I punch the number. It rings three times.

Come on, witch. Fucking answer.

"Hello?" A woman picks up, sounding annoyed.

"Is this Olivia?"

"Lincoln—" She hesitates.

"Still recognize my voice, huh?"

"How could I forget it? You annoyed the hell out of me for years." She sighs. "So, what? Is he finally dead or...?"

It takes all of my willpower not to punch the seat of the car.

This woman is a piece of fucking work. My grip on the phone tightens until my fingers hurt.

"Do you give a shit?"

"Somebody must, I suppose, or you wouldn't be calling."

Goddamn her.

"He isn't dead, but he could be soon. Our feelings are mutual, but this isn't about us. Wyatt's son deserves one last chance to see his father alive, don't you think?" I hold my breath, trying to be diplomatic.

"Hmm. I don't know. I think my son has seen enough of his father's drinking and crazy outbursts."

"He didn't start drinking like a distillery until you abandoned him," I snarl.

"Oh, really? And how do you know? Because I seem to remember that you weren't the one living with him when you have like five mansions to choose from."

"Fuck you," I bite off, shaking in my seat. "I lived with Wyatt when neither one of us had a single goddamned wall to call our own."

"Before or after the war? Because it's not the same. People change, Lincoln. You sound pretty batshit yourself. No offense."

She's trying to rile me up.

I'm silent for a second, drawing in a breath that feels like fire.

"You knew he needed help. You abandoned him before he was even back in the States for strange dick. He told me everything."

"Everything, huh?" She yawns loudly.

"He needed you, Olivia. He tried to work shit out—everything—and he went above and beyond. He even told me about the kid that wasn't his—the kid you got knocked up with he offered to adopt."

Low blow, but it gets her attention.

She falls so silent I have to look at my phone to see if she's still there.

"That's *not* your fucking business, Burns. None of it! He couldn't even handle me or Micha. His stupid ass was constantly crying and the bills...*God, the bills*...they're the reason I miscarried, you fucking asshole."

I look at the floor, remembering how totally fucked up the whole situation was.

She's right about one thing, though.

Everyone suffered.

"Olivia, if he dies alone, that's on your hands," I growl. "And believe me, if I have to wait a decade, I'll tell Micha about his old man. I'll also be sure to let him know *you* kept him away when he was on his deathbed."

I hate that I have to play that card. It kills me, but what alternative do I have?

"You just—you don't even *know!* I begged him to get checked into treatment when counseling wasn't cutting it. He wouldn't." She inhales sharply, sobbing quietly now. "I'm sorry he ended up on the street, but it was either that or let him drag us down. I *begged* him not to enlist in the first place. He wanted to because his stupid dad and his stupid grandfather served. He chose his battle, his life. He lost. I picked mine, and I sure as *hell* don't need your judgment. But your opinion of me is none of my business, just like my life isn't yours."

"His battle was defending his country—right or wrong—and trying like hell to come home to his family. Yours was what? To ride dick and leave? You would've been out the door without so much as a Dear fucking John if he wasn't discharged early. Don't lie to me."

Again, that gaping silence.

Again, I know I'm right, and I hate it.

"Doesn't matter," she hisses. "I *tried* to give my son a normal childhood that didn't involve a mental patient swearing and drinking and punching walls."

"He's not a maniac," I bite off.

"*Wasn't*, you mean. That was true, once."

"Are you wishing him dead?" I ask darkly.

"No. I'll admit that he was sane before the war. He came home a different person. I might be a bitch for leaving him, for messing around, but damn. What can I say? I value sanity in a partner?"

"You should have stood by him. He wouldn't have lost his mind if he had more support," I snarl, sure to the bone that's true.

"Umm—I don't know if you know this, but it's not my job to fix a broken grown-ass man with one leg."

"He loved you, bitch. If you cared about him at all, you should have made sure he got help instead of taking off."

Again, that killing silence.

"What's done is done. Also, Doctor Dubuque isn't a lunatic and he's a good role model for my son, so I can't say I regret anything. So go to hell."

No remorse.

Did the witch ever care about Wyatt at all?

My jaw tightens, remembering why that question stabs me so harshly today.

"Are you bringing Micha to see him or what?" I demand, the only question that matters.

"I don't know. That's asking a lot. I don't really want to tell my new husband we're road-tripping to Seattle to visit my ex. Micha has a few good memories of his father—before he came back batshit crazy—and he has a few bad ones too. He's not at a good age to deal with all that." Olivia pauses and sighs. "How bad off is he?"

"He might have a fifty-fifty chance of survival at best. I'm not sure he'll pull through." I've seen him like this before. She hasn't.

Last time, he only came out the other side for her, for his family. That won't be a reason to fight this time. I have to hope Micha is, if he can hear his son somewhere through his coma-fog.

"Well, I'll think about it. I just don't want my son exposed to that homeless freak and his problems..."

Can she piss me off more?

"What problems? He's not going to be drinking in a hospital

room when he can't even open his damn eyes. He's comatose. You're acting like you're taking the kid to see him in prison, but it's a *hospital.*"

"I'll talk to Doc about it. I'm not sure."

I can't believe she calls her husband Doc. Like the entire world needs to be reminded she hooked herself an MD every five seconds.

"Think fast. If 'Doc' doesn't give you permission, understand that I will have every carnivorous attorney I know forcing a visitation issue. I'll call in every corporate favor I've ever been owed. I'll hire a PI to find out what hospital Doctor Dubuque works for, and if I don't know who owns it, I'll buy out the main fucking stake." I inhale sharply. "You, Olivia, will regret the day you were born if you don't get that kid in here to see Wyatt. This could be their last chance. I'm sorry shit didn't work out for you and Wyatt—actually, I'm not. It was mostly your fault. He loved you too much, the poor idiot. Now, it's time for you to grow the hell up."

There's a chiming sound.

She hung up on me.

Predictable.

I mash the phone back into my pocket and let my head thunk against the window.

She doesn't care if Wyatt lives or dies. She has no guilt for leaving him after he lost his leg and his life.

It's hard to believe they were ever happy. When he wasn't on duty, they were inseparable.

She cried the day we deployed.

Olivia and I never got along, but the day we left, she begged me to bring him home safe.

Whatever she is now, I loathe her.

About as much as I hate the way I haven't had time to deliver Dakota's well-deserved apology. I've been scrambling to take care of Wyatt.

Maybe it's better this way.

If this is where love always leads, fuck everything about it.

If things ever got so bad that Dakota didn't care if I lived or died, if I hurt her, I wouldn't want to keep existing.

You've already hurt her plenty, jackass, a voice in my head hisses.

Regrettably true. I've just got to find the nicest way possible to let her down.

This can only end in a storm of tears and anguish. What's the point in causing us both more grief?

Louis pulls up to the hospital a minute later and lets me out.

Soon, I'm parked in the chair beside Wyatt's bed, my pulse hammering so thick the noise engulfs my ears.

"Micha's coming to see you. You'd better wake up to see him. Will you do that for me, man?"

No response.

I take a deep breath and lean back into the chair.

"I talked to Olivia today to get the kiddo to come. No fucking clue what you ever saw in her." I clear my scratchy throat. "I know you two loved each other once. When the divorce first hit and you took it so hard, I thought you were overreacting. But now—shit."

Total silence.

He's asleep, Linc. Just get it out.

"I finally understand. If I woke up with Dakota in my arms every morning and she just up and told me one day she didn't want it anymore—you'd have to make room in that bed. I'd lose my mind. I couldn't run my company. I couldn't function."

I lurch to my feet, moving to the window, looking out at Seattle.

It's a clear, vibrant day that already looks like summer. It contrasts sharply with the darkness swirling in my soul.

I don't know why I'm here.

I'm just talking to myself.

This shouldn't be so hard.

"She's pissed at me, Wyatt," I say, looking over my shoulder.

"Nevermore, I mean. It's my fault. I deserve it and I haven't figured out how to apologize yet. I don't even know if I should."

I pause, hanging my head.

"After seeing what you've been through, should I risk it?" I whisper. "My plan was to let her down gently, but what's the point if it'll just bust her up again? The best thing I can do is stay the hell away. She'll get over it in time. I'm just one more asshole who tried to break her heart."

XIX: DARKNESS THERE (DAKOTA)

"Go ahead, call me an idiot. I should have trusted my instincts. There was no way this fake engagement fling was ever ending in anything besides disappointment."

Eliza looks at me like she knows that's a massive understatement.

Disappointment is when you go to Sweeter Grind and ask for a Regis roll, but come home with a bear claw because they're sold out.

Disappointment is when your fiancè decides he needs to follow his dreams the morning of your wedding.

Finding out that this thing with Lincoln was always a game? That's not a disappointment.

It's an ax blow to the heart.

Eliza hands me a coffee infused with so much vanilla sweet cream it smells like a scented candle.

"He put on a good show, didn't he? The man sucked you in. It's not your fault. And are you *sure* he didn't just freak out? You typically don't push in some stabby moron's face over a girl you don't care about. The cold shoulder could mean more even if it definitely means F-you at the moment."

I shrug and sip my drink.

I desperately want to believe her. Pathetic hope flutters in my chest.

"...but if that's it, then why haven't I heard from him?"

Her mouth forms a rigid line.

The hope unfurling in my chest hits a cavernous pothole and dies.

"See? No good explanation." I sigh.

The oven dings and makes me jump.

"Ready or not, here comes brownie therapy." She walks over and pulls out a tray of colossal fudge brownies. "Give them ten or fifteen minutes to cool."

"This is my fault, Eliza." I prop my head on my hand glumly.

You know it's bad when godly brownie fumes can't dispel bad thoughts.

"Nope, and I don't want to hear it again," she says sharply. "When you're under my roof, you don't get to beat yourself up."

"Technically, we share the same roof."

"Whatever! You told Jay Fuckboy five million times to leave you alone. He didn't listen and got himself in a world of hurt. You aren't responsible for how he reacts or the bosshole, either."

"Have I been too passive?" I ask.

"What do you mean?

"I don't even know what I saw in Jay. It was a small town and he was like the first guy who appreciated words to come along and show interest, so I just rolled with it. Somewhere along the line, I got serious and he didn't. I never should've opened myself up to that abuse. God, I even replied to his weak attempts to make up—"

"Wrong. You told him to get lost and blocked his number when he turned into a stalker nut. He could've *stabbed* you, Dakota. What else were you supposed to do? If the guy who won't take the hint starts brandishing a knife, that's not your fault. Ever."

I laugh dryly because she's too right to argue back.

"Well, it turned into my problem and someone else's by letting it fester. I played along with Lincoln, too, without enough thinking. I just let him sweep me off my feet, and he dropped me like a feather."

She goes quiet for a minute.

"He didn't give you much choice. What were you supposed to do? Beg him to change his mind in front of everyone you work with? Right after a dude came at you with a knife? Dakota, you're not responsible for his stupidity or anyone else's."

"He's definitely no Honest Abe."

"Have you been to the office since it happened?"

I look down at my drink. "It was just a couple days ago. I couldn't stand showing my face after that. Cheryl had the driver bring me home, thank God. Otherwise, I would've been a sobbing mess in front of everyone. Not to mention useless for work. I called in sick."

"Will you face it tomorrow?"

Ugh, don't remind me.

"I don't know that I have a choice. I've only worked there a couple months. No huge pools of PTO banked besides what they give you starting out..."

"It pays more than your last job, right?"

What's the point? To prove Lincoln may not need me, but I still need him?

"Yeah," I say miserably.

"Could you ask for a week or two off even if it's unpaid?"

I hadn't thought of that.

"Probably. Since he's had me working two full-time jobs, I've been making way more than my old salary and working too much to have any time to spend it. I can totally take unpaid time off if they'll let me."

"Do it. Use the downtime to hunt for another job. Unless you're really okay with going back to work for this guy, forget about the pay. You should have some savings now, so if it doesn't pay as much, oh well."

"That's a very Eliza solution," I say glumly.

She's good at grabbing life by the horns and shaking it around without getting smashed. I wish I was that bold.

That rock that's been sitting in my throat starts choking me, and I blink back tears.

I realize how pathetic I must look moping around like this after a man I never truly had.

The hope that died earlier has turned to dust.

"You said his silence could mean anything, right?" I ask bitterly.

She nods, sipping her coffee. "It could. But if, by some miracle, he realizes he's been a blockhead and comes crawling back, and you guys figure your crap out and live happily ever after...is it a good idea to keep working for him? That's a ton of pressure."

I sigh. "What if he ends the radio silence?"

She shakes her head like it's obvious.

"Dakota, if he tries to get in touch, hear him out first—that is, if he starts with an apology. And make sure the talk happens on your terms. If you're still his employee, it can't be equal. Not when he controls your schedule and your income."

I blink at her. "Maybe you should give up on coffee and become an advice columnist."

"Not on your life. I love the bean too much. Now, are you ready for Dr. Brownie or what?"

I let her bring me one of those chocolate monsters and dig into it while I finish my coffee. Panic eating is surprisingly helpful today.

She packs up a few more treats for me to take home. I don't argue because they're decadent. Heartbreaks are always a sliver less awful with heaps of chocolate.

When I'm back in my apartment, I sit down in front of my laptop and stare at the screen. I open an email to Anna, close it, and reopen it.

What do I even say?

Dear Anna, I'm a slutty-slut-slut who slept with her boss and it ended badly, so can I have some time off to process this even if it has to be unpaid?

Yeah, guess how that'll go over.

If I said I have mono, would she ask for a doctor's note?

An informal text seems less daunting and humiliating than an email, I decide.

So I pick up my phone and hit her contact.

Anna, hi. Off the record, if I have mono for a week or two would you ask for a doctor's note?

I get up to wash a few dishes and wipe down my stovetop before she replies about twenty minutes later.

Anna: Off the record, how about I give you administrative leave for workplace trauma from being threatened with bodily harm? I'm sure it qualifies after your boss and some lunatic came to blows in close proximity with a knife. I don't see HR turning you down, if only to avoid a lawsuit. She sends a smiley face emoji and a heart for care.

Dakota: I won't sue. Don't worry.

Anna: Shhh! Don't tell anyone that. God, I'm on your side here. Another smiley face emoji followed by a gif with two big furry monsters hugging. **How are you holding up, anyway?**

Dakota: Fine, considering the circumstances. Really. Thanks for helping me out with the leave. I'll let you know in a couple days.

With that, I move to the couch, turn off the alarm on my phone, and switch on Netflix.

Time to chill, and not the kind that involves any moron with a penis.

Job surfing and life can wait.

* * *

AFTER A FEW DAYS of movie binging and pecking at poems with lines so depressing they could win an angst match against a teenager's diary, I need to get out.

I'll be back tomorrow, I text Anna.

Are you sure? she replies later.

I can't stay home forever and I want to work. Whatever happened with the big boss shouldn't keep me away from helping the main marketing push.

Anna: Okay! I'll see you tomorrow then. Oh, and of course we've shelved those photos for now until we figure something out. So no worries about seeing them.

My throat knots. I'd half forgotten the pictures where Lincoln and I played at being newlyweds.

God, I hope I can live up to my word, keep my head down, and work without cracking.

The next day, I bike to work like the old days before—

Before.

I stop at Sweeter Grind and order two coffees and Regis rolls.

Just like *before.*

When I show up, I'll have the bosshole's order, a straight spine, squared shoulders, and a smile so effing bright it could blind the stars.

Lincoln Burns won't get the satisfaction of a distraught, emotional mess. I'll show him just how little power he has over my life.

...only, I find his office locked and the lights off when I show up.

Hmm. I check the time.

I'm not late. He couldn't have left for a meeting already?

Since when is Mr. Stick-Up-the-Ass late?

Whatever. I'm better off not having to deal with him.

I set his breakfast down on my desk, power up my laptop, and clock in.

Hours pass before I look up and notice he still hasn't arrived.

Weird. I guess Shrek needed an extra day in the swamp to yell at somebody else.

My desk is in front of Linc's office, and we're secluded from most of the company. He likes it this way. He has fewer interruptions and more quiet, orderly space. But it's extra lonely over here today.

A few other C-level employees have offices near us, but they rarely poke their heads out. The CFO, an older man named Reed, flies past. He's oh-so-careful to keep his eyes focused straight ahead so he doesn't make eye contact with me.

By early afternoon, I've cleaned out the executive Inbox, which was oddly lighter than usual, and caught up on ad work.

With Lincoln out today, there's technically no one to assist in my EA role and I can't stand it here any longer.

So I pack up my laptop and head down to the main floor where the copywriters work. That has to be better. But even down here, people look away as I pass them.

Nice. Avoid eye contact with the freak who seduced the boss but couldn't keep him around.

She's a plague rat. Her drama might be contagious.

My stomach tries crawling up into my chest.

Why did I think I was brave enough for this again? Anna would've given me as much time off as I needed.

After a painfully long walk around the building, I sit down at my old desk beside Cheryl.

"Dakota? Welcome back. I didn't expect to see you back for a while." She flashes a friendly smile.

I don't know what to say, so I keep my mouth shut.

"How is Mr. Burns?" she ventures.

"I wouldn't know," I bite off too harshly.

"Oh." Her face falls and she nods. "I hope everything's okay. He's hardly been back to work since the day your ex showed up. He came in very briefly the next day but ducked out fast, I heard. Everybody's freaking out about it because Burns never leaves early. And it's been years since he missed a single day of work..."

That does raise my eyebrows.

Is it possible the asshat feels a little guilty, but he's too proud to say sorry like a normal human being?

I mean, he did save my life, right before he stabbed me through the heart in a way Jay couldn't.

"Eh, I don't know. He probably hoped the drama would die down while he was out," I say. "Laying low makes a lot of sense."

Will I ever learn? I will always attract guys who can't get their shit together—not even when they're billionaires. And I fall for them every time like the gullible, moonstruck romantic I am.

There's a tap on my shoulder, and I turn to see Anna.

"Hello, hello. Do you have a minute to talk to me in my office?"

I nod and follow her.

She motions to a chair across from her desk and I fall into it.

What now?

If she's brought me here for a pep talk, I'm not interested, even if she means well.

"I'm proud of you for coming back," she starts, glancing up at me with her head low.

Is she really? If I had an employee in this mess, I might hope they'd stay away and save everyone the awkwardness. But I know that's my anxiety talking.

"You're a talented writer, and we can't afford to lose you. I just called you in to let you know we're behind you all the way. The whole marketing team and especially me. Whatever you need to make this easier, just ask. You want to work from home? Good. You want a private office? Also cool. I'll be personally reviewing your copy before passing it on, so if he has a problem with anything, he can take it up with me directly."

I nod, more than a little stunned at her support.

"I'm grateful. Thank you." I plant my feet on the ground and I'm about to stand, hoping that's it.

But, of course, it never is.

Anna puts up a hand, urging me to stay. "Wait. That was my little support talk as your boss."

"There's more?" I ask quietly.

"Dakota, as your friend, that was such a shit move he pulled." She goes quiet for a moment and her face stiffens. "Honestly, I'm still floored by it. I've never seen him lose control like that. To be fair, he had to wrestle a guy with a knife, but it was way out of character."

"Yeah, I was there," I say, trying not to sound bitchy.

"I think he cares about you...but rejecting you in front of an audience like that was a low blow. I hope he comes to you on his hands and knees before you ever speak to him again." She gives me a menacing look.

Harsh. Is this what's driving Lincoln into hiding? Hostile work environment?

"I doubt that'll be an issue," I say softly.

"Have you heard from him?"

I shake my head, mouthing a *no*.

"Well, probably for the best. He can't cause more drama that way, but I do hope he clears the air before he shows his face around here again. The tension is so freaking thick it's stifling."

"That would be great, but don't get your hopes up, Anna."

"He's barely been back since the day it all went down—"

"I heard."

"He came in the next day and left early in a rush. He hasn't been back since and he's never been out like this before. The message he sent was so vague. Some kind of 'personal emergency.' I sent a response to let me know if he needed anything, but he never even replied."

My heart sinks in confusion.

I don't even know how to hash that.

"I think he just wants the scandal gone before he comes back," I say, echoing my conversation with Cheryl.

"No point in waiting then. This weird extended absence after the incident has got people talking nonstop, especially since you were out for a few days, too." She sighs like she's legit overloaded from the drama flying around.

I can't even blame her.

"Do you think people would look at me again and stop treating me like a pariah if Burns came back?" I ask.

She lays her elbow on her desk and rests her head on her hand.

"No one thinks you're a pariah, Dakota. They just feel bad for you and don't know what to say. We've never run into this situation before."

"That's almost worse."

She sighs. "I know. I'm sorry. But to answer your question, I think it would lighten things up if he came back and restored some normalcy. It's pretty cowardly for him to let you deal with the aftermath alone. But like I said, the email was vague, and he's never been out unscheduled before, so something might be wrong."

Something *is* wrong.

He doesn't want to deal with the dumpster fire he caused, and he doesn't care if it burns me alive.

"Thanks, Anna. I'll keep working from here. We can't both be ghosting the place. But as long as he's out, I'll be down here at my old desk. It doesn't make sense to linger upstairs with no one to assist while I'm still doing Lucy's job."

"However you want to play it. I'm sure the acting CEO won't have a problem either if this turns into an extended absence on his part. Say, do you want a coffee before you head back out? I can order from the place up the street."

"No, I'm well caffeinated."

"Go be the best wordsmith ever so that jackass knows you're better than him," she says with a ruthless smirk.

You've got to love her energy.

Somehow, I don't think I'm a better anything than a princely CEO.

Once I'm at my desk, I decide to get this over with and text the loser.

Yeah, I know.

I'm supposed to wait. Let him come to me. Play the game.

I've already forgotten about him, but if Anna thinks his sorry ass returning will make people act normal around me again, he's going to hear about it.

Why aren't you at work? I send.

He doesn't answer.

Hours go by, and I'm more annoyed by the minute. By the end of the day, I can't resist a follow-up text.

You could show your face. It's not a good look vanishing like this. Everyone thinks you're a coward.

Surprise, surprise. He doesn't answer that one either, maintaining radio silence.

At five thirty, Cheryl stops by and says, "Don't tell me you're staying here all night?"

"I was out for a while. I have plenty to make up," I lie.

"Oh, don't worry about it. If you're behind, we'll help you catch up."

"Thanks."

She looks at me for a long moment without speaking before she finally says, "Maybe someone should call his mom."

Oh my God.

That's the last thing I want.

"Why?" I look up, meeting her eyes.

"He's just never out like this. What if it's more than Burns having a hissy fit? If *you* haven't heard from him, something could be wrong—"

"I doubt that. He made his opinion of me perfectly clear."

"You're probably right," she says weakly before slipping away.

He sledgehammered my heart in front of the entire team, and by not showing up, he's making it worse. Now Cheryl feels sorry for *him*.

On the way home, I stop at Sweeter Grind. The jackass might

not respond to my texts, but I happen to know he frequents this coffee shop.

I order the largest caramel latte they have and bunker down at a table, waiting to see if he shows up. This is usually one of the evenings when he makes his cinnamon roll runs for Wyatt.

I wait for nearly an hour before I can't stand it.

No sign of Lincoln Burns.

I hate myself for it, but now Cheryl's words have me concerned.

What if something crazy happened to Lincoln and everyone just thinks he's waving his dick? He never struck me as a coward.

I get up and ask the barista girl if she's seen a suit come in lately for a large Regis roll order.

She knows exactly who I mean.

When she tells me he hasn't been by in a few days—very unusual—my heart skips. *What the hell is going on?*

I take off, tossing back what's left in my cup as I fly out the door.

At the park a few blocks down, I find Wyatt's tent. It's crumpled and empty, his meager belongings picked over.

Oh my God. What happened?

A rustling noise behind me makes me turn.

A girl comes out of the pink tent where we left flowers once. She gives me a friendly wave.

I return it, even with my brain stuck on panic.

Should I call Lincoln? Does he already know? Is this why he's gone?

"Hey there. Any news about Wyatt?" the homeless girl asks.

I blink, clearing my throat. "No. I'm sorry. What happened?"

"You don't know? I found him. He was pretty sick and out of it, so I called an ambulance. I rode to the hospital with him, but then Lincoln came and I couldn't stay there forever. I just want to know how Wyatt's doing." She gestures to the collapsed, empty tent.

A rock forms in my throat.

"What hospital did they go to?" I ask.

Before she's even done rattling off a name, I'm racing into the night.

Lincoln Burns might be the bastard child of a cactus and a rabid wolverine, but I can't leave him hanging with those stand-offish texts if his best friend is dying.

I need to find him ASAP.

XX: THAT MELANCHOLY BURDEN
(LINCOLN)

Knock, knock, knock!

I jerk up in my seat, almost welcoming the interruption. It's a good reason not to write this stupid email I've been struggling with for days.

I go to the door, assuming it's a nurse or doctor here for another check-up. I find Olivia and Micha instead. The boy's face is hollow, empty, and scared.

My heart sinks. I'm glad he's here, but I know it can't be easy.

I reach down, tussling his hair with my hand.

"I haven't seen you in a while, little man. You've gotten so big."

He looks up slowly with a small sniffle. "Is my dad gonna be okay, Mr. Lincoln?"

"He's been through worse, I promise you that," I say, wishing I had the heart to lie to him with lofty guarantees about Wyatt springing out of bed tomorrow. "Why don't you go on in and see for yourself?"

"Thank you, Burns," Olivia clips. She's just as fabulous as ever, wearing a smile that looks like it wants to chew my face off.

You'd never guess the man she made a son with is lying behind us on his deathbed.

I hold the door open, ushering them inside before I let it shut behind me and walk across the hall.

I want to stay as close as I can while I wait for them to leave. Wyatt shouldn't be alone when there's always a sliver of a chance he could wake up.

They're in the room for less than half an hour.

Micha's strung-out sobs are hard to miss, even in the hall. When they exit the room, Olivia's face is redder than her son's. She swipes a tear off her cheek.

I want to believe those tears are real.

Only, she's so self-centered. She's probably just pissed Wyatt found a way to force himself back into her life—back into Micha's—even if he's horribly close to leaving this world.

I move over as Micha tries to shrink into the wall, his arms clasped tightly around his small body.

"You going to be okay, bud?" I ask, leaning down with concern.

"Yeah," he mumbles without looking up.

Olivia sighs.

"I just knew he'd end up like this if he kept living like a pack rat. He looks *terrible*." Her words are soft and strained.

"You're blaming a homeless guy for having pneumonia in front of his son?" I growl, standing and lowering my voice so the kid can't hear.

"No. I'm blaming a man who refused to hold down a job after Iraq, and who used to pop painkillers like dinner mints. He's lucky it's just pneumonia. I don't even want to know what his liver looks like."

"He couldn't work. He lost his leg—" I choke on my words, knowing I have to be calm for the boy's sake.

"But not his brain—"

"You abandoned him," I bite off.

"Oh, sure. It's not like his issues were any better when he was drinking himself stupid. Somebody had to support our son, and you're looking at her," she says bitterly.

"Whatever. Micha doesn't need to hear you trashing his old man like this while he's laid up in the room behind you. It's not fair to anyone."

Micha's small, hurt sobs are audible again. He looks at us with wide, glistening eyes.

"Is Daddy gonna die?"

"I don't know, honey," Olivia says quietly.

I shake my head firmly.

"He's a human ox. He'll pull through. Count on it, Micha."

He looks up at me, his eyes conflicted.

Goddammit, this sucks. Every last rotten bit of it.

I'm not sure what else to say. I don't deal with kids often.

I meet Olivia's eyes, hoping she'll come to the rescue. This is her son, her family, whatever the hell happened between them to cause grudges.

She stares straight ahead for a solid minute before her eyes flick to me.

"Well, we have to get back. Will you call me if he—if anything changes?"

My jaw tightens. I want to rip her a new one so bad.

"That's it?" I whisper, my voice low. "You'll let the boy visit one time for half an hour and run home?"

She closes her eyes for a second. When she opens them, she scoffs.

"Burns, would you want to see your father like that? Would it do anything besides give you nightmares for life?"

I roll my eyes, making a frustrated sound.

What the fuck ever. I get it.

She wants to fly back to her fancy new life with another sucker she'll probably screw over eventually the same way she did Wyatt. That's cool. But why use the boy as an emotional shield?

"Your choice," I bite off, crossing to the door and pressing my hand against it.

It's all I can do to keep my rage in check.

"You'll call me, right?" she calls after me.

Fuck no, I'm tempted to tell her.

If that's her attitude, she can find out Wyatt's fate from the staff.

Of course, I can't do that to my friend, though.

"Will you care?" I ask, moving back to the room.

"Lincoln, wait!" My name comes out like an expletive.

I don't stop, pushing the door open. I reenter Wyatt's room without continuing this pointless conversation.

I return to the hard chair I've practically lived in for the last few days and open my laptop again. Let's try this email one more time.

One of the monitors beeps.

I glance up at my friend, this motionless mass of tubes and paleness. His condition hasn't changed the whole time I've been here.

The lines move up and down the same way, the machines churning with faint hisses.

I exhale. "Get better, man."

With my eyes back on my screen, I confront a different torture, inhaling sharply.

Okay. Fuck. Let's try this again.

Dear Dakota,

I'm sorry I was a jackass.

My nose wrinkles. I punch DELETE. It's true, yeah, but there's no point in getting her hopes up just to crush her again.

Dear Dakota,

I can't see you again.

I snort, knowing how stupid that sounds.

My hands push the laptop shut again.

Who am I kidding?

Dakota Poe is the *only* person I want to see, and I shouldn't. I don't deserve her.

Even if I knew full well the sheer torment of watching a comatose Wyatt the past few days would have been easier with her here. And she'd be here if I only asked.

You'd think the hardest part of this past week would be staring at Wyatt, wondering if he'll ever leave his bed.

The hard part should've been tracking down his heartless ex and threatening her with legal destruction so she'd show up with their son, who I have an ugly feeling won't be back again.

I look at that mess of a man again, hanging my head.

"I'm sorry, Wyatt. I wish I'd done you better..." When I look up, I'm biting my inner cheek until I taste blood.

Wyatt Emory saved my life.

The hardest part should be watching, waiting, and praying he'll cheat death one more time.

But it's not.

It's only a close second to my other nightmare—trying to decide what to tell Dakota without gouging out my heart with a rusty serving spoon.

I'm not completely stupid.

Yes, I need to apologize, but more importantly, I can't crush her.

The text she sent calling me a coward speaks volumes.

I'm no fucking coward.

Doesn't she understand I'm trying to protect her from me?

Somewhere along the line, I forgot that romantic relationships are a sick joke.

Ma and Dad.

Olivia and Wyatt.

Regina and me.

They make me a worse man. A frustrated, explosive beast prone to outbursts that could wreck my life—and Dakota's by default.

They're a few years of flirting, sweet words, and guilt-free sex. All followed by a shattered lifetime in a tent because your other half gave up on you, leaving you stalking the world like a hollowed-out phantom.

I don't want Mother's fate, and I damn sure don't need Wyatt's.

I won't have that destroying Dakota, either.

I'm still brooding, staring out the small hospital window, when the door clicks. The doctor comes in, a wiry man with greying hair at the temples. He nods at me.

"You're a loyal visitor, standing watch like this," he says.

"Not half as loyal as Wyatt Emory."

He sets down a thick tablet on the bedside table, checks the monitors, and takes out a flashlight and shines it in Wyatt's eyes.

My friend doesn't stir.

I suck in a breath that burns and hold it while Wyatt snoozes through the rest of the exam.

After the doctor punches a few notes into his tablet, I can't stand the suspense.

"Any clue when he'll wake up?" I ask point-blank.

The doctor frowns.

"It's hard to say, I'm afraid. I'm mildly surprised he hasn't regained consciousness yet. Believe it or not, I have good news."

"You do?" I'm almost afraid to ask.

He motions me over to the screen in the corner and pulls up what looks like a digital X-ray. He points at the two white cloudy spots floating against the faint outline of Wyatt's chest.

"These are Mr. Emory's lungs," he says.

"Okay?"

He points to a foggy bubble on one of the ghostly balloons. "That's ground zero, where the infection is being fought. It was significantly worse forty-eight hours ago. It's clearing up, little by little, which means the drugs are working."

Shit.

Positive news has been so scarce lately I almost fall over.

Propping a hand against the wall, I stand and move closer to the screen, taking a good, long look.

"You're sure about that? I'm no doctor, obviously, but both of those lungs look pretty fogged over to me," I say.

"I'd say the fluid is roughly thirty percent less than it was yesterday in the worst areas," he assures me, pulling at his collar. "You see the bubbles, but what's not so clear in the image is the infection-free tissue, which appears rather healthy. We may have caught him just in time before permanent damage set in."

I pinch the bridge of my nose, exhaling slowly.

"Mr. Burns? Are you—"

"I'm fine, Doc. Damn. I'm just relieved. This is the first good news in a while."

He smiles. "Well, with the infection fading, he should be on the mend, especially once he's off the ventilator. This time next week, he should be breathing freely and regaining his strength."

"Hope you're right. Thank you," I say, leaning against the wall.

I haven't felt this relief since I was facedown in a combat zone, my ears ringing with a deafening blast, and that heap of shit crushing me was suddenly lifted away.

"No problem." He looks at Wyatt and back at me. "He's your brother?"

"Yeah," I mutter.

The doctor frowns. "According to his chart, he was brought in from the streets. When he's discharged, he'll need real care, or he could wind up right back at square one."

I toss my head, already determined to ensure that won't happen.

"Understood. I won't let him limp back to his tent, no matter how much he fusses. I've been trying to get him to move in with me for a while now, but he's stubborn as a mule." I heave out a sigh. "This time, I'll just drive him straight to my place."

"Good plan. I have to make my rounds, but I'll be back this

time tomorrow unless there's any abrupt change in his condition." He moves to the door and pulls it open.

That's my cue to get the hell out of here and find some fresh air. I head down to the lobby, my mind numb.

When I step out, I think I'm hallucinating.

A blond pixie rushes over and comes to a dead stop in front of me.

"Lincoln?"

"Dakota?"

We toss each other's names at the same time.

Shit. I wondered if my silence would bring her to me sooner or later.

This is not how I wanted to have this conversation, but the time for choosing is over.

She looks down, up, and covers her mouth with both hands as she meets my eyes.

"Oh my God. Is Wyatt okay? I heard something happened to him, but I didn't realize he was in the ICU." Her eyelashes flutter, soft green eyes misted with grief.

For a hellish second, I think she might cry.

She shouldn't be here.

But since she is, I make the only move I can.

"Let's talk outside," I say, placing a hand on her arm and escorting her to the nearest door and the cool, waiting night.

She follows, darting small glances at me as we walk. When we're finally outside and alone in the too-bright parking lights around the hospital, she looks at me and sighs.

"Is he...?"

"He'll be fine. Supposedly. The doctor just gave me an update. He caught a nasty case of pneumonia, but it's clearing up with the stuff they're giving him. I'm sure he'll pull through, even if he had me damn worried for a few days."

Her green eyes are marbles, reflecting the same worry and relief I know too well.

"I'm sorry, Lincoln. If I'd known—I would've been here with

you right away. But after what happened at the park, I just thought—" She stops.

I move my hand off her arm. I need the distance, and so does she.

The only thing more entanglement can give us is death by ten thousand cuts.

It's slightly humid tonight, the air thick with tension. That's not why it's hard to breathe.

How the hell do I do this?

"The doctor says Wyatt should be a lot better off in a week, so you don't need to worry." I take a deep breath, knowing what I have to do. "Dakota, you'll be better, too. I meant to contact you sooner. If it wasn't for this emergency, I would have."

"You had your reasons." She rolls one sleek shoulder. "Though you could've at least texted...I would've understood. You had me scared, and you worried the rest of the office, too."

A soft rain starts. I grab Dakota's arm, pulling us both under the awning before I release her like she'll burn me.

Distance, dammit.

Separation.

We need it.

"That brings me to my point," I say slowly, gathering my words. "What happened last week can't ever happen again."

I wait for her to nod, her eyes glittering in the quiet rain and hazy lights.

"I've made a hard decision. All I can ever give you is baggage, Dakota. I won't trouble you with that shit anymore."

Her face screws up in shock. Instant hurt.

"What baggage? What are you talking about?" She holds a fist to her chest.

"I'm leaving you alone. You won't have to—"

"Oh my God! You're...are you stupid?" she sputters. "Lincoln, I'm pissed because you stopped bothering me with anything. You verbally shot me in front of the entire staff and then you disappeared. You said we were *nothing*."

It's like a fucking movie.

Right on cue, lightning rips the sky. That early summer rain turns to an all-out storm, beating the air.

Dakota stares out at the mess and looks back at me.

How do I make her understand?

"I'll be the first to admit mistakes were made. Entirely mine. Not yours." I jab a thumb at my chest for emphasis. "What happened when that asshole showed up swinging a knife—I had to step in. That part was right. The rest of it was where we went wrong. I crushed a man's face and just between you and me, the outcome would've been the same whether he rushed us or not. I can't be that person again. I panicked."

"You panicked? *You* panicked?" She shakes her head violently. "My psycho ex could've killed us if you hadn't punched him. Then you stabbed me anyway with that stupid denial in front of everyone. And you think you get to panic?"

"I only—fuck. It never should've escalated to that point, whether it was necessary or not. Maybe the little idiot wouldn't have charged if I hadn't pushed him." I clamp my mouth shut. "Don't you get it? It's hard to think straight when I'm around you. You make me too insane, too reckless, too passionate. That's a side of myself I unleashed once, and it almost cost me everything."

She looks at me, totally bewildered.

I haven't told her about the man I beat when I caught him cheating with my ex, but that's not the point.

I'm not admitting what she's really done to me, horror of horrors.

She made my dumbass fall in love.

What else is there to say to that?

We should be done. More words can only make this worse.

"Oh, Lincoln. You sad, strange man..." She steps toward me.

I take a halting step back, and I'd rather break my own leg.

Goddammit, will she stop making this so hard?

If she gets any closer, I'm boned. Because I'll kiss her, and that's a one-way ticket to ruin.

Her bottom lip quivers with rejection, this faint, desperate hope fading in her gaze.

Damn, Dakota, please don't cry.

Don't waste your tears and your love on the rain, on me.

Don't make me lose my resolve.

"I'm so sorry. I never meant to hurt you. You're the last person I *ever* wanted to hurt, sweetheart." I pause, my tongue on fucking fire. "I can't undo what's happened, but I can prevent more damage."

"I—I still don't understand. What do you mean? What happened that's made you so afraid?"

I set my jaw so hard I'm about to crack a molar.

More explaining won't help.

She wears the same heartbroken expression she did on the street that day. At least she isn't crying yet.

"For you, I'll make this easy because it's my fuckup and it's unforgivable," I say. "I'm stepping away from the company. A long leave of absence. Your job will be safe and you won't report to me anymore. I never should've gotten involved with an employee, but it won't come at your expense—"

"Just an employee? That's all I am to you?"

Her face is *killing me.*

She's not "just" anything and she knows it. I need to get this over with.

"I'm saving you from the fallout. Your life was trashed once by a big dumbass leaving you out in the cold. Not this time. I'll go into total exile before I let that happen. Honestly, Wyatt deserves my time off, too. Whatever support I can lend to his recovery, but—" I can't finish. My throat knots, cutting off my air supply.

I thought I was stronger.

Evidently, I can fight a war and run a multibillion-dollar

brand, but I can't break it off with this little poet without turning my insides into thorns.

"But?" she urges.

Do it, Lincoln. Take the shot.

"But—I'm done with it. All of it, Dakota. I've made a big goddamned mess of things. I tore up your heart and mine along with it. That's not something I'll keep doing while it's still in my power to stop it."

For a single second that feels like an eternity, she's quiet.

"So that's it then?" she mutters.

I don't answer.

Maybe she was right when she called me a coward.

"You got your wedding campaign out of the deal." Her face goes red. "And your *fun*, and now you're just tossing me aside." Her eyes glisten with fresh, molten tears.

"Dakota—"

"Just like before. You...you used me," she whispers. Then she throws her head back and stares at the sky, cloudy and unsettled with distant thunder. "I should be used to it by now. I'm such an idiot. When will I learn? I never fucking will, I swear."

She turns and starts moving away.

Fuck, I can't let it end like this.

"Wait. I'm mangling this. It's coming out wrong." How do I make her understand?

I *can't* love.

I can't.

Cupid, that rat bastard, doesn't hit people with cute arrows. He blows up their lives with lethal missiles.

He's not doing that to mine. He's not reducing her life to rubble.

"Dakota, I hate this. Listen, I can handle fucking up myself, but I can't do that to you. I can't ruin your life while you're still young and beautiful and so smart. You still have a chance with a better man than any I'll ever be."

Tears stream down her face now, each breath racking her entire body.

"Lincoln?" Her voice is barely audible as she stops and turns.

"Yes?"

She flips me off, her eyes glowing like hellfire, and then she's gone, one more shadow in the storm.

"Wait! I'll call a car for you."

She doesn't stop.

She doesn't even throw me a backward glance.

I start after her, but she doubles her pace.

After she's out of my sight, I walk back inside the hospital, a drenched mess of a human being in every way imaginable.

I'll go sit with Wyatt. I don't want him to be alone when he wakes up, though tonight would be one hell of a time.

My laptop sits in the chair I've lived in for days. I pick it up and collapse into the chair. At least I don't have to worry about sending that email anymore.

Still, now I need to work out what stepping away from the company looks like, and who can take my place without running the empire into the ground.

The worst part is, Mother is still the majority shareholder. I'll have to talk to her and I'll get a nuclear earful when she finds out why I'm leaving.

I could tell her I need to help Wyatt, but she won't like that one bit. She'll probably also tell me to take a month off instead of backing away completely.

I'm not even sure a temporary leave will work unless Dakota quits, which is always a grim possibility. She moved out of state after her last breakup.

Something about running her out of this city wrenches my gut.

So does that last parting look with the one-gun salute.

No woman has ever looked at me with such contempt before. Any chance I had with Dakota Poe in my next five lifetimes was slaughtered outside this hospital.

"Burns, you are one dumb SOB," I whisper.

It's far too easy to imagine Wyatt saying those words.

Whenever he wakes up, he'll probably invent new ways to call me a fucking fool.

And if Dakota can't hack it—if she packs up and heads home to North Dakota—will that little jagoff be waiting for her?

I already agreed to avoid pressing charges if and when they assure me he's set up with a therapist, a job, and a place to live at least five hundred miles from Seattle.

Dammit.

Dakota basically said I'm just like him, and I can't even argue.

He ruined her past, and I just flattened her whole future.

I push my face into my hands, pressing my knuckles into my eyes.

I'm doing everything humanly possible to make this right. To let her walk away with minimal damage.

Whatever she chooses next shouldn't bother me.

It shouldn't, but it does.

It's her life, and she's better off without the pond scum named Lincoln Burns.

XXI: STILL BEGUILING (DAKOTA)

*W*elp, the asshat actually did it.

He stepped away from the company without even the courtesy of showing up for one last all-staff meeting. He just blasts an email to the entire crew.

Dear all,

I've recently found myself dealing with a personal tragedy that requires all of my attention and my heart. It wouldn't be fair for me to stay on at the helm of Haughty But Nice dividing my time. I can't do that to you.

That's why I'm stepping away indefinitely to tend to personal matters.

I hate that my time with you has come to an unexpected end. I'll sincerely miss each and every one of you. Some of you, I've known my whole life. Rest assured I'm leaving you in the most capable hands.

Sincerest wishes,

Lincoln Burns, Chief Executive Officer

. . .

I READ THE EMAIL, blinking back tears, and turn to Cheryl.

"So who's our new CEO?" I ask.

"Oh, God, I have no idea. Did you know about this?"

I shrug glumly.

"...he said he might do this, the last time we got into it. I just didn't think he was serious." I bite my lip, hating the instant crash in office morale I can feel in the air.

The COO strolls right past us to Anna's office.

That's never happened before. We stare after her.

"Why is she down here?" I whisper.

"How should I know?"

I try to glue my eyes back to ad projects on my screen, but I'm too distracted by the impending doom. We whisper back and forth, wondering why our lowly marketing team is being visited by C-level staff.

"I *knew* something was seriously wrong," Cheryl moans, rubbing her face. "We're going under, aren't we? We took on too much with that wedding line. Burns knows it, and he's jumping ship before we're underwater."

"Lincoln wouldn't have resigned if he thought we were going under. He'd stay and fight until he turned it around." I may loathe the man for using my heart as a punching bag, but I'll give him his professional due.

I also know the real reason for the turnover in leadership.

Linc just doesn't know what to do. He'd rather exit his family business than deal with me.

Sure, there's also the Wyatt factor, but ugh.

I used to think I hit my all-time low when Jay ghosted on my wedding day. Anything had to be better after that.

I was wrong.

Cheryl stares through her computer screen and glances at Anna's door. "She's been in there for a while."

The COO comes out of Anna's office and goes straight to the elevator without speaking to anyone else.

Anna steps out about a minute later and walks up to us.

386

"Dakota, do you have a few? I'd like to talk." she asks.

My stomach sinks.

"Good luck," Cheryl mouths from her desk.

I nod, square my shoulders, and head to Anna's office, ready to face the music, although I'm not even sure what I'm facing the music for. An HR formality, probably. They want some kind of statement to cover the company's butt based on whatever Lincoln said about us.

Hell, maybe they think I should resign, too. That would tie up any loose ends.

"Why are you so tense?" she asks as I pass her.

"...I don't know."

She smiles. "Have a seat. I'm not here to put you in front of a firing squad."

Not a huge relief, but I comply.

"So, Lincoln's departure is a pretty big surprise. No one expected it." Anna moves to her desk and sits. "The board will work to hire a new CEO, but in the meantime, leadership is being reshuffled."

"Reshuffled?" A lump forms in my throat. That doesn't sound good.

I should have just quit when crap went down.

"Jane's going to be our acting CEO—"

"Jane?"

"The COO."

"Oh, right." I see her around but never knew her name.

"I'll be acting COO in the meantime. It's not permanent. Jane will return to her position when it's all said and done." She whispers, even though we're alone in her office. "But just between you and me, I'm confident she's planning to leverage her temporary CEO experience to take a stab at being CEO somewhere else once Lincoln is replaced. And if that happens, I'll be staying in Jane's position permanently."

I nod. What does any of this have to do with me?

"While I'm COO, you're going to be marketing manager."

My heart jumps, sticking in my throat.

"What? But there are people who have been here way longer—"

"Doesn't matter. You already review other people's work when you don't need to. Your suggestions are always good. People find it easy to ask you for advice and accept your criticism. There's no one better for this role. It may be temporary, but it'll be awesome experience on your resumé."

I'm stunned, glued to my seat.

"Thank you. Um, when do I start?"

Anna clasps her hands and leans forward. "Today, if you're ready."

After Lincoln, I don't know that I'll ever be ready for anything again. But I wanted a distraction, didn't I?

Ready or not, here it is.

* * *

It barely takes a few weeks to figure out I hate the new job.

All I do is go to meetings, approve creative from multiple teams, convince them they like their job, and run reports. I miss writing so much it hurts.

I also miss sparring with Lincoln over Regis rolls every morning. Anytime I go upstairs, I fight back tears at the sight of Jane in his office.

A whole month passes before I can blink.

No one's heard from Lincoln since the day he disappeared.

I definitely haven't. I don't know what I expected, though.

He made it clear that I don't matter. I'm the dirty little secret who blew him up and pushed him out of his career.

Anna and Jane have my back, working hard to shut down any lingering gossip. But it's almost like they don't need to. He's been gone so long we're creeping into *life goes on* territory, when news becomes memories and memories start to fade.

I head downstairs with a sigh, ready for another dull day.

Cinnamon and butter punch me in the nose when I hit the marketing floor.

Jesus. It shouldn't still remind me of him.

I've avoided Sweeter Grind like the plague lately. Now, that's impossible with everyone holding one of those stupid colossal cinnamon rolls.

"Hey, Dakota." Cheryl smiles and follows me on my way to Anna's office—technically now mine. "You want me to grab you a Regis roll?"

"No. I'm—trying out this low carb thing. It's pretty brutal. The entire diet is bacon and cabbage." I stick my tongue out.

"Woof! You're braver than me," she says with a laugh. "Are you okay?"

I nod briskly.

"Do I not look okay?"

"You're smiling, but your eyes aren't. It's okay to be upset."

Part of me loves her for going into office mom mode when she sees me having so much as a quiet moment. The rest of me feels annoyed.

"I'm fine, Cheryl. No reason to be upset."

"I mean, I'd still be raiding the drugstore every night for ice cream. Do they have a bacon and cabbage flavor?"

I look at her and blink.

"I don't want to find out. Also, it's been an entire month. I'm over it, lady. If I can get over a crazy, cheating scumbag leaving me at the altar, I can also get over Lincoln freaking Burns."

I wish those words sounded sincere.

Who am I kidding? Lincoln Burns is everything I ever wanted.

He's everything Jay isn't, and now he's gone in a flash of shattered hearts.

I try not to scoff.

"If you ever want to talk, I'm here," Cheryl says gently.

Oops. I guess that scoff was audible.

"Yeah. Thanks."

"And thank you for your feedback on the latest copy. I'm correcting it today, and I'll have it to you by lunch. It's way easier working for you!"

I plaster on a smile that doesn't feel real.

People keep telling me I'm a natural in this role, but it makes me hate it more.

Just because you're competent doesn't mean you're happy.

I want to sling words—not manage people—and I desperately hope maybe Jane decides she wants her old COO position back so Anna will have to fall back to this. I'll gladly give it up the second she asks.

"Your work rocks, Cheryl. Tons of improvement," I tell her, ripping my mind off bad thoughts.

Cheryl beams, her soft silvery eyes twinkling. "I think it's because you showed me I'm not afraid to take chances. If something doesn't work, you let me know without any ego in the way. We just change it up."

My lips twist in thought. Her posts have gotten funnier recently.

"Can't wait to see what you bring me. I'll see you later," I say as I push open my office door.

I've barely been at my desk for fifteen minutes when someone knocks.

Now what?

"Come in!" I call.

Whoever I expect, it's definitely not Tillie Burns marching through the door in a green blazer and gold necklace that look like they were just jacked from a runway model.

Can this day get any worse?

"Mrs. Burns? What a surprise. I wasn't expecting you." That's an understatement.

And Tillie is a nice woman but her sudden presence is like a sucker punch.

The biggest reminder of Captain Dipshit yet.

"Hello, dear. I'm sorry I haven't been around the last few

weeks to check in on everyone since Lincoln left. He asked me to lay low, actually, and thought it would make the transition easier. I agreed. I love this company, though, and I simply couldn't stay away forever. I'm sure you've had one of my cinnamon rolls?"

"Um, bacon diet. I wish I could." I wrinkle my nose. "But the whole office loves them. You're pretty much the hero around here anytime you bring Sweeter Grind."

"Oh, the pleasure is all mine. It's the least I can do to support my grown-up baby. I want this company to thrive with heart and soul for many years to come—even if my dearest son is a horse's ass."

I bite back laughter, giving her a curious look.

Somehow, I have a feeling this isn't just about cinnamon rolls and waxing nostalgic.

Without hesitation, Tillie closes the door behind her and takes the empty seat across from my desk.

"Dakota, I'm so sorry," she says abruptly.

Wait, what?

So that's what she wants. I was afraid of this.

I glance at her, guarded, and shake my head.

"You can't apologize for your son's behavior, Mrs. Burns. It's not your fault. If he really wanted to apologize—please don't take this the wrong way—but he'd man up and do it himself."

I try to keep my anger in check. It's not easy when I know he hasn't done it because he doesn't want to.

"Oh, I'm not apologizing *for* him," Tillie says smoothly.

My eyebrows go up. "Then why did you say you're sorry?"

"Because I feel responsible for this dreadful outcome." Her body ripples with a sigh.

A single surprised laugh slips out of me.

"This is not your fault in any way, shape, or form. Not even indirectly. It's partly mine for being stupid enough to get involved, to believe him. And a lot of it was his for being—" I remember I'm talking to his mom. "Umm—well—so *Lincoln.*"

She gives me a knowing nod.

"The boy can be maddening. I know, considering I'm the one who raised him. His father was the same way." Her lips curl in this half smile, and her eyes are somewhere else. A different time and place.

"Lincoln told me you adored his dad..."

"Oh, I still do." She shrugs. "That didn't make him any less infuriating at times. But that's not my point. I'm here to apologize for my role in this mess. I'm the one who talked Lincoln into entertaining this fake engagement marketing ploy while I hoped it would turn into something else. If I'd just kept my meddling mouth shut, the rest of this drama might have been avoided."

I don't follow.

"You did?" I whisper. I was under the impression Lincoln Burns doesn't do anything he doesn't damn well want to do.

Tillie nods slowly, frowning.

"Do you remember the first day we met?" she asks.

"How could I forget? You found me crying..." She must think I'm such a loser. The first time we met, I was having a nervous breakdown at work. Now I've had a tryst with her son that pushed him out of her company.

"That's the day. Lincoln came around the corner, saw you upset, and was ready to kill someone—"

"Your son was the *reason* I was hurt," I tell her.

There's no point in hiding it if we're spilling truths all over the place.

"Yes, I guessed as much." She smiles sheepishly. "It bothered him, though. Deeply. I know when he's upset. In fact, the only time I've ever seen him so flustered is when that young man he looks after gets in real trouble—"

"Wyatt?"

"Yes," she says with a knowing smile.

"Not to change the subject, but how's he doing?" I sincerely want to know.

"He's on the mend. It hasn't been an easy recovery, but when this all started, it wasn't even certain he had another chance in the cards."

I exhale pure relief, thankful that something went right.

"Anywho, back to business. I'm sorry I talked Lincoln into the fake wedding. He's a grown man and he makes his own decisions, but I can't help feeling like I might've been the decisive factor in his thinking. It's just a trope in so many movies, and you two played off each other brilliantly when I saw you together." She dips her head and looks up at me with big, sad eyes. "I had no right to intervene, Dakota, even if I'm obsessed with seeing my son happy. I just knew if he had to spend time with you—if he let his shields down, it wouldn't stay fake for long.'"

"Yeah, well..." I can't find the words to respond to that, so I shift in my seat.

"I assure you, I didn't expect him to go and muck it up so dreadfully." Again, she pauses and sighs, raw grief in her face. "I never knew it would trigger bad memories for him. Let alone bring him so close to making the same awful mistake twice..."

"What mistake?" I lean forward, my mind flashing back to that last horrible conversation with Lincoln and his cryptic comments about becoming someone else.

Everyone keeps dancing around some big forbidden secret.

Tillie looks at me sadly.

"You know how his last relationship ended, yes?"

I nod slowly. "He mentioned it. Cheating fiancée. Nasty fight. He said he caught her with her lover... It must've been pretty bad."

"That's putting it mildly." She straightens in her seat, her mouth drawn tight. "I suppose he never mentioned the hideous aftermath?"

I shake my head, baffled at what she means.

"He's an honest man, Dakota. When he goes all into something, he gives his entire heart, and it was like that with Regina, too. When he caught them together, he couldn't hold back, right or wrong..."

Oh, God.

What *is* she getting at?

Tillie holds up a hand. "You didn't hear this from me, but that poor excuse for a man he found her with, he had the nerve to laugh in Lincoln's face when my boy ordered him to get out. Then he threw the first punch."

Holy crap. I'm getting flashbacks of what happened with Jay and the knife.

"That's awful, Mrs. Burns."

"It's Tillie," she corrects sharply, taking a deep breath. "And that impulsive little rat almost wound up in an early grave. The second after he struck first, Lincoln pushed him to the ground and beat him senseless. He didn't stop until half the bones in that man's body were fractured."

"Oh my God," I whisper, my hand coming to my mouth.

She nods like her head weighs a ton.

"You can guess what came next," Tillie says. "A criminal report. Lots of accusations and lawyers. Lincoln was lucky he wasn't arrested, and luckier still when the man agreed to drop all charges for an appalling settlement. My son came an inch away from losing his reputation, his job, his entire life..."

When it clicks in my head, it twists like a knife.

Especially when Tillie says, "He knew how narrowly he dodged a cannonball. He worked hard to never put himself in that position again, to keep his anger from taking over. But regrettably, when your ex came along and tried to hurt you..."

"He panicked," I finish weakly. "No wonder he freaked."

"I only wish telling you could make it better, but I'm not delusional," Tillie says. "Here, this should do more than any words ever will."

She pulls a large envelope from her pocket and pushes it toward me. I'm so numb I can barely reach for it.

"What's this?"

"Open it," she tells me. "It can't make up for the emotional tizzy I've had a hand in, but it's a tangible apology."

I open the thick pink envelope and pull out—a contract?

Huh.

She's offering me a "creative fee" of five percent net profit from the wedding line.

Wait.

That's a product line projected to profit at least half a billion dollars. Five percent of a conservative five hundred million is— *holy Hannah, I don't even know.*

It's a crapload.

I throw the contract back at her like it's burning my hand.

"Mrs. Burns—*Tillie*—no way. This so isn't necessary. I'm fairly compensated for my work on the wedding line, and anything else that happened outside work is—"

"Nonsense. There's no earthly way he could've paid you enough for a sham that ended in tears. I know about your ninety-day work arrangement, too, and he'll still pay you for that since you've reached the deadline. I feel horrible about this whole thing. If I was even a teensy bit to blame, I *must* make amends."

Her eyes flash, a hazel-brown shade lighter than her son's.

I've seen that same defiant look before, too.

Now, I know where he gets it...

God, I hate this.

She's such a nice lady, and she's his mother. It's not her fault her son is a complicated jerkwad. Also, I don't want to upset her, but there's no point in denying the obvious.

"Well, I did get hurt, but money can't fix a bad breakup. I mean, this is overkill. I don't need to be a freaking millionaire because Lincoln broke up with me."

"The ad concepts were your idea, Dakota."

"But the fake marriage was Anna Patel's!" I throw back.

"Lincoln told me you wrote most of the copy, or approved it." Her eyes are unwavering.

"I did." My voice is shrinking.

"And you were in those pictures with my son. You crafted a large part of the social media push that's beginning now. Help me understand why you don't deserve this?"

I don't say anything, but I'm still holding out the contract.

She doesn't take it.

"I hope you realize this money is yours. I won't take it back, and if you refuse payment...well, I'll be so offended I'll never speak to you again."

Dang.

Tillie Burns can do a supermom guilt trip so intense it could curl your hair, and she's not even *my* mom.

I drop the contract on my desk with a conflicted sigh.

So this is my life.

Forced into reluctant riches, something I used to dream of in college.

"I wish I could turn back the clock, but money can't buy time. I should have stayed out of it like Lincoln told me to," she says.

"No, ma'am. It's not your job to make me feel better. The only person in the world who can do that has made it pretty clear where he stands—as far away from me as possible." I pull at my collar awkwardly, wondering why it feels like a steam valve.

"That terrible breakup with his ex and everything that came after left him a guarded man. Even before that, he wasn't good at relationships, at feelings. I know my son."

She's so genuine.

Unfortunately, I know men.

"Tillie, he hasn't spoken to me since the day he ditched me in front of the hospital. Not the actions of a man who cares. It's fine. I always knew I wasn't the kind of girl handsome CEOs end up with," I say.

"I have no idea what you think my son's type is, but I'll tell you this. If he didn't care, he wouldn't have ended it and slipped into the ether. Dear Lord, do girls not read romance novels anymore?" She smiles.

"My tastes run darker, and romance is fantasy way too often. That's why the fake wedding scheme didn't work."

"If he didn't care about you, Dakota, it wouldn't matter to him if you ran away with a biker. He left so you could continue on here with peace of mind. He had something to lose, so he took the loss the best way he could in his own misguided way."

Oh my God. Is she right? I want her to be right.

Shut up, Dakota. It's wishful thinking and you know it.

But she's rubbed this wound raw again. I blink several times, my eyes stinging.

"So, I hate to cut this sort, Tillie, but I have a meeting."

"But—"

I stand, needing to get out of here.

"I really have to go. Sorry." I race out of the office, leaving her behind.

In the bathroom, I lock myself in a stall and ugly cry. Once it's out of me, I fish my phone out of my pocket and panic text Eliza.

Dakota: I wish I was dead.

Eliza: What happened??? I'm shocked you're still working there. I couldn't hack it. Are people trash-talking you?

Dakota: Maybe. Probably. I don't care.

Eliza: What's wrong then?

I give Eliza a quick rundown on everything that just happened, including Matilda Burns' bonkers apology offer.

When I tell her the amount, there's a three-minute pause before my phone buzzes again.

Eliza: OMG. Take it and run! Dakota, you can write your heart out forever.

She sends a gif with a jolly pig rolling around in a pile of money.

Technically, she's right. I should be euphoric.

I basically hit the jackpot, only, this is a lot more personal than any faceless lottery win.

I send a one-word response. *Why?*

Eliza: Uh, if being an instant millionaire isn't incentive enough, how about being able to quit? Not being reminded of Lincoln Burns on a daily basis? That might help you get over him.

I frown, knowing she's right.

That's why it's been a month and I can't get him out of my head. Everything here still breathes Lincoln Burns.

Dakota: I don't know. I'm in management now. And it feels like an even crappier move if I take the money and run.

Eliza: You hate management. You're a Poe.

Fair point.

When I was writing ads, it wasn't poetry, but at least it was writing.

Dakota: Another issue, quitting would be like admitting all the rumors are true, right?

Eliza: Well...they are.

Dakota: But no one else needs to know that.

Eliza: But they already do!

Before I can reply, another message dings.

Eliza: And why did this woman show up to randomly apologize for convincing her son to fake marry you? That's weird.

Dakota: She felt bad. She just wanted to make things right. I'm pretty sure my cut is coming out of hers, and it's not like anyone named Burns is hurting for money...

Eliza: You haven't texted me from the bathroom crying for over a week until now. I just decided I don't like his mom any more than I like his stupid face.

I laugh. I didn't meet Eliza until I moved here, but she's so loyal. I pity the lunk who ever tries to date her.

Dakota: His mom is very nice. Don't hate her on my behalf.

Eliza: She upset you. What are you going to do? I hope you don't move out of state like you did after Jay. You're the only person in the building I like.

Dakota: LOL. No worries. I hate moving, no matter how much money I've got. I have you, my bike, and a really awesome savings cushion.

Eliza: Gotcha. What's next then?

Dakota: I'm going to wash my face so no one knows I've been crying when I walk out of this bathroom. And I'm going to start applying for writing jobs. When I find something, I'll jump.

Eliza: Only in Seattle?

Dakota: Yes. Relax, I'm stuck here.

I've known ever since I moved here that this was the place to be. The rain, the disappearing mountain, the cool breezes, the lush greenery surrounding the city, the art scene... This place may have its problems, but it just vibes *writer.*

For a while, I even thought I might find someone here to put Jay to shame.

Oh, I got my wish in the worst way.

But I also met Eliza, Cheryl, Anna, and a few more cool people. Until I got promoted, I made a nice salary doing what I love. There are plenty of reasons to stay, and Lincoln Burns won't scare me away from rebooting my life.

I scrub my face with cold water and head back to my desk.

Acting like memories of Lincoln aren't looping through my head is harder than it seems.

By afternoon, I duck out early and go for a long bike ride in the early summer breeze.

My legs pump until breathing hurts. I want to imagine I can sweat out heartbreak.

I'll get over this jackass one way or another, richer or poorer, better or worse.

Thanks to him, I'm stronger than I was when I first showed up in this city.

If his gift was heartbreak, I'll mend it by building a life worth living.

XXII: BIRD OF YORE (LINCOLN)

I forgot how cozy the guesthouse can be until I brought Wyatt home.

It made sense and it gives him plenty of space while he recovers. Plus, the place is single level, so it's easier to take care of him until then.

The nurse steps out of Wyatt's room.

"How's he doing today?"

"Definitely better. His vitals look excellent today. I'll be back in the evening to check in," she tells me.

"Is he awake?"

She smiles. "Yeah, you can go on in. I'm sure he'll love the company."

I walk her to the door, and once she's gone, I retrace my steps and enter Wyatt's room. He's sitting up in the bed, leaning against the frame, only half as ghost-white as he was a few weeks ago.

I grin. "This is the longest I've seen you up. Looks like you'll be running around in no time."

He looks at me but doesn't say anything.

"The nurse says you're doing better. With any luck, you should—"

"Lincoln Burns, you are a fucking idiot," he growls, cutting me off.

I can't say I mind the insult. I haven't heard him talk smack since before he got sick. If I needed a real sign, here it is.

"Good morning to you too?" I roll my eyes. "At least I know you're feeling better."

"I said you're a damn idiot," he snaps, pulling at his newly trimmed beard.

"I heard you the first time, pal."

He holds my gaze.

I fold my arms. "Am I supposed to ask why you're calling me stupid?"

"How long have you been glued to my side?"

"Glued to your side?" I don't follow.

"Telling me old war stories like I didn't live through that shit with you, and bad jokes that are never funny for anyone but you. Can't remember the last time I heard something besides your voice."

"You're talking about the coma? I didn't want to leave you hanging, and I figured if you could hear anything while you were out cold, I thought you'd appreciate the entertainment."

"Burns, you have a life to live. You were finally starting to do something besides work." He huffs out a breath. "What happened to Raven?"

"Raven?"

"Blondie. Worker bee. The chick with the raven tattoo."

My lips turn up.

"Nevermore, you mean." Then I remember she's truly *never more* and my smile vanishes. "I—well—it didn't work out."

"Why not?"

Fuck.

I stare at him, unblinking.

"Why didn't it work out?" he repeats. "She had a husband she forgot to mention? Because anything short of that, and you're one dumb bastard."

"I ruined it, okay? Are you satisfied?" I bite off. "It was bringing out the worst in me and I left her in a good place. She's in management now."

I clamp my jaw shut, not telling him I'm basically out the door. He might have a heart attack if he hears I'm no longer on the corporate train.

Wyatt chuckles. "What the hell ever. I don't doubt you left her better off than you found her. That's not the point."

"What is?"

"Your voice is almost cracking like a sixteen-year-old kid just talking about her, man. I might be stuck in bed, but shit. If I find out I'm the reason you dropped that girl, I will beat you to such a fucking pulp you'll wish like hell I'd left you buried in Iraq."

I snort at how ridiculous he sounds.

"You're a Nevermore fan, huh?"

He glares at me. "I'm a Burns fan. And you don't have many of 'em who aren't interested in your bank account, so it might benefit you to tune in and listen for once, you stubborn cock."

"Those drugs make you nicer than usual," I grumble sarcastically.

"Without them, I'd be dead because I'm dealing with you. Now tell me what happened with Raven."

I cross the room and drop down on the window seat next to him.

"I won't deny I miss her. Walking away from her was hard as hell, but it's for the best. Trust me." I shrug quickly. "It was going to hurt far worse later, if I'd let her linger."

"Uh—I'm the guy on drugs. What kind of *hurt* you mean?"

"The kind you know," I say, trying to be gentle and failing. My gaze hardens. "You loved Olivia more than life, way back. She came to the hospital one time while you were sick, and only then because I threatened her with everything I could think of if she didn't bring Micha. You loved her so much and she just fucking abandoned you. How can anybody believe in love after that?"

"She saw me three times."

He's confused. I shake my head sharply.

"She came once, Wyatt."

"Nah, she came again the next day, before they had to catch a flight. She apologized for everything. For such a brilliant man, you can be one dense motherfucker."

"Not possible. I barely left the hospital. They came once."

"You must have just missed each other then. I'm the guy who was laid up with nothing better to do than listen to people talk," he says, tossing his body back against the pillows.

"I don't believe she apologized. She fought with me like crazy in the hall."

Somehow, he laughs.

"You just have a hard time concealing your venom, and Olivia was never one to take shit."

I don't answer.

Arguing with him won't do either of us any good.

"Seeing me so busted must have stroked whatever mouse-sized soul she has left," he says. "She apologized for everything and said as soon as I'm well, she'll make sure I see Micha again. We'll never be best friends or whatever, but I can respect that."

I stand slowly, pulling at my shirt.

"Respect? After everything she's done to you, you're going to forgive her? She was crying over a man in a coma. Who knows if she'll follow through—though I hope she will."

Wyatt looks up at the ceiling and laughs, falling into a brief coughing fit.

"Careful," I whisper. "You know, it's not important—"

"Burns. How have you survived on the planet this long? You really are clueless. Forgiveness is earned. I don't want a second chance with Olivia. But for my family's sake? Yeah, that apology is the start of something better for everyone." He pauses, stroking his beard. "Now that you've burned up my energy, I need to sleep."

He rolls over and turns his back to me.

Goddamn, this is frustrating, but he's also right.

Wyatt isn't furious at Olivia anymore. *I am.*

What if she's not his personal Satan?

Maybe I am a certified fool.

What if I'd tried harder to work through my crap, my constant doubts about love? Would I still have Dakota Poe warming my bed?

I hate that I'll never know.

I might never stop regretting what I did to her, either.

* * *

A Regis roll stares up at me from Mom's best china like it's a radioactive tumor on a plate.

I don't go to Sweeter Grind anymore.

Since I've finally got Wyatt expanding his palate beyond pure sugar and it reminds me of Dakota like a knife to the face, there's no need.

Thank God.

Ma, on the other hand, still damn near worships the things. She bites her roll in half with an excited smile, chewing as she looks at me.

"Are you okay, Lincoln?" she asks after she swallows.

"I'm peachy." I'm just not here.

I'm still beside a campfire with Dakota in a homeless camp.

I'm still watching her eyes glisten in the rain.

I'm still on a moonlit overlook, trying to kiss her, but some jackass who can't buy a muffler steals my thunder.

I'm still driving into her, a gentle hand on her throat, waiting until she looks at me before I unload inside her so hard I see stars.

I'm—

Pulling my head out of the gutter, apparently. Because I'm having coffee with my mom and pretending to stuff a mess of sugar into my mouth.

"You've barely touched your cinnamon roll or your coffee. No appetite today?"

"I'm fine, Ma. Just not hungry."

"I'm worried about you, Lincoln. You should be learning to unwind without a company to manage. This past month is probably the only time in your life where you haven't been workaholicking."

I look up. "You can't make workaholic a verb, Ma."

"I just did," she says, putting her fork down with a decisive clatter.

I shake my head, muttering under my breath.

"Okay. Whatever. It's not like this is a vacation. It may be the rest of my life," I tell her. "Plus, Wyatt still needs a lot of care."

Mom nods. "You're a good man, Lincoln, which is why I don't understand how you could be so horrible to that poor girl."

Oh, yeah. Here the fuck we go.

"I told you, I did the best I could. I left her a better job than the one she had. I would have made her a frigging exec if it were up to me, but she doesn't have a lot of experience at that level, so I couldn't force it."

"The job makes her miserable, son. She didn't even show a flicker of excitement about the profit share I gave her."

That grabs my attention.

"What? She told you that?"

"She didn't have to. She was pale, Lincoln, minus the dark lines under her eyes..."

I rattle a fist under the table, wishing I had one of those stress balls right now.

"Ma, just because you *think* something doesn't mean it's true. You thought the fake wedding was a good idea."

"In another universe, it might have been. One where Miss Poe didn't have a stalker and you didn't have such a sorry past that turned you into a short-fused grizzly bear."

Damn. I roll my eyes.

Everyone's calling me names today.

"I did the best I could for Dakota, all right? I even had you pitch her that fee out of *my* stake in the company, didn't I?" I take a loud slurp of coffee to shut my yap.

"She doesn't want money. The young woman wants an *apology*—and if you have it in that brain of yours, a makeup kiss or two wouldn't hurt."

"Not happening. Love—especially the office kind—leads nowhere good. I did us both a favor and saved us a flaming tragedy."

It's Ma's turn to roll her eyes.

"I swear you get that stubborn streak from your father because you've got my brains."

"What?"

"Lincoln Burns, you're no martyr. You're acting like a fool who walked away from a wonderful young creature who adored you." Her face tightens before she continues. "I'd give anything —*anything*—for one more hour with your father, and watching you give up on a woman you obviously care about, who loves you—" She throws up her hands. "If you weren't almost three times bigger, I'd spank you right now."

Brutal.

And of course she's desperate for another hour with Dad. That's because she's heartbroken and too blind to see it—to see what I'm saving us from.

She holds my gaze and says, "The biggest lesson I learned after your father passed was how bitterly short life can be. You can't waste it living in fear—"

"I'm not afraid, Ma."

She laughs and takes a hurried bite of her cinnamon roll. "Keep telling yourself that."

"What does that mean?"

"You were afraid of losing Dakota—"

"No, I wasn't. We weren't even together. It was a sham. I didn't have anything to lose." Yeah, right. Even I don't buy it.

"Whatever you say. Either way, you ended it. Now, you don't

have to worry about it. But love is a gift, Lincoln. The only way it ends in tragedy is if you choose to go through life without ever loving because you're scared to death you might get hurt. That's the real tragedy, son. I just hope you figure that out before it's too late." Her voice softens.

I don't know why that annoys me so much.

"Can we drop this?"

"Not likely. Dakota might've been the best chance for grand-kids I'll ever get. Also, I don't care what you say, dear. You were happy with her. It was clear as day in every photo."

"Huh? They were supposed to destroy those pictures," I growl, irritated that somebody didn't follow orders.

"I'm your mother. I told design to keep them locked up securely. How else am I supposed to know what you're up to?"

That fucking figures.

Between Wyatt's earlier comments about "Raven chick" and Ma's two cents, I'm on knife's edge. I've pitched nine-figure deals without this much adrenaline coursing through me.

"I have to get home to give Wyatt his medicine. He shouldn't get out of bed alone."

"Of course." Mom smiles, having said her piece.

I stand.

"So, can I hope you'll at least think about calling that girl?"

"You can hope whatever you want. Doesn't mean it'll happen."

She glowers at me, her eyes dark with disappointment.

"One day, I'm going to join your father. Then you might be sorry you never had your own family."

"You're so ornery that won't be for a while. Heaven thinks you're too entertaining here and you scare the pants off the devil." I lean down and kiss her on top of the head. "I love you, Ma."

"Bah. If you did, I'd have a grandbaby by now."

I leave her to lick my wounds in peace.

With my car on the ferry back to Seattle, I have plenty of time to think.

I've already met the Reaper face-to-face once, and again when I thought he had Wyatt's ticket. I'm fearless in business, take risks, and always land on my feet.

So how the hell does one little blond with a spear for a tongue bust me up so much?

Dakota damn Poe runs through my head in chaotic scenes.

Arguing over cinnamon rolls.

Red-faced and crying because she sent the wrong attachment.

Pulling a greedy moan that tastes like pure honey from her mouth.

Standing beside me in a white dress that's so goddamned beautiful it stops clocks.

My heart stops, too, because I know.

I know if I ever wanted a woman beside me in a white dress, it's Nevermore, and no one else.

It's that dress she wore like an angel sent to render me boneless.

Then I went and ruined what could've been by conning her into a fake-ass engagement. I let her worm of an ex get in my head and rattle me into shoving her away.

Why?

Dumbass, you know the answer.

I feel sick, and I never get motion sickness on these ships.

Fuck. What have I done?

Before I can regret it, I pick up my phone.

How are you, Nevermore? I text.

No answer.

No surprise.

How are you liking your new role? I try again.

That's a genuine question. Mother said she's miserable, and I thought she'd be happy being promoted.

There's no answer by the time I'm driving off the ferry thirty minutes later, my jaw tight, every nerve bristling.

A bullet to the face would hurt less than wondering if I damaged Dakota Poe so much she's given up completely.

I can't leave it like this, even if I can't even fathom how to fix it.

* * *

I sit in a chair beside Wyatt's bed, glaring at my phone every five minutes.

"Has your girl called yet?"

I roll my eyes. He knows damn well she hasn't.

"Quit acting like a lovesick fool and up your game," he tells me.

"I've sent texts. She won't answer."

He jerks forward with a snort so hard it makes him cough.

"Burns, I'm beginning to get how a pretty rich boy manages to stay single."

"I have no idea what you mean."

He barks laughter. "Like hell! You denied her in front of your people, and then you kicked her while she was down. Sending a text is—"

"A cop-out," I cut in.

He nods, a hard smile on his face like he's amazed it's getting through to me.

"What would you do then, love doctor?"

"Only you can figure that out." He slumps back, waving a hand.

Before he can sling more crap at me, an alert for the gate chimes on my phone. I pull up the camera view.

Whoever it is stands in the shadows, a slow night rain pelting them. I'm not expecting anyone, so it must be important, or a huge scam.

"Someone's here. I'll be right back." I get up and hit the

microphone icon to speak to them. "Burns residence. Who's there?"

"Uh, Meadow. From the park?"

Oh. I unlock the gate remotely and dart outside, waving her toward the house.

A minute later, Meadow stands on my porch shyly, not saying anything.

"Come on in and dry off," I tell her, ushering her inside. "What brings you here?"

Timidly, she looks up at me and lets out a deep breath.

"...I heard Wyatt might be staying here. He always mentioned you bothering him to move in and it took forever to find your place, but...I had to try. I had a little help. Sorry for any intrusion."

"It's fine. He's in my guesthouse. You want to follow me over?"

She nods. "Thank you."

"Who helped you find my place?" I ask.

"Oh, uh. I can't say."

I chuckle. "Can I ask why?"

She holds up a hand like she's apologizing and says, "Well, I don't think it's true, but *she* says you're a giant douchenozzle. And if I mention her name, she'll never tell me anything ever again." She laughs lightly. "Hard to argue with that, right?"

I know who Meadow means.

Dakota.

I nod. "Did you see her at the park?"

"No, that coffee shop up the block. Sweeter Grind. Sometimes they donate their used grounds for compost." She squeezes her eyes shut and hangs her head. "You won't say anything, will you?"

"I'm no rat."

She follows me to the guesthouse, where I open the door for her. I hear Wyatt stirring before we're even down the hall to his room.

"Well, hell. I guess it's not your damn girl, is it? I couldn't be that lucky, could I?" Wyatt calls loudly through the cracked door.

Meadow grins, covering a giggle with her hand.

I put a finger to my lips to shush her.

"Keep giving me hell, Emory, and you'll regret it," I say, poking my head in the room.

"Burns, I've regretted plenty in my life. None of it was *ever* giving you shit."

"He sounds better!" Meadow whispers.

She has no clue.

"What's taking so long? I need my meds. I damn near broke a rib hacking up a lung and it hurts all the way down to my ass crack."

"Wyatt! I'm going to suggest you shut up. You've got company. Are you decent?"

He goes dead silent.

As soon as he calls "Yeah," I lead Meadow into his room.

"Who—oh. Miss Green Thumb."

It's brutally hard not to laugh when the big bad badass blushes. His face reddens under his beard, a stark contrast against his body's lingering paleness.

And he's not alone. Meadow's cheeks are redder than cherries as she snickers.

He glares at me. "You couldn't have warned me *she* was here?"

I cross my arms in front of my chest. "And miss you making a fool out of yourself? Nah, that's payback."

"Whatever, dude." He turns to Meadow. "You weren't at the hospital," he says softly.

"I—" She looks down. "They only let family in the room. Lincoln said he was your brother—"

"She rode in the ambulance with you," I add.

"Eh, I don't like hospitals anyway. I couldn't stay too long.

But are you okay?" She's so shy, this small thing approaching this rude hulk occupying my guest bed.

"I'm fine, lady." His tone is soothing.

He's stuck in a bed, but he's comforting her.

She leans down and hugs him. His arms close around her. I can't help staring.

Damn.

After everything Olivia put him through, if Wyatt can find the strength to mend his black lump of a heart under that broken body, what the hell is my excuse?

I don't have one.

I turn to exit and give them some privacy.

"You're not gonna stay and hang out with us?" Wyatt asks.

"You guys should catch up. I just realized I have something to take care of." I *need* to get Dakota's attention.

"Someone, you mean," he says with a laugh. "About time."

I ignore him, moving to the door.

"And if she won't take you back, remember—grovel more!" Wyatt yells after me.

"Oh, stop. I'm not sure today is the day for that," I hear Meadow tell him. "I don't think she's ready to talk."

I block out her words and keep moving.

If I want to send up a flare, I'll need a real plan.

I won't stop until she's mine again—or until I believe she's happier without me.

How the hell do I talk to a woman who won't give me the time of day?

I know where she works, yeah. That's a start, but I sure as hell won't become her stalker ex.

I *need* to be the man she can count on.

The man she turns to.

The man who restores what we had before I went and fucked it all up.

Since I don't know what else to do, I reach for inspiration.

"Lincoln? To what do I owe this late-night call?" Ma answers the call like she's waking up from a dead sleep.

"In those silly movies, if a guy pissed off his fake fiancée, what would he do?" I can't believe I'm asking.

Mother gasps.

"Oh, dear! You've come to your senses."

"Ma, no. This isn't about me," I lie. "Wyatt's fighting with his girlfriend."

"Oh, Lincoln. You may bend the truth at conferences and get away with it, but I'm your mother. You can't lie to me."

"Answer my question, then. What happens in the movies?"

"I'll tell you a few you can watch. You'll figure it out," she says, mischief in her voice.

Six hours later after I've watched the titles she rattled off, I'm only sure of one thing. I'd be better off if I were a prince from a country no one's ever heard of.

Since I'm only the Duke of Dickheadistan in her eyes, I have to find a better way to lay out my soul. To show Dakota Poe she's everything.

All the constellations in my life, all the light, all the soul I'll ever need.

Even above my own pride and dignity and coldhearted logic.

XXIII: QUOTH THE RAVEN (DAKOTA)

*M*y phone dings, tearing me from a delicious dream of kisses and soft words with a man who once held my universe together.

I blink my eyes open.

Just a dream—no, a memory from the day on the boat—*again.*

I grab my phone with a sigh to see who wants what. The first text I see guts me.

Lincoln: Can we talk?

Hell no. But I guess ignoring his last few messages for days hasn't gotten the point across. He's certainly not done.

I've done some thinking, Dakota. A lot of thinking. I know this is all my fault.

Still clutching my phone, I freshen up, get dressed, and run downstairs, beating on Eliza's door.

She opens it with a yawn. "What's up?"

"I have a question—does every man ever born have the same script?"

"What's wrong?" She moves aside so I can enter.

"Nothing."

"Will vanilla bean make your nothing better?" She pads into her kitchen and starts pawing around for coffee.

"Please."

"Seriously, tell me what happened?"

"I need to block his number. That's what," I say. But there's no chance I will.

Unlike Jay, it doesn't feel right.

As if to prove my point, the phone pings again. I shouldn't look because I'm sure it's him. On the other hand, I've been scouting jobs I'm not sure I'll even take just out of curiosity, so...

I look down.

Bad move.

Lincoln: Will you trade an hour of your time for a year's worth of Sweeter Grind?

I can't roll my eyes hard enough.

"Great. Now he's trying to bribe me with Regis rolls."

"Yikes, he's playing his best card already?" she jokes. "Are you going to talk to him?"

"Nope."

Her eyebrows dart up. Does she think I'm overreacting?

"I mean, this feels too familiar," I lie. "He's blowing up my phone after he said it was over. He freaking resigned rather than deal with me, which just made the rumor mill spin—and when an office romance goes wrong, everyone always blames the woman. Then he disappears for over a month and thinks we can pick up just like *that?*" I snap my fingers. "I'm so over it, Eliza. I bet whoever he really wanted dropped him and now I'm Backup Girl again. Screw that. Not having it."

"Who did he want?" she asks quietly.

"...I don't know." I shake my head. "There's usually someone. In Jay's case, it was band girl. Lincoln probably has some lightning-hot Instagram model or a scary power CEO who eats nails for breakfast."

Eliza laughs at the image.

I shrug, hating how paranoid I am. Hating that I still care enough to be upset.

"This could be completely different. What if Lincoln fell

down the stairs and the bump on the head knocked some sense into him?" she ventures.

"Why step away from his job then?"

"His friend from the park was in the hospital, wasn't he? Maybe he wasn't lying and he was actually tied up." She gives me a careful look.

I know what she's doing. She's being the good friend, the devil's advocate, making me think with my head rather than a wounded heart that just wants to bleed.

"I don't know. I doubt Lincoln really would've left work for that." I frown, unsure if I believe it.

"Well, if you don't talk to him, you'll never know, will you?"

"If I do, I'm just giving him another chance to suck me back in. It's pointless. He made my place in his life crystal clear. I'm not his plan B. His mom—*his mom*—felt the need to apologize before he did. That's bonkers."

Eliza nods. "Yeah, she knew about it, didn't she?"

"Everyone knew. After Jay got all stabby and caused a scene, it wasn't a big secret," I say.

"Have you ever done something wrong and blamed it on somebody else for your mom's sake?

"Um, hasn't everyone?" I laugh.

"And did your mom believe you?"

"Yeah."

"So, she wouldn't have gone apologizing to the person you weren't speaking to with a monster check in hand unless you admitted it was your fault, right?" Eliza leans back against the counter and stretches her arms.

"What's your point?"

"I bet he told mama he blew it. That alone means he's not Jay."

I narrow my eyes at her.

"Whose side are you on?"

"Mine, of course," she answers with a cheeky grin. The timer she set for the coffee goes off and she pours it into two mugs with a generous splash of vanilla cream. "Dakota, if you love him—"

"Love? I never said that!" Her tiny apartment suddenly feels like a sauna.

She cocks her head.

"You didn't have to. You're smitten. I'm just not sure what you get out of shutting him out. You have to go back to that office until you decide you're done." She takes a slow sip of coffee and says, "You're not getting him out of your system like a bad bout of food poisoning. And it's not like I care if he's happy, but I *hate* seeing you miserable. Hearing him out might bring some closure."

I stare down at my coffee, heavenly vanilla wafting up my nose.

"I just don't get it. Why couldn't he have texted before now? Why come crawling back after he swore we were done?" Tears brim my eyes and I swipe them away, pretending to scratch my nose. "Hell, I don't even care. We knew the whole thing was a sham, but the sex was ludicrous and he started talking like it meant more. Maybe I set the bar too high. I hoped for too much when I should've just enjoyed the moment."

Eliza nods slowly, my diligent therapist.

Technically, I suppose she is when food therapy works wonders.

"If he didn't care, he wouldn't have gotten in your ex's face before the little creep even pulled a knife. And as for playing it down...well, we know guys are dumb. He probably didn't want his coworkers to know he's whipped."

"That would make sense if we were stuck in eighth grade," I say sharply.

She purses her lips. "Dakota, I think he's blowing up your phone because he doesn't want you feeling cornered at your job. It's kinda sweet if you think about it."

"How can I be cornered if he doesn't even work there anymore?"

"Did he actually resign? Or did he just take a leave of absence? Everyone is temporary, so—"

"I don't know," I admit. "It's all the same to me. The email was just a goodbye without a lot of specifics."

"Maybe he just doesn't want you feeling trapped. He wants you to choose him," she says.

"Maybe you've seen one too many bad movies. That's not how the world works. People aren't that pure with their motives." Yes, I'm plunging into my natural pessimism right now, but I don't care.

"What do you have to lose by talking?" she asks softly.

"My pride. What's left of it, anyway."

She holds up a finger. "A dark unfathomed tide, of interminable pride—"

"Eliza, no. Now you're quoting Edgar Allan? I'm pretty sure my six-times great uncle is about to come back and haunt me for being so dumb."

"Hey, just trying to help." She gives me a pained smile.

I turn away. It's too hard to say what's on the edge of my tongue when she can see my face.

"I'm worried about my heart. He could trample it again, and I'm not sure I'd survive that. Since you're so keen on reminding me I'm a Poe, you know what happened to Edgar Allan after his wife died, right?"

Eliza winces. "Yeah. Bad end."

"Exactly. Love doesn't treat us kindly. With Lincoln, it's not even more rejection that would kill me. It's having hope again, a future I buried years ago resurrected—only to be snatched away." I sigh.

She stares into her steaming mug.

"If you're a hundred percent certain he'll break your heart again, you're right. You can't talk to him. I didn't think we were ever going to get past the crying."

I nod. "Yeah, I'm better now. No good reason to relapse."

"Block his number. But only if you're sure."

Ouch. Why haven't I already done that?

I blocked Jay's first number fast. Why can't I bring myself to block Lincoln?

"I can't," I whisper.

"Why?"

I go quiet, taking a long pull from my coffee. Even vanilla sweetness won't bring easy answers.

"You're not ready for it to be over, but you won't listen to him either," she says. "You're living in this weird grey zone of maybes. You can block him and be done with it, or you can let him run his mouth for a whole year of Regis rolls. That's not a bad payoff."

"Says you," I throw back, side-eyeing her.

"I'll say this—if you keep holding your breath for every text, you'll keep being miserable. You're not giving yourself the chance to move on, but you're also not ready for the final word."

Damn her logic.

I slurp my coffee, pondering her words.

"What would you do?" I ask when I set down my cup.

"Hmm, well...I'm not sure. But I'd probably give the dude a chance to explain, if only for those rolls. Dead serious." She grins again. "I'm too emotional to stay firm like you, and I don't like being miserable when there's a glimmer of hope."

"But what if it's *false hope?* What if it's just another chance for him to break my heart again?"

"I can't say because I've never met the guy. It's hard to give you advice, but I'd probably take a crack at heartbreak to help ease the pain."

"You know how you said you're not sure you're strong enough to ignore the texts?" I ask.

She nods.

"I'm not sure I'm strong enough to give him a second chance to burn me."

"Only you can decide," she says with an empathetic look.

"God, you're right. This is bad, Eliza. You'd think I'd have learned not to trust men after being stood up in a wedding dress. Maybe I'm just not as smart as I like to think I am."

"Don't let Jay make you distrust all men. You had no clue Lincoln would hulk out after acting like he cared. You can't blame yourself."

"He got emotional over cinnamon rolls. Big red flag," I remind her.

"You know now why he needed them, though. For his friend, right? That makes it slightly less crazy..."

"You're not helping. I need reasons to hate this man." Yes, I'm whining, and I don't care.

Eliza laughs. "Why?"

"Every time he texts me, I try to remember why I hate him. It's how I keep myself from responding."

"If you have to convince yourself not to respond...I think you know what that means," she says firmly.

"Sure. I'm playing with fire and we know how that ends, too. One day, I just hope I can despise Lincoln Burns enough so it doesn't even matter."

* * *

I GO INTO MY—WELL, Anna's office—early the next morning.

I have to run numbers for another meeting guaranteed to put me to sleep.

I'm not expecting a flash of excitement when I see the cup of coffee and a Regis roll on my desk.

What the what?

Whose sick joke is this? I've made it pretty clear I'm done with anything that involves masses of cinnamon, sugar, and heartbreaking beast-men.

But the dark roast with a big dab of caramel makes my stomach growl like a cougar. I didn't have time for breakfast this morning, so what's the harm?

Then again...I stare down into the cup and notice something off.

Do we have a new intern? Who leaves coffee with no lid next to a computer?

I answer that question before I take a single sip.

The words *Sorry, Nevermore* swirl around a heart in white foam.

Jesus. I don't even know how he got the cream to stay like that long enough to be readable unless they made the drink right here in the building?

And now he's taken to dicking with my coffee? Really?

My stomach gurgles again impatiently.

Whatever. It's caffeine and sugar and I gulp down a mouthful.

It's warm, sweet, and delicious, never mind who it's from.

I sit down and start peeling back the first layer of the Regis roll with the fork next to it. But apparently, breakfast is full of surprises.

Lincoln's office is edged in the dough.

Dear God. He's here?

And Lincoln's office is technically Jane's now. So much for Eliza's theory about being cornered at work.

I won't go. He can't make me.

If he wanted to talk to me this badly, he'd come here and face me. He knows where to find me.

I get through all of ten minutes working, reviewing slides for that presentation, when I get a call from the COO's office. I pick up my desk phone, expecting Anna.

"Hello?"

"Dakota, can you come down to Lincoln's office?" a smooth voice asks.

"Jane? Where are you?"

My heart skips a beat at the phrase *Lincoln's office.*

She sighs. "Back in my old office today. It's...well, you'll see."

"What's this about?" I ask faintly.

"Is she coming?" I hear another voice in the background, high-pitched and concerned.

"Wait. Is Anna in your office with you?" I pause. "Guys, what is going on?"

"We're having a meeting," Jane says, clearing her throat.

"Umm—what's this about? It sounds pretty urgent."

Silence on the other end of the line. Dread and hope blow through me in equally heady doses.

"Well, will one of you come with me?" I ask.

"She wants us to go with her," Jane whispers, probably to Anna.

"No, we can't! Tell her..." Anna's voice fades out.

"Dakota, I'm confident you won't need the backup," Jane says.

I glare at the phone.

"O-kay. Well, tell Anna if I'm being set up, I'll never speak to her again," I say sharply.

"Will do. We'll talk after...you'll see." Again, with that cryptic phrase, she hangs up.

I slam the phone down and groan.

Oh, well. I might as well get this over with.

I swear, I'm going to give this colossal bonehead a piece of my mind for dragging me into this. He can't just drop in and out of my life on a whim.

If he's returned to mess with me, I may just quit on the spot.

With the payments starting from the wedding line in a few months, I'll have more savings than I could ever dream of to tide me over until I find another job—or shut myself away from the world in a cave to hack out poems.

My knees feel like cement as I hitch an elevator ride up to the C-level suite.

I storm past Lucy, who's back from maternity leave, stalk past my old desk, and throw Lincoln's door open.

It's—empty?

My breath heaves out of me.

I don't get it. Why go through this much drama just to get me here if I'm alone?

Wary, I walk in for a closer look. I peek under the desk. I'm not sure why because jumping out of a closet seems a bit much even for him. It's quiet, though.

Too freaking quiet.

Until a small dark shape moves behind the window and stops on the balcony.

"Holy shit!" I mumble, falling back and catching myself.

My heart races. What was that?

It's way too small and fast to be a person...

Moving to the glass door in front of the balcony, I push it open cautiously.

"Caw!" A huge raven barrels at me.

I throw my arms up, shielding my face like I just became an extra in Hitchcock's greatest film. "Aaahh!"

Swoosh.

Something drops near my feet as the bird darts over my shoulder.

Its deafening calls fade as it flies, soaring through the space between a couple tall buildings across the street.

I drop my arms, trying to catch my breath as I see it.

A rolled-up piece of paper, tied with what looks like a gold ribbon, lays beside my feet.

...a scroll?

No way. He had a carrier pigeon—*a carrier raven!*—deliver a message?

I pick it up, too curious not to read it.

Nevermore,

I realize the bird drop was probably over the top. I'd apologize for the theatrics, but I had to get your attention somehow. Texting wasn't getting the job done.

I'm sorry I hurt you.

I was an asshole of the highest order. Worse, I was a total fool.

When I said there was nothing between us, I let the past get the best of me. I was rattled because for the first time since shit went down with my ex, I lost control.

I know my mother told you about that.

In the heat of the moment, in self-defense, I became an angry, uncontrollable wreck. A monster I swore I could never be again.

I'm not the sort of man who loses control easily. But when I'm around you, I can't help it.

You make me feel things I didn't know I could.

You give me passion, and that scared me at first. Only, now I've realized true stupidity is pushing away the only woman I've ever loved.

When I stepped away from my position here, it was to protect both of us.

I tried to shield our hearts from the ravages I've watched love inflict on so many good people. Let me explain.

Wyatt loved a woman more than his own life. She abandoned him, left him broken, and he descended into chaos.

The only thing my parents ever loved as much as each other was me. When my dad died, my mother lost her spark. She might take no crap from anyone and live an active life, but she's not the same woman.

Then my own engagement with Regina. Her betrayal savaged me. I beat the man she was fucking within an inch of his life when he goaded me into a fight. It damned near cost me my own life.

This was my fear—a fear I won't be ruled by anymore.

I also won't make any grand promises.

If you hear me out, I can't promise you perfection. I can't guarantee I won't screw up.

The only thing I can offer with certainty is all my fucking heart.

I thought if I just stayed away—if I kept us apart—I could spare us the pain.

Wrong. This exile is killing me.

Dakota Poe, you scare me, and you also keep me honest.

My recklessness speaks for itself. The truth of how deep my feelings are for you.

You're the spark I needed to come along, shine right through me, and show me that what's truly frightening is spending my entire life denying my biggest passion—you.

Woman, I need you back in my life.

I'll do whatever you want except walk away without another word.

Love,
Lincoln

Holy crap, holy crap, holy crap!

Hot tears run down my cheeks in rivulets.

God. How could anyone not cry after that?

And how am I supposed to stay strong when he's sending love letters by raven?

I clutch the letter with one hand, wiping away my tears with the other.

I'm about to retreat into his office so I can get back to my desk and hide, but I see Anna, Cheryl, and Jane standing behind the glass door gawking at me. They've got what looks like a peanut gallery of twenty people behind them.

Just flipping great. There's no escape.

My choices are stand on this balcony forever, fling myself over it, or slink back inside and deal with a barrage of awkward questions like I'm the President of Bad Decisions holding a press conference.

Diving off the building looks more appealing all the time. *I'm joking.*

Maybe if I just stand here long enough, they'll get bored and go away so I can make my way in with my tail between my legs?

"Dakota?" A velvet voice vibrates behind me like distant thunder.

Uh-oh.

I know it's him before I even turn around.

The few stray tears streaming down my face burst into a harsh sob that racks my entire body.

My hands shake. My being trembles. My heart knows this is it.

It's either turn around and face him or run.

I'm not sure which is worse.

Until he says, "Nevermore, if you keep crying, at least do it where your head belongs."

I turn toward his voice.

He comes at me with his arms outstretched. He closes the distance between us until his fingers brush my arms, gingerly clasping them, pulling me in.

It's the hardest thing I've ever done to bury my face against his wall of a chest.

Harder than wearing a wedding dress in a honeymoon suite with no husband.

Harder than sparring over cinnamon rolls.

Harder than watching that last pained look on his face as he told me to get out of his life.

But I push my face into him.

I lay my cheek against his warmth, his strength, his every-thing, and *breathe*.

I'm inhaling Lincoln Burns like it's the very last time, because God, it might be. I take a few deep, rattling breaths of his mascu-line scent before I lurch back.

His eyes glow like dark amber, searching mine, asking so many questions.

The letter was sweet, sure, but it's not a conversation.

I can't just run back to him so easily.

"Dakota?" His face tightens and his arms drop to his sides. "I don't blame you for being scared—*for* questioning me. You didn't want to be hurt. We're on the same page. I just do a better job of hiding my emotions."

Why is he making this so hard?

I gather another reluctant breath into my lungs.

His eyes are so intense today, heat lamps that melt me into a puddle right here on the balcony.

But even if I'm boneless, I can't go down this road again.

I can't be stupid.

Dakota, find your strength.

Lincoln Burns shared his truth in that letter, and now, it's my turn.

XXIV: ALL MY SOUL WITHIN ME
(LINCOLN)

*D*akota takes another step away from me.

It might as well be a thousand miles.

My heart slams against my rib cage.

Fuck, what if she doesn't care? What if she refuses to give me a second chance? What then?

"You—you had to force your way in with a trained raven? Seriously?" she spits, beyond exasperated.

I smile faintly and shrug one shoulder.

"Do you know how hard it is to find trained messenger birds in Seattle in the twenty-first century? Something had to drive home how much I care." I flick my eyes to the window, where every woman in the office and even a few men stare out at us. I lower my voice so no one in our unwanted audience hears me. "Do you remember the night in my office when I traced your tattoo?"

She tries hard not to smile, but she can't stop her lips from turning up as her face reddens.

Dakota gives me an awkward nod.

"You said it was a work in progress. The raven clutching a broken heart, something you added after that sorry little fuck threw away your love. Nevermore." I come closer, taking her hand in mine and pinning it between us against her chest. "Let me give you fresh ink. Never more will your heart be broken in my hands. You have my word."

She bites her bottom lip, trembling.

"Bold words. I'm sure it took you a while to practice that..."

"Dakota—" I flare.

She puts her hands up defensively and steps back.

"No, Lincoln. How do I know you won't just change your mind again? I can't survive it a second time." A single hot tear streams down her face.

My heart sinks. I'm the reason this beautiful woman is crying.

How the hell do I convince her? The right combination of words must exist.

"That's why I'm here. I came to tell you I'm making my leave of absence permanent," I grind out.

She blinks at me.

"What? Why?"

"I've spent too much of my life working, not living. I need to start existing again—ideally with you—and I can't do that as your boss. I need to put you first, second, and third. I can't do that as a workaholic. So, I'll step down, because I need you infinitely more than I need Haughty But Nice. I need you more than anything, Dakota Poe."

For a second, she stares, too stunned to move.

Then, I'm hit with a small cannonball.

She *hurls* herself at me so hard I'm winded, her arms thrown around my neck.

I close my arms around her with a slow smile.

"Sorry. Maybe I should have led with that," I say.

She laughs erratically and then sniffles again.

I pull her tighter against me, pushing one hand against the small of her back, ready to keep her there forever.

"What's wrong?"

"You can't just up and leave for me—this is your family's business. I can't take it away from you. It's not fair. And...and everyone is doing the best they can, but things are pretty rocky here without you. Morale sucks so bad, you don't even know," she whispers.

I frown. "Like I said, you're my first and last priority. They'll have to rough it."

She throws me a desperate look, slowly shaking her head.

"No. You'll resent me for it later, and so will they."

I kiss her eyebrow, her forehead, her cheek.

"Never. It won't happen. And if it does, we'll figure it out."

"But—"

I kiss her lips, silencing her worries.

"Sweetheart, I have a plan. I'm not leaving anybody high and dry."

"O-of course. Of course, you do," she stammers.

I grin. "I always have a backup, but I haven't seen you in a month and—"

She tilts her chin back.

"You missed me too," I whisper.

She doesn't answer as her eyelids flutter shut.

I cup her face with my hand, bring her mouth to mine, and savor her sweetness, her coffee-rich breath, the eager way her tongue flicks against mine and the moan she spills in my mouth.

Goddamn, I'm going to savor this woman until the universe goes cold.

I hear a faint slapping sound behind us. Everyone perched inside my office claps. A few whistles make it through the thick glass.

Dakota bolts away from me and groans, her face rivaling a tomato.

"Yikes. How could I forget them?"

"I've got this," I say, stomping over to throw open the door to the balcony. "Show's over, people. Everyone out of my office."

Cheryl, Jane, and a couple other women go reluctantly, beaming back grins too big for their faces.

Anna lingers, her hands on her hips as she meets my eyes.

"Yes?" I clip.

"Don't you dare hurt her again, Mr. Burns."

"Noted, Miss Patel. Now kindly leave."

She stands there, looking at me for an uncomfortably long moment. I fold my arms and glare back.

"It won't happen again. I'd rather die a thousand times."

Her death stare lightens.

"That's so sweet," she muses, slowly walking away.

"Anna?" I call.

She glances over her shoulder.

"Thanks for caring so much about her. You're a good friend," I say.

She smiles and leaves my office.

I look back at Dakota. "Now that they're gone..."

She closes the space between us.

"Yeah. So what's your big plan?"

"We'll have a meeting with the senior staff and HR in the afternoon. I have to work out a few last details first."

She nods. "Lucy's back, so I'll be downstairs working on this stupid meeting."

"No, you won't." I grab her gently by the hand.

"Oh?" She raises a brow.

"You're not going to be a marketing manager much longer anyway. And because I haven't seen you in a month, there's no damn chance you're leaving my office this morning."

She smiles. "But we're at work."

I pull her closer and wrap my arms around her again, closing my eyes with a thick sigh.

"Um, are you okay?" she asks with a laugh.

"Yeah. I just—I've never been this happy." I run my lips up her neck. "It was a long, lonely month."

"I know. It was hard for me too..."

This time, she attacks my mouth first, all teeth and

wandering tongue. I find her lips with mine again, relishing how tightly she clings to me.

She breaks away, drawing in air as my grip on her intensifies.

"Smooth. Now there's no chance you're getting away from me before the meeting," I growl.

"Lucky you, there's nowhere I'd rather be."

Her green eyes flare with a heat I can't wait to ignite the second we leave the building.

With my soul on fire, I return to my desk and type out the proposal with Dakota in my lap the entire time. Her ass teases me, pressing my hardness, bringing back memories of when I took her in this very office.

When I finally press print, my lips are on her neck again, my fingers pushing through her hair.

"You're coming home tonight," I whisper, digging my teeth into her bottom lip so she knows it's not an invitation.

It's a demand.

"I know," she whispers back.

I turn her in my lap so I can see her face. I've made a big decision.

"I mean permanently, Nevermore." I take a deep breath. "We should go to your place first and get your stuff." I may have lost it but I don't care.

Her eyes become two jade moons, wide and bright.

"Wait, you're saying I'm moving in with you?"

"I said you're coming home, didn't I?" My lips cascade up her throat again, stopping to nip at that sweet spot just under her ear.

"But—"

I shrug. "No buts. You don't want to move in with me, fine. I'll stay at your place."

"My shoebox apartment?" She presses a hand to my forehead. "Do you have a fever? Linc, you can't be serious..."

"When it comes to you, I don't joke. I also don't give a single solitary shit where we're living, as long as it's together. My place has a lot more room, but if you don't trust me enough for that, I'll—"

"Lincoln?" She waits for me to go quiet. "Shut up and kiss me."

Agreed.

Just like that, her lips find mine, sealing our fate.

She kisses me frantically, and I swipe my tongue across hers until I'm fucking dizzy. Her hands grasp at my hair.

If we didn't have business to tend to, I'd throw her on my desk, open her legs, and take her right here.

Shame that has to wait.

I'm rasping when I pull away, cradling her to me, pushing a hand up her skirt. She's so drenched I shudder when I squeeze her pussy through her panties.

"Hold on, Nevermore. Just a few more hours, and I'm reclaiming this tonight. This time, forevermore."

* * *

WE SIT side by side at the conference table, our hands joined under the table.

Ida, my HR head, meets my eyes, scans the room, and looks at me again.

"Mr. Burns, I don't think anyone here quite understands what you want us to do. Can you walk us through it again to make sure we're all on the same page?"

"Sure. I'd like to make Dakota a very well-compensated independent contractor under her own LLC. She'll help with copywriting and marketing part-time for Haughty But Nice, according to our needs and her heart's content. The rest of the time, she'll be freed up to pursue her poetry career. I'll remain CEO—mostly for insights and branding—but since everyone in this room is extremely talented, I'll be delegating a lot more to my executives and managers. While I was out, you've all proven you can rise to a challenge. That means I'll be working from home at least a few days a week. Thoughts?"

Dakota squeezes my hand so sharply my breath almost catches.

"It's workable and sensible," Jane says.

We talk among ourselves with a few other executives I've pulled in from sales and legal. While Dakota looks on, we draft up a blueprint for how Haughty But Nice will be run in the future with the personnel balance it deserves.

By the time we're out of the room, her hand smolders mine, holding on like her life depends on it.

Honest to God, it does.

With everything in place, we have a new freedom I've never imagined.

It's cavernous, honestly. A life teeming with possibilities and dreams.

Without this woman, I know how lost I'd be.

That's why I push my fingers through hers, matching her grip with my own, ready to march into our future together.

* * *

I BARELY MAKE a fuss loading her bike up in the trunk of the town car.

"I still hate you biking all over town," I tell her.

"Why?" Dakota stands behind me. "It's healthy. We should get one for you."

I snort. "What if you get hit by a car?"

"Our ride could be crushed by a semi on our way home, too."

"This vehicle has airbags." I open the door for her, contemplating how pissed she'll be if I buy her a ride with four wheels.

She climbs in. "Since when did the big bad Marine get so concerned with safety?"

I get in beside her and shut the door behind me before I answer.

"Since you, Nevermore."

That shuts her up. Her eyes dance when she smiles.

"Lovesick fool," she mutters.

She has no idea, but she's about to. I grab her soft legs and pull her onto my lap.

"Told you I'm bewitched. I must've been under somebody's spell when I hired a damn bird guy to apologize."

"And I loved every bit of it. I've missed you so much," she whispers, looking up through her lashes.

"Me too—"

"It took you an entire month to text me."

"I—" There's no good explanation for that. "I was a coward, and I'm sorry."

"What changed your mind?"

"Ma helped. She told me losing someone you love isn't a tragedy. The tragedy is never loving. Sappy as it sounds, there's some truth there."

She sighs. "I don't know about that. If something happened to you, I'd never be the same."

"That's another thing I was worried about. That's why I thought I should keep my distance. What my mom said made me think, but it wasn't the final answer."

"Yeah? So, what was?"

"Wyatt. He has a huge crush on Meadow," I say, grinning when I think of that clown with the little gardener.

"That's sweet, but what does that have to do with us?" Dakota asks.

"You remember how Wyatt lost everything because of his ex-wife and bad habits? I never thought he'd survive, honestly, let alone make the turnaround he has. If *he* can still find it in him to love after everything he went through...why can't I? Especially when I've got one hell of a gorgeous reason to live to my fullest."

She kisses me, softly and sweetly, tempting me with that mouth.

"How's he doing, anyway?"

"Much better. He's holed up in my guesthouse, mostly watching bad TV and messing around with Meadow when she visits him..." I run my fingers through her hair. "Enough about them. There's an angel in my lap, and I haven't seen her in a fucking month. Wyatt is *not* what I'm wasting breath on."

When we pull up to my place, our lips are fused, my hand running up her thigh. Every time I feel her wetness, I sink my teeth into her lip.

Louis has to gently tap the privacy screen down to remind me we're home.

I climb out first with a muttered apology, holding the door for Dakota, and then roll her bike to the garage. I pull her to me and hold her for a long moment before leading her inside.

"Damn, it's so good having you home."

She shows me she knows, leaning up on her toes and pressing her lips to mine with wild abandon. She flicks her tongue against my lips, and when I open my mouth, she sucks my bottom lip.

I sigh out my soul, my hands falling to her ass, digging my fingers into her curves.

I'll mark her tonight, I swear to God. Possibly for life.

My jealousy, my greed, all my darker impulses can't be bad if they're all for her, can they?

I wonder.

And I wonder a lot more when she looks up with her eyes so hot, so shiny, her lips parted.

"I love you, Lincoln Burns." She swallows hard. "I...I had to say it."

I pull her in, holding her like she's closer than my own shadow.

"I love you too, Dakota. Love you so hard it drives me batty. You have no idea."

"I don't know. The raven with the scroll gave me *some* idea."

"The bird doesn't scratch the surface." I lead her inside, thinking we'll sit on the balcony for a minute or two.

We'll see how long it takes for the madness in my balls to drive us to bed.

We get exactly two steps outside before she's pinned against the wall, whimpering real sweet for me.

I'm on my knees, flicking up her skirt, my mouth roaming up her thighs.

Neither of us care if half the city can see. I'll eat her until she *screams* with the entire world watching, and the moon for good measure.

"Lincoln," she whispers, raking her nails through my hair.

It just encourages me to take her panties down with my teeth. I don't even let her step out and leave them on the ground before I go to work.

My tongue sweeps up her seam, tasting her hot little cunt.

There goes my mind.

There go my fingers, a knuckle pressed to her clit, adding fire my tongue can't.

There goes my girl.

I catch her as she slides down the wall, holding her up while I tongue-fuck her to kingdom come.

And goddamn, does she *come* for me.

When I feel her tension, her rhythm, and that puff that's half curse and all groan in my ears, I quicken my lashes.

I tear her orgasm out like I want it to hurt. She goes off, all molten pleasure, trembling against my face as I grab her ass and mold her to my mouth.

Fuck yeah, Nevermore.

I make her ride my face to the last tremor.

Then she slowly, sweetly, deliriously collapses in my arms. I pepper her face with kisses, bringing her home.

I love that I can afford to be slow and tender, even if my pulsing cock disagrees. From this point on, we have the rest of our lives.

"Ready, sweetheart?" I whisper when she finally looks up.

With my fingers laced through hers, I help her to her feet,

leaving her panties on the ground. We move back into my place, and I start heading to the kitchen for the glass of water I'm sure she needs.

Dakota stops, though, centering her weight against my side.

"You're going the wrong way," she says.

"I am?"

She nods, gives me a heavy look, and walks in the opposite direction that leads to my room.

"Straight to the point today, huh?"

"Don't get too excited. It's been a month, and I need you. Not just *that*, I mean, I haven't slept well alone since—yeah." She doesn't finish the sentence. The words hang in the air between us.

"Me either," I admit, pulling her to me, winding my arms around her waist.

"I'm going to sleep like a kitten tonight," she says, butting her head gently against my chest.

"Wish I could say the same."

"Why not?" She looks up at me, startled.

"Like you said, it's been a month. That means I'll be too busy watching you, woman. My eyes are starved to see you in my bed, where you belong," I tell her.

Her face screws up with laughter, but her body is tense.

She's home. She's drenched. She's waiting.

She's finally mine, but she's not the same.

"What's wrong?" I ask.

She shakes her head.

"Liar. What is it?" I urge.

She gives a tiny shrug. "I just keep thinking what if you freak out again? Or what if—"

I silence her with my lips, an aggressive kiss of denial that makes her limp in my arms.

"Dakota Poe, listen. There's no chance I'm strong enough to lose you again."

"But you almost were once..."

"Before, I had no clue what it was to live without you. Or how perfectly you fit in every corner of my life."

"I do?"

I chuckle. "Wyatt threatened to kick my ass for spending so much time at the hospital instead of with you. Ma tore me a new asshole in her bless your heart way. I'm pretty sure if this doesn't work out, I'm getting disowned by everyone."

She laughs. "Your mom loves you way too much for that."

"There. Now you know how I feel about you."

She smiles softly. "So, this is real." Her words are a statement and a revelation.

I kiss her again to drive it home.

"Nothing's ever been this real, and I'm looking forward to every moment of it. Now, if we're done flapping our mouths, I'm pretty sure another part of my anatomy wants to be heard..."

She nods as I pick her up, throwing her over my shoulder.

"Do you remember the first time you carried me to your room?" she leans up, purring in my ear.

"How could I forget? It was almost this intense."

"What do you mean *almost*? I was about to combust before we even made it to bed."

I grin, gobsmacked at what comes out of her mouth.

"Dakota, you own my soul. I love you."

Her nails graze down my back.

"I love you, too," she whispers.

Once we're through the door, I kick it shut behind us and lay her on my bed. "One key difference from the first time and today," I tell her, staring down in wonder.

"Yeah?"

I stroke her hair, letting my fingers fall through platinum silk as I say, "That was mostly physical but this—this is with my entire heart."

She takes my hand and urges me down, kissing my knuckles. "You've owned mine for a while."

"How long?" I demand.

"I don't know. At least since the first time we made love—"

"Definitely one of the best days of my life." I smile at the memory.

"And the others?"

I press my lips to her forehead. "This is one more. I got my girl back."

"You didn't let me finish," she whispers.

"Bull. You finished just fine that day, as I recall. Your nails sank into my back and your body clenched around me. This time, you'll finish harder," I promise, nipping at her shoulder.

She covers her face with both hands and laughs.

Little minx.

I grab her, pulling one hand away, and bring it to my lips, kissing her knuckles. Slowly but steadily, I uncurl her fingers and kiss them one by one.

She moves her hand away, quivering. Wrapping her arms around me, she drops her face to mine.

The kiss that comes is one long concert of harsh breaths and wicked desires.

Dakota trembles when my fingers brush her skin, too greedy to control.

I yank her dress over her head. She's left in a lace bra and nothing else, her panties still on the balcony.

My face moves down the bed to her tits. I take one nipple through the fabric, dangerously impatient.

Sucking, biting, teasing, I do what I promised.

I bring her *home.*

Two minutes in, she's a gasping mess, barely able to unhook her bra. When she finally frees those perfect mounds, her nipples pucker under my tongue.

I think she might come on the spot.

Before that happens, I roll her on her back, tearing off my clothes piece by piece. I climb over her with a hunger, taking her tits in my hands and pushing those nipples between my fingers as I stare down at the feast before me.

Fuck, this woman.

It's not just my heart and soul that's hers.

She's got the rights to my balls for life.

My tongue returns, rolling across one firm peak. She drags my head tighter against her, low whimpers becoming loud, insistent moans.

Her fingers curl through my hair, down my neck, and graze down my back. I love how her fingernails dance on my skin, urging me to do my best, my worst, my everything.

Tonight, she'll get my all.

My tongue massages her supple skin until I can't stand it.

Until she's bucking her hips against my leg, grinding against the rigid hardness she's roused, begging me to take what's always been mine.

"Fuck," I whisper, tearing away to shift my weight.

I glare down at her, this fragile thing, that tattoo inviting me to take her every which way from Sunday and into the next week.

"Lincoln, please," she urges, winding her legs around mine.

She's asking for my fuckery. All of it.

So I grab the base of my cock, glaring down. I smack my swollen tip against her clit several times, teaching her she's only on the first level of begging.

She's speechless by the time I move in, claiming her pussy, no condom between us. Her pussy clenches me, taking me deep, snapping the last thread of my control.

I *bite* her lips when my head comes down and my hips go to work. It's animal, primal, and somehow still so human it hurts.

Each thrust shakes her down, faster and faster, hammering her into the mattress. It isn't long before she blows, going off in a flurry of gasping breaths, her nails digging into my back until it hurts.

Glorious.

Her pain, I love.

I don't care if she cuts me to the bone, just as long as I'm buried inside Nevermore, pillaging her from the inside out with punishing thrusts. My pubic bone drags against her clit every time I press to the hilt, and soon, I'm baring my teeth.

She looks up with a question flaring in her eyes, too lost for words, but I hear her loud and clear.

Will you? Will you come inside me?

Goddamn. Could I do anything else?

"Hold on, sweetheart," I growl, rearing back so I control my finish, so I can heave every last drop from my balls in her womb.

She makes me that insane.

She makes me so sure that if we're meant to have kids, I want to start early, even if a cooler head suggests something different.

Tonight, fuck cooler *anything.*

I'm pure molten steel as I drive into her and her mouth falls open, her eyes roll back, and her pussy steals my soul.

My cock swells in her chaos, jerking, pulsing, spilling into her.

We come together in a ballad of flesh, pure white-hot delirium fit for two lost souls made whole.

Edgar Allan, eat your fucking heart out.

Or don't.

Because I'm making better poetry than any I ever imagined with Miss Poe, and it's all I need.

XXV: FORTUNATO AND I (DAKOTA)

Months Later

*C*risp wind nips at my fingers, but I won't give in just yet. I'm in my writing groove, brain vibing, heart in flames—and most importantly of all—words flowing.

I cross out a line and replace it. This journal has been a godsend, far more intimate than writing on a computer or hashing out words in my bargain notebook.

We found it at an estate sale in good condition.

Since it's come into my hands, the black leather is slightly battered, the pages softly tanning with light exposure and good use.

Lincoln planned this getaway, and it's brought my muse to life.

I don't know what it is about the coolness and majesty of Mt. Rainier or the vibrant autumn leaves spiraling in the wind, but the verses flow, streaming from my soul.

He slides open the deck door, wearing a tight burgundy button-down shirt, unclasped at the top with his throat exposed.

The man doesn't even need to call "Come in, it's almost supper!" to get my attention.

"Just give me a sec. I'm wrapping up..."

"That means another hour in Nevermore time. Get your sweet ass in here before you freeze," he growls.

I look up, gazing into his honey-brown eyes and smile.

Will the effect he has on me ever fade?

"I'm blaming you. When you said I'd get a lot of writing done here, I didn't know I'd be glued to my pen and paper," I tell him.

"I was right. What else is new?" He huffs out a rough breath. "You came here to spend time with me, remember?"

I wince. Even after all these months and so many changes, he's still got an elephant-sized ego.

"I came to spend time with *Fortunato.*"

He rolls his eyes.

"Poe, you're a freak for naming that journal," he says.

"And you burn for me, Burns. Even when I can't fathom why."

"Oh, no, sweetheart. You burn. If you've got another poem or two about falling into bed, I'll remind you how easily I can turn you into ash."

My face throbs with heat.

Big words from a really big lunk—and yet, they're horribly *true.*

"Well, I do like being in bed with you," I blurt out, quickly adding, "that is, when you're not snoring like a hibernating bear."

"There's a cost to pleasure." He grins, his eyes bursting with sweetness. "For the record, you're my favorite way to warm my bed, too. Now if you get inside sometime this century, we could enjoy it rather than talking."

I hold up a hand. I need to finish these lines before I lose my mojo.

The bond.

The tether

Always together.

"Fair warning," he rumbles impatiently. "If you're cheating on me with Mr. Fortunato, I *will* push him through a shredder."

I glare at him. "Don't you dare, Lincoln Burns."

"Woman, don't try me." He steps off the deck, plodding down the short staircase and comes barreling at me.

I grab the journal, hop on top of the table I'm sitting at, and plod down the bench on the other side, running as fast as I can.

Lincoln chases me.

I sprint away, surprised I can still run when I'm doubled over laughing.

He's gaining on me fast.

Crap. Here comes the hill, covered in freshly fallen leaves and emerald greenery still peeking through. Only one escape—and it's also the best way to piss my man off.

I tuck Fortunato in my sweater, drop to the ground, and *roll* like I'm all of twelve years old again.

"Dakota!" he screams.

Before I can tumble three solid times, strong hands grab my sweater, tearing me back and blunting my momentum.

He scoops me up with ease, holding me like a naughty puppy.

"Are you crazy? Do you see how steep that drop is? You could've gotten hurt." He jabs a finger down and—oops, yeah. He's right.

It's steeper than it looked in the heat of the moment, especially with the leaves carpeting everything.

"But I wasn't." I smile at him slowly.

"Only because I caught you in time," he grumbles. "Don't tell me I have to pull double duty as your boyfriend and your bodyguard? This is getting weird considering I've been your boss."

"As long as you're nice to Fortunato...we'll see."

He daggers me with a look so dirty it's hysterical.

I slide my hand under my sweater, expecting to pull out my journal, but—

"Oh, crap. It's gone! I must have dropped Fortunato when I rolled." My heart climbs into my throat.

"Guess you deserve it then."

"Lincoln, this isn't funny. Put me down! I have to find my journal. I can't lose my work." My throat goes tight, and a hundred ways the little booklet could wind up waterlogged or carried off by a mischievous fox spin through my mind.

"Who's the workaholic now?" He wraps his arms around me, holding me to his chest.

I lean up and kiss him before my panic resumes.

"Dude. As cute as that is, if I don't find my journal, I'll never forgive you."

He sets me down with a slight exasperated sound.

"Hold on. I'll go rescue him," he promises.

"You will?"

"Like I'd risk your wrath, Nevermore. There's a hell of a lot of places out here to hide my carcass, and I'm sure you'd find the worst," he jokes.

"You're so dramatic." I laugh at him anyway, marveling at how his dumb jokes can brighten up even scary times like this.

"And you're the one who named your damn journal."

We walk together, staring at the ground, searching. Lincoln starts down the steeper incline, pulling his former Marine card and demanding I stay put.

Insanely annoying, but also sweet.

"I think I see it!" he calls up from the bottom of the hill, kicking leaves aside. He bends down, grabs it, and starts back up.

Delicious relief floods my system, cool and peaceful. I almost don't notice the tiny flakes prickling my skin.

Just a handful at first, and then a proper dusting that swirls through the trees.

Weather gets intense at these elevations, and in late October, it isn't unheard of for the rains to turn to snow.

I pull the tops down over my fingerless gloves and stick my

tongue out as Lincoln approaches. "See what you did? I'm blaming this weather on you, Captain."

Beside me, he chuckles. The last couple months, I've taken to calling him that. But he's anything but a dipshit now.

Lincoln Burns is the light of my life, the first and last man I'd follow into hell.

"Careful or you'll ruin the magic," he warns, eclipsing me in those massive arms that always feel like they hold up the sky.

"Not possible. You saved Fortunato," I whisper, taking the journal and giving it a good hand wipe.

"There's enough magic inside, where it's warm. I made a fire," he whispers in my ear.

I look up with a grin. "You knew it was snowing?"

"Been in the forecast all week with more than a ninety percent chance," he says.

"Wow. I'm surprised you went through with the trip."

"A little winter never hurt anybody. Also, I plan on keeping you plenty occupied in the cabin for heat. Tomorrow, if you're lucky, you'll wake up sore as hell with a cup of coffee in hand and a nice view of the mountain in glittering white."

I lace my fingers through his. This man is the best thing that ever happened to me, even if I have a hard time putting it into words.

As soon as we step inside, I'm engulfed with cozy warmth, the orange flames twinkling in the fireplace.

"I love how you're so thoughtful—when you want to be," I tease.

My heart skips as he smiles back.

He pulls the door shut behind us, kisses my lips languidly, and moves past with a playful butt swat.

"Go put your journal somewhere safe and I'll make you coffee," he orders.

"Hmm, okay. But I can think of better ways to warm up than getting wired..."

He chuckles and kisses me again.

"Soon," he whispers, low and firm.

He's so perfect. I can't help but stare, wondering how I ever got swept up in this whirlwind.

I haven't even given up the lease on my apartment, despite all but living with Lincoln since the day he won me back by raven messenger.

If I were still a starry-eyed college girl who believed in weddings, he'd be the man I'd want to swap vows with, hands down. But something tells me we're better off this way, easy and slow, committed with no formal, hard commitment yet.

I head into the bedroom and lay my journal on the desk. When I return to the living room, Linc has two cups of steaming coffee and a huge Regis roll on the coffee table, apparently warmed up like it was just made.

He lounges on the couch as I sit beside him, my curiosity rising.

"Whoa. You really thought of everything. When did you stop for this?" I ask, staring at the roll with my stomach growling.

"The morning we left. They sold it raw and I just had to pop it in the oven. I wanted this weekend to be perfect, and I know my girl loves pastries more than money."

I laugh at him, suddenly suspicious.

"Lincoln, what are you doing?"

He holds his hands up like he's innocent. "Nothing. Why?"

"You're up to something."

He shakes his head fiercely.

"You're wrong. Scout's honor."

"Lincoln Burns, you're no Boy Scout. How many times do I have to remind you?"

"Dakota Poe, eat your cinnamon roll and shut it," he says playfully.

"What if I'm allergic to cinnamon now?"

"Liar."

I pick up the ceramic plate he's laid the Regis roll on. There's a small silver fork next to it, waiting.

"Dig in," he orders.

I do, and the cinnamon roll all but crumbles apart. I take a bite, but it's weirdly flaky, almost like there's something odd with the dough. I cough, sputtering small crumbs into my hand.

"Are you okay?"

I nod.

He slips an arm around me, pulls me closer, presses his mouth to mine, and traces my lips with his tongue.

I open my mouth.

He glides his tongue across mine.

I drop the fork and put my hand in his hair.

He covers my palm with his hand and pushes my hand back to the plate without breaking the kiss. He's still tracing my tongue, the inside of my mouth, with his.

I sigh, already delirious as he breaks away.

"You need to eat," he whispers, curling my hand around the fork with his own.

Together, we stab the cinnamon roll, closer to the center.

What's he doing?

He kisses me again, this time deeper, his tongue flicking over mine.

Oh, God. I can't care what he's doing.

We pull at the cinnamon roll again, and this time the fork hits something solid. He guides my hand, lifting away the flaky layer.

He pulls away, sighs, and draws in a deep breath. "Dakota, look at your plate."

What? I blink.

"Now?"

"Please?" The word is barely audible as it leaves his mouth.

I catch my breath and look down.

The fork hits something metallic almost like a small metal disc. I tap the fork again, peeling back more roll.

"Um, that's a pretty big screwup for customer health. I think we should sue," I joke, my head whirling with possibilities.

"Let's see what it is before you sic the lawyers," he says slowly, his eyes locked on mine.

I scrape cinnamon roll away from the rest of it. There's something on top as I pry it out.

It's...some kind of box? There's a raven shape engraved across the top.

My breath catches.

My eyes flick back to Lincoln.

"Go on." He gives me a half smile and shrugs. "Open it, Nevermore."

Breathe, Dakota. Just breathe.

My fingers shake as I pull the box closer, touch it to make sure it's cool, and gasp as I run my pointer finger over its seam.

Ready or not...

The hinges pop as I push it open.

Hello, vintage ring. A gorgeously large oval diamond clustered by smaller diamonds in a halo around it.

"Lincoln, this is—it's *beautiful*," I stammer, tripping on my words.

He leans over with a firm nod, lifting the ring from the box.

"Looks a hell of a lot better if you're wearing it, beautiful," he whispers.

I look at him, unsure what he's doing, even if part of me knows.

I'm transfixed as he gets down on one knee and slides the ring on my finger.

"I told you I can't live without you. That gets truer every day. I love you with all the heart I'll ever have, woman. Now I just want you to be Mrs. Burns."

"I love you too—I love you *so much*—but—" Hot tears push up my throat in a strangled sob.

I can see his dark-brown eyes fall.

Oh, no.

"L-Lincoln," I stammer.

He stands with a soft smile, pulling me into his arms, even though he must be paralyzed.

"But what, sweetheart? Isn't love enough?"

"It's just—I don't like weddings."

He strokes my back with his hand. "You trust me, don't you?"

"Of course, I do." I nod sharply. "I want to marry you, I guess I'm just scared..."

"That makes two of us then. Nevermore, if you give me forever, we'll get through this together. I promise. You're the only one I'd *ever* trust to do this with."

"But what if you freak out because you have to wear a tux—"

"It's still a semi-regular occurrence at Ma's charity events," he says softly.

"Oh. Right. But there are so many people—"

"Also normal. If you want, we can do our vows without an audience," he says, his voice so torn, so determined, so *sweet.*

"But what if you wake up with huge regrets? Like, 'Oh my God! I'm going to spend the rest of my life with this woman. I'm never having sex with anyone else again, and if I wanted to go bum away boating with Wyatt for a week, there goes my chance.' Would you run?"

He laughs for a solid thirty seconds.

"First of all, an entire week is way too damn long to be with Wyatt Emory on a ship—"

I look at him, my breath stalled, trying to bury my stupid fears so I can give him the firm *yes* he so truly deserves.

Then he nips at my neck and I jump in his arms.

"Ahhh—what was that?" I sigh.

"You think too much," he growls against my ear, all hot breath and saintly patience. "For the record, I wake up every goddamned day with zero regrets. I just *know* you're the woman I'm spending the rest of my life with. Whether that means we're tying the knot today or in ten years, you're never getting rid of me."

I. Am. Ugly. Crying.

"Y-you mean it?" I whisper.

He nods.

"Promise?"

"Cross my fucking heart. I want to spend the rest of my life with you, and I want that life to start *now*."

"I just—oof. I didn't think you were the marrying type."

His jaw clenches. "Is that a no then?"

"God, no! I love you. I don't want this to end."

"So, you'll marry me?"

There's a long pause where my heart stops.

"I want to. With all my heart." My lip quivers. "But Lincoln...I'm really bad at weddings."

"Wrong. Your jackass ex was bad at weddings." He beams pure confidence into my eyes, and oh God, it's infectious. "If we do this, my mom will plan it, or I'll hire a planner. Anything you want, Nevermore, as long as you're mine."

"I want to elope," I blurt out, pushing my hands into his.

"What?"

"I want to elope. Just us."

He pulls me to him. "Ma will have my head on a silver platter if I deny her the wedding she's been planning for twenty years, but for you—"

Laughing, I push my hand softly in front of his lips.

"You swear you won't chicken out?" I whisper.

He cups my face with his hand.

"Dakota, if I don't show up to our wedding for any reason, I'll be dead. And even then, I'll probably come back and haunt your ass all the way to the honeymoon suite. Listen to me very closely."

He takes the other side of my face softly, clasping my head in both hands. Smiling, I sigh.

"I. Cannot. Live. Without. You. Not today. Not tomorrow. Not in a thousand years. Am I getting through yet? I need you like oxygen."

My lips turn up. "I love you."

"So, is that a definitive yes?" He presses his forehead to mine.

I wrap my arms around his neck and nod, sealing my agreement with a kiss that curls my toes.

Our lips are fused for what must be ten solid minutes before we slowly, breathlessly pull away.

"Only you could convince me," I whisper, finally looking down at that strange, yet magnificent ring on my hand that's starting to feel just right. "Oh, and I have a surprise for you!"

"Yeah?"

I bite my bottom lip. "It's kinda cool here. We should move closer to the fireplace."

He side-eyes me so hard I laugh.

"What's this surprise?"

"Only one way to find out..." I walk toward the fireplace, motioning for him to join me.

Lincoln follows and grabs the back of my sweater. "Nevermore, you have no idea what you do to me."

Heat pumps under my cheeks and I grin. "I think I have some idea."

I pull my sweater off then, revealing a hunter-green teddy underneath.

His breath catches and he swallows hard.

"You're wearing lingerie under your clothes."

I nod.

He traces the silk cup over my breast while his eyes stay on mine.

"This color looks good on you, but so would a paper bag. Your eyes glow." His voice is husky.

"You're still looking at my eyes?" My lips quirk up.

He loops his fingers into the waist of my skirt and yanks me toward him.

"Fuck no. They're hypnotic, but so is the rest of you." His mouth comes to mine.

My fingers go to work, hot and nimble, undoing his shirt buttons.

His tongue slides across mine as his fingers rip down my gown.

He wraps his arms around me then, pressing me greedily against him, making me feel his hardness.

Holy hell.

As long as I live, this will *never* get old.

I work the button of his pants free as he kisses me senseless, his lips moving to my throat.

We slink to the floor together with a mess of throw blankets stolen from the couch under us.

I push his jeans down and then his boxers.

He lies over me, his eyes bright and fiery and unrelenting.

I tremble under him.

His hands come to my breasts, and he undoes the first row of clasps running down the front of the teddy.

"I'm going to unwrap you—" He undoes the second. "Piece." The third. "By piece."

Four. Five. Naked.

His tongue sweeps the hollow space between my breasts, running along each side.

His rough fingers glide down to my belly button and dart up again, hands made for sex. He gazes at me like he could devour me. Sensuous, but sweet.

"Nevermore, this was the best surprise of my life," he rumbles against my ear.

"Maybe I'll wear green on our wedding night. If you're lucky..." The words are out before I realize I'm starting to *believe* there *will be* a wedding night.

Oh, boy.

He gives me a smug look. "Already planning it, huh?"

"Yeah, I guess so." I smile back.

He picks up my left hand and kisses the ring. "I like that. About as much as I like you wearing my mark."

Singing.

Deep down inside, I'm vibrating with euphoria—or is it just this happy lust for the only man worth owning my soul?

He drops my hand and returns to where he started.

"I need you inside me," I whisper.

His fingers trail down, arching over my pussy to the round, throbbing bead in my center. He presses his fingertip against it, drawing slow, intense circles.

In three seconds, I'm almost in the zone, my head bent back and breathless.

His lips take mine. Our tongues meet, but his finger never strays from my clit, winding steady circles that push me closer to the edge.

"Lincoln," I whimper.

His teeth grab my bottom lip, making me a willing hostage while he slides his fingers inside me.

It doesn't take long.

Soon, I'm grinding against him helplessly, so close to a devastating O my legs shake.

Then he slides his arm under me, pushing me up, shoving my legs apart.

He holds me closer, his eyes dueling flames locked on mine as the head of his cock brushes my clit.

"Oh, God."

His mouth moves to mine, teasing me while he holds back. So painfully close to filling me, but only moving up my seam with a hard-on like steel skinned in velvet.

Lips.

Tongue.

Breath.

Teeth.

His tongue sweeps the seam of my lips, tasting me with a slow torture that makes me writhe.

"How is it you look so damn sexy when you beg?" he whispers, returning his mouth to mine with a deeper, sweeter kiss before I can answer.

I'm rampant now, hooking my arms and legs around him, urging him *to take me, please!* any flipping which way he chooses.

His hands shift to my ass, squeezing both cheeks, spreading me open and deepening the way he claims me when his hips thrust forward and—

"Lincoln. *Lincoln!*" His name is the only word I manage through the delicious madness lodged in my throat.

The only word I can even comprehend when his tongue sweeps mine again.

I grasp at his hair, pulling him closer, melting in our kiss as he drives inside me with frenzied strokes that match the sear in his eyes.

"Goddammit, Dakota," he snarls against my mouth.

Deeper, deeper, and *deeper still.*

Even if we wanted to take this slow, there's no hope of that now.

We're too needy. Too desperate. Too hungry to feed the same flame consuming us both.

My hips arch up, meeting his rapid strokes as my core tightens and my eyes pinch shut.

He sinks into me, his thrusts so swift and intense they might break me—and God, do I *want them to.*

Still kissing my forehead, he tucks his chin over my head and plunges in to the hilt, his body flexing like a storm made flesh.

Holy shit!

My body clenches in surrender.

That wave of absolute bliss has to be Lincoln emptying himself inside me, his masculine force vibrating through me like thunder.

My fingers, my toes, my *everything* curls.

I'm airborne—hopelessly in love—and even when the convulsions subside and I'm back in my body, I just know.

Now that I'm wearing his ring, I will never, ever come down.

"Love you," Lincoln whispers, still catching his breath. He twirls my ring between his thumb and forefinger.

"You love that I'm wearing your ring."

"Hell yeah, I do."

"Good. Because so do I." Bringing his hand to my mouth, I kiss the palm, and then each finger.

"I thought you were scared?"

"I am, but I was also being stupid. You'll never leave me, and I know it."

"You're mine for life. My only regret is not shoving a ring on you sooner," he says, taking my hand and kissing it in turn.

We lay there spooned together for a good long while. Eventually, we move to the bed, where Lincoln Burns reminds me just how easily he guides me into the inferno.

* * *

I WAKE up to frigid air and pull the blanket up, snug around my shoulders.

I move to snuggle into Lincoln, but he's not there.

Weird. I slide out of bed and throw on the oversized white bathrobe I found in the bathroom and leave the room.

"Lincoln?"

"In here, sweetheart."

I'm smiling before I find him in the kitchen. Through the glass door, I can see how right he was yesterday. The whole mountain gleams with fresh white powder, the same beautiful sight that's right outside the cabin.

"Do you think we're snowed in?" I ask.

"One can only hope."

I laugh. "You *want* to be snowed in?"

"With you? Sure."

I pad into the kitchen. "What's for breakfast?"

"French toast."

"Hmm, nice, but what if I prefer French kisses?"

"Let me get this off the stove first, brat." He presses his lips to my cheek.

My toes curl happily against the cool floor, a question hanging on my tongue.

"...so, um how soon do you want to get married?" I ask shyly.

He chuckles. "As soon as you're ready. Looks like you've gone from wanting to elope to looking forward to the wedding in the space of one night, huh?"

Blushing, I nod.

"I'm so sorry for the way I reacted. It wasn't fair to you or us. I love you more than anything."

He moves the French toast from the pan to a plate before he hooks an arm around my waist, drawing me close.

"For a split second, you scared me. You don't have anything to apologize for, though. I put you through hell once. I know that."

"It's behind us," I say eagerly, pushing my nails gently into his shoulders.

"What changed?" he asks, his eyes searching mine.

"When we were on the floor last night, I just realized how very much you love me."

With a smile brighter than the sun-splashed snow outside, he nods vigorously.

"Damn right. I'm just glad I've got the rest of my life to prove it," he says, finishing with a kiss so brilliant it's almost blinding.

XXVI: EVERMORE (LINCOLN)

Three Months Later

J fumble with the tie, which is knotted and lopsided.
Groaning, I untie it, clenching my fingers around both ends to try again.

"Easy, tiger. It's already dead." Wyatt moves closer, a shit-eating smile plastered on his face. "Let go. I've got it."

"Whoever tailored this suit should have left more room for the tie. It's too damn long."

He laughs. "Isn't this your brand?"

He removes the tie from my neck, lines the ends up, restrings it, and ties it.

"Hell, I didn't design them personally. I just market them."

"Don't say that too loud. Bad publicity." He sits down on my couch. "You know the tie isn't what you're fussing about, right?"

My eyes dagger him.

"What, now you're my shrink? Okay, Doctor Emory. Enlighten me."

"Burns, you're a nervous wreck. You're gonna be fine. Raven—"

"Will you ever call my wife by her name?" I grumble.

"Raven sounds cooler, but maybe I'll reconsider once you get through your vows without barfing all over that sweet outfit. She loves you, idiot. You've got nothing to worry about." His words are the usual Wyatt crap, but the brotherly slap on my shoulder doesn't lie.

He means well, and he's also the closest thing I'll ever have to a brother.

"You got cold feet?" he asks gently.

I look at him flatly.

"You're worried she does?"

"...or that she'll outgrow me," I admit harshly.

"But you're willing to risk it?"

"Obviously. I need to know she's mine."

"Listen, man, everybody freaks out about starting a new life till one day they wake up, and they're already living it. You'll be fine, Burns."

"But what if—"

"No. Don't even. You're not me, and she's damn sure not Olivia," he growls.

I check my watch.

"We've got to get the hell out of here. If I'm late, Dakota might keel over, and I can't do that to her."

Wyatt follows me outside to the limo. Louis waits with a bright-red boutonniere pinned to his lapel, holding the door for us.

"I'm sure you'll want privacy with your new lady," Wyatt says in the car, leaning in. "So I'm taking Meadow camping for a few days while you're starting your honeymoon."

I roll my eyes at him.

"There's practically an acre between the guesthouse and mine. It's not like you'll be interrupting anything. Besides, our flight leaves the next day."

"Lincoln, this was never meant to last forever. I'm back on my feet, and you might need a place to put up your in-laws for a few days if they want to go sightseeing after you're gone," he says.

"Nevermore won't let them stay in the guesthouse. She wants them in a spare room in my house." I shrug. "It works. We have plenty of space."

Wyatt laughs and punches my arm. "Since I'll be gone by the time they get here, maybe you can convince her."

"How are you liking the mailroom, anyway?"

"It's a decent living. I have grunts to boss around. Everything's done neat and wrapped up at the end of the day. It's nice feeling useful again. Meadow got a job too."

"Nice. Where at?"

"A daycare. Turns out she's really good with little kids."

More good news for Wyatt. I smile.

"Has she met Micha yet?"

He shakes his head. "Nah. When school breaks in the spring, he's coming for a couple weeks. They'll meet then."

"You're doing well for a change, Emory. I'm happy as hell to see it," I say.

"Yeah, no shit, because I owe it all to you."

I laugh. "Karma repaid. I'm only alive on my wedding day thanks to you."

We both look away like we've said too much. It's one of those awkward man moments where you're so damn happy it's hard to keep a lid on anything.

My phone buzzes, and I take it out of my pocket to glance at the screen.

Dakota: Where the hell are you?

Lincoln: Still early and on my way, Nevermore. No need to worry.

The phone rings a second later and I swipe the green icon.

"Talk to me," I say, expecting my girl.

"My new daughter is freaking out. Where are you, son?" Ma practically screeches in my ear.

"About five or ten minutes out. Can you put her on?"

A pause.

"Hello?" Dakota's voice quivers.

"Are you crying, sweetheart?"

"No!" she lies with a sniffle.

"Why are you freaking out?"

"You wouldn't elope, and you're not here yet."

"Dakota, if the town car gets hit by a bus before we get there, I will crawl out of the wreck and carry Wyatt on my back." I nod at him. The look he throws back says he'd totally be the one carrying me.

"What if you're struck by lightning after that? There are hazards to marrying a Poe."

Her voice is no longer shaky.

I laugh. "Woman, you've already bewitched me. If lightning strikes after surviving the bus, I'll put the fire out and keep coming."

"How?"

"What do you mean how? Stop, drop, and roll. Did you skip elementary school?"

Wyatt laughs beside me. "You want me to tell her I'll get you there?"

I shake my head. I enjoy flirting with my wife-to-be even if she's being ridiculous. The huge, splendid house attached to the golf club slowly comes into view.

"Nevermore, we're pulling up now. I'll see you soon."

"We're in the woods," she says absently.

"I know. You'll be the one in the white dress, right?"

"Um, well..."

"You're not in a white dress?" I can't tell if she's joking as I say, "I thought we picked the new Haughty But Nice line?"

"We did. I just had it dyed black. It felt right."

For a second, I'm planted in my seat.

462

"You dyed your wedding dress black?"

Wyatt barks laughter beside me, head back and fingers in his eyes.

"Mm-hmm. But I have cool peacock feathers in my hair! Hair accessories by day, pens by night."

One more look at Wyatt and I lose my shit. I'm doubled over in my seat, laughing so hard I need to wipe my eyes.

"Lincoln?" she says for the fifth time.

"You're lucky I love you. See you soon," I promise.

"You're not upset I dyed the dress without telling you?" she asks in a small voice.

"Surprised, yes. Not upset. As long as you're mine today, I don't care if you show up in palm leaves strapped together."

"I'm already yours," she whispers happily.

I smile. "And I want that on paper, Mrs. Almost-Burns."

We're passing through the gated entrance, winding up to the walkway that will bring us to our spot in the woods where we have everything set up for the big show.

"See you soon," I tell her one more time, already throbbing at how she'll look in that dress.

Wyatt looks at me with some insufferable bullshit clearly on his lips.

"What?" I prompt.

"You're getting married in the woods at dusk and your bride's wearing a black dress. You really are wifeing up a Poe, dude."

"Shut up," I warn, trying not to smile.

Because he's too right, and I wouldn't have it any other way.

He gets out of the car ahead of me when Louis looks back and gives me his best wishes.

I trail behind my best friend and we start down the walkway. He moves quicker than I expect, well adapted to his new leg now.

The walkway takes us to a circular clearing tucked in a thicket of huge old trees. A judge stands in the middle of the circle with the Bible. Two lines of tall white folding chairs are arranged neatly around the paved circle, and my mom waits at the end in a lace dress.

I take her arm. "Let's find you a seat. I'm sure you've been running your tail off."

"Oh, Lincoln, she's so beautiful today. You'll cry when you see her." She blots her eyes, already shedding enough tears for the entire guest list.

I laugh softly, pleasantly surprised.

I expected Ma to be taken aback by the black dress. Apparently, she's so happy I'm tying the knot that she doesn't even mention it.

Wyatt and I lead her to the front row seating, and then I wait next to the judge. Wyatt stands beside me, adjusting his tie.

Then, with a swell of violins, my future begins.

Eliza steps out of the trees at the end of the aisle in a sleek blue Haughty But Nice bridesmaid gown, slowly walking toward us. She carries a small bundle of white baby's breath and moves like she's gliding on air, only stopping when she's next to us, leaving a space for my Nevermore.

Dakota and her dad come out of the trees next, and she's—not wearing the black dress she promised.

My eyebrows pull down as I swallow a chuckle. My heart hits my rib cage at the same time.

"You fell for it," Wyatt whispers conspiratorially.

I'd dart him a look if I wasn't transfixed on the angel in front of me.

"She loves to harass me," I mutter, grateful that I've got an entire lifetime of that ahead.

The dress she actually wears is white, flowing around her flawlessly like silk fog. With tiny rosebuds pinned in her blond hair, she'd be the envy of every runway model up and down the West Coast.

"She's...breathtaking," I whisper, my voice stolen.

Wyatt smiles knowingly.

Her father, a large pleasant man with a round face and rounder gut, walks her to me and places her hand in mine.

"Take care of her for me," he whispers, clasping my hand so tight in his it almost breaks.

"I will, Harold," I promise.

"We wrote our own vows," Dakota says.

The judge smiles. "Go ahead and get started, if you please."

"I'll go first," she offers.

Oh, shit.

Dakota's first poetry book is already racking up acclaim with the critics. I don't want to go after her since it'll be a tough act to follow.

"Sweetheart, let me," I whisper, taking her hand in mine as she nods.

I'm grateful it's a small audience now.

The entire world seems to shrink and fall silent, condensing around us in this weird, remarkable bubble that's just her drumming heart and mine.

"Dakota Poe, I never knew I needed anyone else in my life until the day you refused to give up a cinnamon roll—"

She giggles, so does everyone else.

"You were beautiful and feisty and strong. I never expected to see you again after our run-in. Then you danced into my office and wrapped my staff around your little finger. You made me think. You opened my eyes. You rocked my entire world. I love you more than life because you made me whole, and you still do every single day we're together. I know better than anyone that I'm a work in progress. You, sweetheart, are *my* muse. Will you be my forever?"

She smiles and nods vigorously with a heavy tear shining in her eye.

"Yes," she says breathlessly.

Then she pulls her hand from mine and finds a folded piece of paper inside the bouquet she's still holding.

"I'm not done..." I remind her.

Though I wish I were because then I wouldn't be rendered nearly speechless. Her soft smile becomes a wide grin, and those dazzling emerald eyes stare up at me.

"From today forward, we'll love with a love that's more than love."

Her smile deepens, even as she looks a bit puzzled at how I've butchered Edgar Allan's line from "Annabel Lee."

I don't think that's how it goes, her eyes say.

"Had to tweak it," I tell her, leaning in to meet her eyes. "With us, it'll never be past tense."

I'm not quiet enough. Mom laughs, and our entire wedding party beams at us.

"I love you," she whispers, looking down at the piece of paper in her hand. "I've never been good at big speeches, but I did write this..."

She clears her throat and begins to read her latest epic while I stand there like a stone, listening.

"She lives between the black of night and shades of grey.
Then comes an ivory Adonis, all spinning light.
He, who woke a heart from cold dead.
Her white knight.
Her heaven thread.
He made a withered heart beat red,
Terrified, she curled in dread.
"This is no game," he said.
"Please take my name."
Fear begs, "But what if you change your mind?
Change your life? Leave me behind?"
"Nevermore, get a clue.
I can't live without you."
"This is no game," he said.
"Please take my name."
He's a white knight, but she's not hunting for a wedding night.

Still, he made a withered heart beat red.

Woke it from dead.

"Yes," she said.

She wasn't hunting for a wedding night.

She's afraid to take flight.

But she owes him her life.

And he cherishes a wife.

Play with magic.

Dance with fire.

You must pay.

A lesson that slowly burns.

Burns who? Burns what?

Burns, me.

Burns, we—

Both of us, Burns be."

FUCKING FLOORED.

It's a small miracle I'm still standing.

Without thinking, I reach out and cup Dakota's face, guiding her closer.

I can't wait. I bring her lips to mine, kissing her like I've wanted to ever since she sent the first draft of that poem. The words have changed a lot, but somehow without the sex, it's even hotter.

Her flowers brush my back, skimming over my suit's fabric with a *whoosh* as they hit the floor.

A throat clears somewhere.

I'm too preoccupied to care.

"We usually exchange the rings before the kiss, but go ahead," the judge says.

I pull away from her.

"Sorry," I whisper.

"I'm not," she says intently.

God. This woman drives me certifiably insane even when she's completely innocent.

"Exchange rings," the judge urges.

I turn to Wyatt, who hands me the ring.

Dakota takes the ring from a grinning, teary-eyed Eliza and slides it on my finger.

I push Dakota's ring on her hand, then bring it to my mouth and kiss gingerly. Even her little finger feels more precious than gold.

"This is where I'd normally say 'kiss the bride,' but we've already done that part. I now pronounce you man and wife!" the judge says.

With applause bursting around us, I clasp my wife by the hand and march forward.

I lead her down the patio pavilion where the reception will be with a bigger group of our family and friends. It's in a massive heated yurt tent thrown up to dampen the winter chill.

The sun slips toward the horizon as we come up to the patio, glowing with twinkling lights.

"See? I told you this was the perfect time of day for a wedding," she says.

"Hell, marrying you would've been perfect at three a.m." I tighten my hold on her fingers.

She wraps her arms around my neck. "You've been very sweet today."

"What? I'm always sweet. You just got yourself a husband without going to pieces. I'm proud it's me, Nevermore," I whisper, stopping to steal a kiss.

When we resume walking, I see her wipe away a glorious tear.

When we arrive, the first thing I see is a massive three-tier cake. It's white and decorated with a nearly life-sized black raven perched on a black tree that spirals down all three tiers. The groom's cake is decorated with photos of us posing for the Haughty But Nice wedding line.

Eliza runs up later, holding Dakota's bouquet. "I think you forgot this!"

Nevermore takes it. "Thanks, lady."

"Look who I found." Wyatt appears next with Meadow clutching his arm, her worn flannel and jeans traded for a sleek purple dress that accents her slender frame. Emory looks like he could have her for breakfast, lunch, and dinner, and I'm sure they'll be ducking out early.

"I rode over with Dakota's family. I didn't want to crash your special time," she explains.

Mom runs toward us with her arms outstretched. I move to hug her, but she closes Dakota in her arms. "You're sooo gorgeous! The daughter I always dreamed of."

"I don't know," my mother-in-law says. "She was grounded her entire tenth grade year."

"Oh?" I pull my wife closer to me. "I knew Nevermore had a naughty streak, but now I have to hear this story."

"I do not!" Dakota lets out a mortified laugh. "And no, you don't."

"That's nothing. She cost me two thousand dollars in ER bills after she jumped out of a second-story window," her dad says.

I look at her.

"I wanted to go to a party. He was like a prison guard."

I plant a kiss in her hair. "Surely, you could have let her go to a party."

"A frat boy came home for the summer. It was his party and everyone there was older than twenty, not that she made it there," her father explains.

"Oh, let's just get through this reception, so you two birds can take off." Mom grabs Dakota's hand. "As soon as you're sick of this, you guys should go and we'll handle the rest." Ma leans in, never one to be shy. "Plus, I need grandbabies, Lincoln, and I'm not going to get them with you here gabbing."

Goddamn, she's not subtle.

Dakota overhears and turns bright red.

469

"Ma!" I whip out.

"Oh, sorry."

It's an interesting night. Mother keeps trying to shoo us off to make her a grandkid ASAP.

Meadow and Wyatt make out in a corner, while Eliza fights three other women out of the way and grabs the bouquet at the toss.

"I'd *better* be next now that Dakota abandoned me," she says.

I'm just glad when it's over and I finally get to have my wife alone.

* * *

Three Days Later

WE SIT on the patio together, exhausted after two sleepless nights wearing each other out and then the world's longest flight.

Damn if it isn't worth it, though.

Crystal blue water washes over our feet, ripples back, and repeats.

"I've never seen water so blue," she whispers with awe.

"The Maldives is a special place. I'll show you around tomorrow. You're going to love it," I say, smiling because it's only my third time here.

"I'm sure I will." She yawns, covering her mouth with one hand as she stands. "I'm going to go get ready for bed."

I stand and draw her to me. "I'll be inside soon."

I kiss her cheek and then her lips, tugging her close.

"I love you," she says with a parting squeeze.

Nevermore heads in while I linger outside, watching the waves swirl like they're carrying away the last of our old lives.

Good fucking riddance.

I glance down at the simple solid gold band on my finger and grin.

Until I met this blond pixie, I never thought marriage was for me.

Now, I don't want to know what my life would be without the other half of my soul.

The waves must hold my attention longer than I think with a lukewarm beer in my hand, because the next thing I know, a soft voice behind me says, "Lincoln."

I look over my shoulder.

My wife stands in the doorway, wearing nothing but a soft blue bathrobe that barely covers her chest. She's left it loose deliberately. There's a body made for sin that's ready for me, and I'm already aching.

I swallow the last dregs of my beer, stand, and draw her to me at the door.

My lips find hers like starving wolves.

She slides her tongue in my mouth, just as eager, her earlier tiredness gone.

I fall into the kiss, sucking and stroking, reminding us both that this is real.

This is mine.

This is us.

Dakota moans, thick and honey-sweet, without breaking the kiss.

When her leg goes around me, I move my hands under her ass and lift her.

Our bodies align perfectly.

Tongue to tongue, chest to chest, her all malleable softness while I'm so fucking hard I think I have a lethal weapon attached to my body.

With a growl caught in my throat, I throw her down on the bed.

She giggles as I tear her robe shell loose, hurling it to the floor, baring her like the delicate flower she is.

This may technically be the third day we've fucked since saying our vows.

I don't care.

With this woman, every time is just as electric as the first time, and as soulful as the last.

She looks up, her eyes wide, yanking my swim trunks away.

Once I'm free, she traces my shaft with one finger, gliding it up my length in a slow, teasing stroke.

"Fuck," I grind out, capturing her eyes.

She draws a gentle circle around my throbbing head, looking up with a devilish smile.

There goes my last thread of control.

My mouth meets her as I rear up, climbing on top of her, my throat like sandpaper as I flick the head of my cock at her entrance.

My erection coats itself in her wetness and smacks her clit.

Goddamn, do I love that little pleasure sigh that always falls out of her.

She winds her fingers through my hair, pulling me closer, deepening the kiss with a hot moan against my tongue.

Her other hand rests above my bare ass.

Her knees come up and she arches under me.

The woman is a human radiator, burning for my fullness. I'm happy to oblige.

I break our kiss, releasing a slow breath as I sink into her.

Her arms clasp my neck and she kisses my chin, shuddering under me.

With a silent look that's all fire, I drive in, bottoming out with my balls on her ass, claiming every last inch of her.

Our breaths come harder.

We're melded together, deliriously still, connected for God only knows how long.

I don't need more. I don't dare ask.

How could I when I'm living in heaven?

I lower my head closer to her ear.

"I love you, Mrs. Burns." A laugh falls out of me. I'll never, ever get sick of calling her that.

"Show me how much," she whispers back, drawing my thumb into her mouth and sucking it.

Fuck.

I'm thrusting like a madman by the time her fingers rake through my hair, tugging, each moan falling out of her louder than the last.

Our bodies go to war, giving and taking, seething and sweating and pulsing in happy chaos. My hips crash down on hers with a mind of their own.

I'm famished, and so is she, her little body twisting under me as my pubic bone drags friction against her clit.

Her pussy clenches like a second mouth, dragging me to madness, begging me to come with her with an illusion of choice.

I couldn't hold back to save my life.

Not today.

Not when she's like this.

Not when I want to mark my wife with seed she'll still be leaking when we shower tomorrow morning.

"Dakota!" I thrust so deep my spine bends.

"Lincoln! Oh God, oh yeah, *come inside me.*"

I fucking explode in a mess so hot I think she'll have to peel me off the bed later.

Her body spasms around mine, a firing spring, all of my senses gone except the raging need to pour myself inside her.

She wrings me out for a small eternity before I pull away, still hard, and crash down on the bed next to her.

"Nevermore." I sigh. I tuck her head under my chin and hold her as we both struggle to find our breath. Once I've regained control of myself, I roll beside her and pull her into my arms.

She trembles as I trace a finger down her back.

"What? I just touched you."

She shrugs. "My senses are in overdrive after *that.*"

"And I love the way your senses react to me."

Dakota falls asleep in my arms.

I run a finger through her hair and slowly fade off to sleep, my eyes drifting to that raven tattoo last. When we're back in the States, she's getting that touched up.

The heart no longer broken. My name around it, a seal of trust and love she's promised as a wedding gift.

It's beautiful and it's also sexy as hell.

My dick goes hard again as I fade out, thinking about taking her while she's branded with my name.

When I wake up in the morning glow, Dakota sits across the room, already wearing her swimsuit and a see-through wrap.

"You're too far away," I tell her.

She smiles, holding up a small plate with a glazed bun. "I got you breakfast. No Regis rolls here, but they do have these Japanese cinnamon buns."

"Fuck pastries, sweetheart. I want you."

"Oh, I think you'll want to eat this one, hubby," she tells me with a wink. "Just come here."

My eyes narrow, wondering what she's up to.

"Lincoln." She holds up the plate again impatiently.

Fine. Whatever.

I stumble to the edge of the bed and take the roll from her hands.

Then I pick it up, take a huge bite, and—almost break a tooth as she gasps.

"Oh, be careful!"

Too late. I spit something into my palm. It's...a tiny plastic person?

"What the hell, Nevermore?"

I look at the object in my hand. It's a small smiling baby.

When I look up, she smiles, her face turning vibrant red.

When it hits me, I fall back on the bed with a heavy bounce.

"Oh, shit. Oh, Jesus, are we—" I pause, sitting up to look at her, probably with eyes bigger than marbles.

Grinning shyly, she nods so briskly her hair flaps.

"How long have you known?" I ask.

"I found out the day before the wedding, but I thought I'd save the news. There aren't too many things you can get a billionaire bad boy he doesn't already have, and besides a tattoo job, I figured this might make the list."

"This *definitely* makes the list." I reach for her, damn near bursting with excitement like a kid on Christmas. "Come the hell here!"

This is how I hope it'll always be with us.

When we're too lost for words, we just kiss.

Of course, it has its hazards. Neither of us remembers I'm holding a cinnamon bun until the warm, sugary mess is sandwiched between us when I peel back.

"Shit, sorry," I mutter.

Dakota tries to brush smashed pastry off her swimsuit. It's not really working. When she looks at me, laughter bursts out of her, explosive and bright.

"It's perfect," she says, drawing in a breath while I give her a puzzled look. "Look at us, Lincoln. Hot, messy, and still pretty sweet. I wouldn't have it any other way."

"I would," I whisper, plucking a strip of flattened roll off my abs and popping it into her mouth.

When we kiss again, it's not just sugar and spice I'm tasting.

It's Dakota Burns.

It's all of my tomorrows.

Both of us, Burns be.

FLASH FORWARD: ONE BOSSY LITTLE BIRD (DAKOTA)

Months Later

I open my eyes to a sight that's never looked better after the hell I just went through.

Lincoln stands over me, his jaw clenched and his eyes glossy.

Oh, God. Wait. My chest tightens.

"Linc? Where's the baby?"

He picks up my hand softly. "She's sleeping like a little angel. Are you okay?"

"Is she okay?" I whisper again, clasping his fingers.

He smiles, his mocha-brown eyes gazing down in wonder. "She's fine. I asked if *you're* okay?"

"Yeah." I nod. "I think so."

"How much pain are you in?" he asks.

"Umm—I'm not."

He raises a brow.

I smile. "I'm sure. Whatever they gave me, it did it's job."

"Shit." He sighs with what sounds like relief, raking a hand through his thick dark hair. "Dakota, your blood pressure nose-dived. I was scared shitless."

I throw my arm around his neck, kissing him for being so sweet.

There's another noise across the room, a little cry. The baby?

I try throwing my legs to the side of the bed.

A knife stabs into my stomach instantly.

"Oooo-uch." I take a deep, shaky breath and release it. "Holy crap. Maybe I lied about being fine."

"You need to stay put, woman. You had an emergency c-section. It was rough, but the doctor swears she's never seen a baby so healthy, and you've both been stable since the surgery."

The baby wails again.

I try to get up again, but don't manage to get a foot over the bed before that hot knife rides through my guts again.

"God! I wish someone had warned me...is she...?"

"No worries, sweetheart. I've got her." Lincoln moves to the hospital bassinet at the end of my bed.

"But—"

"Hold on. I'll bring her over." He scoops the little bundle up—so small in his ginormous arms—and walks back to me, placing her lightly in my arms.

I gaze down at my daughter with my breath stalled.

She's tiny and bright and wrapped in a fluffy pink blanket with a head of what can only be described as peach fuzz. "Hey, Lin. Mommy loves you."

She screams like a banshee, whipping her round head from side to side. *Hello to you, too, mommy dearest.*

"Ah. I bet you're hungry." I tuck her inside my gown to nurse.

"Lin? That's not her name," Lincoln says.

"I know. But we agreed Lin would be a nickname, right? I wanted her to have your name one way or another. You're the best man I know, but she probably won't like being called Lincoln."

"Lin's a fine nickname for Lincoln. It's just that she didn't get named Lincoln, did she?" He smiles.

I blink at him slowly. "Oh, God. What's her name?"

"I thought I might lose you for a minute, and then you were doing better but you were completely under and out of it. You had lost so much blood. Didn't seem right naming the baby after me with any of the variations we discussed when you did the hard part."

"Lincoln, what did you name her?" I insist.

"I named her after you," he says matter-of-factly.

"What—so she's Dakota? Can't say I love that. I never found my roots in North Dakota."

"Not exactly. Try again." He grins with that smug smile only I could fall in love with.

"Lincoln Burns, what *did* you name our child?"

"Evermore," he whispers.

For a second, I'm dumbfounded. Then I throw my hands up.

"You did not!"

"Well, I couldn't name her Nevermore, could I? That's you."

"Oh my God." I think I'm turning pale. "She'll be the butt of every joke all the way through high school. She'll hate you forever."

He raises a brow coolly. "You're telling me a chick named Lincoln wouldn't have been mocked until her dying day?"

I shake my head, trying to process my new reality.

"Evermore Burns. Wow," I say slowly.

A weird, quirky part of me can't deny it has an interesting ring to it, though.

"You left out her middle name," he says.

I nod. "Evermore Alice Burns. Right. See? That sounds even more morbid."

He closes his eyes. "Yeah. Good thing it's not her name."

I glare at him, my strength suddenly returning.

"Linc, you're lucky there's a hungry kid latched to me. I'd

jump out of bed and come after you right now, otherwise. *What's her flipping name?*"

"Poe."

"What?"

"I wanted to name her after you. You're amazing. I want her to be like you. And since poetry is so much of you and the family name fits—"

"It's only coincidence I was born a Poe.'"

He smirks. "Maybe."

"Lincoln, I'm hardly any relation to the real Poe."

"Sweetheart, at this point, I think you *are* the real Poe. You're the one winning awards now."

"Evermore Poe Burns? God. She's going to murder you, you know. And someday when she asks me how she got this curse of a name, I'm going to say I was unconscious and your dad did it without talking to me first."

"How could I talk to you? You were out cold."

I hate that the lopsided grin he pulls out of me blunts my urge to smack him square across the face.

"We had a deal," I say miserably.

"Yeah, well, shit changes. That deal went out the window when I had to watch your blood pressure drop for *hours.*"

"I bet that was hard for you, Captain. Soon you can tell me if it's as bad as having your freaking blood pressure flatline." I hold up a fist.

Lincoln stares at the floor, holding in a smarmy laugh.

"I'm sorry. Look, if you really fucking hate it, we can always change it."

"It's fine. It'll grow on us, I'm sure. I think our little girl is probably the one you should apologize to."

He grins. "She'll get over it."

"You hope."

Knock. Knock.

"I hear you in there! I know they're both awake. You better let me in, or I'll take you over my knee—"

I giggle. Lincoln laughs too.

"Oh, let her in. This is her dream come true."

He laughs and takes half a step away from me.

The door swings open before he can go any further.

Tillie Burns claps her hands together with a gasp.

"Oh, dear! I have a granddaughter. I'm so excited!" She bustles over to my bed with her arms outstretched.

"She's eating," I say cautiously.

"Well, darn, I need to hold my baby. How are you doing, lovely?"

"I'm fine."

"Your parents are here. They just went down to the cafeteria for breakfast."

"Oh. Good, I was afraid it would be hard for them to get here."

"You kidding? People will go anywhere to see their first grandchild. Seattle is barely a skip away from Dallas when there's a baby involved!"

I laugh. All I can think is how I hope I'll have her energy if I live to be her age.

Tillie stares at the baby, completely awestruck.

"She's so beautiful." She looks up at Lincoln. "I only wish your father could see her."

"Me too, Ma."

"Wyatt and his young lady just arrived, too," she tells him.

"They have?" Lincoln asks.

Tillie turns to me. "There's also your friend Eliza and several people from the office."

"The office?" I glare at my husband. "I wasn't going to talk to anyone from work until I was like home and showered with my hair up."

He holds up a hand. "Wasn't me. I was going to send an announcement the day we came home like we talked about."

"Cheryl called me just to see how we were. The poor thing

sounded panicked. I couldn't not tell her my grandbaby was on the way," Tillie says.

I roll my eyes.

"Of course not, Ma," Lincoln says with a huff.

The baby falls away from my breast and burps.

I giggle and wipe her mouth with my gown.

Matilda holds her arms out, and I put the baby in them. "Here she is, Tillie. Evermore Burns."

"Oh, Evermore! You're grandma's forever more, aren't you, sweet pea?"

I blink at my mother-in-law. "Your mom knew the baby's name before me?"

Lincoln shrugs sheepishly.

"Ma was awake when we left the operating room. You weren't."

Grandma pats the baby in her arms. "He asked if I thought it was okay. I thought you'd think it was cute the way you are. Sorry to disappoint. Maybe I should have told him to stick to the plan."

I grab for Lincoln's hand.

He immediately laces his fingers through mine.

I smile up at him. "It's okay. There are worse things than your husband having a desperate urge to name his baby after you."

He kisses my fingers. "I love you, woman."

"Love you, too, even when you're *horrible*."

The door bursts open and my parents come piling in.

"Why does she get to hold the baby first? I'm your mother, Dakota!" My mom squeals.

"She didn't go for breakfast."

Mom rolls her eyes.

"I had to feed your dad." She walks over to Tillie who stands over my bed, holding the baby. Mom stretches her arms out. "Okay, okay, my turn now."

"But I just got her!"

"You live here. You'll see her way more than I'll get to."

Matilda sighs. "Oh, you're right."

She passes the ball of baby to my mom.

The door pops open again. Wyatt stands in the doorway holding Meadow's hand. "Everything good, man?"

"Never better. Come in," Lincoln says.

Eliza, Cheryl, and Anna trail in behind them, each with a smile bigger than the last. I think I make it through a minute of frenzied questions and frazzled fussing over me before I've hit my limit.

I "accidentally" punch the nurse's button.

A stout older lady comes in and runs everyone out. *Thank God.*

The room is back to just me, my husband, and our lovely new child nestled in my arms.

"Lincoln." I'm so tired his name barely comes out.

"Yeah, sweetheart?"

"I have to sleep sometime."

He takes the baby from me with a gentle smile.

"Come to daddy, duchess," he coos. He kisses my forehead in slow motion, strokes my brow, and whispers. "Rest up. You've got a whole life ahead of you being her mama and the best thing that ever happened to me."

* * *

Five Years Later

LINCOLN GRABS me and pulls me closer, spooning us together.

He kisses my shoulder and runs his finger over my tattoo.

"I've always loved this, but I love it even more since you filled the heart in and added the ampersand Lincoln under Nevermore." He kisses my shoulder again.

This man.

Somehow, he still manages to make me happy shiver like it's the very first time he's discovering me.

"Careful. If you keep kissing me like that, I'm going to need an encore."

He helps me turn in the bed so I'm facing him and brings his lips to mine. "I'm okay with an encore."

Thud!

"Ugh. The kids are up." I push the comforter aside so I can get up and get dressed.

He locks his arms around me.

"Wait." He quickly catches my bare breast in his mouth and rolls his tongue over my nipple.

I sigh. "Why? Why would you do that when you know we have to get up and deal with them?"

"So you won't make plans for naptime."

Thud!

This time, the noise belongs to a small body slamming our bedroom door like a battering ram.

"Just a second! I'm coming."

"*Moooomm!* I can't see if Santa came until you get up!" Evermore says.

"He always comes," I remind her.

"Ma-ma!" Little Linc says. "Wanna canny cane!"

"Merry Christmas," I whisper to my husband.

We both scurry up and get dressed before we waltz out to face the day. When we come out of our room, I scoop up our three-year-old boy.

Evermore looks at me carrying the baby and then at her dad, a hilariously grumpy expression on her face. "Pick me up too."

"You're five," he reminds her.

"Not fair! Linc gets carried all the time. I hate being the oldest."

He chuckles and gives in, hoisting her up. "Like this or on piggyback?"

"Fly, Daddy," she squeaks softly.

He nods and holds Evermore out in front of him like she's airborne. She stretches her arms out like the overgrown, incredibly spoiled little bird she is as they start moving.

I scowl at him. "I wish you two wouldn't go down the stairs like that."

"Tell Mommy we'll be careful," he says.

Evermore doesn't follow orders. She just giggles.

Once I've made it downstairs behind them, Little Linc jumps out of my arms and darts for the tree.

"You guys know the drill. Breakfast first," his dad says.

"No! No, no, no!" Evermore says. "Santa came. Santa *then* breakfast."

"Breakfast first, kidlet," Lincoln repeats, his stomach growling loudly for emphasis.

"French toast?" I ask.

"How did I get a wife who doesn't cook?" he teases.

"I believe you lured her with a trained bird. Funny things happen."

"Touché."

There is a knock at the door.

He sets Evermore down. "I'll get it and start breakfast. You corral the kids."

He goes to the door.

Little Linc's chubby legs bounce as he follows his dad to the door.

"Uncle Wy-att!" the baby screams.

"Merry Christmas, little man!" Wyatt says warmly. "We brought breakfast. Hope it's okay to just show up."

"You're always welcome here."

Wyatt and Meadow come in carrying enough Sweeter Grind boxes for a squad of soldiers. He has the coffee and paper cups and she has two pastry boxes.

"Rollies!" Evermore screams.

"Yep," Wyatt confirms.

"They're still Uncle Wyatt's favorite," Meadow says.

We sit around the tree with colossal Regis rolls for breakfast, and less than an hour later, Tillie shows up.

The kids unwrap dolls, trucks, and countless other toys, and when there's only one gift left under the tree, I hand the box to Lincoln.

He unwraps a leatherbound book and raises an eyebrow at me. "Really?"

"Open it, doofus." I smile at him.

He thumbs through pages of us posing for Haughty But Nice, hanging out with Wyatt and Meadow, old engagement pictures at the Mt. Rainier retreat, our actual wedding, holding Evermore and then Little Linc and the four of us together all captioned in verse.

I've spent years putting this together.

He looks from the book in his lap to me.

"Dakota, I love it." He shakes his head. "I love *you.*"

As always, the second I'm in his arms, his kiss is the only gift I'll ever need.

We're in heaven until Evermore yells.

"Gross!" She covers her eyes.

My toddler squeals and wraps his chubby arms around my leg. I pull away from my husband, giggle, and peel my son off my leg.

Around two o'clock, the oven dings, and I go take the ham out. We all sit around the table, laughing and stuffing ourselves with a month's worth of food.

Wyatt and Meadow leave after lunch to head to another party with Wyatt's son.

Tillie, Lincoln, and I play with the kids and their new toys. When her grandma tries to leave, Evermore throws herself on the floor, hugs her ankle, and screams, "Take me! Take me, Gram!"

"Let's see what your folks say." Tillie looks up from the sobbing five-year-old on the floor to me. "Can I take her?"

I laugh and nod. "Sure, but don't bring her home before lunch, because I'll be dead asleep."

"No problem." She looks at Evermore. "Go on. Pick out a nice dress and we'll do tea."

Evermore bolts upstairs and comes back holding her favorite dress so fast it shouldn't be possible.

"Thank you, Gram!" She takes Tillie's hand and they start out the door.

Little Linc wails.

I bend down and pick him up.

"What's wrong?" Tillie and I ask at the same time.

"Wanna go with Ever."

My mother-in-law smiles. "Can he come too?"

I nod and hand over my child gratefully. I love them, but it's been ages since I had any alone time on Christmas with my husband. I've learned to appreciate what an unexpected gift that can be.

Lincoln slips an arm around my waist and we watch them leave.

Once she pulls out of the driveway, he shuts the door, closes both arms around me, and embraces me with all the sweetness of coming home.

"Fuck, we're alone. I can't believe it."

I grin. "I know."

"I haven't given you your real Christmas gift yet."

"What? But you got me plenty..."

"Nevermore, surely you know me better by now. Do I ever fail to surprise you? It's upstairs on the bed. Waiting."

"When did you have time to go back upstairs?"

"I slipped out during lunch, and you didn't even notice. See? You neglect me."

I punch his arm playfully, rolling my eyes. "Oh my God. I'm so sorry, I didn't notice you leave the table while I was force feeding a kid with each hand."

He picks me up. "Enough apologies. They're gone, so I get your full attention now."

I kiss his chin and then his lips. "You always have it."

He carries me upstairs and sets me on my feet when we get to our room. The evening sunset splashes in through the massive windows, turning everything gold, wintry but warm. We only moved into this cozy mansion just north of Seattle a few years ago, but it's become the bright, quiet, homey sanctuary I never knew I needed.

A silver wrapped box lays on our bed, glittering in the light. I run to the bed and open it. I pull out a dark-green teddy that laces up the front.

"Oh, wow." Heat pumps under my cheek. "I haven't seen one like this since our honeymoon."

"I thought it looked a lot like the one you wore when I proposed. I haven't seen it since Ever came, and I think it's been too long."

I swallow past a lump in my throat.

"Umm—after two kids, I'm not sure it will look quite the same."

His face screws up like he can't believe the words coming out of my mouth. "What the hell difference does it make, sweetheart? I'm just admiring it and then taking it right off."

"I could just strip. Wouldn't that be easier?"

He shakes his head. "I like to unwrap you, and you like it too."

I hold his gaze. "Are you sure?"

He closes the space between us, drives me to him, and finds my mouth with his own. He parts my mouth with his tongue, slipping in my mouth and brushing his over my own.

Holy hell.

I sigh.

I always do.

He gently peels away from me. "Trust me, I know. Because when I unwrap you, you squirm and laugh and you come yourself

487

stupid. The way you react is half the fun." He kisses me again in a long, slow teasing slash of tongue and teeth. "But you're right. I don't need a naughty nightie. I only need you, Nevermore."

His lips are on mine again before they move to my neck, then down my collar bone. He inches the zipper at the back of my dress down barely—*just barely.*

His gorgeously greying stubble rakes my skin as he kisses the top of my breast while he tugs at the zipper again.

I moan and start sliding out of the arms like syrup.

"No, ma'am," he growls, pushing a hand under my butt to hold me up.

I meet his eyes. Why would he say no?

"I told you. You're mine to unwrap today. It's Christmas."

He works my arms out of the sleeves. The top of my dress collapses down to my waist. He unclasps my bra, removes it, and places his mouth over my breast, sucking eagerly.

"Oh." I fall against the bed. "Oh, Lincoln. *God.*"

He climbs over me with a feral glint in his bottomless brown eyes.

I know that storm.

I love that storm, and I've learned to worship it.

Grabbing his shirt, I pull it from each side roughly. Nobody cares when buttons start popping off and skittering across the floor.

His relentless mouth takes mine. His rough hands roam every inch of me. He unzips the dress the rest of the way and drags it off from under me.

My hands move to his pants, shaking like they always do before sex, and I undo the button. I push the pants away.

Lincoln moves to the edge of the bed and takes my hand, guiding my fingers to his length, around it, and down. I stroke him until he throws his head back and groans, showing off the beautiful definition in his muscles as they tense.

I'm so wet I could die. Even after all these years, you never get used to making love with a god.

He settles me on top of him and helps me move over him, taking him in.

Our bodies meld.

We slip into the warm, electric blur together. All movement and pulses and slowly rising, feral sounds. I'm held, kissed, and caressed.

It starts off slow and gentle, but soon becomes enough to break me.

More intense.

He never lets go of me as he robs me down to the bone, stealing every breath, pulling sweat from my pores, making me give up noises that used to scare me.

Now, they're just normal.

Now, they're part of being Lincoln Burns' wife, and loving that I am.

Every touch caresses my body, mind, and soul.

Every thrust.

Every mad growl rolling out of him like thunder.

He drives into me with his pelvis, his thumb circling my clit, his tempo matching the fury of his tongue swiping mine into submission.

Coming!

I push my face into his shoulder, clinging to him, murmuring his name with each and every breath.

He holds me tighter, slamming into my convulsions, until I know what's next. If I wasn't completely wrecked, I'd smile, because I always do at the surprise.

"Dakota—fuck!" He throbs inside me.

I dig my nails into his skin. "Lincoln. Oh, God!"

I don't need to say it, even if I want to.

He buries himself in my depths and releases with guttural relief in his throat. His body heaves, emptying everything he has, reminding me with every pulse and molten rope just how we built our beautiful family. And how we might wind up with more than two kids one of these days.

"Shit. Sorry," he says, crashing down next to me with a groan. "Couldn't fucking last with the whiskey I had with Wyatt and—hell, with you. It's been a while."

"I'm not sorry." I gasp. "And it's been like a week?"

We look at each other and laugh before we collapse against the mattress together. We both know we'll do this at least three more times before the kids come home.

"I love you, Nevermore," he whispers. "Merry fucking Christmas."

I shake my head. "*Evermore*. It's not just the name of our little girl. It's us, Lincoln. You gave me that. You taught me how real and how magical love can be. I don't care how cheesy that sounds."

He grins. "I do. Because woman, I love you when you're kind and sexy and so pissed off you could spear me in the face. I love you when you're sad, when you're celebrating, and even when you're napping with the kids. I even love your stupid cheesy shit. That's why I'm telling you I love to fucking love you."

What a flipping charmer.

Before I let him see the waterworks switch on, I push my face against his, drowning us both in a laughing kiss.

ABOUT NICOLE SNOW

Nicole Snow is a *Wall Street Journal* and *USA Today* bestselling author. She found her love of writing by hashing out love scenes on lunch breaks and plotting her great escape from boardrooms. Her work roared onto the indie romance scene in 2014 with her Grizzlies MC series.

Since then Snow aims for the very best in growly, heart-of-gold alpha heroes, unbelievable suspense, and swoon storms aplenty.

Already hooked on her stuff? Visit nicolesnowbooks.com to sign up for her newsletter and connect on social media.

Got a question or comment on her work? Reach her anytime at nicole@nicolesnowbooks.com

Thanks for reading. And please remember to leave an honest review! Nothing helps an author more.

MORE BOOKS BY NICOLE

Bad Chicago Bosses

Office Grump

Bossy Grump

Perfect Grump

Damaged Grump

Knights of Dallas Books

The Romeo Arrangement

The Best Friend Zone

The Hero I Need

The Worst Best Friend

Accidental Knight (Companion book)*

Heroes of Heart's Edge Books

No Perfect Hero

No Good Doctor

No Broken Beast

No Damaged Goods

No Fair Lady

No White Knight

No Gentle Giant

Marriage Mistake Standalone Books

Accidental Hero

Accidental Protector

Accidental Romeo

Accidental Knight

Accidental Rebel

Accidental Shield

Stand Alone Novels

Cinderella Undone

Man Enough

Surprise Daddy

Prince With Benefits

Marry Me Again

Love Scars

Recklessly His

Enguard Protectors Books

Still Not Over You

Still Not Into You

Still Not Yours

Still Not Love

Baby Fever Books

Baby Fever Bride

Baby Fever Promise

Baby Fever Secrets

Only Pretend Books

Fiance on Paper

One Night Bride

Grizzlies MC Books

Outlaw's Kiss

Outlaw's Obsession

Outlaw's Bride

Outlaw's Vow

Deadly Pistols MC Books

Never Love an Outlaw

Never Kiss an Outlaw

Never Have an Outlaw's Baby

Never Wed an Outlaw

Prairie Devils MC Books

Outlaw Kind of Love

Nomad Kind of Love

Savage Kind of Love

Wicked Kind of Love

Bitter Kind of Love